THE NIGHTSHADE

HATTIE JAMES
BOOK 4

STACY LYNN MILLER

Severn River Publishing
www.SevernRiverBooks.com

ISBN: 978-1-64875-693-1 (Paperback)

ALSO BY STACY LYNN MILLER

Hattie James WWII Novels
The Songbird
The Rio Affair
The Secret War
The Nightshade

Lexi Mills Thrillers
Fuze
Proximity
Impact
Pressure
Remote
Flashpoint

Sign up for the reader list at
severnriverbooks.com

To Leslie and Allison.
My daughters and keepers of my heart.
They teach me every day that love is unconditional and enduring.

PROLOGUE

Maryland Eastern Shore, Wednesday, December 10, 1941

The message he received on Sunday had made it clear: get the lists or get exposed. Karl James and his spy rosters had vanished, and his daughter Hattie had arrived from Brazil five days earlier. The Germans believed she had them, and, given Berlin's warning that the war would continue to expand through the week's end, they were desperate to get them. And so was he.

His name could be one among the many on Karl James's lists, so he had every reason to find and secure them before American agents did. Hattie James was the key, and she had made a mistake. She had led him to this remote cabin on the Eastern Shore. Based on everything he knew about her, coming here was odd. She was not on vacation, after all. She and her companion had only stayed overnight, so the rosters were likely inside or with the Professor, the woman she met with there yesterday.

He had spent all night and morning hiding among the trees in the below-freezing temperature. His winter gear had helped, but he still felt half-frozen, waiting for the right moment to make his move. Hattie and her friend had left an hour ago, leaving only his target inside.

Two decades ago, he glimpsed the elusive Professor only a few times while working at the Black Chamber, the joint US Army and State Department cryptography organization established to intercept and decipher communications. When Hattie used that moniker to say goodbye at the car this morning, he was sure he had found the right place and person, despite not seeing the woman's face clearly from the trees. Though he never worked with her directly, he remembered she was petite with dark hair. While this woman's hair was silvery gray, she was about the same height and build. It had to be her, the passage of time aging her appearance.

The door finally opened. The woman from the log house got in her car and drove down the gravel path toward town. This was his chance to search for the documents while the building was unoccupied.

The cabin's warm and welcoming appearance contrasted starkly with the chilly air, but the structure was a picture of rustic charm, with weathered logs forming its sturdy walls. A prominent stone chimney, built from large, irregularly shaped rocks, rose from an end. A heavy wooden door painted black bore a hook with a fishing net hanging from it.

He had scouted the building overnight and had already picked out his point of entry at the back, where passersby could not see the windows upon approach. He smashed a small pane near the latch, opened it, and crawled into the bedroom. The dated furnishings matched the exterior's country feel.

He searched the drawers, cupboard, and beneath the bed. He even flipped up the mattress and inspected the metal frame. Not finding any lists, he continued to the bathroom and main living area, taking care not to leave a mess in his wake. The goal was to get out of there: find what he had come for before the woman returned and, besides the window, not create obvious indicators of having been there.

The space was more functional than decorative, not what he expected from the old woman. Besides painting supplies, it served primarily as a hunter's and fisherman's retreat. However, the telephone was unexpected. It was a sign that the Professor was important enough to have one in such a remote location.

He examined every cranny and was down to searching in the cereal boxes when the door opened, causing him to freeze. He had not expected the woman to return so soon, but there she was. A petite elderly woman with wavy gray hair entered, carrying an overflowing grocery sack in one arm. There was no quick escape without her seeing him, so he pulled his gun, holding it against his thigh out of her view to not pose an immediate threat.

She locked eyes with him, her expression full of surprise, not recognition. Maybe he could get what he came for without having to kill her now that she had seen his face. "I wasn't expecting visitors."

"Hello, Professor. I've come for the lists."

"For what?"

"Don't play coy. If you're smart, you'll give me those lists now."

"What lists?"

"I warned you." He raised his pistol and stepped toward the woman.

Panic swam in her eyes. She dropped the bag, causing a loud crack. Milk mixed with the bread and the fresh vegetables at her feet. She turned to run. He lunged forward, grabbing her by the arm as she reached the door. She struggled to break his grip and shrieked bloody murder.

The cabin was quite a distance from the road and the nearest neighbor. However, the lack of city or traffic noise might let her screams travel far enough for someone passing by to hear. He slammed the door shut and wrapped a hand around her mouth, but she continued to thrash against his hold.

"Don't fight it. Give me the lists and the cipher, and I'll go."

She screamed again, but his hand muffled the sounds of deep-seated terror. She was too small and frail to overpower him, so her resistance was baffling. He had seen the Professor referenced in a top secret report, her name associated with wit and intelligence and as the protector of Karl James. The Professor must have the lists and know how to decode them. Surely, she understood that she could not win this battle. The prudent choice was to give him what he wanted and hope to communicate the loss in time to do some good. But this woman continued to resist, acting out of fear, not with logic as he expected.

He doubled the pressure on his grip and pulled her tightly against his body. "Where are the lists, Professor?"

Her breathing was erratic, but she slowed her squirming and sucked exhaustedly for air with her nose.

"When I release my hand, no screaming. Do you understand?"

She nodded hard.

He slipped his hand from her mouth. The next second, she elbowed him in the gut and darted toward the door, shrieking. He dashed up behind her and slammed her head against the solid, thick door. Her body went limp and fell to the floor. The dull crack he heard when her skull hit the wood was unmistakable. He had fractured both.

Hoping he had merely knocked her unconscious, he checked for signs of breathing but found none. He had killed her. He sneered and spat his words. "I told you not to scream."

He searched her clothing, purse, and every inch of the place but could not find what he had come for. "You're a damn idiot," he cursed himself and the mess he now had on his hands. It would be light outside for another five or six hours. He could not bury the corpse without risking a passerby seeing him, nor could he wait until dark to hide his actions. Putting her in his trunk to drop it somewhere in the remote woods was a possibility, but he also wanted to send a message.

After scribbling a note that read, "The lists or more will die," he positioned the woman's body in the overstuffed armchair. He pinned the paper to her shirt with a safety pin from the bathroom.

He went out the front door to his car, hidden half a mile away in shrubs off the main road into town. Hattie James must still have the lists. There was still a way to get to her and get hold of them; he was sure of it. He simply had to find it.

1
___

One week earlier, Washington, DC, Thursday, December 4, 1941

The early morning whirr of activity in the Stanton household reached a head-splitting level today. Eugene had thought the house was noisy when the kids were younger, but toddler tantrums did not compare to teenage rants. The sharp ringing of broken glass that followed the slamming of a door in the hallway felt like daggers through his eyes, which were battling the lingering effects of last night's whiskey.

Partially dressed in his shirt and boxers, he stomped to his bedroom door, flung it open, and focused on the retreating backside of his college freshman. "Can we go one day without the dramatics, Ben?"

"Tell Princess Pamela. She spent an hour in the bathroom again, and I still have to brush my teeth. My ride is almost here."

Eugene went to his nightstand, grabbed the half-eaten roll of Life Savers, and tossed them to his son. "Try these and get up earlier. Start keeping a toothbrush and paste in the kitchen like every man in a house dominated by women."

Ben grunted and slipped his book satchel over his shoulder before stomping down the stairs.

"That boy will never learn," Eugene mumbled as he picked up the broken picture frame on the hallway floor and dumped the glass in the bedroom trash can.

His son was smart enough to get into Georgetown to study economics, yet dumb enough to let the twins get to him. Eugene had grown up with only sisters and learned the hard lesson. He had had to outsmart them if he wanted any semblance of a happy life. Why he had not done the same with his adult tormentors until now was a mystery. Eighteen months ago, a man named Sam had bullied him into doing things that turned his stomach. The demands he made this week had crossed a line Eugene had sworn never to flirt with—and yet he had. It remained to be seen if his risky maneuver to neutralize what he had done had worked.

He slipped on his olive trousers and low-quarter army russet shoes, buttoned his darker drab dress shirt, and slung his black tie over his collar. He opened his bedroom door again and stepped into the corridor, discovering one of the twins still in her nightgown and pink fuzzy slippers. "You're going to be late, Pam."

"I know that, Father."

"I don't have time to drop you and your sister off at the high school today, so you had better ride the bus."

"Why didn't you say so last night?" Pamela's eyes got extra round before she turned, panicked, and scurried down the hallway. "Susie," she shouted. "We have ten minutes to catch the bus."

"Ten minutes?" A shrill, muffled voice came from the girls' room.

Eugene descended the stairs smiling, having given his daughters a taste of their own medicine. The staff meeting was not for another two hours, but he needed to teach them a lesson and stick up for his son.

In the kitchen, he found his wife dressed and at the stove. Ben was already eating a big stack of buttered and syrupy pancakes. "Morning." Eugene kissed Jill on the cheek before pouring a cup of coffee from the percolator.

"Did you put the trash can on the curb before going to bed? The garbageman refused to open the gate last week since Scruffy bit his leg."

"I did, and I left a six-pack of Natty Boh on top with an apology note." Eugene preferred bourbon over beer, but National Bohemian was cheap and on display at the front of the liquor store on the way home last night. He was sure the trash guys would appreciate the gesture.

"Nice touch." Jill returned his kiss and resumed preparing breakfast for the Stanton herd.

"Honey, not vinegar." He sat at the table across from his son and poured syrup over his pancakes.

The twins rushed into the kitchen and made sandwiches using flapjacks, toast, and sausage patties. They snatched up the lunch sacks prepared by their mother and kissed each parent on the cheek. "Bye, Mother. Bye, Father," both said before they scampered out the front door as the bus stopped at the street corner next door.

"You're not driving the girls in this morning?" Jill asked, taking a seat at the table beside him.

"They needed a lesson in time management." Eugene winked at his son, who snickered after shoving in another mouthful. "Stanton men stick together."

After putting the first bite into his mouth, Eugene picked up the early copy of the *Times Herald*, unfolded it, and fixed on the big, bold headline: "F.D.R.'s War Plans." It took him a moment to absorb the story's content. He spat his food onto his plate, staring at the article as his belly twisted into a knotted mess. His plan worked, but he never thought it would happen this fast.

"Eugene?" Jill touched his forearm. "Are you all right?"

A sinking feeling squeezed the air from Eugene's lungs. He tried to suck in more to form words, but nothing helped. He agonized over whether he had done enough to cover his tracks.

"Are you choking?" Jill slapped his back between the shoulder blades. The force allowed him to take a breath.

"Holy Moses." He scanned more of the article.

Smaller headlines read, "Goal Is 10 Million Armed Men" and "Proposes Land Drive to Smash Nazis." The War Department's top secret strategic plan, the plan he had been working on for the last year, was on page one. He fixated on the line saying this was a "blueprint for total war on a scale unprecedented, taking place on two oceans and three continents—Europe, Africa, and Asia."

The report went on to say that July 1, 1943, was the date fixed for an Allied invasion of Europe. That the plan called for an American military force of more than seven times its current strength, with half slated for Europe. Rainbow Five was all there, and the byline noted the same article was also appearing in today's edition of the *Chicago Tribune*. That meant the secret plan was now in the homes of at least 450,000 readers. Going back was impossible.

"What's wrong?" Jill's pinched expression telegraphed her concern.

"I gotta get to work. Crap has hit the fan."

Eugene left his breakfast on the plate, hurried to the entry hall, and looked in the wall mirror to finish putting on his necktie. He fumbled with the tabs, but he was too upset to concentrate.

Jill walked from the kitchen. "Let me." She grabbed both lengths of the thin black fabric. "You're never good at this."

"You would think after twenty-one years in the army that I would learn how to tie a half-Windsor."

"That's why you have me." Jill did her magic, flipping the ends over one another, and patted him on the chest when finished. "There." She snatched his dark olive drab uniform jacket from the coat tree and held it while he eased his arms into the sleeves.

He secured the four buttons and the Sam Brown belt around his waist. He liked how the leather matched his shoes but hated the cross strap that went over his right shoulder. It served no real purpose other than making him look more trim and square-shouldered like he was in his youth.

"I'm guessing from the headline this might be a long day," Jill said.

Eugene put on his green wool army overcoat and service cap and picked up his briefcase next to the front door. "I would suppose so. I'll call if I'm going to be late."

He drove his Buick Special to the Munitions Building and located a parking spot in the farthest row. That was his punishment for not coming in at sunrise on a day like today. The morning headlines seemed to have prompted a lot of personnel to show up earlier than usual. He had stopped doing that eighteen months ago when his life went to hell. The colonel's eagles on his shoulders would have earned him a reserved slot at any army camp. However, as a member of the War Department's General Staff, he barely rated a private office. He went to the closest entry point and showed his military identification card to the armed guard. This corporal had checked him in before, but Eugene never bothered to learn anything about him or the other guards beyond their rank. It did not matter. Those men came and went with great frequency.

He removed his outer coat, slung it over his left arm, and doffed his cap, sliding it to his armpit on the same side. The building buzzed with the typical weekday activity of army, navy, and civilian personnel, but the corridors were void of idle chitchat. Each face he passed held a long, solemn expression, and everybody walked with a sense of urgency. Detailed government secrets were not supposed to be the subject of national headlines.

After ascending the stairs to the second floor, he entered the offices of the War Plans Division, where he shared the small suite with a secretary, his boss, Major General Leonard Gerow, and the two company-grade army officers who directed the duties of a dozen lower-ranking personnel.

"Good morning, Mabel." She was pecking away diligently at the typewriter on her desk. He hung his outer jacket on the coat tree inside the door, along with his cap. "Is he in yet?"

Mabel was always the first to arrive in the office, getting the coffee brewing and sorting through the mail, internal distribution communications, and the classified messages the duty noncommissioned officer picked up. Eugene typically was a close second. However, considering today's earthshaking headline, it would not surprise him if General Gerow had beaten everyone into the building today.

The secretary looked up from her typewriter without stopping her work. He felt her frosty chill from across the room. As far as he could tell, she had never really liked him, but he couldn't put his finger on why. Then again, he never stayed in an assignment long enough for office dynamics to become a priority, so he never bothered to ask, and this was not the day to try to remedy their dysfunctional working atmosphere.

"The inspector general is with him. He said to send you right in."

"Thank you, Mabel. I better get in there."

"That would be wise."

He dropped his briefcase inside his office, returned to the reception area, and eased open his boss's door. Rich woods adorned the stately office with an ample seating section and a large desk. It also had one of the building's few decent views of the Lincoln Memorial.

General Gerow waved him over. "Gene, come in."

"My apologies, General. I only read the article an hour ago."

"It caught everyone by surprise." Gerow gestured toward Major General Virgil Peterson. "Can you get the IG up to speed on Rainbow Five?"

Eugene acknowledged Peterson with a respectful nod. "What do you need to know, sir?"

"How many copies of the plan are there?"

"Thirty-five."

"Can you account for all of them?"

"Yes," Eugene said. "The custodian conducts a daily end-of-duty-day count."

"Who has had access to them?"

"I can get you the list. It changes quite often."

"How many people have authorized access to the Rainbow Plans?" Peterson asked.

"Between the army and navy, I'd say over two hundred."

"I'm assigning Colonel Price as the lead investigator," Peterson said.

"Bob Price. He's a good man. I'll call him and get a list of everything he needs." Eugene stood, facing his boss. "Will that be all, sir?"

"I want you two working together on this. Find out how the hell something like this happened and nail the son of a bitch who created this washout."

"You can count on me, sir."

Eugene went into his office. It was much smaller than his boss's but average-sized for his rank in the Munitions Building. The furnishings surpassed expectations, though, a perk of working for a two-star. The inbox on his desk was brimming with file folders, but all that would have to wait. Two of the highest-ranking generals in the United States War Department had just assigned him to help investigate the illegal release of the country's most guarded top secret documents. To uncover the person responsible for the crime. He was that culprit, but he knew precisely how to steer the investigation away from him.

Wiping the nervous sweat from his brow, he wondered if he had done enough to cover his tracks. Eugene was familiar with the security procedures in the War Plans Division because he wrote them. The officer managing the classified documents room ensured personnel signed out each document before removing them from the secure room. Policy required they return the file by the end of the duty day, where a clerk would check it in. The enlisted clerks lacked the clearance to read the report, only to safeguard it, so they ensured the title on the top page matched that on the folder and checkout sheet. No one questioned what was inside if its thickness was about the same as when it left. Eugene could have stuffed a collection of his wife's holiday recipes in there, and the man would not have discerned the difference. Procedures did not allow him to look beyond the cover page.

The IG inquiry would stall because his staff had accounted for every copy. The records would show that the Rainbow Five plan had never been missing, though Eugene knew the opposite was true. Colonel Price would have to concentrate on a pool of over two hundred army and naval officers who had access to the document and may have released its contents. It was a group too enormous for even the most skilled investigator to wade through.

Eugene had Mabel connect him to Colonel Price's section. His secretary told him to come to his office at once. When he got to the inspector general's suite, Price invited him inside. After some pleasantries, Eugene arranged a time for Price to inspect the documents room, inventory the plans, and question everyone in his unit. Price asked about their security procedures.

"We account for every copy at the end of every day, but once it leaves our safe room, Bob, we have no idea what is done with it," Eugene said.

"Maybe that's the problem," Price replied. "We should never allow the documents to leave the secure room."

"I've been saying that since day one on the General Staff, but everyone with a star on their shoulder is too busy to come down here and ignores my requests. They want to read our files in their cozy offices."

Everything he was saying was true. When he first arrived at his current duty assignment, before his life went to hell, he had recognized the gaping procedural holes. He had tried to implement improvements but faced massive resistance. Maybe this would serve as their wake-up call, and security would tighten. That possibly would get Eugene off the hook in another way. If he could no longer slip things past the guards, his blackmailer might stop asking him to do so.

"It sounds like you've been fighting this battle for a long time," Price said.

"Perhaps more will join me now to make genuine changes around here." Eugene took a virtual page from the nation's war-planning approach —the best defense was a good offense. Sounding outraged was Eugene's only option at this point.

"Heads definitely will roll over this," Price said. "The IG has brought in the FBI to mirror my investigation. The president and secretary of the War Department are looking for someone to blame."

"How can I help?"

"The FBI has an army of agents. They will question any person who ever glimpsed that plan. My job is to fix things so it doesn't happen again. That's where you come in. I need every report you made going back from your first day on the job that outlines weaknesses in the system."

"I'll dig them up." Misdirection was Eugene's strong suit. He planned to cooperate with Price and the FBI. However, he would subtly manipulate the information to implicate a flawed bureaucracy and protect himself.

"Thanks, Gene. I knew I could count on you." Price stood, signaling the meeting was over.

When Eugene returned to his duty section, Mabel gave him another dagger-filled stare and handed him a phone memo slip. "Your dry cleaning is ready."

"Thank you, Mabel." He glanced at the message. It said the store would close from twelve to one today. He looked at the wall clock. "It's almost noon. I'll pick up my uniform on my way back from lunch. Would you like anything from the 14th Street Deli?"

"I brought my meal like I do every day." She harrumphed, telegraphing her dislike for him. "Secretaries can't afford to eat out."

"Suit yourself. I'll be back in an hour."

After grabbing his coat and service cap, he went to the parking lot. It was 12:15. Forty-five minutes remained for the meeting window—ample time to make his stop. He drove straight to the sandwich shop, picked up a pastrami on rye, and threw it in the front seat. After circling the block twice to ensure no one followed him, he found a slot close to the Smithsonian Castle.

Before beginning his brisk walk, he put on the dark olive-green wool gloves to counter the frigid December air. The trees in the garden were utterly bare, but no one had swept the leaves from the concrete pathway. Clouds of steam escaped his mouth with every exhale. He sat on the first park bench and checked his watch. It was 12:45, still within the window mentioned in the message.

He had brought along the morning's newspaper in order to appear occupied, so he folded it to hold it in one hand and scanned the front-page article again. The journalist reported that an anonymous War Department source claimed victory over Hitler would require the United States' involvement alongside Britain and Russia. Eugene took a deep breath because those had been his exact words when he made arrangements to hand over the top secret plan. He had no idea a reporter would end up using them in a hard-hitting news story that would shake up all of Washington.

Minutes later, a man sat on the other end of the park bench. He had angled his fedora low and flipped up the collar of his wool coat, blocking most of his facial features. However, Eugene knew it was him. It was Sam. Eugene believed the probable Nazi agent had chosen the name to thumb his nose at the finger-pointing recruiter in the Uncle Sam posters.

"Quite the headline," Sam said.

"Yes, it is."

"Was that you?"

Sam's accusation hung in the chilly air, a threat intended to scare Eugene into compliance and make him so terrified that he would pee himself. That was precisely what he felt like doing.

"No," Eugene answered tersely. He had not leaked the information to the newspaper, but it was the byproduct of actions on which he had risked his and his country's future. "You're not the only one who wanted to get their hands on those plans."

"Whoever did made a grave mistake. Now the information is useless."

He flashed back to the humid summer evening that marked the end of life as he knew it. The night he had made his way to the street outside the Old Ebbitt Grill after several drinks and a quick, passionate interlude with a blonde he had never met before in the men's room. The encounter was unexpected but not out of the blue for him. He loved his wife but could not pass up opportunities when they presented themselves. What red-blooded American man could? A man standing on the corner glanced at him when he stumbled a bit, but he had thought nothing of it.

Eugene Stanton had never been so wrong. The next morning, he found an envelope in his car containing a photo of the tryst and a note to meet at this bench at noon. Sam showed up and made it clear that he had Eugene's neck in a noose and would tighten it anytime he wished.

It had been eighteen months of hell. The demands started small, with Sam asking for organizational charts of the War Department. Anyone could have pieced together most of what he initially asked for through public documents, so Eugene had not felt guilty. However, when he asked for the list of American spies in Germany a year ago, Eugene knew he had dug himself into a hole. Then, the day Sam asked him to run over an aide to Vice President Henry Wallace two weeks ago and make it look like an accident, he knew he would never get out of the quagmire.

When Sam approached him on Monday, ordering him to get him a copy of Rainbow Five, Eugene stopped in his tracks. The title itself was top secret, as was the United States' strategy for entering the war. It centered on building strength for offensive operations in Europe and defeating Japan while initially losing the Philippines. This strategy assumed an alliance between the US, Britain, and France.

Filling the request would have made Eugene the country's worst traitor since Benedict Arnold. His name would forever be associated with treason. Failure to surrender the documents would not only destroy his marriage but result in a life sentence at Leavenworth for the tryst and his previous disclosures. He had considered handing over a fake plan but worried that Sam might have another source for them and would compare it to what Eugene gave him. As far as he could see, the only way out was to comply and make the plans useless by publicly compromising them.

Eugene had spent the rest of the duty day on Monday following Sam's ultimatum locked in his office, copying Rainbow Five word for word onto paper. After returning the classified plan to the safe room, he needed to find someone important who was careful and knew they were committing treason to do his dirty work. A speech on the floor of the Senate the previous week informed him exactly who to target: Senator Burton Wheeler. Wheeler, an isolationist, believed President Roosevelt was itching for a reason to enter the war, a theory that Eugene had to agree with. The Lend-Lease Act, which the president advocated for and signed into law in March, had made supporting the Allies a top priority. It had brought the United States another step closer to joining the conflict. Wheeler was also a staunch supporter of the America First Committee, an influential isolationist pressure group in the United States that opposed American involvement in the war underway in Europe. He had been ripe for the picking.

Tuesday, after officers had checked out twenty copies, he signed for the original, which his section kept in a uniquely colored folder to distinguish it from the others. Once in his office behind closed doors, he swapped the plan with an old, declassified report but saved the cover page. He handed back the file an hour later, showing the custodian the front to identify it.

When he had gone out with the plans wrapped in brown paper in his briefcase, he had intentionally grabbed the wrong winter coat on the tree stand. He had taken the captain's jacket, so if any investigation led them to the station, witnesses would say they saw a captain. Only someone familiar with army uniforms would have detected the incorrect insignia.

He had left the building late in the day and called the senator's workplace from a pay phone. He had convinced Wheeler's aide that he had crucial information about a deception of massive proportions by explaining his work on the War Department General Staff had exposed rumors amongst high-ranking officers that the president was planning a troop deployment without Senate approval. They had arranged for Eugene to place the information in a locker at Union Station the next day by noon and tape the key under a toilet in the men's room. Eugene had stipulated that he needed to receive the document back at the same time the following day and return it to the safe.

After observing the pickup, Eugene proceeded to the Smithsonian

Castle park bench, met with Sam, and handed over the handwritten copy of Rainbow Five.

Wednesday had passed as expected, with him returning the plans without anyone knowing they had been missing. He had gotten drunk as a skunk that night, sick to his stomach over what he had done. He had turned over the most classified documents in the War Department to Sam. Sam had never said as much, but Eugene knew in his bones that he was a Nazi spy. Though Eugene had relied on Senator Wheeler's hatred for Roosevelt and armed conflict to make them useless, he had given the enemy their secret plans. There was no getting around that damning fact.

He had gone to bed intoxicated, praying for a miracle, and woken hungover, to find his prayers answered. The world knew the United States' strategy. Now, the secretary of war would task his office to devise another plan just as grand.

That deserved a toast.

After leaving the park, Eugene went to a bar that was not the Old Ebbitt and ordered a double bourbon, neat. He raised his glass and silently said, "Thank God for pompous old senators."

2

Washington, DC, Friday, December 5, 1941

Hattie glanced to her left. Maya was asleep with her head leaning against the hard metal of the plane's fuselage. The engines had soothed Hattie to sleep several times, but now, being in US airspace had her too energized to rest.

Thirty-six hours on a military aircraft was tiring but not as austere as she had imagined it might be when Leo said the FBI had sent transport from the army. The agency was anxious to learn everything the Kessler brothers knew. Ernst and Gunter were two German aeronautical engineers whom Maya, Leo, Hattie, and her father discovered at the secret Nazi military plane factory in the Brazilian jungle minutes before destroying it. The Kesslers defected to avoid an SS execution, agreeing to relay everything they knew about the long-range bomber they were working on and other Luftwaffe secrets.

Once it was clear the plane the Kesslers had been working on was designed to attack the United States, and that plan had something to do with a Japanese attack in the near future, time became Hattie's enemy. She had to warn military authorities before it was too late and keep her promise to her father. Before Karl had fallen into a coma after taking a bullet to the shoulder at the factory, he made Hattie promise to get the lists of German and American spies to his mentor. The Professor was the one person he trusted to get them safely into the right hands and unearth the traitor in the War Department.

Hattie, Maya, and Leo were now closing in on their destination. The army crewmen rotated duties from Rio to Natal, French Guiana, and Puerto Rico before they stopped for a twelve-hour crew rest. After refueling in Miami, they were on their final leg to Washington, DC. The co-pilot had come aft a while ago to say they would be landing soon.

This closing part of the trek felt odd to Hattie. So much had happened since she arrived in Brazil ten months ago. She left under a cloud, the FBI having seen to it that the media labeled her the daughter of a traitor, something that had cost her her recording contract. Hattie had been singing at dive bars for pennies instead of the Copacabana club. She had been at the bottom with a broken heart from a cheating lover, and her father was a fugitive. The FBI was threatening her sister's freedom to get Hattie to lure him from hiding. She had hated her mother. And she had trusted David, her pianist and supposed boyfriend. He had been the only one she had entrusted with her biggest secret, which was that she loved women.

She would return to the US within an hour, but everything had changed. In Brazil, her stardom had skyrocketed higher and faster than she had ever dreamed. She had a recording contract with Maggie Moore's new label. She had met the love of her life and was building a life with her. Her father was still on the run, but she had come to know the real him, the man who was a master spy and had been training her to be as good as he was, which came with a disturbing consequence—a body count nearing a half dozen. Then there was her mother. She had developed a profound respect for Eva and was hopeful that she and her father might reconcile. And David, who had betrayed her by working for the Nazis, was dead, killed by Strom Wagner, the mastermind of the Luftwaffe project the Kessler brothers were working on.

She had also met Leo Bell. He had started as an acquaintance who worked at the American Embassy as a naval attaché. He had helped her in so many ways, thwarting the Brazilian president's assassination on the yacht, getting Eva back from Nazi captors, and destroying the secret

German factory in the jungle. Only a few days ago, she learned he was much like her father, a covert spy in the War Department recruited by the Professor. Besides Maya, he had become her most trusted friend.

Looking back now at her old life, she could only see its negative aspects —perpetually challenged to stay off the booze, to keep her sex life a secret, to be as successful as Eva Machado, and to retain that family connection. But now those things came with ease. Maya's love kept her centered and sober. Her parents knew and accepted Maya as her life partner. She was no longer in competition with her mother, and she, in fact, welcomed performing with Eva and enjoyed living with her. She loved that her father shared the part of himself he had hidden from her for decades. Her, Eva's, and Karl's lives now were so intertwined that she could not imagine being apart from them.

The co-pilot poked his head into the main compartment again and announced loudly over the roar of the engines, "We'll be on the ground in a few minutes. Stay in your seats."

Hattie nudged Maya's shoulder and waited until her eyes fluttered open. "Sorry to wake you, but we're about to land."

Maya straightened, sat taller in her seat, and looked out the tiny window.

Hattie followed her gaze. Sparse lights dotted the dark wooded terrain below the clear evening sky but quickly grew in number, highlighting the cityscape in an amber glow. They were over a populated area, and their altitude was continuously dropping. Treetops became discernable in the night with the aid of illumination from the crescent moon and twinkling stars overhead. The trees sped by the glass at an alarming speed as their plane dropped lower and lower. Once they were even with the tree line, the plane's wheels contacted the ground. They bounced twice, and the engines whined louder briefly as they decelerated rapidly. Hattie's pulse raced, and she instinctively threw a straight arm to the seatback in front of her to keep from sliding forward and hitting it.

They coasted on the tarmac for a while before stopping at a sizeable hangar, and the motors sputtered until they were off. A series of light poles illuminated big black letters painted on the building wall, spelling out

Bolling Field. Military vehicles approached the plane, one hauling mobile metal stairs.

An enlisted man popped up from his seat and opened the rear passenger door. Frosty air wafted into the cabin, prompting Hattie to stand and grab her and Maya's coats from the open bin over their row. She stood in the aisle to give Maya room. "Here. Put this on."

"I've never been in cold weather before," Maya said, slipping her arms into the jacket sleeves. "Heck, I've never been outside Brazil. Not until I got on this plane."

"You'll get used to it," Hattie said, putting on her wool winter jacket. "It's nice having four distinct seasons."

Maya burrowed deeper into her coat, raising her eyebrows. At thirty-four, she had only known the tropical paradise of Brazil. Hattie hoped their search for the Professor and the War Department mole would broaden Maya's horizons and give her a first experience with snow.

Hattie returned to her seat and waited for Leo Bell to instruct them on what to do. As a naval commander, he was the ranking officer on the plane and was responsible for the special passengers—the original purpose of the flight. FBI Special Agent Samuel Knight was escorting Gunter and Ernst Kessler from Rio.

Once the enlisted men walked all the luggage off the plane, Leo came aft. "Ladies, I have to go with Agent Knight to take the Kesslers to FBI Headquarters. It will probably be a long night, so I can't take you into town. I can arrange for a cab." He looked at Hattie. "Do you plan to stay at your sister's?"

"I thought we would go to a hotel near Georgetown since our search for the Professor will start there."

"Good. The first thing on our agenda is to brief my bosses on what happened this week and what we learned about the Japanese plan to attack the US. We stick to our stories." He leaned closer and whispered so no one else in the cabin would hear. "And leave out any mention of your father." He handed Hattie a business card, and she glanced at it. "This is the address of my office in the Munitions Building. Be there at ten in the morning."

"It will be Saturday. Does the senior staff work weekends?"

Leo snorted. "Only when crap hits the fan, but my boss alerted all the major players. My boss is hoping to have a full house for the briefing. I'm not as optimistic."

"We'll be there."

"If anything comes up, call me. If I don't answer, hang up and dial my house. I've written my home address and phone number on the back. My wife will get a message to me."

"Ah, Beverly. I'd love to meet her," Hattie said. Although he had only mentioned her a few times, she sensed his devotion to the woman.

"And I'm sure she would love to meet you once I tell her about you being here." He leaned closer again. "I've spoken to the Kesslers about not mentioning your father. They're grateful for us saving their lives, so they'll say that only the three of us got them out."

Hattie nodded. If anyone knew that Karl James had been at the airfield and was in a coma after being wounded there, the Nazis and the Brazilian and American authorities would be hunting for him. It had not been safe to take him to a hospital where someone might have recognized him, so they had taken him to her mother's home, where a trusted doctor had patched him up. Eva had agreed to care for him there until he woke up and recovered enough to be moved.

When she and Maya deplaned, two military jeeps pulled up, and their drivers loaded their luggage in the back. The air outside had to be near freezing. Hattie inhaled. The smell of aircraft fuel was strong, but the frigid temperature was a familiar reminder that she was back home. After being away for nearly a year, she should have missed it more than she had, but with her parents in Brazil and having found the love of her life there made Rio feel more like home.

Maya flipped up her collar, folded her arms across her chest, and shivered. "Wow, this is cold."

Leo gestured to one of the jeeps, where a man was in the driver's seat. "He'll take you to get your passports stamped in the Operations Building. You can freshen up there and call a cab to pick you up at the main gate. He'll run you out there when you're ready."

Hattie gave Leo a brief hug. Maya did, too.

"Thank you, Leo," Hattie said. "We'll see you tomorrow at ten."

Leo, Knight, and the Kesslers boarded one jeep while Hattie and Maya got into the other. Both took off toward a collection of structures, but Leo's vehicle veered right when they got closer. Hattie's continued straight and stopped in front of a two-story facility with a sign identifying it as the Operations Building.

The driver led them inside, where a clerk behind a counter asked for their passports, stamped them several times, and handed them back. Hattie examined hers. The man had backdated the first entry to document her departure from Rio, and the second annotated her arrival in the United States today. She supposed Agent Knight had arranged for their documents to appear proper.

After using the bathroom and washing up, they returned to the counter.

"Can you request a taxi service and have them pick us up at the gate?" Hattie asked.

"Where to?" the clerk said.

Hattie considered giving him the name of the hotel she had in mind, but she decided to remain guarded until she was sure who to trust. "Tell them it's a run to Georgetown."

The enlisted man shrugged and placed the call. "They said half an hour."

"We better get a move on," the driver said. "At this time on a Friday night, that could mean anything from fifteen minutes to an hour."

The clerk filled two paper cups halfway with hot coffee from a percolator behind his desk and handed them to Hattie and Maya. "You might need a little joe in this cold."

Hattie thanked him and hopped into the jeep with Maya. The driver took them to the main gate and waited with them a few feet outside the fence. He did not ask questions, nor did he engage in chitchat. He remained quiet in his army uniform and winter coat, with his arms close to his chest to trap his body heat. Perhaps higher-ups had ordered him not to talk, or maybe late-night military plane arrivals were not unusual after all.

Hattie glanced over her shoulder at Maya, who had huddled stiffly in the back seat, sipping coffee. Her breath rose in a cloud with every exhalation. "Are you warm enough?"

"You're kidding, right?" Maya's hands shook as she brought the cup to her mouth again. "I'm glad I changed out of my dress at the last stop and put on pants."

"We'll get you inside soon," Hattie said.

Minutes later, headlights approached the base's main gate. The taxi slowed and turned around, shy of the guard shack, parking several yards from their jeep.

The cabbie got out when Hattie and Maya stepped toward the car. A muscular younger man with dark hair, he tipped his newsboy cap back as they approached. "Ladies, it's a little late to be leaving the base."

"Long day," Hattie said. "Would you mind helping with our bags?"

"Sure thing." He popped the trunk, and he and the military driver had their luggage loaded in one trip.

Hattie turned to the enlisted man. "Thank you. Stay warm."

He gave her a two-finger salute and drove onto the post.

The cabbie opened the back passenger door and gestured for Hattie and Maya to board. Once they were in and he was behind the wheel, he craned his neck toward the back seat. "Where to, ladies?"

"The Mayflower," Hattie said. She had stayed there a few times when she was in town for a performance and not staying with her sister or father. The hotel, known for its expensive elegance and luxury, was in the heart of the Georgetown neighborhood in Washington. Its security and discretion were exceptional.

"You got it." He grinned, put the car in gear, and drove. He was clearly expecting a big tip from the big spenders.

After crossing the John Philip Sousa Bridge, the driver navigated in the light late-evening traffic in the capital city. The cabbie was a pleasant fellow, pointing out various landmarks and other points of interest. When they went by Union Station, Hattie knew where she was. They passed the Carnegie Library and were soon at the Mayflower's driveway.

A porter dressed sharply in a black suit, bow tie, and bowler cap hurriedly opened the rear passenger door, offering his hand to Hattie. "Welcome to the Mayflower."

"Thank you," she said. "We have six bags."

He helped Maya out while Hattie paid the fare and tipped the cabbie, who replied by removing his hat and bowing slightly with a generous smile.

"Thank you, miss." He returned to the cab but backed it up instead of pulling away, likely waiting to see if any guests exited, needing a ride.

Meanwhile, the porter loaded their luggage onto a cart and followed Hattie and Maya into the elegant two-story lobby. It didn't rival the opulence of Rio's Copacabana Palace Hotel, where Hattie headlined at the Golden Room, but the place was nonetheless luxurious.

Hattie approached the main desk. At this hour of the night there was no line.

A clerk greeted her. "Good evening, miss. How may I help you?"

"I don't have a reservation, but I'll need a room for several nights. Nothing too extravagant." Hattie remembered where she was and how traveling with another woman might appear. "With two beds."

"We're nearly fully booked, but let me see what we have available." The employee flipped through the registration book and glanced at the wall of cubbyholes for the room keys. "I have a small suite available through Thursday. It's on the second floor facing Connecticut Avenue."

"How much is that?"

"Twenty-five dollars a night."

"That's fine. We'll take it."

Maya tugged Hattie's coat sleeve and pulled her back several feet, whispering, "That's too much. Can we find somewhere less expensive?"

Hattie patted her hand. "It's okay. I've got this."

Maya said nothing, but her loud sigh said she was unhappy about staying in a hotel that cost five times what a room should.

"I'll explain in the room." Hattie went back to the desk. The clerk asked her to fill out the registration card. She filled it in with her name and address in New York City before giving it to the man.

He read it and looked at Hattie. "I'll be a moment, Miss James." He disappeared into a room behind the counter, returning moments later with an older man.

He stopped in front of Hattie. "I'm afraid we don't have any rooms available, Miss James." The right corner of his lips twitched upward briefly in disgust.

Hattie had seen that reaction before following her father's arrest and subsequent escape from federal custody. Newspaper headlines had painted his name in a poor light for days, and in virtually every article, reporters pointed out that he was the father of the famous singer Hattie James. Though all that happened nearly a year ago, these two men apparently had very long memories.

Hattie straightened her posture and said in a firm tone, "Check again."

"There's nothing here for you, Miss James." His reply was even snootier than his first.

"Fine. I know when I'm not welcome." Hattie snatched the card from his hand so he would have no record of her and told the porter to follow them outside. When she stormed out, ready to ask the valet for a cab, she saw the taxi they had arrived in. She waved it up.

The car pulled forward, and the driver jumped out. He opened the passenger door and asked, "No vacancies, miss?"

"I'm afraid not."

The cabbie loaded their luggage back into his vehicle and returned to his seat. "Where to?"

"Where can we get a room at this time of night? We're quite tired from our trip."

Midnight approached. They were exhausted and needed a shower. She had wanted the privacy and security afforded by a place like the Mayflower but, at this point, would settle for any room with a decent mattress.

He glanced over his shoulder. "The Commodore still had its vacancy light on when we passed it. It's near Union Station."

"Take us there, please." Hattie clenched her fingers into a fist so hard that her fingernails might have drawn blood from her palm.

"In a jiffy."

When he faced the road and turned into traffic, Maya clutched Hattie's hand resting on the bench seat, squeezed gently, and whispered, "I didn't want to stay there, anyway."

"You're right." Hattie scrunched her nose and smiled. She had spent the last day and a half this close to Maya on the plane, kept apart by the need to be circumspect. They could not hold hands like this with the crew, Agent Knight, and the Kessler brothers on board. Having fretted the entire trip over her father and the mission he had given her, she had needed a touch like this to reassure her that things would be okay.

Minutes later, the driver pulled in front of the Commodore Hotel. Hattie had seen worse places, but not many. This was not the level of establishment that provided valet service, so the cabbie ran to the passenger side and helped her and Maya out. "I'll get your bags, ladies. You go on in and make sure the place is suitable. Otherwise, I'll cart you around town until we find something."

"You're very kind," Hattie said. "What is your name?"

"Harold, but all my friends call me Harry."

"Well, Harry, I'd like to think we're friends now. This is my friend Maya, and I'm—"

"Hattie James. Heck, I'd know your face anywhere. My mama has a few of your records."

"And you didn't mind all the news about me about this time a year ago?"

"I paid that no mind, Miss James. The newspapers are constantly screeching about something. I figure whatever they accused your daddy of has nothing to do with someone as sweet as you."

"I appreciate the vote of confidence, Harry. Let me see if they have a room. We'll be right back."

Hattie and Maya went inside. The lobby was plain but clean, with signs of fresh paint. A mop and bucket were in the corner. The clerk behind the desk had his feet up on the counter and his face buried in a book.

Hattie stepped up. "Good evening."

"Geez." She had startled him. "Wow. I'm sorry, ladies. When I get into a good book, I'm really into it."

"What are you reading?" Hattie asked.

He held up the novel. "Agatha Christie. *Evil Under the Sun*. Nothing like a good mystery."

"I can't agree more," Hattie said. "We would like a room with two beds for the night."

"I have one for tonight, but it's on the third floor with a common bathroom. You'd have to share with the rest of the people on three."

"Do you have anything with a private bath?"

"Yes, but it has a double bed. It's on the first floor."

"We'll take it. My cousin and I have shared on occasion."

The man did not balk at Hattie's explanation that they were cousins and brought out a registration card. "I'll need you to fill this out. It will be four dollars a night. Coffee and donuts in the lobby starting at six until they run out."

"That's fine."

"I'll get Harry and the bags," Maya said before she retraced her steps outside the main door.

Hattie filled out the required information using her full first name, Harriet, to avoid being recognized. She paid the clerk when the cabbie and Maya entered with their luggage, asked for an eight o'clock wake-up call, and thanked the man. After he gave her the room key, she approached Harry. "I hate to ask, Harry, but would you mind helping us with the suitcases to our room? It's on this floor."

"Sure thing, Miss James." Harry was big and strong and loaded up with four bags. Hattie and Maya each grabbed one and went down the hallway. Hattie opened the door and turned on the light, revealing a bare-bones hotel room. But the crucial element was its cleanliness.

"You can put the luggage next to the bed, Harry," Maya said.

Hattie pulled out cash from her purse to cover the cab fare and another sizeable gratuity, but Harry waved her off. "Just the dollar, Miss James. You've already tipped me way too much tonight."

Hattie laughed. "That's the first time anyone has refused a tip from me."

"It wouldn't be right otherwise."

"Are you working tomorrow, Harry?"

"Yes, miss. I start at nine."

"That's perfect. Maya and I have to be somewhere at ten. Could you pick us up at nine thirty?"

"It would be my pleasure."

Hattie thanked him again before he left, locking the door after him. When she turned around, she discovered Maya had closed the drapes and was unpacking her smaller overnight bag. Hattie went to her and placed a hand on her arm. The condescending attitude of the man at the Mayflower reopened old wounds, not to mention reminding Hattie of her father. She wondered whether he was still alive and, if he was, what his chances were of recovering enough to be whole again.

"Tell me my father will be all right."

Maya put her folded clothes down and pulled Hattie into a tight hug. "Karl is strong. He's as stubborn as you are."

Hattie laughed. "Stubborner."

"Is that a word?" Maya chuckled. "But I'm sure his body is healing. He will wake soon, and your mother will drive him stir-crazy to the point that he will do anything to get better."

Hattie laughed again. "They still love each other but have yet to tell the other as much."

"They will. Who knows? You might have a baby brother or sister this time next year." Maya snickered.

Hattie pulled back, thrown off at the thought of her parents having another child at their age. "Is that even possible? My mother is fifty-five."

"Have her cycles stopped?"

"I don't know." Hattie plopped onto the mattress, finding it as stiff as a board. Images of her mother pregnant and dealing with diapers made her giggle. "She would go bonkers."

Maya sat beside her and patted her leg. "It's good to hear you laugh."

Hattie grazed a finger down Maya's cheek. "You always know exactly what I need."

3

Rio de Janeiro, Brazil, Friday, December 5, 1941

Eva Machado stepped into the wings, waiting for the band leader to announce her name over the club's ultramodern sound system. It had been over a year since she had performed at the elite Golden Room. Before that, she had only periodically appeared on a big stage over the previous three years. After she turned fifty, performing regularly had taken a toll on her voice and body to a level she had never experienced, requiring lengthier periods to recover. Doing performances day after day had become impossible. Eva had been giddy with maternal pride when Hattie signed up to headline at the club, widely considered the best in South and Central America. Hattie was following in her footsteps, living the life Eva could no longer revel in.

Yet here she was, about to go onto the stage again. As ready as she had been to step down years ago, she was as willing to step up when her daughter needed her. Hattie's contract had allowed her to give her notice to the hotel owner and only forfeit two weeks of pay when she had had to return to the States. However, she had hated leaving the club in the lurch and tried to soften the blow by convincing Eva to perform one day a week. Thrilled to have Eva on their roster again, the owner had added her name to the hotel marquee and placed ads in newspapers throughout the region. Eva was giddy with the results. Well, she was as giddy as someone her age could get. Tonight's show had attracted guests from thousands of miles away. She still had it.

The band leader's voice came over the speaker. "Ladies and gentlemen, the Copacabana Palace Hotel and the Golden Room are proud to present Brazil's greatest treasure, Miss Eva Machado."

The musicians began playing her opening song. As the curtains drew open, Eva walked onto the stage gracefully and confidently as if her lengthy absence had never existed. The guests roared with applause and whistles. As she walked past the piano, she nodded at Zoya, one of the most talented students she had taught since she started teaching music. Zoya's face beamed as brightly as the spotlight Eva stepped into. Tonight marked the first time she and her star pupil would perform together in front of an audience, and Eva was equally excited about the experience.

Eva hit the center mark at the microphone right on cue to belt out her first note. The band was impeccable during the ninety-minute show, the crowd was exuberant, and Eva felt energized, like she was thirty years younger at the start of her career. And when she walked off, that electrifying high followed her through the wings for a few extra moments.

A server in the backstage corridor congratulated Eva on an incredible show, jolting her from the performance haze she had been in. The next instant, exhaustion hit her like a freight train. Reality had sunk in: She was still fifty-five and had given up full-time performing for a reason. The strain of worry and caring for Karl, no doubt, was taking a toll as well.

She reached her dressing room—Hattie's old room—and collapsed on the couch. She barely mustered the energy to pick up the towel on the side table and wipe the sweat from her forehead.

A knock on the door drew her attention, but she still lacked the strength to rise and open the door. "Who is it?" she shouted in Portuguese.

"It's Zoya. May I come in?"

"Yes, of course." Eva put all her might into it and sat straight when the door opened. "Come in, young lady, and close the door."

Zoya walked inside. She was a cute thing. When Eva took her on as a student, she had barely turned eighteen; she must have been about twenty-one now.

"I don't know where you get your energy," Zoya said, "but that was an amazing show. You brought the house down."

"I tapped out my strength, so I doubt I'll be able to match the performance next week."

"You're too modest. It was an honor playing for you."

"The honor was mine." Eva patted the cushion beside her. "Sit."

Zoya did.

"I knew from the first day you came to my music studio that you would become one of the country's best pianists. Tonight proved my prediction. Your performance was flawless."

"Thank you, Miss Machado. You're too kind."

"Please call me Eva. We are colleagues now."

Zoya laughed. "That will take some getting used to."

Working with her on Hattie's stage reminded Eva of another responsibility she had taken on when Hattie and Maya left for the States two days ago. They were rebuilding the Halo Club, which had been burned down last year by arson, and had yet to piece together a band for the nightly performances that Hattie and others would give there. She could think of no one more qualified at the piano than the woman sitting beside her.

"Tell me, Zoya. Are you happy here?"

"I'm thrilled to be playing for you."

"You didn't answer the question."

"It's an honor to play at the Golden Room. When I played for Miss James and Miss Reyes ran things, it was an amazing experience."

"I hear a 'but' coming."

Zoya sighed. "But the men in the band can be... how shall I say... condescending."

"It can't be because of your age. Several of the musicians are in their twenties."

"It's not that." Zoya looked away. She appeared hesitant to voice her concern.

"Is it because you're a woman?"

"I believe so, yes."

"I understand the pressure you're under. You have to be twice as good to receive half the recognition, and I'm sure that makes you mad as hell. That same righteous anger fueled most of my career."

"There's not much I can do but deliver flawless performances."

Eva hated to see the defeated look in the eyes of such a talented pianist. The business would beat this woman down in a few years. Eva had had one advantage when she clawed her way up the ladder. The world knew her face and name as a front singer. As a behind-the-scenes musician, Zoya did not have throngs of fans chanting her name, demanding encores. Eva now understood why no older female musicians existed in the band circuit. The old male guard had browbeaten them into giving up.

"I think there is another prospect, or there will be." Eva clutched Zoya's hand. "Don't give up, young lady. An opportunity will fall in your lap soon."

Zoya grinned. "I won't."

"Now, can you help this old woman unzip this stage dress?"

Once Zoya left, Eva changed into the slacks and silk blouse she had arrived in. She checked in with the club manager, who thanked her for a top-notch performance, and they agreed on her performing at least another two weeks of Friday shows. "I'll see you next week."

Eva hopped in her coupe and started toward home. A few minutes into the drive, she remembered that the site foreman overseeing the Halo Club's construction had mentioned he would finish the floors today. She was anxious to see them, so she detoured to the Lapa district and parked near the side entrance. The exterior light illuminated the delivery door and the tiny metal bowls Maya had left out for the club mascot. She bent down, discovering they were empty. She knew the contractor gave her food every morning, so she picked up only the water container.

When she fumbled to find the right key on her ring, a fluffy orange-ringed cat nuzzled Eva's leg. "There you are, Coco. Have you been chasing the mice?"

Coco purred and brushed against her again before taking off toward the trash bins.

"I'll bring you more water in a minute."

Eva walked inside and turned on the overheads, revealing the checkered floor in the entry that, according to Maya's notes, had been in place for a while. More interested in seeing the results of today's work, she continued to the main room. After turning on the central bank of lights, she paused to take in the finished look.

The Honduran mahogany flooring had stunningly beautiful, rich hues with a glossy sheen. Its surface revealed an array of tight, straight grains with occasional eye-catching swirls. The contractor had it polished to perfection to a mirror-like finish, exuding a timeless sophistication. Tables and chairs would cover a good portion of the planks, but this rare view of the cavernous dining hall was breathtaking. The room was in an entirely different league than the Golden Room.

"My girls have made excellent choices."

As Eva stepped farther inside, she paused to consider the words she had just spoken. They had simply flowed from her mouth without thinking about them. She had said "my girls" as if she thought of Maya as her own daughter. Like she thought of Olivia's husband, Frank, as a son.

At first, Hattie and Maya's relationship seemed wrong to Eva, as the church's teachings had molded her initial reaction. However, the fear of losing Hattie after reconnecting with her following a thirteen-year estrangement had left her open to trying to understand it. The more time she spent with Maya, the more Eva could see the love she shared with Hattie. What had pushed Eva to total acceptance, though, was when Maya worked with the doctor in the middle of the night to save Karl's life. Eva was forever grateful she was in their lives. Maya had gained a special place in Eva's heart and was now a daughter to her.

She continued into the dining room, heading for the bar. The foreman used that area during the day as a makeshift office to reference the construction plans and keep his lists of his workers, materials, and things that needed doing. There, he also deposited messages for the owners.

She read the handwritten note at the end of the counter. The contractor said the granite slabs for the bathroom countertops were on a ship from Mexico and would arrive next week. He had arranged for two craftsmen to take measurements and complete the fabrication on site. Eva smiled. Hattie and Maya were close to resurrecting the Halo Club, but they needed to wrap up construction a month before Carnival started on February 13. Brazilians would still want to celebrate even if the government didn't sponsor an official celebration because of the war. This would give them enough time to finish the last touches and train the staff. Everything was proceeding on schedule, and Eva could not have been prouder of her girls and this venture.

She jotted a reply to the foreman's note, adding that she had chosen to go with the second choice for the bathroom fixtures. Maya's last words on the topic before leaving Rio: "I trust whatever you choose for the Halo Club will be the right one to set it apart from the Golden Room." That meant polished gold and brass were out. Antique brass and black would give the place the sleek, modern look the middle-aged and younger crowd craved.

Eva filled the cat's water bowl from the kitchen, placed it outside by the door, and locked up. Coco came over again, rubbing her side against Eva's leg. She stroked the cat from head to toe and purred back, "You be a good girl and keep the mice away."

Once in her coupe again, Eva drove to her house. She saw the sedan she expected in the driveway and pulled into the garage, securing the door behind her. Once she was in the breezeway in the backyard leading to the house, a light in the living room was visible through the double patio glass doors. The home nurse she hired to tend Karl during Eva's absence lounged on the couch, engrossed in a book while sipping a drink.

Eva entered through the private entrance close to Hattie's room, the one she shared with David Townsend when they first arrived and were faking their engagement for appearances. Learning the truth about that had angered her. She had genuinely liked the man and had thought Hattie was using him until events revealed they had entered into a mutual arrangement. She discovered later that he had been working for Strom Wagner, the senior Nazi officer who, among other horrible deeds, had held Eva captive in exchange for Karl's spy lists. Though David's association with him was against his will, it was still a devastating blow. Yes, he had tried to protect Hattie in the end, but he had also endangered Karl and Maya, and that was unforgivable.

She passed Karl's room without looking in on him and continued down the hallway, emerging into the living room. "Hello, Maria," she said in Portuguese.

Maria Mendes looked up, put her book on the coffee table, and stood from the couch. She wore casual clothes, not her nurse's uniform. Eva had given her strict instructions to tell no one she was working there and to disguise her appearance so no one would see a nurse coming and going. The only one to know was Dr. Navarro.

"Welcome back, Miss Machado."

"How is our patient?"

"No change, I'm afraid. I administered another IV of fluids and changed his dressing. His wound is healing fine with no signs of infection."

"That's good to hear." Eva placed her clutch on the entry hutch. "I'm in for the evening, so you can go and see that husband of yours."

"Thank you." She put on her light sweater. "Will you be needing me tomorrow?"

"Take the day off. I plan to stay at home this Saturday. But if you wouldn't mind coming on Sunday, Dr. Navarro will come by around noon after church service. He would like to discuss the patient's progress and go over your concerns."

"Of course. Noon it is." Maria gathered her purse and a nurse's bag camouflaged in a woven shopping sack.

Eva walked her through the front door. A single outdoor light illuminated the garden and the route to her car. She gave Maria's hand a firm squeeze. "Thank you for taking good care of him."

After Maria drove away, Eva secured the gate and returned inside. She whipped up scrambled eggs in the kitchen and gobbled them down along with some bread and a few slices of mango and avocado. Once she cleaned up the dishes, she peeked in on Karl. He was still unconscious but breathing normally and appeared comfortable, so she prepared for sleep.

After a quick shower, she changed into a nightgown, brushed her teeth, and applied face cream. She grabbed her eyeglasses and a hardback novel from the nightstand. Padding in her slippers, she returned to the guest room. Karl was on one side of the double bed, so Eva slipped between the covers, kissed him on the forehead, and put on her spectacles.

"Now, where were we?" She flipped to the page with the bookmark and read aloud a new chapter from Agatha Christie's *Evil Under the Sun*. Nothing rivaled a good mystery.

4

Washington, DC, Saturday, December 6, 1941

Hattie looked around her and Maya's hotel room one last time to ensure they had not forgotten anything. Her gaze alighted on the bed, if anyone could call it that. It more resembled a park bench draped in sheets. While the room was clean enough to want to stay, the way her back felt after only one night on that plank mandated finding another place.

She grabbed the rest of their suitcases and walked them to the lobby. Hattie saw Maya fixing two cups of coffee at the table in the corner. She dropped the bags with their other luggage and joined her.

"There's only one donut left. Would you like to share?" Maya asked, handing her a cup.

"You can have it. My stomach is always a little off for a few days when I travel."

Maya placed the pastry back in the box. "Let's leave it for the next guest. We can grab something later."

They sipped their coffee until a taxi pulled up to the front door precisely at nine thirty.

Harry walked inside, holding his newsboy cap. "Morning, ladies." He glanced at the assortment of suitcases. "Not staying another night?"

Hattie looked around to ensure a staff member was not close by. "My back can't take the bed."

"I'm sure sorry about that, Miss James. I'd heard good things about this place, but I guess I won't be recommending it anymore."

Hattie touched his forearm. "Don't get me wrong. It's a pleasant hotel. Clean and safe, but the mattress needed some breaking in."

"Good to know." He gestured toward the door. "You ladies ready? Shall I get your bags?"

"Yes, please."

Hattie and Maya each grabbed a smaller bag while Harry again lugged the others. He loaded everything in the trunk and helped them board. "Where to?"

"We have to meet a friend at the Munitions Building at ten."

"That's about fifteen minutes away. I'll get you there in plenty of time." He hopped in behind the wheel and held up a lumpy paper napkin. "My mama made fresh sweet rolls this morning. When I told her about having to pick up Hattie James for my first stop, she insisted I bring you some. Care for one?"

"That's truly kind of you, Harry. We would love some," Hattie said, accepting the offering.

She and Maya nibbled on the pastries and chatted with Harry, who pointed out more interesting city sights as he drove. Familiar with the area, Hattie set her attention on Maya's awe of the nation's capital and wished she could be the one to show Maya the city. Before they left, she would have to make time to tour the Tidal Basin and National Mall with Maya on foot. Even in the winter, the views from the walking trails were spectacular.

Soon, he turned onto Constitution Avenue and asked, "The Munitions Building is mighty big. Do you know which wing? I'd hate to have you walking a long way in heels."

Hattie pulled out the business card Leo gave her last night. "I'm afraid I don't know which wing. I only have the main address."

"Is your friend army or navy?"

"Navy. Why?"

"I'll drop you close to 17th Street then. That's the Navy side. What do you plan to do with your bags?"

"Thanks, Harry," Hattie said. "Our friend lives in the area and has a car. I'm sure he'll help us."

He stopped the taxi closer to the far end of the building near an entrance. "I guess you won't be needing my services any longer."

"We might. If I have to call the cab company and want you to drive us, who should I ask for?"

"Harry Cooper at your service, ma'am." He hopped out and, after helping them to the curb, brought their luggage inside the doors, placing the bags against the wall.

Hattie paid him the fare with another generous tip and extended her hand. "You are a gentleman, Harry Cooper. Thank you for your help and kindness. If you or your mother are ever close to one of my shows, I want you to send a message backstage saying you're in town. You will be my guest."

Harry laughed, shaking her hand. "That will make me son of the year." When she tried to return the rest of the pastries, he patted his belly and said, "Keep them. Otherwise, I'll put on a few extra pounds."

Maya thanked him and rested them on her purse.

"You ladies take care of yourselves."

As he drove away, Hattie took Maya inside to get her out of the cold. Besides the two enlisted navy guards at the check-in station, the building looked empty, much as Leo had predicted. Hattie rubbed Maya's arms through her winter coat sleeves to help her stop her teeth from chattering. "You're really cold."

"This isn't Rio."

"Far from it." Hattie laughed. "Harry sure is a nice man."

"He has a crush on you." Maya snickered.

"Who has a crush?" a male voice said from behind Hattie. She turned her head to see Leo approaching, dressed in his black service dress uniform. He glanced at the stack of suitcases. "What's up with the luggage?"

"Long story," Hattie said. "Where can we keep them until after our meeting?"

"Hold on." Leo went to the guard desk and called someone on the phone, saying he needed two enlisted men at the northeast door of Wing One quickly.

While they waited, Hattie filled in Leo about the debacle at the Mayflower and Commodore, highlighting the kindness of their cab driver.

"Harry sounds like a fine man," Leo said. He turned when two in navy uniforms approached. They stood straight at attention to receive their orders. He gave one a set of keys. "I need these bags put into the trunk of my car. I'm in space 142. Return the keys to my office when you're done."

The one with the keys popped straighter. "Aye, sir."

Before the men rushed off, Hattie called out. "Wait." She gathered the remainder of the sweet rolls Harry's mother had made from Maya's purse and handed them each one. "For your trouble."

The men beamed from ear to ear and said, "Thank you, ma'am." They stuffed them into their mouths, picked up their bags, and disappeared down the hallway.

Leo laughed. "Where's my pastry?"

"Sorry, that was the last of them." Hattie cocked her head, giving him the side-eye. "Besides, I don't see you hauling a bag."

He smoothed the lapels of his uniform jacket. "I can't afford to get this dirty. We have our meeting in a few minutes." Once the guard gave them visitor passes, Leo led them down the main corridor to the third wing. They passed no one in the hallway.

"Is anyone working today?" Hattie asked.

"It's Saturday. This place is a ghost town on weekends unless you're on the watch desk or called in for something hot." Leo stopped at the door marked Naval Intelligence. They went inside, but no one was there.

The ample room had six metal desks, each neatly arranged in two rows, and the tops were uncluttered. Filing cabinets lined two walls. Three other doors led to different areas, one labeled as "Classified Room" and the other "Briefing Room."

"We're supposed to start at ten thirty," Leo said.

"Who will we be speaking to?"

"After I told my boss what we stumbled across, he called a meeting of all ranking officers in Military Intelligence and operations for the army, navy, and the War Department General Staff. We'll see who shows up on a Saturday."

Maya snorted. "They sound like every government official in Rio.

Unless something bad happens or the newspapers make a big fuss, there's no urgency."

"Some are like that here," Leo said, "but I like to think that we take things a bit more seriously in Washington."

Maya snorted again, which Hattie understood. Many officials in Brazil were corrupt, lazy, or both. Maya's interaction with the man who was supposed to investigate her sister's disappearance had reinforced her impression. He refused to act on anything until the newspapers or the country's president breathed down his neck.

Leo opened the door to the conference room and let Hattie and Maya inside. "Can I get you some coffee?"

"We had some at the hotel," Maya said, removing her jacket, "but thank you."

"Did you get to spend much time with Beverly last night?" Hattie asked.

"A few hours before I had to change and come here." Leo took their jackets and hung them on a coat tree in the outer office.

"I'm glad." Hattie patted his hand. "I'm sure she was happy to see you."

"I definitely surprised her." He laughed. "She nearly hit me over the head with my three iron when I walked in the door."

Hattie chuckled. "You didn't tell her you were coming?"

"I couldn't. Our trip was classified. I probably shouldn't have gone home until I knew how long I'd be staying. She knows my job can take me anywhere at a moment's notice. I hate getting her hopes up and having her think I might be around for a spell."

"You haven't told me much about Beverly, but you should have more faith in her. If she's anything like you, she'll temper her expectations and take whatever time she can get with you."

He sighed. "You're right. I need to cram in whatever time we can so she can enjoy it."

"And you." Hattie stabbed his arm with her index finger to emphasize her point.

While they waited, Leo filled them in on the Kessler brothers. "Agent Knight had several agents there interrogating them through the night. He even brought in aeronautical engineers from the Army Air Forces and the Martin Company."

"The Martin Company?" Maya asked.

"They are one of the largest American aircraft manufacturers, plus they have a government contract to build a new medium-range bomber for the army. Martin has a headquarters in Baltimore, so it was easy to get a specialist there to help with the interrogation. They spent hours picking the brains of the Kesslers." Leo turned to Hattie. "That was the right call at the airfield saying we should bring them."

"When I met them in the Golden Room, they seemed like two good-hearted men who were good at their job." Agent Knight had twisted her arm to pump them for information. Gunter's infatuation with her was charming. His brother, Ernst, was on the quiet side but was equally entertaining when he spoke.

"Well, they are singing like canaries. They are a treasure trove of intelligence on the Luftwaffe."

Someone behind them at the door cleared their throat loudly. Hattie pivoted. It was the men who had taken their luggage. One gave Leo his car keys while holding his other hand at his back. "You're all set, sir."

Leo said, "Thank you. You're dismissed."

One man's expression turned sheepish. "May I ask a question, sir?"

"Sure."

The man fixated on Hattie, appearing starstruck. "Are you Hattie James?"

"Yes, I am."

The other man elbowed the bolder one in the side. "Told you. Ask."

The first produced a Leica camera in a leather carrying case from behind his back. "Can we get a picture with you, Miss James?"

Hattie grinned. "Of course. Anything for our men in uniform." She turned to Leo. "Would you mind?"

He rolled his eyes and took the camera. "Anything for our men in uniform."

Hattie asked the men their names and where they were from. After shaking their hands, she stood between them and smiled for the camera as Leo snapped several pictures.

"This isn't a USO show, gentlemen," a voice said at the door behind Leo.

Leo turned around and quickly handed the camera to its owner. "Dismissed, men." Once the enlisted men departed, he addressed the older man in the same naval garb as he wore. This man was a bit shorter than Leo but carried himself with some importance. "Sorry, sir. The fellas were starstruck. Admiral Drummond, I'd like to introduce Hattie James and Maya Reyes."

Drummond had his service cap stuffed under his left arm. His right was free, but he did not offer his hand. If he intended that to be an insult, it worked. "Yes, I read your reports. You've had several active months down there."

Leo straightened his posture and rolled his neck, a sure sign the admiral's surly reception had agitated him. "Yes, sir. We thwarted an assassination attempt against the Brazilian president and an undertaking intended to halt the construction of our naval base in Natal. Miss James and Miss Reyes were instrumental in this success. Most recently, they helped me uncover the secret Nazi bomber factory about which we will inform you and the General Staff today."

"Yes, well, that's not going to happen."

"What do you mean? You said you had called for an urgent intelligence briefing."

"I did, but over half of the flag officers are out of town this weekend. The response I received was that unless I can present evidence of a credible, imminent threat, it can wait until Monday." Drummond sat at the head of the table and unbuttoned his uniform jacket. "Brief me."

Maya said nothing, but her harrumph said everything Hattie was thinking. Lazy. Complacent. Entitled.

Leo remained professional, closed the door, and invited Hattie and Maya to sit across from him. He walked the admiral through how FBI Special Agent Knight had identified several German nationals as possibly being the Nazi aeronautical engineers who had mysteriously disappeared from Berlin. Knight had tapped Hattie James to engage the targets to milk them for intelligence. The first two were the Kessler brothers. Two days later, Armand Klein, another engineer, arrived.

"Back up, Commander Bell," Drummond said. "When did you get into a scrape with Vice President Wallace and go on the run for the murder of his aide?"

"That would have been on the intervening day, sir."

"I was there when it happened, Admiral," Hattie said, speaking at last. "We both heard the shot, and Commander Bell went after the shooter."

Drummond waved Hattie off in a dismissive, condescending fashion. "Yes, yes. I read the report. Continue, Commander."

Leo glanced at Hattie with apologetic eyes before starting again. "Miss James, Miss Reyes, and Mr. Townsend were instrumental in helping me outrun the authorities until we could discover what those engineers were up to and clear my name."

"Speed this up, Bell. If we have enough credible intel, we can try to convene senior staff tomorrow."

"Yes, sir. Miss James engaged the second target last Saturday night."

It was hard to believe nearly a week had passed since Wagner had shot Karl at that airfield. Hattie needed to telephone her mother to find out whether he was awake.

Leo rubbed the back of his neck because this was, Hattie knew, where he had to get creative in his storytelling. "Miss James manipulated Klein into inviting her to his hotel room so she could get information out of him."

He told the story about how they learned about the secret plane factory and a strategic bomber the Nazis were building to strike the United States to coincide with some kind of Japanese attack. He detailed how they located the factory but omitted any mention of Karl's involvement.

"They called it Operation Amerika. Klein claimed, before his death, that all the attacks would be made to look like a Japanese plot. He said this would divert US resources from Europe to the Pacific. I can also report that Strom Wagner, who spearheaded the endeavor, was killed during our raid. Unfortunately, Mr. Townsend lost his life, too, and we could not recover his body. As we were about to leave the facility, we found the Kessler brothers, and they came willingly with us."

A lump formed in Hattie's throat at the mention of David's name. Leo had left out that Wagner had been manipulating David to feed him the location of the spy lists, which Hattie still hid in her purse. It was an enormous betrayal, even though, in the end, David had acted primarily to protect her.

"That is quite the story, Commander Bell. Do you have any concrete evidence beyond the ramblings of a dying man that a Japanese attack will take place tomorrow?"

"While planting the explosives, we discovered some interesting personal items that belonged to SS agents. These were all American—books, cigarettes, cash, and fake driver's licenses. We believe the Nazis intended to drop agents via parachute once over the border and continue on to their bombing run."

"That sounds like conjecture, Commander."

"It's an educated conclusion based on the intelligence gathered, which is what you pay me to do, Admiral."

"Without something more tangible, I won't recall the General Staff. Write up a report, and we will distribute it first thing Monday morning. I want you back in Rio by the end of the week."

Leo stretched his neck again. "Aye, sir. I'll have it on your desk within an hour."

When Drummond left, Leo slumped back in his chair, his face pale.

"Are you okay?" Hattie asked.

"I have a sinking feeling that something horrible will happen soon."

Maya leaned back, flopping her arms against the armrests. "I do, too."

Hattie focused on the doorway Admiral Drummond exited through moments ago. His lackadaisical attitude about a potential attack on the United States had her thinking now that he could be the traitor. She was likely off base with that conjecture, but one thing was for sure. The infiltrator worked in this building. "What if we went around your boss and found someone higher up who would listen?"

"That would be General Marshall, the chief of the War Department. That won't happen this weekend," Leo said. "We've done everything we can and just have to hope for the best."

Hattie sucked in a breath to calm her frustration. "So that's it?"

"For now. We need to focus on finding the Professor and getting her the lists. Then we find the mole." Leo popped up from his chair. "Wait here while I write up that report. I won't be long." He disappeared into a smaller adjoining office. The sound of his typing kept Hattie and Maya company as they discussed options for their search for the next forty-five minutes until Leo reappeared. "All done, ladies. Let's get you settled somewhere. Afterward, we can start our search for the Professor. I only have one week. So where is it going to be?"

"I think hotels are going to be hit-and-miss in this town," Hattie said. "Half the people love me. The other half hate me."

Leo rubbed the back of his neck—his tell that he was anxious about something.

"Spit it out, Leo," Hattie said. "What has you worried?"

"I'd offer up the fold-out couch at the apartment, but it's the sleeping arrangements. Telling Beverly about... Not because of that, you know, but... well, I'd be in the doghouse forever if she found out and I didn't tell her."

"I understand," Hattie said. "I can stay at my sister's. Besides, I need to check in with Eva to see how my father is doing. I should place the overseas call at Olivia's, not here where people might be listening in."

"All right." Leo gestured toward the door. "Let's get you to Olivia's. I'd love to see her again."

Two hours later, after having lunch at a nearby restaurant, Leo pulled up to Olivia's Alexandria home. The quaint two-story house offered extensive front and back yards for the children to play. The trees had lost their leaves, and the perennials had gone dormant, as had the lawn, which was meticulous in appearance. Hattie's brother-in-law took pride in maintaining a well-kept lawn.

They retrieved the suitcases from Leo's trunk and walked up the concrete pathway. Hattie rang the bell. Moments later, the door swung open to reveal her sister, clad in a house dress, sweater, and an apron, with her dark blond hair up in a bun. Her mouth fell open when she set eyes on Hattie. Her eyes were wide with shock.

"My Lord. What in the world are you doing here?" Olivia was giddy with excitement.

"Are you going to invite us in?"

"Gosh, yes," Olivia squealed before hugging Hattie. "It's so good to see you. Come in. Come in."

Everyone filed into the house with the luggage, and Olivia greeted each one with a long hug. "Maya. Leo. It's wonderful to see you." She turned to Hattie. "Where's David?"

Hattie swallowed the lump that had formed in her throat. Sadness swept over her, thinking about the things she had to tell her sister and imagining her response. "I'll tell you later. We have important business in DC, but first, we need to talk. Is Frank home?"

Olivia's expression went slack, and her face went pale. "Is it Mother? Did something happen to her?"

"Mother is fine." Hattie caressed her sister's arm, put on a reassuring smile, and turned her tone sugary sweet to keep Olivia from panicking. "Is Frank home?" she asked again. "I want to tell you both why we're here."

"He's raking leaves in the backyard with Matthew. I'll call them in."

While Olivia went to the back of the house, Hattie invited Maya and Leo into the living room, where they sat down. Moments later, a thumping on the stairs drew everyone's attention. The cutest toddler, with pink bows in her brown pigtails and dressed in a skirt and a mint-green knitted cardigan sweater, came scampering down. Sarah reached the bottom, peered into the room, and came to a screeching halt.

Her eyes got extra round like her mother's had. She brought her hands, now fists, to her chest and shook them in elation. "Auntie Hattie," she squealed and raced toward Hattie's open arms.

"Come here, you." Hattie pulled her into a tight hug. "You've gotten so big." It had been almost a year since she had seen her niece, and the transformation was mindboggling. Hattie had still imagined her in diapers but now envisioned her on the playground with the other little girls. "You're so pretty."

"Did you bring us presents?" Sarah said in the most darling little voice.

"I did, and I also have something from Grandma Eva. They're in my suitcase, but they will have to wait until I talk to your mommy and daddy."

The girl pouted but became a ball of excitement a second later when her brother bolted in through the kitchen.

"Auntie Hattie! Auntie Hattie!" Matthew shouted, still bundled in his wool winter coat, mittens, and beanie. The picture of adorable, he collided into Hattie's embrace. Though he immediately asked for a present, he transitioned quickly into telling her about the new tricycle he got for his fifth birthday. "And it's red. And it has white tassels."

"That sounds wonderful. I can't wait to see it."

"Give your aunt some breathing room," Olivia said.

Frank entered the room behind his wife, removing his leather work gloves. "You kids go upstairs to play while the adults talk. Pull out what you want to show your Aunt Hattie, and I'll get you when we're done."

The children groaned and objected, but Frank used his stern voice, which was not very firm in Hattie's opinion. He was always a softy with them. Nevertheless, they raced up the stairs, jabbering at each other.

Frank removed his wool utility jacket and gave Hattie a hug. "It's great seeing you."

"It's good seeing you, too." Hattie introduced Maya and Leo as good friends from Rio.

After handshakes, Frank said, "Olivia said you wanted to talk to both of us."

"I do." Hattie gestured toward the living room. "Let's sit." Once they settled into their seats, she started. "I assure you that Mother is fine, but I need your word that what I'm about to tell you stays between us. You cannot, under any circumstance, discuss this with anyone outside this room. Other than Mother, of course."

"You're scaring me, Hattie," Olivia said.

"Do I have your word?" Hattie studied her sister's eyes. "I know you are bad at keeping secrets, but this is one you absolutely can't tell. You must promise me, Olivia."

Her sister clutched her husband's hand. "We promise. I promise."

"I've been in contact with Father. We all have for some time."

Olivia stiffened. "For how long? How is he?"

"I saw him a week after I arrived in Rio, and we've been in communication since."

"You didn't say a word of this in May when I was in Brazil. Does Mother know?"

"Yes, she knows. We didn't say anything because we didn't want you to lie if someone asked you about him. And be honest with yourself. You have a tough time keeping a secret."

Olivia's expression turned harder, and she gave Hattie her offended glare. "For this, I would have kept my lips shut. But why are you telling me now?"

Hattie reached toward the nearby couch and squeezed Olivia's hand. "Father is alive, but he's been hurt."

"Hurt how?"

"He was shot five days ago. He lost a lot of blood, and when we left Rio on Wednesday, he still hadn't regained consciousness."

Her sister gasped and threw her hand over her mouth.

"Mother's old family doctor is seeing to his care." Hattie avoided sharing the frightening details that they could not take Karl to a hospital for fear of someone recognizing him and that his treatment was occurring in Eva's home. "Mother has a nurse tending to him when she's not with him." She calculated the two-hour time difference between DC and Rio and figured this would be a good time. "I need to find out how he's doing. May I place the overseas call from here? I'll pay for the charges."

Olivia could only muster an emotion-filled nod.

"Of course." Frank stood and stretched the phone cord from the other end table to where Hattie sat.

She lifted the handset, raised the operator, and arranged the call. The operator said she would ring the house when she had made the connection, adding that it could take minutes or hours, depending on the availability of circuits.

After he hung up the phone, Frank said, "Tell us what happened, Hattie."

She started by telling them how the FBI had forced her into going to Rio in February to lure Karl out of hiding, threatening to jail him and Olivia if she refused. Both shifted uncomfortably on the couch.

"What about the children? What would have become of them?" Fear was in Olivia's voice.

"The FBI would have seen to it that a court deemed me unfit to take them, so the foster system would have scooped them up."

Olivia gasped, and Frank clenched his teeth, the muscles in his jaw rippling with pure outrage.

"I've been doing the FBI's bidding for months but have managed to keep them off Father's scent."

"Was that how you got tangled up in that mess at the plantation and with the attempted yacht bombing?" Olivia asked.

"In a way, yes. Most recently, the FBI had me butter up some Nazis who came into the nightclub and attempt to gather intelligence from them."

"Isn't that dangerous?" her sister asked.

"It can be," Hattie said. "One thing led to another, and Father got involved. The same man who shot Father also shot David and..." Hattie paused, dreading her next words, but she had to say them. "David is dead."

Olivia's hand went to her mouth again to cover a gasp, and tears filled her eyes. "I'm so sorry, Hattie. I know how much you loved him. Will there be a service?"

"Not here," Hattie said. "It's all very complicated, but we will get word to his parents in Germany about his death."

"Germany? I thought he was from New York."

"We can get into that later. The important thing now is to check up on Father and do what he asked of me before he fell into a coma."

"What is that?" Frank's question gave the impression he was skeptical. "I want no more trouble here like we did after he escaped custody and killed those two FBI agents."

Hattie understood his concerns for his family, but his words were infuriating, nonetheless. "He did not escape willingly, Frank. Leo here can attest that the SS broke him out, killing those agents, and forced him onto a Rio-bound freighter. Karl has been hiding since."

"What about the secrets he handed to Germany?" Frank asked, still testing Hattie's patience.

"That wasn't him," Leo said. "I work in Naval Intelligence at the War Department and can tell you that Karl James is innocent. He has done everything in his power to protect his country and family. Which is why we are back in the States."

"To do what exactly?" Frank still appeared skeptical and protective of his wife and kids.

"I'll take it from here, Leo." Hattie gave him a nod filled with appreciation for stepping in. Before she could continue, the telephone rang. She looked at Frank for permission to answer. It was the overseas operator. "Yes, please put her through."

"I have your party," the operator said, presumably exiting the call.

"Hello, Hattie?" Eva said.

"Mother, I'm at Olivia's and wanted you to know I arrived safely. This call is expensive, so I'll keep this short. I know I left you with a handful with the club and all. Have you encountered any problems?"

"No problems. No changes either. Things are going as expected."

"That's good to hear." Hattie let out a sigh of relief. Before leaving Rio, she and Eva had worked out a secret code to discuss Karl's condition in case someone was listening. It seemed to be working.

"I'll call if I run into any hitches."

"Thank you, Mother. I have to go. I love you."

"Love you, too, sweetheart."

The call disconnected. Hattie turned to Olivia, who was leaning forward on the couch with an expectant expression.

"Father is doing fine, but he still has yet to come to. The night the doctor patched him up, he said it could take a week or more before his body healed enough to allow him to wake."

"That's not much of a comfort." Olivia had no way of knowing how hearing he had not taken a turn for the worse was a tremendous relief. She had not seen their father the night Wagner shot him, nor had she been along for the harrowing three-hour ride through the jungle to Rio.

"On the contrary," Hattie said, "it's excellent news."

Olivia reached out and squeezed Hattie's hand. "Good." She appeared a bit more at ease.

"I'm glad Karl is doing okay," Frank said, "but we still don't know why you're here. And why now?"

"I understand your concern, Frank, but it's a long story."

"Give us the *Reader's Digest* version," he said.

Hattie shifted in her seat to push back on the familiar suffocating feeling she encountered during interrogations. "Father has suspected since last Christmas that a Nazi mole was working high up in the War Department. They were after the lists of spies the United States and Germany had in the other's country, lists he had control of."

"Why would Father have lists of spies?" Olivia asked, narrowing her eyes in confusion.

"His job at the State Department is his cover. He really works in Military Intelligence."

"He's a spy?" Olivia cocked her head back, even more confused.

"Yes, for at least twenty years." Hattie continued explaining why they had appeared on her sister's doorstep without revealing too many specifics. "Father didn't know who he could trust, so he made the lists unreadable, but not before copying and encoding them. For reasons I can't get into, it's now imperative we get the original lists to the right person. That's why we're here."

"But you said there's a mole. Aren't you afraid whoever you give them to might be the traitor?" Frank asked.

Olivia sat quietly, slack-jawed.

"Father said there is one woman he trusts. I'm supposed to find her and hand them over to her, and she will help us unearth the mole. I'm not sure how long it will take to find her, but I was hoping you could put Maya and me up for a few days. The hotels were a hit-and-miss last night."

"What about Leo?" Olivia asked. "Will you need a place to stay?"

"I have a small place in DC with my wife," Leo said. "Unfortunately, we don't have a guest room."

Frank leaned back on the couch, rubbing both hands roughly down his face after glancing at the luggage at the base of the stairs. "I'm sorry, Hattie, but I want you out of here. I don't want you endangering Olivia or the kids."

"Frank." Olivia drew out his name. She had, finally, broken from her stupor. "Hattie is family."

"I have to work, which means I can't be here to protect you, Olivia, if someone comes snooping for those lists. I don't want a repeat of the night the FBI raided our house looking for your father."

"The only ones who know we have the lists are Eva, Karl, and the people in this room," Leo said. "Everyone hunting for them is in Brazil and searching for Karl."

"But for how long?" Frank leaned forward, his elbows on his knees, shaking his head. "Somebody is bound to figure out you're here, and the FBI will come around."

"They already know we're in the country," Leo said. "We flew on a military plane with an FBI agent from Rio. They think we're here for another reason and have no idea about our true purpose."

"That's not very reassuring."

"It is for me," Olivia said. "If we can put up your drunk college buddy who tore up the bowling alley during a brawl, we can put up my sister and her friends. I will not turn family away, and that's final."

When Frank sighed and stooped his posture, Hattie knew Olivia had won the argument.

$$5$$

Rio de Janeiro, Brazil, Saturday, December 6, 1941

Otto Klaus, bandaged after taking a bullet to the arm five days ago and recovering from smoke inhalation, was finally well enough to travel and was on his way to Rio. Well, if he were being honest, he could have started the trek days ago, but he was a coward. He had needed time to figure out what to do.

Following the ambassador's instructions days earlier, he had transported Karl James to a secret airfield to enable him to negotiate with Strom Wagner for the lists of covert operatives Germany and the United States had within each other's borders. Things had been going as planned until Karl's daughter and the others had shown up.

Guards had captured Hattie James and the other woman at the gate, presumably while trailing Hattie's father. And then Wagner's patsy had appeared. The piano player was someone in Hattie's inner circle whom Wagner had strong-armed into locating those lists. He had failed to do so up to that point, and it had not taken long to learn that he was in love with Hattie, which explained his inaction.

Finally, a guard had brought in another man. Wagner had believed he was an SS agent, a second spy planted close to Hattie. He was the last to arrive in that hangar briefing room and said he had what Wagner wanted, claiming to have hidden the photos of the coveted spy lists in the nightshade. Otto had no clue what "nightshade" meant or where it might have been. So, when Wagner sent him and his driver to collect those documents, he had rightly feared a forthcoming wild goose chase. It had taken only minutes for the latecomer to catch both off guard and knock them unconscious, proving he was a fake. He was an American naval man, through and through.

Otto had woken up in a dark closet, his hands bound by twine, next to his partner, who had been similarly tied up. Though he had considered trying to break free, he was all too familiar with how the SS dealt with failure, and he had definitely failed. That usually ended with a bullet to the head, so he decided to do nothing.

He had become concerned after smelling something charry and seeing vapors seep through the crack at the bottom of the door. However, waiting until his partner stirred had been a more palatable option than facing the consequences of his failure. They had untied each other, coughing as the smoke had begun to eat up most of the oxygen in the confined space. After discovering their sidearms missing, they had tested the knob but found the closet locked. The driver, the stronger of the two, had tried to break the door without success. The smoke had grown thicker, and Otto had feared he had waited too long to free himself. In a desperate move, they had sat on the wooden floor and kicked the door in unison, forcing it open on the third attempt.

A toxic cloud was blanketing the hallway, and gunfire had erupted somewhere in the building. It had been impossible to detect anyone's presence, so they had crouched low, seeking better air, and followed the wall to its end. The smoke had become too much for Otto, and he dropped to the ground, fearing death was coming for him. He had looked up in time to see the driver burst through the door and be riddled by a barrage of bullets. A bullet had found its way past his partner and hit Otto in the arm. His body had jerked, and he had fallen to his knees. When he opened his mouth to scream in agony, he had inhaled more smoke and passed out.

Two days later, he had come to in the hut of a local coffee farmer. The farmer had seen the explosions and rescued him from the wreckage before authorities arrived. The kind stranger had cared for him, providing food and water until Otto felt well enough to leave his bed.

He was ill-prepared to be on the run. He had no money, no identification papers, and no means of making it somewhere he could fit in to start a new life. His best option was to return to Rio and make it appear he was an innocent victim who had escaped the devastation only through the kindness of a stranger.

This morning Otto had asked the farmer for a lift to the nearest town. From there, he had hitched a ride on a coffee bean delivery truck bound for Rio's port. The three-hour trek had been quiet; the driver only knew Portuguese, and Otto spoke only German and enough English to get by in a bar or restaurant.

They had entered the city several minutes ago and were nearing the docks. Otto recognized the street names and gestured for the driver to pull over and drop him off. He thanked the man by patting him on the arm, receiving a smile before they drove off.

After getting his bearings at the nearest corner, Otto figured the German Embassy was four or five blocks away. He had no cash, so flagging down a taxi was not an option unless he wanted to deal with a beating from the cabbie for not paying his fare. Walking, though challenging, seemed to be his best choice.

Otto began regretting his decision when he was within sight of his embassy. Rio was humid, and the sun was at its peak in the cloudless sky. Perspiration had soaked his filthy, tattered shirt, and his limbs felt like lead weights, but he had to forge ahead. He had already been gone too long, and his tardiness would not please the ambassador. Otto figured, however, that he could play up his exhaustion to his advantage. It would prove his determination to return to town and explain what happened at the airfield.

He arrived at the embassy entrance exhausted. He did not have his identification papers, which he supposed he had lost in the airfield destruction, nor did he recognize either of the sentries, so he spoke to the German, not the Brazilian.

"I am Untersturmführer Otto Klaus. My papers are missing. I have an urgent report to give to Ambassador Falkenberg. Have the duty officer meet me at the gate," he said in German.

The German guard eyed him with skepticism but lifted the phone inside the shack and contacted the security office. Minutes later, an officer a grade junior to Otto, someone whom Otto knew, came to the front and authorized his entry. The officer helped him toward the building, throwing Otto's uninjured arm over his shoulder and steadying him with one around his waist.

They were soon in the embassy's secured area. Staff offered him food and drink, which he welcomed but took slowly to avoid recovering too quickly. Otherwise, the ambassador might not believe he had been too weak to return earlier. While he waited, his supervisor came in, demanding a briefing.

"I'm sorry, sir," Otto said, "but Ambassador Falkenberg's last order was that I report directly back to him. Only him."

His superior, furious, stayed in the office with Otto, eyeing him with suspicion. He had been gone for five days, and the farm he had recuperated at, he said, had had no phones or newspapers. He was anxious to learn what had happened beyond the airfield's destruction and guessed the others there had perished. Logic suggested Karl James and his helpers had escaped, a fact that could still get him killed. However, he was confident his story would hold up.

The sweat-producing wait was awkward until the ambassador appeared.

Falkenberg waved his hand dismissively at Otto's superior. "Give us the room." Once Otto's boss left, he sat across from Otto, meticulously straightened what he was wearing, and said calmly, "Explain what happened and your five-day absence."

"We took James to the airfield and directly to Herr Wagner as you instructed. Guards there took custody and dismissed us," Otto said, taking quick breaths to play up his weakened state. "We went to the support building to await further instructions. Soon afterward, we heard gunfire, and Herr Wagner ordered us to investigate. Attackers had infiltrated the facility and set the buildings on fire. Multiple explosions followed. An attacker wounded me in the arm and killed my partner in a shootout. I then passed out from the smoke and woke up days later in the hut of a farmer who had found me in the debris. I later learned he had taken me to his farm and patched me up. When I recovered my strength, I returned to the site but discovered local authorities were there combing through the wreckage. It seemed those blasts had destroyed the entire fleet of aircraft, so I hitched a ride to Rio. And came directly here."

Most of what Otto said was true, but he had sprinkled in enough embellishments to make himself appear a fortunate hero. Regrettably, Falkenberg's stonelike expression meant he likely was doubting his story. This made Otto think that perhaps his dead partner was the lucky one.

"Was I right in assuming the planes were all lost and everyone killed?" Otto asked.

"The aircraft, yes. However, we've received reports that several mechanics and pilots survived the incursion and that Brazilian police took them into custody. Authorities are still questioning them. They will presumably consider them prisoners of war after tomorrow."

Otto was unsure what the ambassador was referring to but knew enough to not ask. "Do you know what happened to Karl James?"

"That is a mystery, Herr Klaus, and it is the only thing keeping you alive."

Otto felt the strangling hand of failure wrapping around his neck, but the ambassador seemed to have given him one last opportunity to redeem himself. "What do you want me to do, Herr Falkenberg?"

"Locate Karl James, no matter the cost, and get those lists."

"I will need a team of men."

"How many?"

Otto had no idea how he would find James, nor how much muscle would be necessary to make that happen. Thinking back to his childhood when his father had taught him that a sign of a good leader was to sound self-assured, he threw out a number he thought Falkenberg could spare. "Five."

"Pick whomever you want, but get the job done. Start tomorrow. You have one week."

"Yes, sir."

Once the ambassador left, Otto reported to his superior. He detailed his special mission but received a salty response after asking for help to select the men for his team.

"You got yourself into this mess. Get yourself out of it."

Otto returned to his office, where he washed himself off with a wet towel from the restroom and changed into the clean suit he kept on a hook on the back of the door. Once he was presentable, he went to the administration section, where they made him a new set of identification papers and issued him a Luger.

Otto then visited the personnel unit and scanned the embassy roster. He chose men who were young and fit, figuring this job would require more brawn than brain. After leaving instructions that they were to report to him in the morning, he grabbed some cash and his car keys from his desk drawer. He drove to the nearest bar, ordered two double schnapps, and downed them in succession. If he failed his mission, he knew his life was over.

6

Alexandria, VA, Sunday, December 7, 1941

Hattie showered, dressed, and headed to the kitchen hours before her typical rise-and-shine time, which was already well behind the household pace. Usually, no one rose earlier than the mother of toddlers. Indeed, Olivia was already at work, frying the last bit of bacon, stirring the hash browns, and chiding Matthew for playing army man at the breakfast table.

"But they're from Auntie Hattie," Matthew said in a whiney tone. "I want her to play with me."

"I'd love to," Hattie said, walking into the room. Sarah was beside Matthew, serving her new teddy bear a sip of orange juice. Maya was buttering toast at the counter across the galley from Olivia.

The kids snapped their gazes up simultaneously and shouted, "Auntie!" They put their toys down, shimmied from the built-in bench along the window wall, and scurried toward her. She lifted Sarah onto her hip, but Matthew had gotten too big, so she pulled him close while he hugged her around the waist. He hurried back to his war games soon afterward.

"Have you two had breakfast yet?" Hattie asked the children.

"Mommy makes us wait for Daddy," Sarah said.

"And our guests," Olivia said, bringing the rest of the food to the table.

"Where's Frank?" Hattie set Sarah down on the bench, leaving her to her stuffed friend.

"He's scraping the ice off the car windows. We need to leave for church right after we eat." Olivia spooned out eggs and potatoes onto the kids' plates.

"We will handle the cleanup," Maya said. "Leo won't pick us up for a few hours."

"That's very kind of you," Olivia said, "but you're a guest. You've done enough already."

"No buts," Hattie said. "It's the least we can do after you convinced Frank to let us stay. I'm enjoying seeing everyone."

Olivia patted Hattie's hand. "And we've loved spending time with you."

Frank entered the kitchen, peeling off the same wool work coat he had on yesterday. "Morning, ladies. Did you sleep well?"

"Yes, we did, thank you," Hattie said. "We'll be out of your hair after breakfast. We'll be back, but I promise we won't stay much longer."

Frank sighed. "Look, Hattie. I enjoy having you here. The children do, too, but as long as this craziness is going on, I can't afford to take any chances."

"I get that, which is why Maya and I will find a hotel that will take us, somewhere the bed won't break my back."

"Don't go, Auntie." Sarah's lips quivered.

"You have to go?" Matthew asked, tears building in his eyes. "You just got here."

Hattie rubbed the top of his head, messing his hair. "I promise to come by before I fly back to Brazil."

Matthew and Sarah sniffled and cried, begging Hattie not to leave.

"You've upset them, Frank." Olivia consoled her children by inviting them into her open arms, where they continued to sob.

"All right, all right." Frank bit off a mouthful of bacon. "Stay as long as you want."

"Thank you, Frank. We've got the dishes." Hattie smiled with gratitude as the little ones cheered and jumped up and down on their seats. As much as she wanted privacy with Maya, she wanted to soak up as much time as possible with her sister and the kids.

Olivia did not have to rush to get the family out the door for church since Hattie and Maya cleaned up the kitchen after breakfast. They were waving goodbye to the family at the door when Leo pulled up to the curb, arriving a few minutes early. He was always prompt no matter their arrangements.

He jogged up to the door and wagged his thumb over his shoulder. "Darn, was that your sister's family?"

"Yes, it was."

"Sorry I missed them today. I wanted to arrange a time to introduce Beverly to them before I have to return to Brazil."

"I'm sure they would love that," Hattie said. "We just need to grab our things. Then we can get our search for the Professor underway."

Minutes later, after locking up the house, Hattie and the others hit the road, heading toward the district. Once they were across the Potomac and were in Washington, Leo suggested they not start in Georgetown, where the Professor might have lived. "I met her off and on in Anacostia. We should begin there."

Hattie and Maya agreed. His information was more current.

They crossed another bridge over the Anacostia River, passing the navy base there. Leo took them through a run-down and sparsely occupied industrial section of town, weaving through several unkept roads and past a half dozen deserted buildings. He stopped in front of a rusty warehouse with broken windows and weeds growing wild around it and the parking lot. The place appeared abandoned.

"Why are we here?" Hattie asked.

"This is where the Professor and I held SS Agent Erik Weiss for weeks after he broke your father out of federal custody."

"You mean this is where you tortured him," Maya said.

Hattie craned her neck toward the back seat to look Maya in the eye. "That's not fair."

"No, Maya's right." Leo twisted the steering wheel and sighed deeply, clearly regretting what he had done in that building. "We used tactics that I'm not proud of, but once we broke him, he told us what we wanted to know, including that he was supposed to report to Brazil to continue the search for Karl."

"Where is he now?" Maya asked.

"He hung himself in his cell. I then assumed his identity when I arrived in Rio, letting Wagner believe I was Weiss."

Hattie recognized the anguish in Leo's voice. She had heard the same tone a week ago in a Rio hotel room while he was looking at a picture of the wife of Armand Klein. The German aeronautical engineer had died from injuries after falling out a second-story window. Klein would not have been in that situation if she had done a better job of extracting information from him about the secret airfield and plane factory. She understood Leo's regret. Armand Klein and Erik Weiss might be alive today if she and Leo had done something different.

"Then why are we here?" Hattie asked softly.

"We may have left something here that could lead us to the Professor." Leo opened his car door, got out, and slammed it shut. He retrieved a flashlight from the trunk.

Hattie and Maya followed Leo to the building. He moved a stack of old, cracked wooden crates leaning against the exterior wall, unearthing a leather pouch buried an inch below the surface of the dirt. He removed a small key and used it to unlock a padlock on the nearby door.

They went inside.

The room appeared to have once been a foreman's office. Sunlight through the smudge-covered windows, some broken, reached halfway down a corridor. Leo led them down it, flicking on the flashlight when the space got dark.

He went to the center of the building, turning down another hall illumined only by the light in his hand. The deeper they went into the structure, the creepier the surroundings felt. The floors here were dusty, though free of debris. Leo walked through an open hallway door, closing it after Hattie and Maya passed through. He flipped on a switch on the wall, activating the ceiling lights to the end of the passageway.

"Electricity? Isn't this place abandoned?" Hattie asked.

"It's supposed to look that way, but it's owned by the government and operated by Military Intelligence as one of our playgrounds."

"Playgrounds?" Maya asked.

"Special interrogations. It's far enough away from anything else that no one can hear things or see us coming and going."

"So, Erik Weiss wasn't the only one brought here." Hattie said this as a statement, but she intended it as a question. "Did my father bring anyone here?"

"I don't know. You'll have to ask him."

She might do just that if her father ever woke from his coma.

"We primarily used the first three rooms on the left," he said. "Let's walk through them to see if we can come up with anything."

They entered the first room. Leo turned on the light, a single light bulb strung to the ceiling.

"Lovely accommodations," Hattie said, though she supposed this place was a step up from the favela shack her father first rented when he arrived in Rio.

The passage of time had grayed the paint in the room. Two wooden desks, pushed together against the far wall, faced one another. An armchair was beside each one. There was a waste can near the door, a 1941 Shell Oil calendar hung from the wall above the work area, and a radio was sitting atop a desk.

"I've been in worse," Leo said. "We used this as our office. The desk on the left was the Professor's."

Hattie went there, and Maya went to the one on the right. While Leo sifted through the garbage can, they went through the desk drawers. Hattie discovered pencils, paper clips, and a collection of empty Tootsie Roll and M&M wrappers in the drawers. "The Professor certainly has a sweet tooth."

"That's an understatement." Leo chuckled. "She's thin as a rail, but that woman always has candy with her. I swear, sometimes that was all she ate."

"Nothing here," Maya said, turning her attention to the wall calendar. She took it down, flipped through the months, and stopped on a particular page. "Nothing here either except for some markings during February. What happened then?"

"That's when we had Weiss here." Leo stepped closer and peered over Maya's shoulder. "X marked the day we started. The smiley face was the day we broke him."

"That's eight days of torture." Maya pushed back from the desk, her voice brittle with anger and expression laden with shock.

"I know," Leo replied in a somber tone. "Let's move on to the next room."

He led them to a smaller room one door down. It had a metal armchair, a water bucket, a crusty towel, and a car battery with jumper cables. Dark specks and stains surrounded the chair.

"Dear Lord," Maya said.

She must have come to the same conclusion as Hattie, that the battery had been used as a torture device and the spots were blood. Her experience with her father had taught Hattie that sometimes the good guys had to do horrible things for the greater good, including things considered inhumane. Though they were repulsive, Hattie knew even heroes could sometimes justify horrific acts when the lives of loved ones or thousands of innocent people hung in the balance.

Thankfully, after finding nothing else in the windowless room, they moved on to the third room.

Leo did not have to explain the room's purpose. A foul smell, a lumpy mattress on the floor, and a makeshift toilet confirmed Hattie's suspicions: This was where Leo and the Professor had held Weiss between interrogations.

One corner contained a pile of food wrappers. Hattie bent her knees and started inspecting them. Maya did too. Leo stood by watching. Sandwich and burger wrappers and a few used paper cups comprised most of the trash.

"Who brought him food?" Hattie asked.

"We split the duty," Leo said. "I brought him breakfast from the house. The Professor would pick up a little something in the afternoon or evening."

"So the paper towels and plain brown bags are yours?" Hattie asked.

"Yes."

"That means the restaurant wrappers came from the Professor." Hattie separated the stuff, isolating what the Professor might have carried into the facility. Most had no markings; two of the bags had an image printed on them, but there was no indication of the establishment's name. Hattie pointed to the design. "This Liberty Bell. Is there a diner nearby that uses this logo?"

"I'm not sure, but we can check the Yellow Pages at a phone booth," Leo said.

"Great idea."

Leo turned off the lights, retraced their route, led Hattie and Maya to his car, and drove out of the warehouse area. They located a corner drugstore in the Capitol Hill neighborhood and went inside. A payphone was there. Hattie flipped through the phone book attached to it by a metal cord and turned to the restaurant section. None of the advertisements she saw matched the logo on the bag. She went down the list of local eateries, stopped at the *L*s, and grinned. A quick scan of the remaining names revealed no other establishment that might fit the symbol.

"I think I found it. There's a Liberty Café in Georgetown."

"Let's go," Leo said. "Besides, I'm hungry."

"You're always hungry." Hattie laughed.

"What?" He shrugged. "It's almost one. I had breakfast at six."

"Fair enough."

Leo maneuvered through town, heading northwest on Pennsylvania Avenue. He found a parking spot two blocks from the restaurant, and they walked the rest of the way.

The place was more of a diner with a checkerboard floor than a café. Several servers wearing all white, with aprons, skirts for the women and pants for the men, were working behind a chrome-accented counter lined with a dozen red-topped stools. Matching leather booths were along the windows on three sides. Patrons packed the dining room, and it buzzed with the din of a multitude of conversations.

The hostess greeted them and seated them in a corner booth.

It was two o'clock.

Minutes later, a waitress came to their table and dropped off glasses of water. She pulled an order pad from her apron pocket and a pen from behind her ear, where her updo of dark hair had held it in place. "Welcome, folks. What can I get you?"

Once everyone provided their orders, Hattie said, "Before you go, I have a question."

"Sure, hun. What is it?"

"I'm trying to find an old family friend, but I've lost her address. She lives in Georgetown, and she mentioned coming here several times."

"Did you try looking her up in the book?"

"I did, but she's unlisted. Her name is Vicky, and she has quite the sweet tooth."

"Sweet tooth describes about half the people who come here." The waitress laughed. "Sorry, hun. I only know a few customers' names, but no Vicky."

"This might be asking a lot," Hattie said, "but if you get a chance, could you ask the other servers? It's important that I find her."

"I'll do my best." Fifteen minutes passed before the server returned with their selections. "Enjoy your meals." She focused on Hattie. "I asked some of the girls about a Vicky, but no one seems to know her."

"Well, thank you for trying."

They dug into the food on their plates. While they were eating, Hattie noticed the conversations in the café slowly quieting and people huddled near the radio behind the counter. Moments later, the hostess turned up the volume, and the place became deadly quiet.

The announcer said, "Attention, everyone. We interrupt this program to bring you a special news bulletin. This just in from the Pacific: Japanese forces have attacked the United States Navy base at Pearl Harbor, Hawaii. Initial reports indicate significant damage to naval vessels and aircraft, and there are numerous casualties among our brave servicemen.

"President Roosevelt will address the nation shortly to provide more details on this grave situation. We ask all citizens to remain calm and stay tuned to their radios for further updates. Please keep all those affected by this devastating event in your thoughts and prayers. We will pass along more information as it becomes available. Remain with us for continuous coverage."

Several women gasped. Others whimpered, and their male companions tightened comforting arms around their shoulders. Some men turned pale as the horrifying assault began to sink in. The country was under attack, and Americans would soon be in a global war. That same country would call many of them into service, and some might not return home. For everyone in the room, one thing was certain. This momentous event forever changed their lives.

Hattie clutched Maya's hand beneath the table, her shock turning to anger.

"I have friends at Pearl." Leo's eyes took on an angry yet determined look. Hattie rubbed his forearm with her free hand, feeling the tenseness in his muscles. He sat silently, but the growing redness on his face meant a rage was coursing through him.

The very thing they had tried to warn the War Department's General Staff about had become a terrifying reality. She knew that even if they had listened yesterday, there would not have been enough time to stop the attack. However, perhaps units could have taken defensive measures. The radio report had said there were multiple casualties. Was it a handful or an unfathomable multitude of dead and wounded? Some lives might have been saved if the generals had attended yesterday's meeting and heeded their warning. Even one life. Maybe that one life saved could have been Leo's friend.

7

Rio de Janeiro, Brazil, Sunday, December 7, 1941

Forgoing another church service felt odd but not as sinful as Eva had once considered the omission. Until this year, she feared being struck by lightning for missing mass. However, faced with a choice between accepting her daughter or adhering to the church's teaching, she had decided that the church was not always correct in its interpretation of the Bible. She missed the sense of belonging and community that being a member of the church had provided, but the truth was that she refused to give up on the piece of her heart that would always love Hattie like a mother should.

The morning came and went without any sign of change in Karl's condition. She had given him a sponge bath and dressed him in fresh night clothes, taking care not to disturb his catheter. Seven days had passed since traumatic blood loss from a gunshot had caused him to lose consciousness. The IV fluids ordered by Dr. Navarro seemed to be helping; his skin color had returned to its normal tone. She had also been rubbing his lips regularly with ice chips to prevent them from chapping, yet despite all the attention she had been giving him, he remained unconscious.

The doorbell rang, announcing her expected visitors. She went through the front garden and opened the gate, finding that the doctor and nurse had come together. "Joaquim. Maria. Please come in."

In the guest room where Karl had been since Hattie rushed him home after the shooting, Navarro dug into his physician's bag, retrieving a stethoscope, and began his examination. He checked Karl's heart, pulse, temperature, breathing, and reflexes, the last of which were nonexistent, and looked for signs of infection.

He turned to Maria. "When did he last have a fever?"

"Wednesday," she said.

"And his urine output?"

"Normal and clear."

Navarro shifted his attention to Eva. "Have you been exercising his legs and muscles like I suggested?" he asked, putting his things away.

"Three times a day," Eva said. She had been moving his limbs for him so much in the past week that she had developed stronger arms of her own.

"Very good," the doctor said. "He is much improved compared to a few days ago."

"Will he wake soon? I'm starting to worry that he may never do so."

"It's looking promising. I could give him a stimulant to see if it will wake him, but it's better for him to come around on his own. His body needs time to heal." Navarro stood. "Call me if you see any change. If I don't hear from you, I'll return on Wednesday."

"Thank you, Joaquim." Eva walked him and the nurse out, handing each an envelope with their pay and hush money. "Thank you for coming, Maria. I'll stay with him today. Can you come back on Tuesday at noon? I have to be at my studio for lessons."

"Of course, Miss Machado."

After they drove away in Navarro's car, Eva went inside and peeked in on Karl, who had not moved. She then entered her home office and began preparing for this week's instruction. She liked to review each student's progress on Sunday and tailor their time with her to keep growing them as artists. Watching young musicians grow into their innate talent had become a joy in the last few years, some more than others. Eva hoped to continue working with Zoya professionally at the Halo Club once it opened in two months.

When she finished the lesson plans, she checked on Karl again, exercising his arms and legs and wetting his lips with more ice chips. She straightened his thinning grayish-blond hair and stroked his cheek before clutching his hand.

"When will you come back to me, Karl? I miss your smile and your needling me about being kinder to Maya. You'll be happy to know how much I've come to respect that woman and her love for our daughter. She helped save your life, sweetheart. Maya put aside her grief and anger over her sister's death to get you here and assisted Joaquim in patching you up. Now, she's gone with Hattie to the States to find Vicky and give her the lists you've kept safe all this time. If that isn't love, I don't know what is. That's why I'm overseeing the Halo Club's construction while they're away. After all that, I can't let her creation wither."

Eva swore she felt Karl squeeze her hand, but when she called his name and rubbed his chest, he did not stir. She did not fight the tears that had formed, letting them fall and dampen his fresh T-shirt. "Don't you break my heart again, Karl James. Wake up soon, because if you don't, I will haunt you through eternity."

Eva kissed him on the forehead and returned to the living room, looking for something to occupy her time. She enjoyed cooking, but she had already filled the refrigerator with meals she had prepared, enough to last her several days. Her plants, on the other hand, were desperately in need of attention.

She changed into work clothes, gathered her shears, weeder, and bucket, and went to work. Tending to her garden was more than a time filler. She loved nurturing them from seedlings and seeing their plain stems transform into vivid displays of art. It mirrored motherhood, watching daughters blossom into vibrant women, at least the snippets she had been there to witness. Her greatest regret was missing out on a good portion of their lives, particularly Olivia's formative years. She supposed that was why she appreciated her flowers to the degree she did. She got to experience their lifespan in such a short, satisfying amount of time.

Eva cut back old blooms and pruned the wild growth to give the new buds room to grow. Their beautiful colors would soon brighten the garden.

The afternoon heat bore down on her, causing her to sweat, but being outside among her flora was good for her.

She worked for an hour, stopping only to take in water—and when she heard the rumble of vehicles coming up her access road. She went to the tall stone wall surrounding her home and peeked through a hole in the mortar, watching as two dark sedans approached and parked at the top of her driveway. Men got out, six in all, all carrying Lugers. One man spoke German, barking orders and gesturing toward her house.

Panic set in. The Germans had come for Karl, and he was helpless to defend himself. The stone perimeter would slow them down, but eventually, they would gain entry. There were a few small pistols in the house, kept for protection, but she would be no match against half a dozen armed intruders hell-bent on getting to her husband. Ex-husband. Her best option was to hide, but she refused to leave Karl vulnerable.

Rushing inside, she eased the door closed quietly and locked it. After retrieving a pistol from the living room cabinet, she ran down the hallway to the guest room. "Sorry about this, sweetheart."

She threw back the covers and pulled on the bottom sheet, causing Karl to slide to the edge of the mattress, his legs dangling. After wrapping the sheet around him, she gave the section near his head another tug, caught his uninjured shoulder long enough to let gravity do the work, and eased him onto the wooden floor.

He thumped a little. Eva grimaced at the thought of hurting him before she remembered he was in a coma and felt nothing, at least according to the doctor.

She grabbed more blankets and pillows from the closet and stuffed some under the side of the bed facing the door, adjusting the decorative skirt so they were not visible. Circling to the other side, she pushed Karl, still swaddled in the sheet, and centered him beneath the frame. She smoothed out the top of the bed to make it appear unused, then crawled underneath with the extra linen, tucking it at her feet and along the side.

She cocked her pistol, held it against her chest, and waited in the dark. Moments later, she heard glass break and the sound of approaching footsteps. The intruders were close. Their shouts in German were unintelligible to her, but she could tell they were searching for her and Karl. The sound of destruction mounted, each shatter quickening Eva's pulse. There was a commotion outside the bedroom door, footsteps unmistakably loud and clear, and then... Somebody was inside the room.

Eva's heart thudded rapidly against her chest wall. Someone was there. Inches away. Seconds away from discovering their location.

Her space under the bed became suddenly brighter. Someone lifted the bed skirt to look underneath. She held her breath, fearing the sound of her exhalations might give her and Karl away. A blanket on her side shifted a fraction, and she directed her pistol toward the sunlight seeping through the fissures in her concealment. She stiffened, hoping the intruder had not noticed her move.

Then, the brightness fluttered, and her refuge darkened again. Footsteps creaked on the wooden floor, their sound growing weaker and less intense. They were moving away from her.

Eva finally took a breath. She released one sweaty palm from her weapon and searched with it in the darkness for Karl's hand. They stayed in their cocoon, hand in hand, waiting for the noise to stop and the intruders to lose interest. Even after a door had slammed and the house had gone silent, Eva remained motionless, thinking someone might have stayed and been lying in wait.

Once she thought an hour had passed, she pushed out the blankets and pillows concealing them and shimmied out from underneath the bed. After replacing the bedding and hiding Karl, she held her pistol in a ready position and peeked into the bathroom shared with Hattie's room. It was unoccupied. She tiptoed into the next bedroom, looking for an intruder, then continued into the hallway.

Eva knew which slats creaked in the wooden floor and avoided them as she made her way toward the front of the house. She froze when a noise came from the kitchen. It sounded like the refrigerator door had closed. Someone was still in the house.

Her hands shook as she leaned slowly around the corner at the end of the corridor that opened to the living room. Her quick peek revealed no one there. She took a long breath to steady herself. It had been years since she had handled a gun, let alone fired one. To be sure of hitting it, she would have to get close...remarkably close...to her target.

Pressing her back against the wall that terminated in the kitchen, she inched her way forward. The thumping in her ears from her racing heart became instantly more prominent, so much that she feared it might drown out noises that could warn her of an approaching foe. She dug deep into the well of courage she had seen Hattie and Karl dip into many times in recent months. She needed to be strong. To stay strong for them. For him.

Another thud echoed as someone opened and closed a cabinet door. Then a drawer.

Eva surmised the intruder who had stayed behind was rummaging for food. He likely would go somewhere to sit to enjoy his findings. The primary options were the dining area or the living room couch. If she heard the—

The next sound she heard provided the answer.

Wooden chair legs screeched against the floor. Something thudded, and a medium rattle followed by a high-pitched scrape indicated that the intruder had tossed a dish onto the table and was devouring his food with her silverware.

With his hands occupied, this was Eva's best chance.

Only one seat had an unobstructed view into the living room and the front garden. She had spent many lonely meals in that chair. In a way, she hated it. It represented all the mistakes that had led her to sitting at an empty table.

She thought of Karl lying helpless beneath her guest bed, stuffed between old pillows and blankets, and of the Nazi who had pulled the trigger that put him there. That steadied her hands. Her turn to take action had arrived.

She held the weapon in both hands, as Karl had taught her years ago. Now she understood why. Wheeling around the corner of the wall, she pointed the muzzle toward where she suspected the intruder would be. Her guess was spot on.

He was raising a spoon to his lips, helping himself to her favorite ice cream...in the middle of the day, for goodness' sake! Enraged, she aimed for the utensil and pulled the trigger repeatedly while stepping toward him. His body twitched, and droplets of blood spattered her table. She stopped firing when his head slumped lifelessly into the bowl of melting mess.

Her hands shook for a moment. Taking a life was a mortal sin, but her and Karl's lives had been in grave danger. God would forgive her, she was sure. Yes, God would forgive.

She hurried to him and grabbed the Luger lying beside him. Blood was everywhere. It would take forever to make her kitchen spotless again. Pulling his hair to raise his head, she made sure he was dead. That should have bothered her, but she was too angry at the situation to dwell on the fact that she had killed a man.

Nazis had invaded her home, prepared to kill or capture her and Karl. A Nazi had put a bullet in Karl's shoulder. A Nazi or someone doing their bidding had framed Karl and had him hiding for nearly a year. Nazis had destroyed their marriage and almost killed her entire family. She knew hate was wrong, but she hated everything about the Nazis and what they represented.

Instead of grieving over the life she had taken, she sneered at the dead man and said, "Ice cream is an after-dinner treat, you fool."

She went to the wall phone near the refrigerator, picked up the receiver, and then paused. She considered calling the police, but bringing in the authorities would endanger Karl even more. Staying here was not an option. Having left a man here, the Nazis would likely return to check on him. Moving Karl was imperative. But she could not do it alone.

Joaquim and the nurse came to mind. They already knew about Karl. However, the law obligated them to report the dead man in her kitchen.

This was a mess. She could think of no one else she trusted with Karl's life.

Eva pounded her fists against her temples to knock more ideas into her head. "Think, Eva. Think. What would Hattie do? Who would she trust?" A name popped into her head. "Javier."

Javier was a valet at the Palace, and his wife, Monica, was a server in the hotel's Golden Room. Hattie had gotten them jobs there because they were kind to her when she first arrived in Rio and sang at the old Halo Club. Hattie once mentioned that she thought of the two as family. Eva hoped Javier and Monica reciprocated that level of appreciation.

With no other viable options, Eva called the hotel and spoke to the manager in charge for the day. "An emergency has arisen, and I need to reach Javier, one of your valets. Is he working today?"

"Yes, he is, Miss Machado. I will get him."

Eva remained on the line. Minutes later, a voice came over the phone. "Hello? This is Javier."

"This is Eva Machado, Hattie's mother."

"Yes, Miss Machado. I know who you are."

"Javier, please listen. Hattie told me you and Monica are family to her and would do anything to help you. She is out of the country, and I am in desperate straits. Would you help me? I have an emergency that requires extreme discretion."

"Yes, of course."

"I know you are working now, but I need you and your wife to come to my home immediately. I will get the manager to excuse you from work and cover your pay for any missed time."

"May I ask what this is about?"

"I'll explain when you get here, but I assure you this is a life-or-death situation. Can you come quickly?" She provided her address.

"I can pick up Monica and be there in twenty minutes."

"Thank you, Javier. I won't forget this. I'll see you soon. Please put your supervisor back on." When he picked up the phone, Eva hinted at a home emergency requiring Javier and Monica's presence. Her offer to compensate the hotel for the salary of another valet and server convinced the manager to let them go.

After hanging up, Eva returned to the man at the table and confirmed again that he was dead. She hurried to the guest room and slid Karl from under the bed. Seeing that he was still peacefully unconscious, she propped his head onto a pillow, covered him with a blanket, and kissed him on the forehead. "I'll get you somewhere safe. I promise."

She dashed to her room and packed several suitcases of her things and some clothes that Karl had left there before. Another bag was for toiletries, and another was for the medical supplies the nurse and doctor had kept at the house. She rushed to the kitchen and filled grocery sacks with food, then grabbed the dead man's Luger, her two pistols, ammunition, and all the cash she had lying about.

She had just finished gathering what she thought they would need when the doorbell at the gate rang. It startled her, though the time on the clock indicated that only about twenty minutes had passed since she spoke to Javier. Remaining cautious, she readied her gun, crept through her garden, and peeked through the hole in the stone wall. It was Javier and his wife.

Eva stowed her pistol at the small of her back in her waistband. She ushered them inside and hugged them both. "Thank you for coming. We don't have much time." She led them into the house, stopping right inside before the kitchen came into view. A dead man at her table, unexplained, could surely scare them off.

"I'm going to tell you something that will sound horrible and a little frightening."

They nodded, confirming they understood that the situation was grave.

She briefly explained that authorities had wrongly accused Hattie's father, Karl, of a crime, and he had been hiding in Rio with Eva and Hattie's assistance. After a shooting that had rendered him comatose, Hattie left the country on a dangerous and urgent mission, pursuing it on his behalf.

"Those same Nazis are hunting him. They came here today. While I was able to hide him and evade capture, unfortunately, I had to shoot and kill one of them. His body is in my kitchen."

"Have you called the police?" Monica asked.

"I can't. They will arrest Karl. I need your help to get him into my car so I can take him to a place where the Nazis can't find him."

"What about the dead man?" Javier asked.

"I suppose whoever left him here will return soon and take him away. They can't afford to bring the authorities into this either." She looked at them solemnly. "Will you help me with Karl?"

Javier and Monica looked at each other, giving affirming nods.

Eva led them farther into the house, passing by the luggage she had lined up on the floor near the couch. They walked past the kitchen, and, after a glance, Monica covered her mouth with her hand. "Oh my."

"It's best not to look," Eva said as she continued down the hallway to the bedroom. Karl still had not moved. "We must work together to carry him.

Javier, you take his uninjured shoulder while Monica and I take his legs, keeping him wrapped in this sheet."

Minutes later, after several rest stops, they had ensconced Karl in the back seat of Eva's sedan and the luggage in its trunk. The logistics hereafter would be tricky. Eva would require a vehicle while she and Karl were in hiding, but she could not risk returning home for Javier and Monica to reclaim their car.

"I need help getting Karl to the place I have in mind," she told them. "But first I have to ensure no one follows us. Park your car at the grocery store at the city's north end. I will pick you up there once I know it's safe." She hugged them and squeezed their hands. "I can't thank you enough."

After they left in their car, Eva pulled out of the garage, closed the door, and coasted down her driveway. She turned opposite from the way Javier had gone and meandered around town for twenty minutes to be sure no one was following her from the house. She glanced in the rearview mirror, noticing a vehicle behind her. A memory bubbled up of her harrowing experience in the passenger seat with Hattie driving when she needed to lose whatever secret agent had been following them. Eva made a series of quick turns to observe the reaction of the car behind her, and it mirrored her moves. Someone was tailing her.

Eva had been driving these roads for years. She had to detour many times because of Carnival, repairs, or accidents and was familiar with nearly all side streets. Whoever was pursuing her would have to work hard to keep up.

At the next corner, she downshifted, negotiated the turn, floored it, and outmaneuvered another car. The vehicle behind her did the same and closed the distance Eva had put between them. The thick traffic in the shopping district slowed her escape, so the best way for her to lose the tail was to take a page out of Hattie's handbook and outmaneuver them.

She turned onto a street where she knew there would be lots of pedestrians and spotted two large gaggles of people. The first was crossing in front of an alley she had taken before in her coupe. Eva maintained her rate of travel, waiting for the last person in the group to clear the entrance. She braked, shifted gears, and swung into the alleyway between the two bunches. She picked up velocity again and glanced in her mirror. Despite rabid horn honking, the second cluster continued their walk and blocked the car following her.

At the end of the passageway, Eva made a quick turn and another until she was sure she had lost them. The thrill of the chase had her pulse racing so fast she had forgotten how tired she was after the ordeal at her house. She now understood why Hattie enjoyed it so much the day they went to Karl's secret cabin in the jungle. The danger, speed, and hairpin turns. It was exhilarating.

She picked up Javier and Monica in front of the grocery store and drove about aimlessly again to see if anyone was trailing her. No one was. She then headed north out of Rio, going to Karl's cabin. Once they got him settled into the bed in the back room, she handed Javier an envelope with some cash. "Please take this. You've aided me tremendously at substantial risk of your own."

He waved her off. "We cannot take your money, Miss Machado. We helped because we are family."

Eva smiled, thinking that Hattie had chosen her friends well and placed her trust in good people. "Yes, we are family. So call me Eva. I can see why Hattie is so fond of you two."

"We are fond of her as well," Javier said.

"I will ensure you receive full compensation for your shift today. I'm also glad you two will be working at the new Halo Club when it opens in two months."

"We're looking forward to it," Monica said.

"Hattie and Maya will start bringing on employees after the first of the year. Before they left the country, they mentioned using you, Monica, to train the waitstaff as head server. Is that something you would be interested in?"

Monica smiled brightly. "Very much so."

"Then consider it done." Eva turned to Javier. "Now, let's get you two back to town so you can get your car."

Eva dropped them off at the grocery store, reminding them that everything they had seen and accomplished, including the location of Karl's cabin, was to remain a secret. When she returned to the cabin and checked on Karl, she discovered he had developed a mild fever. She figured it could have resulted from moving him around a lot today. A cold sponge bath seemed to help.

After unpacking and stocking the kitchen, she lit the lanterns as the sun set. She then switched on the battery-powered radio to see if the day's events at her home were in the news. It took her a moment to understand the report she was hearing since she had tuned into the station in the middle of the hour. She heard the word *Japanese* and knew something horrible had happened. It had. The United States was under attack.

Karl had been right about the Axis Powers' plans, but he had been unable to stop them.

8

Washington, DC, Sunday, December 7, 1941

Eugene Stanton loathed few things more than he did sitting in a frigid football stadium. The seats were hard, and the metal radiated the cold to his bottom. At least it gave him a valid reason for not attending church with his wife and kids today. Religion was Jill's thing, not his. He preferred a frozen butt over sitting on a hard pew, dwelling on his shortcomings and the threat of hell from the pulpit.

Sports had never been his thing. He liked cars. However, going with his boss to a number of football games kept the old man in a pleasant mood. Like him, General Gerow also needed an excuse to skip church services, so during the season, he invoked Eugene's name, telling his wife he could not let the man down. Since the situation benefited them both, Eugene never complained.

The Eagles had scored early in the first quarter, so Gerow was not happy, equating the home team's defense today to being akin to Swiss cheese. After the Redskins tied the game in the opening minutes of the second quarter, however, Gerow bought beers and hot dogs from a vendor. Eugene felt he should be enjoying the bonding moment more, but he could not get into cheering for grown men playing a child's game. He likely never would.

Soon, pockets of the crowd began murmuring, their reactions not in sync with the action on the field. Eugene looked around and saw people huddling in groups, not watching the plays. Eugene tapped the man in front of him on the shoulder. "Do you know what's going on?"

"I'm not sure. Someone said there was some big news report on the radio when they went to the concession stand," he said.

The people cheered for some tackle that Eugene did not care about. He turned to his boss. "I'll be right back."

He shimmied to the end of their row and stepped down two rows to where a group of people were huddling. "What's going on?"

"It's the Japs," one man said. "They attacked Pearl Harbor. Lots of dead soldiers and sailors."

"What the hell!" Eugene's stomach twisted as he realized the country had likely suffered a deadly attack.

"Lots of ships destroyed, too."

"Thanks, Mac." Eugene rushed back to his seat and relayed to his boss what he had learned. "Should we head to the office?"

Before Gerow could answer, the stadium announcer's voice came over the loudspeaker system. "Ladies and gentlemen, may I have your attention, please. We interrupt this game for an important announcement. Major General William Bryden, Major General Leonard Gerow, Admiral Lawrence Drummond, and all senior military officers O-6 and above in attendance, report to your duty stations immediately. This is urgent and a matter of national security. Your prompt response is required. Thank you."

"That answers your question," Gerow said. "Let's go."

Once outside, they retrieved the general's car in the Griffith Stadium parking lot and arrived at the Munitions Building an hour later. All the way, Eugene's thoughts bounced between his duties and how this momentous turn of events impacted him personally. He wondered briefly if his office had planned well enough to counter the obsolescence of Rainbow Five, but he fixated on how this would escalate the War Department's search for Karl James's missing spy list.

The corridors were in chaos, with uniformed men dashing about with a sense of urgency that Eugene had never witnessed. They changed into the spare uniforms they kept in the office and reported to the primary General Staff briefing room.

The general took his traditional position at the large wooden conference table. Eugene sat directly behind him in the row of chairs filled by the other lower-ranking straphangers in the room. A bird colonel would have earned a seat at the table anywhere else. Here, however, Eugene would merely be a fly on the wall, listening and taking notes unless a question stumped Gerow. His boss then would turn to his trusty second-in-command, who would whisper the answer in his ear, and Gerow would paraphrase it to the General Staff as if he had known the information all along.

Eugene did not mind the game. His job was to stay up to date on the minutia of war planning, and Gerow's role was to run interference and play politics. Eugene was unsuited for that role, so he never wanted a star on his shoulder.

The room was strangely silent, void of the usual pre-meeting chatter that occurred as the seats began filling up. The flag officers in the room preoccupied themselves with briefing notes, and the support staff wore somber expressions. Each man in that room knew it did not get more serious than this.

When all the key personnel except the big gun and his aide were in place, Gerow leaned back and asked Eugene one more question about the investigation's status into the Rainbow Five leak. Eugene reported that the IG and FBI had yet to find any concrete leads on who had released the secret war plan. He sat straighter afterward, hoping the investigation would take a back seat and not point at him.

A senior noncommissioned officer called the room to attention. Chairs scraped against the tiled floor as people stood. General George Marshall entered the room. His aide followed immediately behind.

"Take your seats," Marshall said. When everyone had settled and the room was deadly silent, he began. "Gentlemen, a grave situation is facing us. Early today, the Japanese launched a surprise attack on our naval base at Pearl Harbor. The damage is extensive, and the loss of life is significant. We must act swiftly and decisively." He turned to Gerow. "Are the Rainbow Plans still viable considering this week's media leak?"

"Yes, sir," Gerow said. "The only plan that saw the light of day was Rainbow Five. We have been working on variations to answer what could address what might be a two-ocean war with the Axis Powers."

"Our immediate priority is to mobilize our forces and direct all available resources toward rebuilding our strength in the Pacific Theater," Marshall said. "I expect each of you to coordinate with your respective departments to facilitate a rapid and effective response. President Roosevelt will be addressing the country soon. It is imperative that we present a united front. Our intent must be clear: We will defend our nation and our allies against this unprovoked aggression. Prepare your units for deployment. This is a critical moment in our country's history, and we shall rise to the occasion with determination and resolve. Let's get to work."

The room came to attention as Marshall departed. Officers consulted each other, unleashing a rumbling murmur. Eugene made his way toward the door but stopped in his tracks when he overheard two colonels talking. One was from Military Intelligence, and the other was from the Operations Division.

The Operations man appeared outraged, holding a rolled piece of paper. "Why didn't we get this G-2 report last night? We could have had units go on alert."

"The threat was nonspecific," the colonel from Intelligence said. "Would you have put the entire army and navy on alert? Be honest. No one would have done that yesterday. They caught us with our pants down."

The Operations colonel stabbed his finger into the other colonel's chest. "Do your job so that doesn't happen again."

The two stood toe-to-toe, looking like they might go at one another physically until their bosses tugged on their virtual leashes. They dispersed before it got overly heated, rejoining their leaders like well-trained dogs but throwing sneers at each other for good measure.

"Come, Stanton," General Gerow said. "We have work to do."

His barking was more demanding than his usual orders. Eugene followed along like the others, attributing his sharpness to the tenseness of the situation. Everyone was under tremendous stress, none more than those in seats of responsibility.

They returned to their office suites. Gerow had recalled everyone to the office for the national emergency. The secretary and other staff members had arrived, ready to continue their work on the modified Rainbow Five. Eugene instructed the junior officers to compile new Pacific Theater asset numbers from Operations to begin their brainstorming. Meanwhile, curious about what had almost caused two bird colonels to brawl in the conference room, he asked Mabel, "Did we receive a G-2 report today?"

"It's in your inbox with the rest of the weekend communiques and another message from your dry cleaners. I never heard of a cleaners that was open on Sunday." Her icy reception was particularly cold today. He attributed it to everyone being on edge.

"Thank you, Mabel. I'm friends with the owner. Considering today's events, I'm sure they're just reminding me that my wife's clothes are ready to pick up tomorrow."

Eugene entered his office and scanned Mabel's memo about the phone call. The coded message told him his handler wanted to meet between six and seven that night. He balled up the sheet and threw it in the trash can with the others he received from Sam earlier that week.

At his desk, he opened the three-page intel report titled Operation Amerika Discovered, authored by Lieutenant Commander Leo Bell of Military Intelligence. The more he read, the better he understood the near fist-fight in the briefing room. If G-2 had distributed this information overnight, Operations might have alerted Hawaii units to look for an invading force. That might have perhaps saved a few assets and lives.

The location referenced in it and a particular name associated with the intelligence operation also caught Eugene's attention. Hattie James was involved. The daughter of Karl James, whom the FBI suspected had fled to Brazil. James was the man Eugene had set up to take the fall for the secrets he had given to the Nazis. The corner those Germans had backed Eugene into in the last year and a half suddenly felt much smaller. If the Jameses were uncovering Nazi operations in the United States, they might soon unravel the truth behind why Karl was a fugitive.

He told Mabel he would be out for an hour. After driving to the National Mall and finding a parking spot close to the Smithsonian Castle, he sat on the bench at six and waited. A few lampposts illuminated the area, but the grassy section was unoccupied. The country was at home mourning. As were his wife and kids, probably. He should have been at work but was here instead, summoned by the people his country was about to go to war with.

Eugene flinched when footsteps sounded behind him. His entire day had been unsettling. The attack, the intel report, and the reworking of the Rainbow Plans leaked by a senator he had manipulated all contributed to his unease.

"Hello, Gene," Sam said, sitting beside him on the bench. "One hell of a day."

"I would say so. What do you want, Sam?"

"Karl James."

"Everyone has been looking for him for a year."

"Trust me when I say you want to find him or at least his lists. Your name could be on them, Eugene."

Sam left, leaving Eugene to his misery. The walls were closing in on him, but he knew how to ensure they did not crush him. Today's G-2 report said that Hattie James was now in Washington, DC, ready to brief the intelligence community if requested. She was the key.

"Get to Hattie to get to those lists," Eugene muttered before returning to work.

9

Washington, DC, Sunday, December 7, 1941

The shock of learning of an attack on American soil had yet to wear off among the café crowd. The murmuring of customers had settled into a solemn silence while listening to the nonstop radio reports. A disaster had besieged the nation, yet a comforting sense of fellowship had formed inside the restaurant. Everyone had learned the devastating news together and had collectively concluded a dark future was in store for the United States. Hattie had a hunch that each man and woman, boy and girl, would vividly remember this day and tell their grandchildren stories about what they were doing on December 7, 1941.

Hattie, Maya, and Leo silently finished only half of their food. Loss of appetite had become a shared side effect of the gut-churning development in Pearl Harbor as a mutual understanding took root. The events had made their mission to find the Professor, turn over the list of covert operatives, and identify the mole in the War Department doubly critical.

Leo tossed three quarters onto the table to pay for their meals and tip the server. The group assembled in the entryway. "Where do we look next?" Leo asked.

"My mother mentioned running into Vicky once at Montrose Park. She told Mother that she lived close to there."

"That's near the Naval Observatory," Leo said. "It's too far to walk in the cold, so let's take my car. We need to find her and quickly."

"Agreed," Hattie said.

They loaded into Leo's sedan. He drove through the district traffic, heading north on Wisconsin Avenue. He glanced in the rearview when they were past the first stoplight. "Someone is following us."

Hattie peered into the side mirror. "Black Ford on our bumper?"

"That's the one."

Hattie kept her focus steady and identified an identical vehicle behind the one Leo had spotted. "There's two."

"Make it three." Leo suddenly swerved into the right lane.

Hattie shifted her concentration to the windshield. Another black sedan of the same make and model cut off their car and turned onto Wisconsin from a feeder street. It sped to stay ahead of them. Hattie checked her mirror. One sedan moved in closer, nearly on their back bumper. The third got beside them, and the passenger, a man in a fedora, motioned for Leo to pull over.

"Who are they?" Hattie asked.

"I don't know." Leo continued straight, pulled a sidearm from inside his suit jacket, and rested it on the bench seat next to him. He reached in front of Hattie and popped the glove box. Two pistols were there. She grabbed them and handed one to Maya in the back.

The side vehicle brushed against Leo's fender, and the fedora man gestured again.

"Hey!" Leo shouted. "That's a new paint job."

The car hit them again. The vehicle ahead of them sped up and stopped halfway into the next intersection, blocking it and leaving Leo only one direction to go. He turned right. A fourth black sedan was on the side street, stopping traffic.

Hattie released the magazine from her weapon, inspected its bullets briefly, and popped it back in. She flicked off the safety and was ready to shoot their way out if she had to. The lists, tucked into a hidden compartment in her purse, had to be protected at all costs.

"It looks like we're pulling over," Leo said, coming to a stop. "Keep the guns low until we know who we're dealing with." He kept his window closed.

The car that hit them pulled beside them. The passenger got out, flashing his government identification and a semiautomatic sidearm. "FBI. You need to come with us." The windows muffled his voice, but his seriousness was loud and clear.

"Pistols down," Leo said. "No one gets hurt today."

"You're sure?" Hattie asked.

"Yes, I'm sure. His credentials are real. They have this week's security marker."

"Under your seat, Hattie," Maya said, meaning she had put her firearm there.

Hattie placed hers back in the glove box.

Leo left his gun on the seat and displayed both hands so they were visible through the glass. "Where to?"

"Leave the car here and come with us."

"I have my service weapon. It's on the seat."

After a cursory search of their bodies and purses, the agents ushered Leo into one vehicle and Hattie and Maya into the back seat of another. One man confiscated Maya's Brazilian passport.

Maya held on to Hattie's hand for comfort as they whizzed through the streets of Washington. Or was it the other way around? They had barely escaped the Germans at the secret airfield a week ago. Leo seemed certain these men were FBI, but a sliver of doubt had wormed its way into Hattie's head. After all, unveiling the German mole in the War Department was part of what her father had asked her to accomplish.

The caravan of vehicles pulled into a controlled parking lot of a building on Pennsylvania Avenue. The markings had gone by so fast that Hattie could not pinpoint where they were. However, she was sure they were somewhere within the Federal Triangle, where many government agencies had their headquarters. Maybe Leo was correct in assuming these men were legitimate.

The agents ushered them inside to the lower levels of the building. A glance over her shoulder confirmed Leo was several yards behind her and

Maya. The corridors seemed familiar, resembling the facility the FBI had brought her, Olivia, Frank, and David to in the middle of the night when her father escaped federal custody. Her shoes clicking against the tile floor created the same haunting echo she remembered from that exhausting night. The FBI had handled her roughly and treated her like a criminal that night, but she did not get that energy today. None of the agents threatened or touched them. However, everyone strode with a sense of urgency.

She expected their escorts to take them into individual interrogation rooms, but entering a small conference room pleasantly surprised her. Her optimism was short-lived; the room had a large mirror on one wall. It was likely two-way. People doubtless would be watching as agents questioned her and Maya.

Her disquiet turned into worry when Leo did not follow them inside.

"Where are you taking Commander Bell?"

"To another room. We want to speak to him separately."

Hattie supposed his Military Intelligence affiliation had something to do with the separation. "Are we under arrest?" she asked.

"You're being detained for questioning," one agent said.

"In that case, I want my family lawyer here."

"That will only delay the process."

Hattie placed her purse on the table, took off her jacket, and sat in a chair. "We answer no questions without legal counsel present. Now, do I get my phone call?"

Maya removed her coat and came beside her.

The agent snapped his fingers and gestured toward another, who left the room, returning moments later with a telephone. He plugged it into the wall jack.

"One call, Miss James," the first one said.

Hattie found the number on a business card in her purse. She spoke to an outside operator, who connected her to Albert Wright's weekend answering service. The woman put her through to Albert, Karl's college chum and personal lawyer.

"Hattie," Wright said, "is everything all right?"

"I'm afraid not, Albert. I need your services again at FBI Headquarters. Agents brought in me and my friends for questioning."

"Give me an hour."

Hattie thanked him and hung up the phone. Turning to the first agent, she said, "He'll be here soon. In the meantime, may we use the restroom?" Her request had two purposes beyond the obvious. She wanted to see if Leo was somewhere close and to tell Maya to say nothing. Maya was not a citizen and might not be sure of her rights.

"I don't see why not." The man directed the other agent to take them down the hallway.

Hattie glanced into all the offices with open doors as they passed. Unfortunately, she did not see Leo. They stopped at the ladies' restroom, and Hattie hurried Maya inside with her before the agent gave them instructions. She bet he would not follow them in since he was a man. Her bet paid off.

Hattie spoke softly in Portuguese in case anyone was listening. "Let me do all the talking."

"Is this about your father or the attack?"

"I'm not sure. Either way, we have to be careful about what we say so we can resume our search."

"Don't worry. I won't say a word."

Returning to the conference room, they waited with two FBI agents until Hattie's lawyer arrived.

"We have to stop meeting like this, Hattie," Wright said when he walked into the room. He had not changed much since she saw him last, though he might have lost a few pounds off his short frame.

Hattie hugged him and introduced Maya, who only nodded her greeting.

Wright sat between Hattie and Maya. The agents took seats across from them.

After introductions, Wright asked, "Now, what is this about?"

"We want to know how your client knew there would be a Japanese assault."

Hattie was relieved this was about the attack, not her father, though the question of his guilt no doubt had made the agents doubly suspicious of her. She waited to respond until Wright nodded his approval.

"Discovering information about a likely attack was precisely why we flew five thousand miles on a military aircraft from Brazil with Agent Knight two days ago. We tried to brief the General Staff yesterday, but no one wanted to interrupt their weekend, so the admiral sent us away."

"Who do you mean by we?"

"Commander Bell, Miss Reyes, and myself. Let me tell you what we told Admiral Drummond at the War Department on Saturday." Hattie repeated the story as Leo had relayed it to his supervisor, avoiding mention of the German safe house in Rio, which could put her and her father in danger. The FBI might question how they discovered the operation and why Hattie had been acting like a spy.

Wright looked on with interest and maybe a little shock as he learned about what Hattie had been involved in.

"What were the German targets?" an agent asked.

"I have no idea, but that's why we snared the Kessler brothers. They were aeronautical engineers brought in to consult on the bomber. We thought they might know more about whatever the Germans had planned."

The door opened, and Agent Knight walked inside a few steps but remained standing, folding his arms across his chest. "The better question, Miss James, is how did you know about the Japanese involvement when the Kesslers did not?"

Knight had pointed his question sharply at Hattie, making her feel like she was under the microscope again. She could tell he was fishing for information about her father or a way to link the two of them so he could finally throw her in a jail cell.

"Because you ordered me to make contact with Armand Klein. I relayed everything we learned from him. You can check his pedigree in Berlin. He was the darling of the Luftwaffe. Of course he would know more about the attack plan than the Kesslers."

"Funny," Knight said. "The Kesslers knew December 7th was an important deadline. Why didn't you mention that? What else haven't you told us?"

The questions made Hattie pause. They were accusatory and roiled her anger. "That's the—"

"Don't answer that," Wright said. "My client has been cooperative. Her actions and those of her associates in the Brazilian jungle were heroic. They uncovered and stopped a German plan and, despite limited information, warned US authorities of an impending attack. You cannot hold them accountable for the military's complacency by not listening. Considering the great lengths Miss James took to get here and ring the warning bell, I think you should shake her hand, not suggest she had committed some wrongdoing."

"Your client, Mr. Wright, is a master at stalling and deception," Knight said. "She frequently evades our surveillance, and I can't believe that in almost a year, she has yet to uncover one damn thing about Karl James."

"I would venture to say that your losing sight of Miss James reflects your incompetence, not her subterfuge. Further, regarding her father, she is under no obligation to volunteer information or assist in your investigation."

In truth, Hattie felt relieved that Knight was harping about her father. It meant the Kessler brothers had kept their word and had not mentioned Karl's involvement, nor him being shot and being taken to Eva's home. Her father was safe for the moment.

Knight set his eyes on Hattie, narrowing his brow. "Is that how you want to play this, Miss James?"

Hattie understood the underlying meaning. He had threatened before to use the fact that her father had inadvertently left classified State Department documents at their house as an excuse to arrest Frank and her sister. It was a threat she had lived with for the last ten months and which had prompted her trip to Brazil.

She refused to answer. Knight could construe anything she said as a tacit admission that she knew more than she had revealed.

"Now, unless you intend to arrest my client on some trumped-up charge, this interview is over." Wright came to his feet, pausing for the FBI to respond.

"You and Miss Reyes are free to go," Knight said.

Hattie stood and whispered to Wright, "They took my friend's passport."

Wright extended his left hand, palm up. "Miss Reyes's passport. Otherwise, I'll file a civil rights complaint."

The first agent reached into his inner breast pocket and handed over the document. "Don't leave town. We may have more questions."

Wright placed a business card on the table. "If that's the case, go through my office to schedule an appointment. My clients will make themselves available at their convenience, not yours."

Hattie and Maya gathered their things.

Hattie eyed Knight. "Your agents picked up Commander Bell along with us. What has happened to him?"

Knight buttoned his suit coat. "Agents have transferred him into military custody for questioning. We'll soon be at war, Miss James. I suppose Intelligence will grill him for a while."

Hattie stepped into the hallway, withholding her reaction. She was worried about Leo. Ten days ago, he had made an enemy of Vice President Wallace by defending her in the face of his rudeness. Hours later, the police had accused him of trying to assassinate Wallace and killing his aide. No one could predict the extent of his scheming to torment Leo.

Once she, Maya, and Wright entered the lobby of the Justice Building, Hattie asked, "Albert, can the navy hold my friend Commander Bell for that long?"

"I'm afraid so. The armed services have different rules."

"Is there anything you can do to help? He hasn't made any friends in the government recently."

"He has the right to a lawyer, but only if accused of a crime. Unless that happens, the military can compel him to stay and answer their questions."

"I don't like this, not one bit."

"Let me give you a lift," Wright said. "Are you staying at your sister's?"

"Yes, Olivia's. That's very kind."

Wright delivered Hattie and Maya to Olivia's at dinnertime. Hattie opened the door using the spare key her sister gave her this morning. She expected to walk into a mix of savory aromas and to find the family at the kitchen table. Instead, she discovered everyone in the living room munching on sandwiches and carrot sticks. That was not like Olivia. Rain or shine, healthy or down with a cold, she always cooked the evening meal.

The children were playing in a corner, enjoying their makeshift dinner. Frank and Olivia were listening to the radio news broadcast, their faces filled with worry. No doubt the local stations had been reporting nothing all day but the attack on Pearl Harbor.

Olivia looked up. "You've heard?"

"Yes. How bad is it?" Hattie removed her coat.

Maya did too.

"Thousands."

Hattie sucked in a rattled breath at the thought of so many lives lost. "Why didn't they listen?" she mumbled.

"What's that?" Olivia asked.

"Nothing."

"Dozens of ships destroyed, including eight battleships," Frank said. "Almost all our aircraft are gone. This is devastating."

"Absolutely horrible," Hattie said.

"Was that Albert Wright who dropped you off tonight?" Olivia asked.

"Yes, it was."

"Why were you seeing him?"

"It's a long story," Hattie said, joining her on the couch. Maya sat beside her. "You should know that today's events make getting those lists to the right person much more vital."

"I can see that."

"Mother said the woman I'm looking for came to one of their Christmas parties, and she might have a picture of her. Can I go through her old photo albums?"

"Of course."

Olivia retrieved the books from the bookcase and a few from a box in the garage. Hattie and Maya spread them on the kitchen table.

Hattie remembered how her mother described the Professor both times she had encountered her. "She's probably in her fifties, wearing a pearl necklace and cat-eye glasses."

"That should be distinctive."

They sifted through years of memories. Maya took extra time to admire the pictures of Hattie as a little girl. "You were adorable in pigtails."

"They hurt my head at naptime, so I stopped wearing them after age three."

Maya held up the image. "Still, look at this. You were a heartbreaker in the making." She lowered her voice. "So many boys who never had a chance with you." Maya turned the page. "And this one. You were the cutest witch. I never really understood you Americans and Halloween."

"It's an excuse to dress up in costumes and eat a bunch of candy." Hattie waggled her finger at the albums. "Back to work."

Half an hour passed, and they were nearing the last of the books when Maya flipped a page. "Could this be her?"

Hattie stopped and looked at the photo. The picture showed Eva singing at the piano with a woman nearby. She appeared to be about the age of her mother now. Short and thin with wavy shoulder-length hair, she wore a thick strand of pearls around her neck and had on an oversized pair of cat-eye glasses.

"This has to be her. This is the Professor."

10

Washington, DC, Monday, December 8, 1941

Hattie's first concerns this morning centered on Leo and whether the military had released him from interrogation. She worried that Vice President Wallace had secretly worked to delay Leo's release as punishment. At the Brazilian president's reception, Leo had refused Wallace's order to throw Hattie out with the trash because she was the daughter of a traitor. She located Leo's business card from their arrival at Bolling. She first called his office, hoping he was back to duty. However, the enlisted man who answered said he was not there. She thanked him and had the operator ring his house.

Leo's wife, Beverly, picked up, and Hattie introduced herself.

"It's nice to finally speak to you, Hattie. Leo has mentioned you often." Her voice was soft and sweet, just as Leo had described her.

"It's a pleasure, Beverly. Leo holds information about you close to the vest, but I think that's his way of keeping you safe. He's completely devoted to you."

Beverly laughed but in a reserved fashion. "He's a mystery at times."

"May I talk to him? We have some important things to go do today."

"He's not here, but when he came home last night—"

"You saw him?" Hattie was relieved.

"Briefly. He came home for a uniform and some toiletries and said he might not be available all day."

"I'm sure every military man is busy these days."

"It's simply horrible what happened." Beverly's voice cracked with emotion. "We had navy friends at Pearl and can't get through to them."

"I hope they're okay. Can you leave a message for Leo telling him that we're returning to Georgetown this afternoon?"

"I'd be happy to. He left an envelope for you before he took off this morning and said you might need it."

"Can you open it?"

"Nope. He got really serious and told me not to open it under any circumstance and that I'm supposed to give it only to you." After expressing Leo's urgency to get the envelope to her promptly, Beverly arranged to have Hattie over in an hour.

Once she finished the call, Hattie went to tell Maya, finding her in the guest room they had shared for the last two nights. She was dressing when Hattie entered, initially flinched, and moved to cover herself. Realizing who it was, she quickly relaxed, dropping her arms and putting her body, clad only in her underwear and bra, on display.

"You're making this hard." Hattie's breathing shallowed as she appreciated her form from head to toe. Yes, they were sleeping in the same bed in her sister's house. However, one stayed under the covers, and the other between, mimicking her private sleeping arrangement with David. Being that close but unable to hold Maya had been her greatest test of willpower. They had not kissed since leaving the hotel room, and she ached to feel Maya's lips again.

Maya slipped on her blouse and said, "We need to keep our promise to each other. Not here."

Hattie reached to trace Maya's skin above the top of her bra with a fingertip but stopped when Maya clutched her hand. "You're right, but we need to find a decent hotel sooner rather than later."

"I couldn't agree more."

Hattie told her about Leo and the envelope they had to pick up. "I called for a taxi. It should be here in fifteen minutes."

When Maya finished dressing, they went to the living room, where the children were playing with their new toys. There would be no school today for Matthew. Most schools were closed today in the wake of the Japanese attack.

Olivia entered the room. "Thanks for cooking breakfast this morning, Maya. It was very kind."

"It's the least I could do, considering your hospitality." Maya grabbed their coats while Hattie spoke to her sister.

"We're resuming our search today," Hattie said. "I'll call if we won't make it back in time for dinner."

Olivia pulled Hattie into a hug. "I pray you find this woman. The country needs the information in those lists."

It had been a long time since Hattie felt this close to her sister. She had aired every lie between them—except the huge one about her and Maya. Their shared experience regarding their parents, despite the high-stakes nature of the situation, had made Hattie feel like their family was whole again. She finally let herself hope for a day when the only thing between them was the truth.

The cab pulled up to the house, and Hattie and Maya hurried toward it. When the driver got out and circled the vehicle to greet them, Hattie sprouted a wide grin. The taxi service had said they would try but could not guarantee that they would fulfill her request.

"Good morning, ladies."

"Good morning, Harry. It's wonderful seeing you again. Thank you for picking us up."

"When the dispatcher said Miss James had asked for me, of course I said I would come." He opened the passenger door for them. "Horrible news yesterday."

"Yes, it was devastating."

"The broadcast had Mama and me glued to the radio all evening." He shook his head. "Just horrible. She's worried the army might draft me, but I got bad feet. I'm not sure if they'll take me even if I volunteered."

"Do you want to volunteer?" Hattie asked.

"It just ain't right. Someone has to teach those Japs a lesson. All the neighborhood men are ready to line up. I should, too, but I'm all my mama has."

"Let's hope it doesn't come to that."

Once he was back at the wheel, he turned and asked, "Where to, Miss James?"

She gave him Leo's home address. "We have to pick up a package there, but we should only be inside a few minutes. I'd like you to wait and take us to Georgetown."

"Can do." Harry was cheery and chatted about his mother's excitement over the possibility of being Hattie's guest at a dinner show. Soon, he parked in front of Leo's charming apartment building near Capitol Hill. He got the car door for Hattie and Maya. "I'll be right here, ladies."

They went up the concrete walkway, located the first-floor unit, and knocked. A minute passed, and Hattie was considering knocking again when she finally heard the knob rattle. The door opened to a darling brunette woman about forty. Hattie glanced down and nearly cried, but she held her exclamation back so as not to look surprised. The heartbreaking sight before her explained so much about Leo Bell and his protective nature regarding his wife and the women he cared for. "You must be Beverly. I'm Hattie. This is my friend, Maya Reyes."

Beverly swung the door farther. "Please, come in." She backed up with her leg braces and crutches, allowing Hattie and Maya inside before shutting the door.

The living room was small but nicely decorated and well-kept. "You have a beautiful home, Beverly. We won't keep you. Do you have the envelope Leo left?"

"Yes, it's on the coffee table."

Hattie considered offering to retrieve it, but Beverly had already started moving in that direction. Whatever her affliction, she was a strong woman accustomed to doing things on her own. She scooped the envelope up and gave it to Hattie with concerted effort.

"Leo told me that you know what he really does for a living," Beverly said. "He never gets into specifics, but I'm glad he has someone he trusts implicitly in Rio."

"He's been a wonderful friend." Hattie clutched and squeezed Beverly's hand before opening the envelope. It contained a house key and a piece of paper with a name and address. She showed them to Maya, who nodded that she understood, and returned her attention to Beverly. "If you hear from Leo, please thank him for this and tell him we intend to follow up on it today."

"I will."

"We must all have dinner soon."

"I would love that." Beverly led them outside, where they hugged her goodbye.

Once back in the cab with Harry, Hattie provided the address of their new destination in Silver Spring, Maryland. He drove and pointed out more tourist attractions along the way. Hattie had grown up in the area and was familiar with the sights, but she enjoyed watching Maya marvel at each location.

When they reached their destination, Hattie slipped Harry the fare and a generous tip. "Thanks for the lift. I'm not sure how long this will take."

"I can wait about twenty minutes before I'm expected to take on another fare, but I'll stay until I'm called away. This is one of the few cabs with a radio, so I'll listen to the president's address to the nation until then. I saw a payphone two blocks down that you can use in case I have to leave. I'll gladly pick you up if you call my dispatcher."

"Let's see how it goes. We'll try to make it quick."

James Cooke's house was a small Craftsman bungalow with a tiny porch supported by columns. Eva's mother would faint over the condition of the shrubs, which were untrimmed.

As they approached the house, Maya asked, "How do you suppose Leo got Cooke's address? He wasn't in the book."

"I'm sure he has access to everyone's address as part of his job."

"That's kinda scary."

Hattie laughed. "You'll get no argument from me."

They went up the walkway and wooden steps to the stoop. Hattie used the key from the envelope to open the front door. They went inside. The living room appeared to be that of a bachelor, though the skewed couch cushions and the wall picture resting on the floor beside the fireplace suggested that someone had searched the space. Whoever did so was kinder than those who ransacked Hattie's apartment after her father escaped custody. They had left her home in shambles several times. This was nothing.

"Let's split up," Hattie said. "Look for anything that might tell us about his mother."

"Right."

Jimmy did not have much in his two-bedroom place. They combed through each drawer, cabinet, closet, and container but found nothing about his mother, not even a picture. The only things they learned about him were that he was a Georgetown graduate, preferred flannel sheets and the color blue for his wardrobe, and liked peanut butter. Lots of peanut butter and white bread. Anything to do with his work was gone, and he had probably kept nothing around that might identify his mother because of *her* work.

When they exited, Hattie was happy to see Harry still at the curb in his taxi. She and Maya hopped in the back seat.

"Thanks for waiting, Harry," Hattie said.

"Think nothing of it. Where to now?"

"Montrose Park in Georgetown."

"That should take us about twenty minutes."

Despite Harry's obvious crush on Hattie, he was a polite and helpful young man. She really liked him. He had many of Leo's qualities. If Hattie and Maya ever ran into trouble in the area, she was sure she could rely on him to help.

Once at the park, Harry offered to wait, but Hattie insisted he pick up more fares. He tipped his cap and drove off, promising to swing back by the park when his cab was available.

"What's the plan?" Maya asked.

"We ask people in the park whether anyone has seen the woman in the picture."

"But that has to be twenty years old."

"We'll wing it."

The park was expansive, with walking paths, open grass and picnic areas, tree clusters, tennis courts, and a playground for children. The park had more school-age boys and girls with young mothers than she expected for a cold late-fall Monday. Then again, with local schools closed because of the national emergency, moms had to do something to burn off their kids' energy. A group of them were nearby, clustered on a row of park benches, keeping an eye on their children.

None of them smiled, and their postures were still while they talked. As Hattie and Maya approached, their conversation became clearer. They were positing a costly aftermath in the wake of the Japanese attack, that several of their husbands would be called into service when the country went to war. One woman comforted another who had broken down into tears.

Hattie approached them with Maya. "Excuse me, ladies. We were hoping you could help us." She showed them the photo from Eva's collection. "We're looking for my elderly aunt from Georgetown. This picture is old, but it's the only one I have. She's the one on the left. Aunt Vicky has memory issues and has wandered away from home. She used to frequent this park and visit a nearby friend, so we hoped someone might have seen her."

"Let me see," one woman said. She scooted closer, inspecting the image. "How old would she be now?"

"Seventy-two," Hattie guessed, but sounding confident would avoid suspicion.

"She looks familiar, but I'm afraid I know nothing about her."

Another woman looked at the picture. "Have you asked the old lady feeding the pigeons?"

"No, I haven't. Where can I find her?"

"There's a fountain in the center of the park. She's there nearly every day at about this time. She's around your aunt's age, so she might know more."

"Thank you, ladies." Hattie led Maya along the concrete walkway.

"You're pretty good at winging it," Maya said.

"I think it comes from hiding my lifestyle for years. I learned to think on my feet." Hattie steered them toward the water feature.

"Do you think that's her?" Maya gestured to a woman dressed in tattered winter clothing sitting on a bench and throwing breadcrumbs at the birds.

"There's only one way to be sure." Hattie approached. The woman appeared to be in her seventies, and her long, frizzy gray hair and facial wrinkles told of many days spent in the baking sun. "Excuse me, miss. May I ask you a question?"

"You just did, young lady." The woman looked at Hattie and smiled, revealing stained and crooked teeth.

"I suppose I did." Despite her urgency, Hattie laughed, showed the woman the photo, and repeated the story about a missing aunt. "I was hoping you might know her and could help me find her."

"Sweet Vicky, salt of the earth that woman is. Yes, ma'am, salt of the earth."

"How is that?"

"She likes to feed the pigeons, too, and she brings me lunch from time to time. No one else around here bothers. I'm just the old bird woman."

"That sounds like Aunt Vicky. You wouldn't know it by looking at her, but she's been ill for quite some time, and we need to find her. When she comes to the park, do you recall from which direction or what road she frequents?"

"Well, sure. Avon Street, by the school. She stops at the corner deli for sandwiches, and we have a grand old time with the birds."

"Is there anything else? Did she ever mention a friend or another home?"

"She was always going on about Cambridge, how she had two places. It never made sense to me." The woman leaned in closer and moved her index finger in a circular motion near her temple. "Vicky might be a little daft like me, forgetting things."

Hattie laughed. "Aren't we all?"

The woman laughed too. "Yes, we are, young lady. Yes, we are."

"I don't have any food on me." Hattie reached into her purse, grabbed a ten-dollar bill from her wallet, and clutched the woman's hands, slipping it to her without fanfare. "A little something for your kindness in speaking with us. I want you to eat well this week."

"Bless your heart, miss. Bless your heart."

Hattie and Maya retraced their steps toward the park's entrance. They walked a little closer together on the return trip. When they were out of earshot of the woman, Maya said, "I could kiss you right now."

Hattie hooked her arm around Maya's and resumed walking as two female friends trying to keep warm might. "I could too." She peered over her shoulder and scanned the area to see if someone had followed them, but nothing stuck out.

They returned to the group of mothers, and Hattie thanked them for the tip about the bird lady. "Can you tell me how to get to Avon Street?"

"Sure," one said, and she passed along directions.

Hattie and Maya continued to the park's entrance and strolled the neighborhood until they encountered the road they were looking for. They walked a few blocks, Hattie trying to think back twenty-two years to the day her father had brought her to the Professor's house, but nothing seemed familiar. They pressed on another block and saw a sign reading Cambridge Place NW.

"Cambridge," Maya said. "We're on the right track."

Hattie's chest tingled at the prospect of locating the Professor's house. Vicky's son had said before he died that she had gone into hiding, fearing someone was after her for Hattie's father's lists of spies. There was little hope of finding her there, but something in the house might tell them where to start looking for her.

She and Maya turned onto the street, discovering a row of historic Victorian homes. Some had bump-outs. Others had rooftop spires. They all had wrought-iron-lined steps leading up to a front stoop. However, only one had a distinctive red door, drawing Hattie's attention. A stubborn memory surfaced, and bits and pieces of an afternoon twenty-two years ago when she had had a stomach bug began to take shape.

Hattie slowed and scanned the entire block on both sides of the street. She distinctly remembered walking up a brick walkway to a set of black stairs while holding on to a metal railing. She also recalled thinking that the door was the color of a candy cane and only needed white stripes to look Christmassy.

She stopped at the pathway leading to the red door. "This is it."

"You're sure?"

"Positive."

They walked up. Another memory cropped up of Hattie clutching her father's hand and the door opening to a petite woman wearing an ornate pearl necklace. She tried to picture the woman's face, but her striking black-rimmed eyeglasses were the only feature she could remember.

Judging by the collection of newspapers and mail stacked on the stoop, no one had been at the house for some time. The name on the envelopes read Victoria Cooke. She rang the bell but did not expect anyone to answer. On her second attempt, she got the same result. She tested the knob with no luck, and Maya tried opening the windows accessible from the porch but found them locked as well.

After going through a short gate, they went around the house and tried all the entry points but discovered everything secured. The backyard was spectacular, with meandering rows of plants and shrubs. They needed some attention, but not as severely as her son's yards. Vicky's garden proudly displayed her care, and Hattie pictured a vibrant spring bloom, echoing her mother's.

They had circled the house and were back at the foot of the steps.

"There has to be a way in," Hattie said, placing her hands on her hips, arms akimbo.

"Vicky sounds like the type of person who would always leave herself a way into her house." Maya went to the front door again, felt around the doorframe, lifted every object on the stoop, and kicked lightly at the wooden slats of the siding. They went to the side and backyard again and checked each nook and cranny, but they found nothing.

Maya stood at the back door, looking at the dormant back garden. She cocked her head to the side. "That's odd."

"What is?" Hattie followed her gaze, but she was unsure what to focus on.

"All the plants and shrubs except for one are dead for the winter. It's almost like she wanted it to stand out."

"I think it's a Christmas rose. My mother used to grow them when she lived here."

They walked to it. The beautiful cluster of white flowers hovering over dark green leaves had nestled among a decorative formation of rocks. Underneath one of the stones, Hattie found a tiny, weathered leather pouch.

"I got something." She pushed up the flap and dumped the contents into her hand. A key fell out.

"I think that's our way in," Maya said.

They returned to the back door. Hattie inserted the key into the lock, felt it turn, and opened the door. "I could kiss you."

They entered the kitchen, closed the door, and continued to the living room. The home looked well lived in. The furnishings and decorations were old but clean and well maintained. Open French doors were to the right. They led to a den that starkly contrasted with the remainder of the house. Stacks of paper on the desk and bookshelves stuffed with books, large and small, old and new, cluttered the room.

"This is going to take some time," Maya said. "You start in here. I'll go through the rest."

The house was cold; no one had turned on the furnace for the season. Hattie started at the desk. The papers and folders all appeared to be related to her work as a professor of political science at Georgetown University. The books looked to be a lifetime collection of historical and philosophical works. She read through the titles on the spines, one by one, and stopped at *Cicero's Letters to Atticus*, the one book that would be within reach of someone seated at the desk. It stirred a memory of what her father had said about the Professor. "She's the only person I know with a Cicero quote for anything."

As far as she could tell from the titles, this book was the only one on the topic of Cicero. Hattie was unfamiliar with Cicero's work other than that he was a statesman and philosopher, but she was confident he meant something to her father and the Professor.

Maya returned to the den. "Upstairs and the kitchen are only clothes and the usual junk. One room is like an art studio, full of paints and easels."

"Were there any paintings?"

"No, not a one, which is surprising."

"They must be significant to her," Hattie said. "Did you find any photographs?"

"Nothing," Maya said. "How about here? Anything?"

Hattie held up the book. "Cicero. This might be important. I'm taking it with us."

"The only place left is the living room."

Hattie pushed back from the desk. "I'm done in here. We can look together."

They looked through drawers and a chest but came up empty-handed. Hattie settled her attention next on the cluttered fireplace mantel. A small picture frame was there, tucked behind the candles and bobbles. She picked it up. It seemed to be the only photo in the house, perhaps forgotten in a hurry to get out of there.

"What is it a picture of?" Maya asked.

Hattie removed the photo and inspected the image. "A cabin near water. It could be the family cabin my mother said Vicky mentioned once."

This was not much to go on, but it was more than what they had when they arrived.

After locking up and returning the key to its hiding place, they called for a cab from the deli and taxied to Olivia's. Hattie was disappointed Harry was not available. The family car was in the driveway, which meant Frank was already home from work.

Hattie and Maya entered the house half an hour before dinnertime. Hattie heard the kids playing upstairs and smelled something savory cooking. They went to the kitchen, where Olivia was busy cooking.

Maya grabbed an apron hanging on the back of the pantry door. "How can I help?"

"Hi, girls." Olivia finished placing biscuit dough on a cookie sheet. "If you wouldn't mind making the salad?"

"I'm on it." Maya went to the refrigerator to pull out the ingredients.

"Thanks, Maya. Did you two make any progress?"

"We found where she lived and got inside," Hattie said. "We discovered a photo of her likely location, but we need to identify the area."

"Happy to help if we can," Olivia said.

Frank entered through the back door, rubbing his hands with a rag. They looked greasy. "What are you signing us up for?"

"Hattie needs help with a photo," Olivia said.

"What photo?" Frank asked.

Hattie retrieved the picture from her purse, returned to the kitchen, and placed it on the table. Olivia and Frank studied the image.

"I have reason to believe it's somewhere on the Eastern Shore in Maryland," Hattie said. "Is this cabin near a lake?"

"That shoreline looks more like a river," Frank said. "The water could be the Choptank."

"What towns are nearby?"

"Algonquin and Cambridge."

"The bird lady was right," Maya said, smiling.

"Two houses! One *on* Cambridge and one *in* Cambridge."

"Who's the bird lady?" Frank asked.

"She's someone we found in the park. What can you tell me about the town of Cambridge?"

"Not much. There's a market there that doubles as a café. The owner there might recognize the cabin."

"This is great, Frank," Hattie said. "How can I get to Cambridge?"

"It's pretty far. You'll have to take the ferry from Annapolis to the Eastern Shore. The trip should take five or six hours, depending on when you hit the boat. I can write down the directions."

"I don't have a car. Can I get there by train or bus?"

"I'm afraid not. It's really remote." Frank went to the sink to wash his hands. "I'm glad I left work today after Congress declared war on Japan."

"That didn't take long," Hattie said.

"Killing two thousand Americans will do that," Frank said. "Anyway, I figured you might need wheels to get around town, so I spent the afternoon getting Karl's sedan running." He dug into his pocket and tossed Hattie the keys. "She's all yours."

11

____

Alexandria, VA, Tuesday, December 9, 1941

Anxious to get on the road, Hattie woke first. She had yet to hear the water running upstairs. Thinking she must have gotten up before Frank and Olivia rose to get ready for work and get the kids up and going for the day, she left the bed quietly and showered in the downstairs bath. When she returned to the guest room, Maya was awake too and gathering her things to shower next.

"This is a first. You're dressed and ready before me." Maya laughed.

"I tossed and turned most of the night."

"I could tell," Maya said. "It was hard not to turn over and hold you."

"You're partially responsible for me not sleeping." Hattie stepped toward her and ran a finger down Maya's cheek. "Soon." She inched her head closer until their lips were a whisper apart. The urge to kiss her was as strong as it had ever been, but she intended to keep the promise she made to herself. She would not disrespect her sister while staying in her house.

"Hattie!" Olivia's voice came from behind her. "What are you doing?"

Terror coursed through Hattie, causing all her muscles to tense. She had neglected to close the bedroom door, assuming no one else in the house was yet stirring. Olivia had been, though. Not only was she up and right behind her, but she had caught Hattie nearly kissing Maya.

She spun around. "Liv, I can explain."

"How can you explain what I just saw?" Olivia's eyes were wide with shock.

"It's... I... I've wanted to tell you for a long time."

Olivia raised her hand in a stop motion. "Don't. It's a sin against God. There's no explaining that away." Olivia's mouth twisted as her dismay morphed into disgust.

Olivia's reaction was exactly what Hattie had feared, what she had hoped to avoid by hiding her attraction to women all these years. Given her mother's arduous path to eventual acceptance, she had let herself hope that Olivia might be willing to try to understand at the onset. After all, they were sisters. And more. After Eva retreated to Brazil, she stepped in and filled the role of mother for Olivia in many ways.

How she wished her mother and father were here to speak with Olivia and show her through example that acceptance was possible if she chose to understand and open her heart. They were not, though.

"I know you're upset. Mother was too, at first."

"Mother knows you're like this?" Olivia's mouth fell open.

"Yes. Father too. They've put aside their prejudices and preconceptions, realizing I'm the same person I've always been. They've also welcomed Maya as a member of the family."

Olivia tugged at her hair. "I can't believe Mother would...would accept this. This depravity."

"She loves me, and I dare to say she's come to love Maya. Why else would she open her home to us and help us rebuild Maya's nightclub?"

Olivia rocked her head, tears streaming down her cheeks. "I can't deal with this. Take Father's car, because I want both of you out of my house."

Maya touched Hattie's arm. "We should leave."

"Please do," Olivia hissed. "And never come back."

Olivia hurried from the room sobbing, leaving Hattie's broken heart in her wake.

Maya closed the door and pulled Hattie into a comforting embrace. "It's okay," she said. "We'll be okay."

"It's not." Hattie let a tear fall. She had lost her sister this morning and doubted she would ever get her back.

Maya hurriedly dressed, and they packed their bags. While Maya took their luggage to Karl's car, Hattie went upstairs and kissed Matthew and Sarah goodbye, telling them she was unsure when she might return.

"But you just got here," Matthew cried.

"I know, sweetheart, but I have something I must do. Now, be a good boy and do as your mommy says."

Leaving those kids hurt her more than her sister had. She was sure Olivia would not allow her to be around them anymore, and they were too young to understand why. They would think that she had forgotten them or, worse, no longer loved them.

Hattie and Maya drove away as the first ribbons of daylight appeared on the horizon. Hattie's stomach was in knots. She needed something to settle it and to keep her alert and focused on the road, not the ugly scene that had unfolded earlier. After pulling into the parking lot of a donut shop, she bought two coffees and several donuts for the long trip facing them.

As soon as the sun was bright enough, Maya reviewed Frank's directions and consulted an atlas he had given them. "Your brother-in-law wasn't lying when he said Cambridge was in a remote part of Maryland. We could easily get ourselves lost."

"You're my navigator today," Hattie said. "Keep me on the right road."

It took her over an hour to get to Annapolis and arrange for passage on the auto ferry to the Eastern Shore. She queued the car at the dock and drove aboard, following the deckhand's instructions, lining up in a row, nearly bumper to bumper. Passengers could remain in their vehicles for the ninety-minute transit or go to the passenger compartment, where coffee and restrooms were available. They opted to stay in their sedan. The argument with Olivia still had Hattie upset, and she was not in the mood to be around people.

During the ride, she studied the map and Frank's directions, reaching out occasionally for Maya's hand. They had more important things to tend to, she reminded herself. They did not have the time to dwell on personal hurts. The country was at war with Japan, and it was only a matter of time before they were at war with the other Axis Powers, Germany and Italy, as well. She had to concentrate on locating the Professor, on getting her the lists hidden in her purse, and on finding the mole in the War Department.

By the time they drove off the ferry in Claiborne, Maryland, they had been traveling for three hours and still had another two or three to go. This leg of the trip would be the trickiest. Though the map showed Claiborne and Cambridge to be just twenty-five miles apart, there were sections of the Chesapeake Bay and multiple rivers in between. Lacking a direct route, they would have to wind through the Eastern Shore's woods and farms via Route 404 and back roads. They passed several cars along the way, and traffic going in their direction had passed them a few times. Hattie checked for a tail periodically, but the lack of decent road markings had her focused more on the route ahead of her, not behind her. She thought a car might have been following them at one point, but then it passed them.

Maya suddenly looked up. "That was our turn back there."

"What? Why didn't you say something earlier?" Hattie's questions were sharper than she had intended, charged by her frustrations about the situation with Olivia.

"It's hard doing the math. I'm used to kilometers, not miles."

"I'm sorry." Hattie took a deep breath and squeezed Maya's hand. "I forget that you only know the metric system. That scene with my sister really upset me."

"Olivia seems much like your parents, so give her time. There's a good chance she'll come around."

"I hope so." Hattie made a U-turn. An hour later, they passed a sign that said Cambridge was two miles away. Frank's directions said the grocery store was about a mile from the city limits, so she slowed to keep an eye out for the landmark.

This section of road was narrow, and the clearing of the forest stopped just beyond the pavement. Around a bend, it widened, and three dated single-story structures came into view. A sign on one of them identified it as a market, coffee shop, and tackle shop. Hattie pulled off, slotting herself between the sedan and pickup truck parked there, and turned off the engine.

She gave Maya's hand a firm squeeze. "You were a brilliant navigator. Thanks for getting us here."

"Good directions helped."

They entered the store, where a peculiar arrangement of aisles and shelves showcased a wide variety of goods. A woman was behind the counter filling a man's coffee mug from a carafe as he sat on a stool, eating a burger. A couple was sitting at one of the four flimsy aluminum tables in the center of the room. Behind the cash register at the entrance was another man reading a newspaper. The headline was about the United States declaring war on Japan. He looked up from his paper and acknowledged them with a nod.

Noon was approaching, and hunger pangs were reminding Hattie that a glazed donut nibbled on while on the ferry did not make a meal. "Let's eat."

The waitress said in a loud, welcoming voice. "Hi, girls. Shopping or lunch?"

"Lunch, please," Hattie said.

"Take a seat. I'll be right with you."

They seated themselves and grabbed two of the menus wedged between the napkin holder and the ketchup bottle. Although limited, the café's options appeared hearty and reasonably priced.

The thin, elderly woman came over with two glasses of water. She pulled a notepad and pen from her apron. "Passing through?"

"We're trying to find my aunt's cabin," Hattie said. "We've been on the road since seven."

"You must be hungry. What will it be?"

"How big is your club sandwich?"

"Good sized. You two could probably split. Would you like fries or potato salad on the side?"

Hattie glanced at Maya with a questioning look. "Potato salad," Maya said. "And split a Coca-Cola?"

"Make it two colas." Hattie winked at Maya.

The woman returned to the counter without writing on her pad. Meanwhile, Hattie removed the two photographs from her purse and studied the one they found at the Professor's house. She scrutinized the structure's shape and composite, the trees, and the body of water behind it peeking through them. Nothing that would help her identify it stood out to her, but a local might know the cabin from a single glance.

Minutes later, the woman came back with their sandwich and two forks to split the salad. When the woman dropped off the bill and cleared their plate, Hattie showed her the pictures. "I'm looking for my aunt. She's the woman on the left with the pearls. She's elderly and has memory issues. We haven't heard from her for some time and are worried about her. I need to find her cabin, but I've lost the address. Have you seen her or do you know where this is?"

The woman squinted and leaned closer to get a better look. "Lots of places close to the river. What's her name, dear?"

"Vicky Cooke. Her full name is Victoria."

"Don't know any Vicky." The woman turned her attention to the picture of the Professor at her parents' Christmas party. "But she looks an awful lot like Penny." She peered over her shoulder and waved the man at the register over. "Hey, Ralph. Come here."

The man approached. "What?"

"Does that look like Penny?" She pointed to the image. "These two girls are looking for an aunt."

The man's eyes narrowed with impatience. "I told you to be minding your own business, Rita. People around here like their privacy, especially now that we're at war. Get back to the other customers."

"Sorry, girls." Rita gave him a sneer. "All this terrible news has Ralph on edge."

"May we use your restroom before we go?" Hattie asked.

"Of course. It's toward the back." Rita walked away and tended to the couple at the neighboring table.

"Let's go, Maya." Hattie laid out enough cash for the meal and a tip.

Hattie used the restroom first. While she waited in the hallway for Maya to finish, she inspected the framed photos hanging on the walls. Most were of Ralph with fishing and hunting buddies standing at a dock with their fresh catch or in the woods behind a recent kill.

One image was different. Someone had taken it in front of a cabin resembling the one in the photo from the Professor's house. Ralph knew the place and likely knew who owned it. However, their server, Rita, did not recognize the name Cooke, which complicated their search. Perhaps Cooke was her married name, and the home belonged to her side of the family.

When Maya came out, Hattie pointed out the image without saying a word. Maya nodded that she understood, and they returned to the car. "They both know something," Maya said.

"I agree, but we won't get anything from her with Ralph around. We wait until one of them leaves. Then we ask Rita again." Hattie moved their sedan across the street close to the trees to lessen the chance of Ralph seeing them when he left the store.

They waited for nearly two hours, during which several patrons came and went and three cars remained parked. Hattie assumed they belonged to local shop owners. Finally, Ralph exited the store and hopped in his pickup. As soon as he drove off, Hattie and Maya walked back inside. With no café customers requiring her attention, Rita was at the cash register.

She smiled at them. "Hi, girls. Welcome back."

"Hello, Rita," Hattie said. "I sensed earlier that you could help us find my aunt. You said the woman in the photo resembled someone named Penny. That's my aunt's middle name. Kids called her Pen when she was little." Hattie grinned in a pleading way. "I promise, we only want to make sure she's okay."

Rita angled her head, staring at Hattie for several seconds. "I've seen you before. Have you been to Cambridge?"

Maya elbowed her side. "Don't be shy, Hattie." She redirected her attention to Rita. "My friend is singer Hattie James."

Hattie was unsure how Rita would react. Half the people she met since her father's arrest and escape hated her. The other half loved her. There was no telling which way this would go, so she held her breath.

Rita's eyebrows arched high, and her face brightened with excitement. "Hattie James? My gosh. This is a treat."

Hattie exhaled in relief. "About my aunt."

"I saw Penny last week, but I'm not sure where she's staying."

"If you have a moment, I want to show you something." Hattie walked Rita toward the restroom and pointed to the picture of the cabin. "This looks like my aunt's place. Do you recognize the location? Where does Ralph usually meet up with his fishing buddies?"

Rita inspected the image. "That's a group of his childhood friends. One of them has a lodge somewhere on the water. I think his last name is Gibson."

"This is a great help." Hattie patted her hand. "Do you have a local phonebook I can see?"

"I do. It's at the register."

Minutes later, Hattie had the address of the Gibson family home and directions on how to get there. The sunlight was diffusing, and the sky would be dark in an hour or two. She and Maya would have to hurry.

She followed the main road through town, passing by the marina and its distinctive hexagon lighthouse. After twenty minutes, they entered a lightly wooded area and spotted a small wood cabin at the end of the gravel driveway, a late-model sedan parked on the side.

Maya patted Hattie's thigh. "I think this is it."

Hattie's chest tingled with anticipation that the Professor might be inside. "I think you're right."

They got out. Their hands touched briefly at the prospect that they had found the Professor, fulfilling the last thing her father had asked of her.

The log cabin had a Norman Rockwell rustic charm and was a stone's throw from a picturesque river nearly a mile wide. The fishing gear on the porch did not look as weathered as the structure's exterior, suggesting someone had used the space recently. Silence hung in the air, joined by smoke curling from the chimney, wind rustling the trees, and a distant birdcall.

She took a deep breath, clutching her purse tightly, approached the door, and knocked.

Moments later, the heavy black door eased open, revealing a petite woman with shoulder-length gray hair who grinned at them. She had on a painter's smock and a pair of distinctive cat-eye-shaped glasses, and her fingers were paint-stained.

"Come in, Hattie." The woman's gaze drifted. "And you must be Maya. You two have to be cold. Let's get you warmed up."

Hattie was almost sure she was the mysterious Professor who had recruited and trained her father to be a covert spy. Before she handed over the lists, though, she needed to be certain of it.

She and Maya went inside, and the woman hung their coats on pegs near the door.

The cabin's main room was a cozy, inviting space where rustic charm met creative inspiration. In one corner, a radio hummed an announcer's deep voice, telling the latest casualty counts from Pearl Harbor. However, Hattie was more interested in what told her she had found the right place. The easel with a portrait work in progress standing in the corner with a palette containing various colors of paint resting beside it was in line with the art studio Maya had found in the Professor's home. Also, the low coffee table next to a well-worn leather sofa held a few books and another pair of unique eyeglasses. These items told her this woman was the Professor, but she had to be certain.

"You're a painter?" Hattie asked.

"I paint." The woman chuckled. "I would not describe myself as a painter."

Hattie studied the half-done canvas more. It depicted an elderly woman with short gray hair, resembling the woman Hattie believed was the Professor, but the face had yet to be completed. "A self-portrait? It's good."

"A friend. Can I get you some tea? I just put a pot on."

"No, thank you."

The woman went to the wood stove and removed the kettle from the burner using a thick dish towel. "Suit yourself." She poured some water into a waiting mug, sweetened it to taste with honey, and returned to the main room. The woman harrumphed. "How did you find me?"

"It's a long story."

"You're much like your father, so guarded. How is he? Why didn't he come with you?"

"Before we get into that," Hattie said, "I have a question."

The woman sat in the armchair and waved Hattie and Maya to the sofa. "Ask away."

"You have a nickname for my father. What is it?"

The woman grinned after taking a sip. "Nightshade."

"Why Nightshade?"

The woman laughed. "So cautious. Your father reminded me of nightshade. It is a plant that can be both edible and toxic. Karl is much like it. He appears safe to the world but can be quite deadly in the right quantity."

Hattie smiled. Her search was over. "Hello, Professor."

12

Rio de Janeiro, Brazil, Tuesday, December 9, 1941

Eggs were not Eva's favorite, but she had wanted to try a dish Hattie had cooked at the house one time. She put the breakfast casserole mixture into a cast iron pot and added firewood to raise the stovetop's temperature. Once confident it was baking, she went outside to the far side of the clearing to fetch wood from the pile. She had run out of small kindling pieces and needed to split a few logs.

Eva had not done labor like this in decades, but she was no stranger to it, having grown up on the jungle's edge cleaning the fish and wild pigs her father had killed for dinner and performing chores like this. The technique returned to her surprisingly, as did her sense of survival at the house when those Nazis had invaded her home. The jungle was a rough place where everyone, including the women, had to learn how to survive.

She aimed for the log's natural cracks, stood with feet shoulder-width apart, and swung the ax with controlled force. She felt as if she had been doing it all her life. As she worked, she sorted through her worries. It had been two days since she had brought Karl to his jungle cabin to escape the Nazis looking for him. She had asked Javier and Monica to notify nurse Maria and Dr. Navarro that she would not be home and to post a note at her music studio, informing students of the cancelation of lessons until further notice because of illness. She had enough food and water to last them a week, so going into town was not an issue. The contractor at the Halo Club was continuing his work, and the Golden Room did not expect her to perform until the weekend.

More worrying was the fact that Karl's condition had not changed. She would have to fetch Dr. Navarro if Karl developed a fever or his condition worsened. Was it time? Maybe she should wait and see. Yes, remaining patient was the right course.

Placing her firewood into a leather carry satchel, she returned to the cabin and began stocking the wood box. She had emptied half her load when the floor creaked, giving her a fright. She looked up and froze, able only to suck in a brief gasp.

"That smells great. I'm starving," Karl said, bracing himself with his palm against the hallway wall.

"You're awake!" Eva stood straight. Happy and relieved did not come close to describing her emotions. She felt like doing cartwheels, shouting joy from the rooftop, and pulling him into a bone-crushing hug. All of those were out of the question. Her husband had just woken up from a weeklong coma. Yes, she still thought of him as her husband.

He moved slowly with a slumped posture but appeared stronger than she expected. Then again, Karl James was a determined man who rarely showed weakness, and Eva was just learning how deep his resilience ran.

She rushed to him, wrapping an arm around his back. "Let's get you on the couch." She guided him to the living room. He put some weight on her but managed to get to the couch and sit under his own power. "I'll get you some water."

"I could use some," he said.

She filled a glass from the pitcher and hurried back. "Here, drink this. Slowly. Are you in pain?"

"My shoulder is stiff, but everything else seems to be working. How long was I out?" He sipped.

"This is day eight."

"Eight days?"

"Do you remember any of it?" she asked.

"Some. I can recall hearing voices, and I think you read to me at times."

"Every bedtime. I didn't want you to be alone at night, so I read to you until I fell asleep."

Karl smiled. "So, we've been sleeping together for a week. Too bad I have no memory of it."

"You are incorrigible." Eva playfully swatted him on his uninjured shoulder. "Breakfast will be done in a few minutes, but you should eat only a little and slowly. You haven't had solid food for days."

"I feel thinner." He sipped more of the water. "So what have I missed? Are the lists safe? Where is Hattie? And why are we at my cabin?"

"A lot has happened. The lists are safe. Leo arranged for an American military plane to take him, Hattie, and Maya to Washington, DC, to report what you and everyone unearthed at that airfield. She's also trying to find Vicky."

"Has she found her?"

"I don't know. Saturday was the last I've heard from Hattie. On Sunday, I had to bring you here. I haven't been home since."

"Why *are* we here?"

"Nazis broke into the house, looking for you. I put you under the bed and hid with you until they were gone, or so I thought. One stayed behind, and I had to shoot him." She grimaced at the memory of the man lying limp at the kitchen table and the spatter of blood dotting the wall. It wasn't the first time she had taken a life, but it was the first time her victim was human.

He patted her hand. "I'm sorry you had to kill him, but that was quick thinking, Eva. Thanks for saving my bacon. How did you get me here? You must have had help."

"I called Javier and Monica from the Palace. They helped get you into the car and into the cabin."

"So they know about this place." He said the words as a statement, not a question, clearly resigned to the fact that the circle of people who knew about his cabin had grown.

"They've sworn to keep everything a secret. Hattie trusts them, and so do I." Eva got up and checked on the casserole. There was enough for two to eat, so she doled servings into two bowls and filled Karl's water glass again.

"I'm not worried about them." He took several slow bites. "This is wonderful. Thank you."

"You're welcome." Eva ate a little. "You were right about the Japanese planning an attack. They bombed Pearl Harbor on Sunday."

Karl leaned back and sighed deeply, running both hands through his unkempt hair. "How bad was it?"

"It was horrible. They killed over two thousand people and injured another thousand. Your Congress declared war yesterday."

Karl put his bowl down, his face contorting with anger. "I have to get to the United States."

"Is it safe for you to go?"

"That doesn't matter anymore. We're at war. Before I go, though, I need to ensure no one will come after you. That means dealing with the men looking for me. Where are the items we recovered from the Nazi house?"

"I hid them in my wardrobe closet at the house. Why?"

"The notecards there contain the lists of agents' phone numbers in Rio. I can use those to get their addresses," Karl said. He still looked weak and pale.

"You're not strong enough to go after them."

"I will surprise them. Pulling a trigger doesn't require much strength."

"I don't like this, Karl."

"You haven't liked much of what I've done in the last twelve years."

"That's not fair. I didn't know the truth."

"Then trust me on this. I'll find the strength."

Neither of them would feel safe until everyone looking for him was dead. There would be no talking him out of it, even if Eva wanted to. And she did not. She wanted them all to pay.

Eva kissed him. "Rest for a while. I'll pack up, because I'm coming with you. We'll leave after dark."

13

The Professor's smile had a maternal quality about it. As if she were proud of her child riding a bike without training wheels for the first time. "I had no idea he had instructed you, but I'm not surprised," she said. "He talked about you so much over the years that it felt like watching you grow up. Your father was right when he told me you're the perfect blend of him and Eva, inheriting both their best qualities."

"I've recently realized that." Hattie brought her purse to her lap but did not open it. "I have something for you. I assume you've been following the news."

"Yes, the Pearl Harbor attack might have come as a surprise to most, but not to me. The signs were there. You merely had to know where to look."

"We learned about an impending Japanese attack on the United States in Rio but weren't able to determine when or where it would happen, other than it would happen soon."

"Interesting," the Professor said. "How did you stumble upon it? I've been out of the intelligence loop for several weeks."

Hattie filled the Professor in about the Nazi engineers Agent Knight had commanded her to get information from and how that led them to Armand

Klein and the secret airfield. She vaguely mentioned Leo's involvement. "Commander Bell said that you had sent him to keep an eye on Father and me."

"I apologize for the subterfuge but keeping you and the lists safe was necessary. I suppose you're here because of them." The Professor put her teacup down.

Hattie opened her purse and removed the half dozen 5x7 photos and Eva's handwritten note from a hidden compartment in the lining. "So, as you know, Father encoded the lists in the sheet music he gave me. He altered the originals once we believed the lists were in danger. I took pictures of them before he made them useless, and this sheet is a transcription of the original code."

"Where are the originals now?"

"Safe with Leo Bell."

"Ah." The Professor smiled. "Sending him was the right move."

"I can't disagree."

"I'm relieved that the lists have made it home safely. We don't want the names and locations of our operatives falling into the hands of the Nazis."

"Yes, I agree. Father said you could decode the list of Nazi spies and get them to the right people."

"Yes, I can do that, and that list is more vital now that we're at war, but why didn't Karl bring them himself?"

"Wagner shot him at the airfield. The last thing he made me promise before he fell into a coma was to get them to you."

"Strom. I'm not surprised he's involved. That man has been a thorn in my side for two decades." The Professor shook her head. "Is Karl all right?"

"He's alive. Beyond that, I'm not sure. Mother is caring for him."

"Eva? My, things have changed." The Professor patted Hattie's hand. "Your father is a strong man. I'm certain he'll pull through." She glanced at the images and sucked in an unsteady breath. "Your father has gone to great lengths to ensure the mole didn't get his or her hands on these."

"Which is why I've brought them to you."

"Unfortunately, the lists would have to go to the State Department and Military Intelligence at the War Department. Until I identify the traitor, it isn't safe to disclose them."

"Have you made any progress on that? Isn't there one person you trust?"

"I trust Leo Bell, but he, similarly, would have to disseminate the information to those who could act on it. That's the rub." The Professor patted a stack of papers beside her on the table. "I've narrowed the list of mole suspects to a dozen people, three women and nine men.

"How did you come up with the names?"

"I used three criteria. They were with the government a year ago, were authorized access to the agent lists, and worked at the Black Chamber when your father did."

"Why those specific people?" Hattie asked.

"Few knew your father maintained the lists kept at the State Department. Whoever framed him must have known about my recruiting him into covert activities. Otherwise, the setup would not have been believable. The mole has to be someone he was close with at the Chamber."

"I'm following," Hattie said. "What's preventing you from narrowing the suspects further?"

"I had told no one at the Chamber about bringing your father into clandestine services, but he might have. I've gone as far as I can. Your father has to do the rest."

"So even after you decode the lists, we can't do anything with them until my father wakes."

"I'm afraid not."

"Can we at least decode them today?"

"That, too, is impossible. In my haste to dump a tail and go into hiding, I'd forgotten the book containing the cipher and cannot remember the numbers I need." She pursed her lips. "I should have refreshed my memory before going into hiding. The older I become, the harder it is to remember things."

Hattie asked Maya for her oversized handbag. She pulled out the Cicero book she had taken from the Professor's home. "By chance, is it this?"

The Professor smiled with an impressed expression but quickly shifted to a serious demeanor. "You've been in my house. Were you followed?"

"I don't believe so. I know how to spot a tail." As Hattie said those words, she ran the events of the last few days in her head. She had been on her game at the warehouse and café. That was how they spotted the FBI agents following them from lunch. She was also careful at Jimmy's house, the park, and the Professor's Georgetown house. However, during this trip to the Eastern Shore, her attention had drifted some as she relived this morning's clash with Olivia. Nothing, though, stood out. She had to trust her instinct and know she had done things right.

"Did your father teach you?"

"He did."

"Did he also tell you where I lived?"

"Not quite." Hattie explained her and Maya's quest to find her home with only an old photo and vague details about Montrose Park and a Maryland cabin. "The bird lady was the key."

"You *are* impressive." The Professor picked up the book. "Has your father taught you about ciphers?"

"Not yet."

"Let me show you."

The Professor flipped to a page that she said translated to "Laelius on Friendship," a text that appeared in Volume One of *Cicero's Letters*, Section Nineteen. She pointed to a passage and read it aloud. "Trust no one unless you have eaten much salt with him."

"That is the quote you had Leo pass along to Father, confirming that he works for you."

"Yes, and Volume One, Section Nineteen is our cipher for this piece." The Professor counted the number of lines on the page until she reached the quote. It was on the fourth line. "Add four positions to any letter in the first half of the alphabet, A to M. Then, Section Nineteen. Add nineteen positions to any in the second half, N to Z. Section Nineteen. But always keep letters in their original half."

"I get it. A becomes E, and M becomes D." Hattie cocked her head, doing the ciphering in her head. "But since the second half has thirteen letters, you're really adding six. Ergo, N becomes T, and Z becomes S."

"Exactly." The Professor smiled.

"What about the numbers?"

"They are all shifted higher by one position. Volume One."

"That's ingenious. Should we start?"

"I'd like to wait until we've unearthed the mole. There's no sense in risking the clear list."

"I understand," Hattie said.

"You've missed the last ferry back to Annapolis, so you'll have to spend the night. I have only one bed here, so I want you two to take it. Fresh sheets and towels are in the cupboard. I'll sleep on the couch."

"We can't take your bed, Vicky," Hattie said.

"You're a couple, right? Of course you can."

Hattie froze, unsure what to say or how to react. "Um…"

"You don't have to hide it, girls. Not here. You are among friends. I saw you outside. We are more alike than you think. That's why I never remarried after Jimmy's father died during the Great War."

Hattie thought back to when she and Maya first arrived and their hands had brushed together ever so briefly. Apparently, that was enough for the Professor. Only those familiar with the New York City or East Coast lesbian subculture would have noticed it.

Hattie grinned, partly because she was happy to be in a safe place. However, she was mostly relieved. This made the idea of an affair between the Professor and her father utterly implausible. "How did you know?"

"I've followed your career and have been to your shows in New York several times. It wasn't hard to figure out since I knew the signs."

"And you never told my father."

"Of course not. We all have secrets, dear Hattie. None but our own are ours to tell." The Professor stood. "Are you hungry? I was about to start cooking supper when you rolled up my driveway."

"Dinner would be lovely." Hattie did not have the heart to tell her they had had a late lunch in town.

With Maya's help, the Professor cooked a light meal featuring a fresh catch from the river behind the cabin. Their dinner conversation flowed from Hattie's father to how Hattie and Maya met.

"When I walked into her club in Rio," Hattie recounted, "I saw this gorgeous bartender putting a thumb hold on a rude, handsy customer in one swift move. Then the man left a hefty tip. It was the sexiest thing I'd ever seen."

Maya chuckled. "Well, I saw this beautiful creature walk into my bar, passing herself off as an out-of-work singer looking for a regular gig. Mind you, I knew exactly who she was and still ran her through her paces."

The Professor laughed. "You two are perfect for each other."

"I think so." Hattie gave Maya a peck on the lips. The small, intimate gesture felt significant. Here, she neither had to hide the kiss nor feel guilty about it. It simply was.

Once everyone cleaned up the dishes and put the last plate in the cupboard, the Professor went to her leather chair to read, and Hattie and Maya readied for bed.

After changing the sheets, Hattie sat at the edge of the mattress and buried her face in her hands, thinking of the horrible news she had yet to tell the Professor. She had kept to her plan to learn the cipher before revealing that the Professor's son was dead, but continuing to hold it back now felt dishonest.

Maya put her arm around Hattie's shoulder and whispered, "We're doing the right thing. There's no telling what she might do once she knows she's lost Jimmy."

"That doesn't make it feel less wrong to be manipulating her."

Maya directed Hattie's chin with two fingers to look her in the eye. "It must be done."

And they kissed and made love…to forget…to not feel regret.

In the morning, Hattie and Maya went to the living room and discovered a pot of coffee on the stove, but no Professor. Hattie checked the porch. The fishing gear was gone. She turned to Maya. "I'll look for her at the river."

"I'll see what I can whip up in the kitchen." Maya kissed Hattie's cheek and offered a somber smile. "Good luck."

Hattie took the footpath toward the water. The frigid air chilled her to the bone. The earthy smells filled her lungs, invigorating her. It had been a long time since she had experienced the coniferous scent. It differed from the Brazilian jungle, conjuring the sense of being home again.

She discovered a small pier at the river's edge where the path ended. The Professor was on a short stool with a book in one hand, bundled from head to toe in winter clothing. A fishing pole rested in a metal cleat on the dock's wooden planks.

"Good morning, Professor." Hattie joined the woman, her gaze at the dark, flowing water. "I need to tell you something." She swallowed a growing lump in her throat, thinking how the news she was about to convey would shatter the Professor's world.

"Of course. What is it?" The Professor placed the book on her lap.

"When was the last time you've heard anything about your son, Jimmy?"

"Weeks. Why?"

"Did you know he had gone to Rio on the trip with the vice president?"

"I did not. I hadn't realized he had made the cut for Wallace's trip." The Professor picked up her cup, her hands shaking. "The radio had reports of an incident there involving Wallace. Details were sketchy, saying only that a member of the entourage..." She dropped her cup, shattering it into a half dozen pieces on the aged, wooden planks. Tears fell from the woman's eyes, streaking her cheeks.

"Vicky, I'm sorry to tell you that the staffer who was shot and killed there was your Jimmy. We're unsure whether he or the vice president or both were the target."

The Professor raked a palm across her face. "Why would someone target my Jimmy?"

"He met with my father that night. He was going to get a message to you about the lists."

The Professor blinked several times and returned her attention to the water. "That makes no sense. The VP had to have been the target. If he died on Brazilian soil, we would never build a naval base there. Who would have known your father was meeting with Jimmy?"

"Leo set it up, but I trust him. Other than him? My friend David could have known," Hattie said. "He never accounted for his whereabouts that night, and I later learned that the Nazis had turned him."

The Professor snapped her head toward Hattie. "The pianist? He was the plant in your inner circle? How did they get to him?"

Hattie explained about David's parents in Germany and how Wagner had threatened to kill them if he failed to cooperate.

"It's possible Jimmy was the target." The Professor stiffened her posture and wiped her cheeks. "But my money is on the VP. What have they done with Jimmy? Is he...his body still in Rio?"

"Leo said he went back on Vice President Wallace's plane and that the White House would arrange his burial if they couldn't locate you."

"I suppose that's for the best." The Professor's hands shook a little. "Since I was a little girl, I've loved this view, particularly in the morning. It's so peaceful. Cambridge has always been my refuge. Jimmy loves it here as well." Her son's death had finally taken root. Pain and this place were all that remained for the Professor.

"That's why you have a house on Cambridge Place in Washington. You're always home."

The Professor broke her stare away from the water long enough for Hattie to see in her piercing dark eyes the lonely life she had led. And how the loss of her only child had made it lonelier. She had no one to share this place with, only memories. Those eyes narrowed, and her jaw set. Something else replaced her grief in an instant. "But home means nothing now. I suppose it will never again, which is why everyone responsible must pay. I'll see to it."

The Professor's facial appearance turned steely while saying those last few words, telling of a possessed determination. She then cocked her head at an angle and studied Hattie for several beats. The scrutiny was unnerving. Her grief had disappeared entirely, replaced by a businesslike expression. The change was oddly quick. "You have many talents, Hattie. You're much like your father when I first met him—perceptive and someone who could read anyone in a room. It's a talent few people have. You should consider becoming an operative like him."

"He's taught me a lot in the last several months, but I don't think I'm cut out for the life of a spy."

"Why is that?"

"Death. I'll never get used to it."

"And that is why you would make the perfect agent. We don't need more sociopaths in this business, which is why I picked your father. He is devoted to his country, but most importantly, he understands that life is a gift. He takes it only when necessary." The Professor turned back to the water.

"Death is a natural conclusion, but its lasting impact on those left behind is devastating. Another thing we need to remember."

Hattie placed a comforting arm around the Professor's back, hating not telling her sooner but also knowing the delay was necessary. "I'll think about it."

They returned to the cabin, the Professor toting a string of catfish she had caught. She put it on the counter atop an old newspaper. "Thank you, Maya, for starting breakfast."

"It's my pleasure." Maya stepped away from the sink to give the woman room to do whatever she needed. "Would you like me to prep your catch?"

"Please, I have to make a phone call. Foil is in the cabinet by the stove to wrap it when you're done."

As Maya cleaned and gutted the fish, Hattie remained in the kitchen with her. The Professor went to the living room, sat in her chair, and raised the operator. Hattie tried not to listen, but the space was small, and absenting herself at this point would be awkward. She busied herself by slicing fruit and buttering slices of bread.

After the Professor rattled off a number, she leaned back on her chair, facing the dormant fireplace. "I'm glad you're home, Celeste... I've received some news about Jimmy... I'm afraid it's bad... Can you come to the cabin?... See you soon."

Hattie waited for the Professor to join her and Maya, but the woman remained seated, weeping softly. Hattie plated some food, poured a cup of coffee, and brought it to her, placing the items on the nearby table. She sat on the couch closest to her. "You should eat. You'll need your strength."

The Professor turned and faced Hattie. She straightened her posture, becoming the very image of fortitude and composure. "Thank you, Hattie. This is truly kind." She sipped on her mug.

"Celeste. Is she a friend?"

"My dearest friend."

Though the Professor did not say it, Hattie knew what her response meant. Her lover was coming. She patted the woman's knee. "I'm glad. You shouldn't be alone. When will she be here?"

"Soon enough. She will take care of things, notify extended family and whatnot."

Maya finished with the fish and brought over plates and coffee for Hattie and herself. "I'm so sorry for your loss, Vicky. I'm no stranger to it."

The Professor studied Maya's eyes for several beats. "I suppose you know it well. The pain behind your eyes runs deep."

"What can we do to help?" Maya asked.

The Professor's expression faltered some, making her appear numb. "I've left the lists and the book on the table for you. Keep them safe until we get word that Karl has woken. Let's meet back here on Sunday."

"Will Celeste stay with you in the meantime?" Hattie asked. "I hate to think of you being alone at a time like this."

"I'm sure she will." The Professor jotted down something on a slip of paper. "This is the number here at the cabin. Call if you hear anything about your father. There's also a chance we might spend some time at her lodge, which is nearby. I love the view from her place, so I wrote her number down as well."

Given how Hattie had left things with Olivia yesterday and the fact that Leo was still unreachable, she considered options for their next move. There was nothing more she could do for her mission, but she did not want to sit idle in DC.

"That gives me a few days to get some work done." Hattie jotted down a name and number on a piece of paper. "Maya and I will be in New York City with my friend Maggie Moore."

"Ah." The Professor nodded. "Singing?"

"Recording. I've signed a contract with Maggie. We're starting a new label."

"I hope it goes well." With the Professor's permission, Hattie called Maggie to let her know they were coming.

After breakfast, Hattie and Maya cleaned up. The Professor handed Hattie the photos of the lists, Eva's handwritten transcription, and the Cicero book. "You've kept these safe this long. Take them with you. We will surface them once we've dealt with the mole."

Hattie placed the photos in the hidden compartment in her purse and the book into a suitcase before helping Maya load their bags into their car.

The Professor joined them.

"I'm worried about you, Professor," Hattie said.

"I'll be fine. Come back on Sunday. Take the afternoon ferry, and we'll figure things out."

As Hattie and Maya drove away, Hattie patted her purse on the bench seat beside her, reassuring herself. She had found the Professor and had the cipher to decode the lists. Discovering the mole was the last thing that needed to be done before she could provide those lists to the appropriate individuals and complete her father's mission.

"Wake up, Father. Wake up," she whispered.

14

Rio de Janeiro, Brazil, Wednesday, December 10, 1941

Karl barely recognized the woman driving him into town in the middle of the night. He had been in love with Eva for thirty-three years and had known since their first kiss that she was the woman for him. Their marriage was far from those in storybooks, but they were a good match. They complemented each other's strengths and found positive aspects in one another's faults. He thought he knew everything there was to learn about this woman, but the things she had told him after waking yesterday surprised the hell out of him.

She had hidden him from an armed invading force, killed a man at close range, knew who to trust and where to take him, and nursed him back to health. His ex-wife, or still-wife, according to the Catholic church, had done this all while he was unconscious and near death. He had believed loving her more was impossible, yet this new Eva captivated him anew. She was strong, loving, and sexy as hell, and after all these years, she still made him laugh. And she still loved him. She was perfect for him. And he was for her. But first, he had to neutralize the people after him once and for all.

Eva parked her sedan on the street behind a tree toward the rear of her house, the same spot where he would park whenever he visited. She offered to help him when they exited the car, but he had improved significantly. The more he pushed himself and used his muscles, the stronger he felt the next time he engaged them. He had a long way to go in his recovery but was well enough and determined enough to ensure she was safe.

Karl waved her off. "I need to do this."

He guided her to a wooden gate and pressed on one slat. The section rotated, creating an opening sufficient for him to insert his hand and release the lock. The barrier opened. He replaced the swivel block and led Eva through the narrow, rarely walked-through passageway. At the end, he unlocked a second gate, using the same mechanism, and entered the back of her property.

"I never knew this was here until you showed me months ago. I'm surprised you found it."

"You shouldn't. I know how to recon a place."

"That you do. I wonder why it was built," Eva said.

"I think the people who owned the house before you also owned the other one and used it as a pass-through. That other house changed hands so many times that I doubt your current neighbors know it exists."

The rise in elevation from the other house made him winded, but he pressed on and drew a pistol Eva had brought. "Stay here."

"No way," Eva said, pulling out another gun. "Your chest is heaving from that walk. You couldn't shoot straight to save your life. We both go."

Karl did not have the energy to argue, so he took the lead toward the house. "Did you leave any lights on inside?"

"All of them," Eva said. "I also opened all the curtains. If I came back, I wanted to see if anyone was there. If any lights were off, I would know someone had been there."

Karl stopped and kissed her on the lips. "You're one smart cookie."

"I was thinking like you and Hattie do." Eva smiled like she did when they were courting, stirring countless fond memories of their younger days.

The back courtyard came into view. Interior lights brightly lit the space. The overheads in every room facing the back were all on. The only rooms still in question were the bathrooms, her study, and the kitchen.

"Stay behind me," he whispered.

They entered through the breezeway door. The first bedroom and bathroom were clear. The second guest room was also unoccupied, but he had expected as much. If he were to hide in the house to catch Eva off guard, he would be where she was the most vulnerable: her shower.

They slid quietly into the living room and inched sideways until the kitchen was in view. She had not exaggerated the scene. Blood stains on and around the table were visible from their position. However, the body Eva said she had left there days ago was gone, telling him that the SS had come back for him. The odds of someone being in the house now or preparing to storm in again were low, but staying cautious was critical.

She tugged on his sleeve with a questioning expression. He signaled that it was okay and for her to wait there. Thankfully, she did not object this time.

Karl continued down the hallway. Fearing someone was lurking in the house gave him an intense burst of energy. The study doors were wide open, and he scoured the room with a glance. He moved on to Eva's bedroom, leading with his pistol. His heart thumped harder; having come so close to death, he was grateful to feel its robust beat. He was alive, and so was his family.

Turning into the dressing area, he peeked first into Eva's god-awful massive closet. It equaled her room's dimensions but was devoid of human inhabitants. That left only her luxurious bathroom.

A noise snapped Karl's head toward the shower. Knowing he was not in any shape to go hand-to-hand with whoever was there, he aimed and fired his pistol, generating three suppressed thwacks. Its frosted glass shattered, and fragments cascaded to the floor. To his surprise, there was no body; there was only the glass and Eva's shampoo bottles. He was relieved because, in his weakened state, he lacked the strength to deal with a corpse.

Eva darted into the room, bearing her pistol. Her terrified expression was clear as day. "You're alive."

"Yep. But your shower door didn't survive. Sorry."

Eva surveyed the mess. Her mouth fell open. "Why did you shoot it up?"

"I heard a noise."

Eva giggled. "I should have mentioned the faucet leak, I guess."

"That would have been nice."

Eva laughed more. "Well, thank you. I've wanted to replace that door for years but could never justify the cost."

"You're welcome, I guess." Karl shrugged and smiled. "Can you get those items from the safe house now?"

"Yes, but you're getting the broom."

Karl kissed her cheek. "Yes, ma'am." Certain enough that he had cleared the house but still aware surprises were always possible, he held his gun at his thigh instead of stowing it in his waistband. After retrieving the broom from the wall clip in the kitchen, he discovered Eva had dumped the things from her safe on her mattress and was sifting through them.

She looked up when he entered. "You said the notecards, right? Anything else?"

"Just those. I'll get to them after I sweep up the mess I made."

Eva separated those objects. "Oh, no you don't, mister. You're still recovering." After scooping the remaining objects back into the pillowcase in which Karl had stored them, she snatched the broom from Karl's hand. She pointed toward the bed. "Sit and figure out how to find those bastards."

"Yes, ma'am."

After returning the rest of the safe house items to her dressing room strongbox, Eva began sweeping the broken glass into the trash and placing the large pieces onto a towel. Karl stole glances at her while he sorted through the Nazi SS cards recovered during their search for Wagner and the secret airfield. As he recalled, they contained phone numbers and letters referring to an agent's designation in Rio. The closer to the start of the alphabet, the higher the agent was in the organization. His goal was to cut off the head of the group and that of anyone who might come after him, Eva, or Hattie. He identified those designators and constructed his hit list. With a phone call—and bribe—to his contact at the telephone company, he would complete the final step, getting the addresses corresponding to those phone numbers.

Eva returned to the bedroom. "I'll make us some decent food."

"I'd like to shower."

"Well, you've limited your options to the guest bath. Towels are in the hallway closet."

Twenty minutes later, Karl emerged from the guest bathroom refreshed but still tired. Eva had a hot meal waiting for them in the living room.

"We're eating here?" he asked.

"I'm not going near that table before it's cleaned and thoroughly sanitized."

"Good choice."

While they ate, Karl found his associate's home number in his wallet and dictated the list to him. They arranged to meet in four hours when his connection would have access to the telephone company's records. That would still give him time to make his assaults before the targets were up for the day.

"We have until three," he told Eva.

"You should get some rest."

They went to her room, where she set an alarm clock to wake them up in time to see his contact. He undressed to his underwear and got into bed. So did Eva. His shoulder was still sore from the gunshot, but the wound and stitches were healing nicely.

Karl turned to her, caressing her cheek. His body tingled with desire, but he was surprisingly apprehensive. They had always been good in bed. That was not the issue. Their history was. They had not been close like this, emotionally or physically, in fifteen years. They were different people in their hearts and in their minds, and their bodies had aged with time. He decided to throw caution to the wind.

"I've never stopped loving you, Eva."

Her chest rose and fell at a faster rate. "And deep down, despite all the hurt, I've always loved you, Karl."

"I gotta say I'm really nervous about this."

Eva smiled. "It's not like this is our first time."

"In a way, it is. You're not the woman I let down so many years ago."

"And you're not the man I betrayed." Eva scooted close, entwining their legs. "Now, shut up and kiss me."

"Yes, ma'am."

And they kissed and made love...to remember...to bury their regret once and for all.

Eva Machado was the sexiest wheelman in history, Karl decided. He hated embroiling her in his business, but she had insisted, saying, "You involved me the day you took the job. I'm just playing a more active role now. I drive. You do the rest."

He had to admit that having her at the wheel was allowing him to conserve his energy. She knew the streets of Rio well and had woven her way to his targets' homes without wasting a second. He had started the morning with six names on his list and was now down to two. Eva had the address of the fifth and was making her way there. Dawn would come within an hour, so they needed to dispose of him and one more before sunrise.

Eva parked two houses beyond the target's residence to make it easy to get away. Karl got out, donning the cap and smoothing the jacket of the telegraph company outfit he had stolen. His black pants did not perfectly match the gray fabric of the telegram men's attire, but they were close enough in the darkness.

"You're quite handsome in uniform," Eva said.

"Don't get any ideas. I'm too old to join the service. I'll be right back."

He closed the door softly so as to not alert any nearby dogs and approached the target's front door. The neighborhood was one step above the favelas, with individual houses and a bit of land, but not much better. Weeds were high and trash overflowed the bins fronting faded and rusted homes.

He knocked and prepared for the man to answer. He was not concerned about family members being there. The SS could not bring them along on foreign duty assignments. The presence of a female companion was always possible, though, so Karl hoped the ruse he had planned would distract this agent as it had all the others.

He pretended to hold a telegram, using the large envelope in his left hand to hide the pistol with a silencer in his right.

A light came on inside, shining through the small glass window above the door. "Wer ist es?" came a muffled voice from the other side of it.

"Telegrama para Frost," Karl said. He had butchered his Portuguese accent but was counting on the door between them to make it not too noticeable.

The door opened, and more illumination poured onto the porch. A man Karl recognized was struggling to stretch his suspenders over his shoulders. "Was ist das?" the man asked.

"Herr Frost?" Karl angled his pistol toward the man's chest.

"Ja." The man put on his eyeglasses.

"A message from Karl James."

Karl pressed the trigger twice, each shot creating a thump like thick books hitting the floor. Frost's body twitched as red spots appeared and spread across his white undershirt. Frost fell back against the interior stairs. Karl took a step inside and fired again, this time hitting him between the eyes.

Frost stopped moving. He was no longer a threat to Karl and his family.

Karl kicked Frost's feet in far enough to close the door. He turned and walked calmly to the waiting sedan. Eva drove away slowly so as to not draw attention. He did not tell her what he had done, and she asked no questions. If the police interrogated her, she had deniability. Some, at least. She could honestly say she only had given her sickly husband a ride around town.

Other vehicles were beginning to trickle onto the streets in Rio's dark early morning hours, a sign they needed to hurry to make contact with the sixth name on Karl's list. Karl would enjoy this one, given his past with the man.

They parked near the home of the last SS agent Karl knew of in Rio, lining up again for a fast egress. This neighborhood, still run-down, was a notch above their previous stop, suggesting this man was higher up the organization and pulled in more money. His residence was a single-story building, so Karl would have to be accurate with his first shot. Otherwise, the target would have a means of escape.

Karl approached the house, using the technique he had deployed with the others. He rang the bell and readied his prop and weapon. The time now was such that Karl expected the man to be up and getting ready for his duty day.

When he knocked, Karl heard a creak from inside the house but nothing further. No one came to the door, asking who was there. Sensing something was off, he stepped to the side of the door, pressing his back against the wall.

Seconds later, the distinctive thwack of gunfire through a suppressor sounded, and holes appeared in the door, splintering it in several locations, all chest high.

A burst of energy surged in Karl. He stretched his arms, aimed his weapon at the doorway, and fired blindly into the house. He kicked in the door without pausing, breaking the jamb and sending wood chunks flying. There was no one in sight, but the porch light revealed blood drops leading away from the entryway.

Karl continued deeper inside, locating a wall switch on the left in the direction of the trail and flicking it on. An overhead light went on in the adjoining living room, and another muffled barrage erupted, shattering picture frame glass and sending it and other décor to the floor. Karl was at a disadvantage—unfamiliar with the layout and running on fumes from his injury—but he had no intention of retreating. He had wounded the agent, and, based on the erratic gunfire being returned now, the man was jittery and getting weaker.

Karl crouched low, making himself less of a target. He peeked around the corner and fired twice, aiming at where he thought the shots had originated. A figure slammed against the wall at the far side of the room and disappeared into the darkened next room through the passageway.

Karl dashed past the couch and a chair, turned on another overhead light in the adjoining room, and paused for a rattled response. A shot rang out, followed by pounding footsteps. He rushed toward them, dodging the dining room table and chairs.

The distinctive racket of crashing pots sounded, and there was a loud "Oof."

This was his chance. He burst into the kitchen. The man was stumbling among the pans on the floor, struggling to get to his feet. Karl fired once, aiming for his leg, nothing that would kill him too quickly. The man fell to the ground, thudding against a pot but getting off a shot as he struggled to hold on to his firearm. The bullet missed widely to the left.

Karl summoned every ounce of energy he had left and knocked the gun from the man's hand before he could fire again. In a second blow, he backhanded him across the face with his pistol, making his body go limp. He slumped against the kitchen counter, feeling his weakest since waking yesterday. When a wave of dizziness threatened to tumble him over, he gulped a glass of water from the tap.

The man on the floor began to stir, but Karl was not ready for him to die.

Now able to focus again, he scanned his surroundings, grabbed a chef's knife from the sink area, and cut a length of string from the window blinds. He tied the man's hands together, then leaned against the counter again, pointing his gun at him.

The man looked up, loosened a glob of red spit onto the tile, and, with some effort, pushed himself to a sitting position. Blood oozed from a leg, an arm, and near his belly on the left side. The blood on his thigh was darker, suggesting Karl had clipped an artery.

"Hello, Otto."

"Karl James." Otto Klaus grimaced.

Karl relaxed his aim but kept his pistol at the ready. "I told you on our way to that airfield that I would enjoy watching you die. That is happening."

"I should have killed you when I had the chance." He coughed and spat up more colored stuff.

"You're a follower, Otto. You never had the balls to take matters into your own hands. Tell me now who ordered you to go after my wife, and I'll make this quick."

Otto went into a curse-filled rant, wasting his energy and making blood flow faster from his wounds.

"Such language, Otto. There's no need to be crass. Wagner is dead. Who is pulling the strings now?"

"No one! *I* had the balls to go after you," Otto yelled, twisting in agony and the reality of death chasing him. "Me. Now, do it. Kill me."

Karl scratched his jawline. "I guess I had you figured wrong, Otto."

Otto grinned in triumph. That was the least Karl could give him.

Karl raised his weapon and fired once more, shooting Otto between the eyes. He retraced his steps through the house, picked up the cap and envelope he had dropped at the doorway, made his way to the car, got in, and slumped in his seat.

Eva drove away, glancing at Karl with concerned eyes. "Are you okay? You're sweating, and you look pale."

"That one took a little more effort than I had anticipated."

"Are we done?" Eva returned her attention to the road.

"Yes, we're done." Karl patted Eva's leg. "You're safe. Now, I can go help Hattie."

15

Maryland Eastern Shore, Wednesday, December 10, 1941

Maya was next to Hattie on the stiff, pew-like benches closest to the portside hull, both of them sipping the hot coffee provided by the ferry. It was satisfying, but it was a world apart from Brazilian fare. Maya occasionally nibbled on the box of popcorn they had bought at the dock before boarding but rarely raised her gaze from the watery scenery of Chesapeake Bay. This was how Hattie wanted Maya to enjoy the ninety-minute trip to Annapolis, not peering the way they had experienced in their car during their eastbound crossing the day before. Today was too cold to sit on the deck and breathe the briny air, so they were riding in the passenger compartment. Despite its salt-encrusted, fogged windows, Maya still seemed to be relishing the ride.

"How far is it to New York City?" Maya asked.

"About four hours by train from DC."

"Why didn't we drive from Cambridge?" Maya glanced at Hattie briefly before turning her gaze back to the water. "Wouldn't it have been quicker and less expensive?"

"Yes, but the train is safer for two women traveling alone, particularly in the winter," Hattie said. "Besides, I want you to see the countryside and not have to have your head buried in a road atlas."

Maya turned her head, giving Hattie a long, emotion-filled gaze. "Thank you. This might be my only trip to the United States."

"And you should make the most of it."

"We already have." Maya gently squeezed Hattie's hand. Sharing bodies last night had been much needed. Maya had said and done all the right things to lessen the sting of Olivia's rejection of them. And Hattie had done what she could to show her appreciation for that.

They arrived at Olivia's home in Alexandria around noon. Hattie positioned her father's vehicle close to the garage, leaving room for Frank to pull into it when he got back from work. She popped the trunk up but left their luggage in it to make it easy to grab when the taxi came.

Hattie rolled her stiff neck and knocked on the door, dreading the scene that was about to unfold. It would not be pretty.

Olivia said nothing when she opened the door, just giving her the same scowl she had when their father had grounded her for a week.

"We're not staying. I wanted to return Father's sedan while we're in New York City through the weekend." Hattie held up the car keys. "May I use the phone? I need to call a cab to take us to the train station."

"Frank can drive you. He came home for lunch and was about to head back to the office." Olivia made no motion to open the door farther to invite them inside, stinging Hattie deeply.

Frank appeared behind his wife, grabbing his briefcase. "Hattie, you're back. Are you going to let her in, Liv?"

"They were just leaving, so I don't want to get the kids riled up," Olivia said. Her tone was cold and uncaring. "They need to catch a train. Would you mind taking them?"

"Of course. I'll be home for dinner." Frank kissed Olivia on the cheek on his way out. "Let's go, ladies. I'm in the garage."

Hattie handed him Karl's keys. "Here. I'm blocking you. We might as well take Father's car."

Once on the road, Frank glanced at Hattie in the front seat beside him. "I don't know what kind of sister drama is going on between you two, but I pray you work it out."

"There's nothing to work out. It's something Olivia has to come to terms with, if she ever does."

He squinted in confusion. "I'm not sure what that means."

"You'll have to ask her."

The fact that Olivia had yet to tell Frank what she saw was significant. She had kept Hattie's secret. It was unclear whether that stemmed from shame over her sister's homosexuality or from the sisters keeping each other's secrets. That uncertainty gave Hattie a sliver of hope that Olivia might come around.

Frank unloaded their bags at Union Station and tipped a porter to help carry them. He turned to Hattie. "No matter how this works out, you're still my sister. If you need anything, call."

"I will." Hattie embraced him and gave him a slip of paper. "This is where I'll be through Sunday morning. I'll leave a message at your office when we return to the area."

Frank hugged Maya and looked at them both. "Safe travels." He waved goodbye and drove off.

Hattie's heart hurt all the way to the ticket window. She had always considered Washington her second home. She grew up there. Her father, Olivia, Frank, Matthew, and Sarah lived there. An invisible family bond had stretched from there to New York for years as she built her career and from there to Rio over the last year. At least it had until now. Olivia's gut-wrenching banishment had frayed all those connections. And with her father still on the run, that bond with DC felt broken, maybe irreparably.

"What will it be, miss?" the ticket agent asked.

"Two first-class tickets to New York on the next Broadway Limited. A private cabin if one's available."

"I can fit you on the two o'clock train today. It arrives in New York at six."

"Perfect."

"That will be fifty dollars."

Maya tugged on Hattie's coat sleeve. "That's a bit much."

"It's only twenty more, and I want the privacy," Hattie whispered in her ear. She turned back to the clerk. "I'll take it."

The train pulled from the station at two, and soon buildings, cars, and trucks were whizzing past their window. Within minutes, the view changed to scenes of rolling farms interspersed with forests filled with green pines and trees that had lost their leaves in the approach to winter. Before long, they were knifing their way through the Allegheny Mountains.

"Is that snow?" Maya pointed to an area on the other side of the glass.

Hattie followed her gaze. The area had received a light overnight sprinkle that had yet to melt in the afternoon sun, a small taste of the grandeur to come later in the season.

"Yes, it is. Just a dusting."

"I've never seen it before."

"I'm glad to be the one to show you." Hattie angled Maya's face toward hers and kissed her.

"I am, too." Maya offered a closed-mouth smile. Then her expression turned serious. "I know this thing with your sister has hurt you deeply."

Hattie fought back tears to no avail. "I'm more than a sister to her. I got her through her teenage years after Eva left. Matthew and Sarah seem almost like grandchildren to me. I can't imagine never seeing them again."

"Give her time, like you did with Eva. If she never comes to accept you, that is her loss."

Hattie caressed Maya's cheek. "I never thought I would love again after Helen broke my heart. I realize now that what I felt for her doesn't compare to what I feel for you. You take me for who I am without trying to change me. You offer kindness and support during my darkest times. You even let go of your resentment toward my father for being the cause of your sister's death. No matter the circumstance, you show me patience and respect."

Hattie brought Maya's hand to her chest. "If that isn't unconditional love, I don't know what is. I hope to show you the same for the rest of my life."

They kissed again, and Hattie held Maya in her arms for the remainder of the trip, watching the passing scenery with her and the sun setting on the Western horizon. It was a magical trip, one Hattie would never forget.

At Penn Station, Hattie weighed calling Maggie but opted instead for the quicker cab ride. A porter loaded their suitcases into the trunk of a waiting taxi, and Hattie gave the cabbie Maggie's address on the Upper East Side.

The driver took them up a less traveled road, bypassing the holiday mess at Times Square. Despite the grim news of the weekend, traffic seemed heavier than usual and shoppers and businessmen wrapped in warm winter garb filled the sidewalks. The only signs that things had changed drastically were the American flags and posters encouraging support for the war effort interspersed among the colorful Christmas decorations adorning the light poles.

When they arrived at Maggie's brownstone, the cabbie lugged their luggage up the front steps, earning himself a sizeable tip. Hattie rang the bell. Moments later, the housekeeper greeted them at the door.

"Hattie James to see Maggie Moore."

"Of course, Miss James." She opened the door wider. "We've been expecting you." The woman offered to get their bags, but Hattie and Maya insisted on helping and brought them into the foyer.

A curvy platinum blonde dressed in blue silk from top to bottom appeared on the stairs. With her shape and height, Maggie Moore would stick out in any crowd, but her long, salon-colored hair was the beacon that drew every ship in the harbor.

"You're quite naughty, Hattie James," Maggie said, descending the steps. "You were supposed to call so I could pick you up."

"I'm sorry, but things were moving fast today. I thought I would save you the trouble."

"It's never a bother, my friend." Maggie pulled Hattie into a bone-crushing hug before offering Maya the same greeting. "It's wonderful seeing you again. How are you enjoying the States?"

"I got my first car ferry ride and saw snow for the first time."

"So Hattie has been giving you the whole shebang."

Maya squinted. "The what?"

"The full tour."

Maya chuckled. "That she has. Though I don't think I'll ever get used to the cold."

"Few of us do." Maggie laughed, too, and turned to the housekeeper. "Thank you, Patricia. Can you see that fresh towels are out in the shared bathroom?"

"Yes, Miss Moore." Patricia hurried up the stairs.

"Have you eaten?" Maggie asked. "We were about to sit down. Aunt Ivie made her pot roast."

"We're famished," Hattie said.

"Then it's settled. Dinner first."

"We should take our bags up."

"Leave them. Wendell will bring them up. I have you on the top floor." Maggie leaned in and spoke softly. "Only I am allowed up there, so you girls can have your privacy."

Hattie grinned. "Thank you, Maggie. How is your cousin?"

"Bound for trouble as always, and since the Japanese attack, he's been insufferable with his bravado."

"Many American men are puffing their chests and are willing to back it up by giving them a good fight." Hattie thought of Harry, their taxi driver, who was more than willing to fight despite his mother's concern.

"That they are."

They entered the dining room. Three place settings were out, alongside side dishes of steamed vegetables, mashed potatoes, and dinner rolls.

Wendell was at the table, puffing on a cigarette, his nose buried in the sports section of the evening edition of *The New York Times* and a box of Camels rolled into his T-shirt sleeve. He fancied himself a wild one, smoking, drinking, and tattooing his arms with images of curvy women. Hattie considered him a leech. He was a gambler who spent half his time riding high on winnings and the other half in debt, borrowing from Maggie or his mother, Ivie. She would have despised the man if not for the sweet way he protected and helped those two.

"Hello, Wendell. It's good to see you."

"There's my girl." He stood and greeted Hattie with the same powerful hug. "It's been a while."

"That it has."

"How long are you in New York?"

"We're taking a Sunday train back."

"That's plenty of time to hit the town."

"She's here to work." Maggie slapped him playfully on the shoulder. "You can light up the night spots with your buddies. Now, go get two more place settings."

The kitchen door swung open, and Ivie entered, carrying a large dish with a freshly cut pot roast and more vegetables. "Hattie, you made it! I hope you're hungry." She put the plate in the center of the table.

"For your roast? Always." Hattie gave Ivie a firm hug, but not too hard. Ivie was thin and a bit frail, but she insisted on cooking to earn her keep since Maggie took her and her son in.

After Hattie introduced Maya, Ivie slapped Wendell on his shoulder. "Why are you standing there? I told you to put out two extra place settings an hour ago."

After pleasantries, a delicious dinner, and a boisterous conversation about the war, Maggie told Hattie and Maya to grab their coats and took them to the lower floor and outside. Her property was a rare double lot with a sizeable main house, a garage, and a carriage house that had housed two horses at the turn of the century. She led them through the courtyard to the carriage house and turned on the lights.

Maggie had spent a year transforming the building into a state-of-the-art recording studio large enough to hold her musicians. It had all the modern technology, including a high-tech soundboard with dozens of switches and levers. The highlight of the space for Hattie was the booth and its sleek ribbon microphone.

Hattie's mouth dropped open. "You got the RCA 44."

"Two, actually. One for the band and one for you."

"They will be perfect for our duets."

This microphone model had many superior features, but its ability to pick up sound in the same quality from multiple directions was unique. It was extremely expensive.

"No sense in pinching pennies at this end," Maggie said. "Our new label will have to vie with the big guys. Go inside the recording booth and check it out."

Hattie walked through the door and closed it, running her hand across the smooth fabric of its insulation. The room had two stools in the center, but it was sizeable enough to accommodate double that. The thick window that kept the external sounds from penetrating was crystal clear without a single smudge. It rivaled any studio she had used at RCA Victor.

She grabbed one of the headphone sets hanging on a wall hook, put one cup to her ear, and stepped up to the microphone. Memories of being in RCA's recording booth for the first time flooded back. That day had marked the start of a new life, one she had dreamed of since the first note she belted out in front of strangers at a recital. Every inch of her skin had tingled with excitement.

She also remembered basking at the time in the thought that she had finally made it to the big time and on the basis of her own hard work, not Eva Machado's reputation. She had wanted nothing to do with her mother back then, only to show her that she could do it all on her own. And do it better. She shook her head. She had been so misguided, sure that distancing herself from her mother was what she needed to get through life. The opposite was true. She needed her mother... And her family. She needed unconditional love in her life, and that was as true today as it had been then. It made Olivia's rejection doubly painful.

Hattie shook off her melancholy as she realized how much she had missed this part of the music business. Her body tingled as it had that first naïve day at RCA. She could not wait to start. Only this time, she would do it right.

Hattie exited, looked at Maggie, and asked, "When can we start?"

Maggie beamed. "Noon tomorrow."

~

The following day, Thursday, December 11, 1941

Maggie's studio musicians began trickling in during the noon hour. Like most musicians, they were creatures of the nightlife; they did not start warming up until nearly two. Maya sat in the band room, watching the activity curiously, while Hattie and Maggie reviewed notes and prepared to lay down their first recording in the booth. They had decided to go with one of the duets they had recorded at RCA before everything with Hattie's father blew up her career. David Sarnoff, the company president, had refused to release them out of spite, saying that no one would buy music by the daughter of a traitor.

"Ready to start?" Maggie asked.

"As ever," Hattie said.

Maggie signaled the sound engineer to begin, and the band members got into position.

Hattie donned her headphones and approached the microphone. "Eat your heart out, Sarnoff."

Two hours and multiple takes later, the technician finally said they had recorded enough to mix and create a guaranteed hit song. Everyone was tired and needed a well-deserved break. Hattie and Maggie stepped from the booth.

Maya joined them. "You two looked like you were having so much fun."

"That's how it always is with us." Maggie grabbed a towel, wiped the sweat from her brow, and bumped playfully against Hattie's shoulder.

"This one could make me laugh in the middle of a funeral." Hattie nudged Maggie's back.

From the first day she met Maggie Moore, Hattie knew they would be friends. Despite headlining shows everywhere as RCA's top female singer, Maggie had mentored Hattie through her first record, providing constant advice and support. Hattie quickly became the label's number two vocalist, and their performances together outsold anything the company had in its catalog. Sarnoff had erred in canning those records and again when he let Maggie buy back the rights to them. Her new label might not bury RCA, but it would make a considerable dent in their sales and make her and Hattie rich.

Hattie's head turned as the murmuring of the musicians huddled in the corner around the radio grew louder. Several glanced toward her. One threw down his sheet music, scattering it on the floor. "I don't care who she is. I won't play for her anymore." A second man did the same, echoing his sentiment.

Maggie approached them. "What's the problem, boys?"

Another man turned up the volume. The announcer was sharing the troubling news that Congress had declared war on Nazi Germany, mirroring Germany's declaration against the United States earlier in the day. The long-anticipated battle was beginning. "Ladies and gentlemen, our country is again at war with Germany. May God bless the United States of America and strike down those who seek to destroy us."

One of the band members scowled at Maggie. "We're at war, Maggie. I won't play for a traitor."

"I won't either," the second man said. "It's her or us."

"Hattie is no traitor." Maggie stiffened, going on the defensive.

"Her father is a damn Nazi." The first man pointed an accusatory finger at Hattie, who stood shocked and numb at the unfolding scene.

"That's it. You're fired." Maggie threw her arm up and pointed out the door. "See my aunt in the main house for your day's pay." As he stormed out, Maggie turned to the other band members. "Hattie stays. Anyone else who wants to join him, leave now. I won't stand for bigotry in my studio."

The second man packed up his things and left. The four other musicians nodded their support for Hattie and Maggie before turning to study their music sheets.

Maggie returned to Hattie and rubbed her arms. "I'll get replacements for those two idiots tomorrow."

Hattie took a deep breath to keep her lips from trembling. Until her father was exonerated, she would have to find a way to tolerate reactions like those from the two men. In the meantime, she was grateful to have Maggie Moore in her corner. "Thank you, Maggie. You're a good friend."

16

New York City, NY, Friday, December 12, 1941

The fire in the main floor's hearth was dying down. The last remaining flame flickered its final sign of life, leaving only rising tendrils of smoke and glowing orange embers in its place. Hattie checked the wall clock. Midnight had passed. The day, or technically yesterday, had started well with an incredible recording session for their first collaboration. It fell apart after the declarations of war and the band members walking out in protest. Maggie had been a champ, defending her at the time. She also entertained Hattie and Maya during and after dinner, telling stories and juicy gossip about what the people in their circles had been up to since Hattie left the States.

Maya yawned, and Hattie struggled to stay awake. Wendell was out, the housekeeper had gone home, and Aunt Ivie had gone to bed an hour earlier. It was time to call it a night.

Hattie stood and offered her hand to Maya. "It's time to get you to bed." She pulled Maya to her feet.

Maggie laughed. "You're getting soft. A year ago, the night would still be young."

"You didn't travel by car, boat, and train the other day. If you had, I'm sure you'd be dragging your butt after midnight too." Hattie made a funny face at Maggie, taking umbrage at the subtle dig of her getting old.

"Fair enough, my friend." Maggie laughed again.

After saying goodnight, Maggie went to her suite, and Hattie and Maya ascended the stairs for their second night in the brownstone. After using the common bathroom one flight below them, they went to the top level, climbed into bed, and melted into each other's embrace. A few kisses later, the need for sleep overtook them.

The day had not been ideal, but nodding off in Maya's arms was perfection.

A loud knock on the door startled Hattie awake. She fumbled in the darkness for the nightstand lamp, finding it after knocking their Big Ben alarm clock onto the floor. "Who is it?" she shouted, picking up the clock. It was two.

Maya popped up beside her.

"Hattie, it's Maggie. You have a phone call. It's your brother-in-law, Frank. He says it's urgent."

"Come in." Hattie rushed to put on her robe and slippers. Maya did too.

The door opened, and Maggie remained in the doorway. "I'm sorry, but I don't have a line up here. You'll have to come down two floors to my room."

"Lead the way."

Maggie took them downstairs and into the primary suite. It was ornate, but Hattie had no time to take in the décor. Seeing the phone receiver off the hook on a small table next to a stuffed armchair, she picked it up and sat down. "Frank? It's Hattie. What's wrong?"

"It's Olivia. She's missing." His voice was frantic.

A knot the size of Texas formed in Hattie's stomach as she absorbed what Frank had told her. She had no doubt that her mission regarding the lists and the mole was at the center of this.

"Tell me what happened." Hattie reached for Maya's comforting hand.

"Matthew developed a nasty cough last night. We ran out of syrup, so I went to an all-night drugstore. When I came back, she was gone. I found a note on her pillow."

"What did it say?"

"It says that you will hand over the lists. Otherwise, Olivia will die. Damn it, Hattie, I knew this would happen. You and Karl brought this on. They were in my house, Hattie. In my house! My kids were there. What if Matthew or Sarah had wandered in?"

"I know you're upset, Frank. I am, too. Have you called the police?"

"The note told me not to. They said if I brought in the authorities, if the cops or FBI showed up at the house, they would kill her. The kidnapper wrote he would call the house tonight."

"Do as instructed. Do not call anyone else." Hattie squeezed Maya's hand tighter, blaming herself for this awful turn of events. "I'll take the first train back to DC. I should be there around noon."

"Then what?"

"We'll regroup. In the meantime, I'll get word to Leo Bell. He'll help us." Hattie heard crying in the background. One of the kids was up. Her gut twisted more, thinking about how this would impact the children. Matthew was sick, and he and Sarah were too little to understand why their mother was not there to cook them breakfast and nurse them back to health.

"I gotta go," Frank said, his tone still sharp as knives. "You need to fix this, Hattie."

"I will." The line went dead, and tears flowed from Hattie like her eyes were open faucets. "Dear God."

Maya and Maggie waited patiently for Hattie to regain her composure and explain what happened.

Maya kneeled inches away and squeezed Hattie's hands. "We'll get her back. Think like your father. What would he do?"

Hattie imagined her father's reaction. He would be stoic, determined, and ruthless until Olivia was back. She straightened and wiped her cheeks, swearing to herself that those would be the last tears shed till she had her sister safely with her family where she belonged.

"We get the job done. We bring Olivia home." She pivoted to Maggie. "I need to make several calls, one overseas."

"Do whatever you need," Maggie said. "I'll get some coffee going."

Once Maggie left the room, Hattie had Maya run upstairs to get her purse. She retrieved the needed numbers, raised the operator, and arranged a call to Brazil. The woman said getting an open circuit would take some time, so Hattie asked her to connect her to another number while they waited. "Cut in if necessary when the call to Rio is ready. It takes precedence."

The operator made the connection, and the phone rang. Hattie hated reaching out at such an early hour, but it had to be done.

"Hello?" A groggy voice came over the line.

"Beverly, this is Hattie James. I'm sorry to wake you. I must speak to Leo as soon as possible."

"He's not here, but I can get a message to him." Leo's wife sounded more alert.

"Thank you, Beverly. I'm not in the area, but I will return later today. Tell him that something has happened. I need him to see Frank immediately. My brother-in-law will fill him in."

"Does he know how to reach Frank?"

"Yes, tell him to go to the house."

"I will," Beverly said. "I hope everything turns out all right."

"So do I." Hattie depressed the receiver hook to end the connection and clicked it several times to raise the operator again. She provided the woman with another number, but the phone merely rang, as did the secondary number she provided. The Professor was unreachable. Hattie thanked the woman for trying and said she would wait for the Rio call.

Maggie returned with a tray and doled out coffee for everyone. She offered sugar and cream, but Hattie waved her off.

"Black. I'm going to need as much caffeine as possible."

As the three sipped on their hot drinks, Maggie and Maya chatted about sights Maya should take in before returning to the States, trying, no doubt, to distract Hattie. She remained quiet, planning her next move and how she would communicate with her mother. She had no doubt that the FBI was monitoring most overseas calls.

Soon the phone rang again. Hattie picked up the receiver and told the operator to put the call through.

Eva answered.

"Mother, it's Hattie. I wanted to check on our project and tell you about my visit."

"It's coming along swimmingly. All the problems have been resolved."

Hattie let out a sigh of relief. "That's wonderful to hear. My trip has not gone as planned. Some issues have arisen that I need help with. Is that possible?"

"Stay positive. Help will arrive sooner than you think. In fact, I was thinking about joining you in the States, but I missed this week's seaplane. Our friend Joseph got the last available ticket."

"I will," Hattie said, "and I'll call when things resolve here."

"I love you, sweetheart."

"Love you, too, Mother." Hattie hung up the phone and turned to the others. "There was no safe way to tell her that someone had abducted Olivia. I didn't have the heart to after she said Karl was out of his coma and recovering. She sounded so happy. He's arriving on the next seaplane from Rio." Hattie focused on Maggie. "I'll need your help."

"Anything."

"Can you meet my father at that plane when it lands? He's traveling under the name Joseph Fuller."

Maggie nodded. "Ah, the cover he used at the president's yacht. Of course, I'll be there."

"Tell him what happened and help him get to my sister's house. He might need cash."

"Don't worry about things on this end. I'll see to everything."

"I knew I could count on you."

17

———

Washington, DC, Friday, December 12, 1941

Hattie and Maya missed most of the scenery passing by their cabin window on the train back from New York. Or at least Maya did. Hattie had gotten in a brief nap about an hour into the trip, but then images of the chaotic hostage exchange that had taken place in Rio earlier this year had invaded her dreams. She had vividly relived every gunshot and the fear and confusion she had felt. Her mother's face, a mask of terror and exhaustion, had transformed into her sister's. A stray bullet had struck her in the head, causing devastating damage. That grotesque mental image had jerked her awake about a hundred miles back, and she could not get back to sleep.

Maya, though, had slept peacefully, watched over by Hattie since she woke up. Watching Maya like this had become a favorite activity. Each muscle in her face relaxed, her worry lines became less prominent, and her expression took on a childlike innocence. Its purity and beauty captivated Hattie, and she could spend all her waking hours looking at it.

When the train slowed, she gently nudged Maya until her eyes fluttered open. "Hey, you."

Maya stretched and smiled when she looked at Hattie. "Hi."

"We're about to pull into the station."

"Thanks." Maya pushed herself up straighter on the seat. "Did you get much sleep?"

"Some. I couldn't stop thinking about Olivia. I shouldn't have gone there after we arrived from Rio."

"Don't start second-guessing yourself. Your sister had a right to know about Karl, and without that photo of the Professor, we might never have located her. Besides, coming to the States and not visiting her would have appeared strange to anyone watching us. You were doing what you thought was best."

"But at what cost? She might die because of it. I could have found another way." Hattie knew it was not her fault that someone had taken her sister, and she was ready for Maya's pep talk. However, she could not shake the guilt that had been clawing at her since receiving Frank's frantic phone call. Everyone she cared about would be in danger until this was over.

"You went through this after Baumann killed Anna and when Ziegler took Eva hostage. The only people to blame are those who have been hunting those lists. I hated your father until I understood why he had to hide them. He was in an impossible position—risk one person to save hundreds or thousands. That same dilemma has passed to you. You did what you had to and will do what is necessary to get Olivia home."

Hattie had sat silently during Maya's speech, sensing emotion settling in her eyes and throat, but she pushed back on it. *No more tears*, she reminded herself. But the power behind Maya's words tugged at her after she finished, and she surmised they would for some time to come.

"I love you, Maya Reyes."

"And I love you."

The scenery outside their window darkened, signaling they had pulled beneath the canopy of Union Station. As the train's brakes squeaked, they crept to a stop. The final jolt forced Maya's upper body toward Hattie's, bringing their lips close enough for them to kiss. Her movement seemed a little exaggerated, Hattie thought, but it was also welcome. A quick glance revealed that the section of the platform visible from their window was empty, so Hattie did not pull back.

"You did that on purpose," Hattie said. "Now you're expecting me to kiss you."

Maya grinned. "What if I did, and what if I do?"

"I'd say your expectations are reasonable...though manipulative."

"Do you have a problem with that?"

"Not one bit." Hattie kissed her, letting it linger and relishing the pillow softness of her lips and the taste of bitter coffee on her tongue. She pulled back. "Feel free to manipulate me like this any time."

"I will," Maya said.

They positioned their bags next to the door and waited for the porter to come for them before disembarking. He loaded the suitcases onto a cart on the chilly, now bustling platform and followed them as they walked toward the exit.

Hattie was unsure who might pick them up, if anyone, until Leo appeared through the crowd. His serious expression telegraphed that the situation remained unchanged. "I brought my car," he said. "I'll pull it up."

Leo jogged off, and Hattie led the way to the station drive-up. Dozens of people milled about, some coming, some going, most of them lugging some form of luggage while cars and taxis maneuvered to find an open spot where their drivers could pick up or drop off their passengers.

Leo pulled up moments after Hattie and Maya arrived. He helped the porter load their luggage and tipped him for his trouble. Once they were on the road, Hattie asked, "No change?"

"No," he said.

She rubbed his arm. He showed no outward signs of having taken a beating during questioning. "It's good to see you. Did they hurt you?"

"The only torture was the food. Military Intelligence ran me through the wringer for days, asking the same question six different ways over and over again. I think they finally believe we knew nothing specific about the Pearl Harbor attack."

"That's good," Hattie said.

"They wanted to know about your father, but I said nothing." He stopped for a red light. "Did you find anything at Jimmy's? Because I didn't."

"Yeah, about that." She pulled the key to Jimmy's place from her purse and handed it to him. "It was a bust, but we hit pay dirt another way."

He stuffed the key in his coat pocket and shifted into first as the light turned green. As he drove them to Alexandria, Hattie told him about her and Maya's search, starting with the picture they found of the Professor, the bird lady at the park, and locating her house. "We unearthed a photo of her Maryland cabin there, and when we got to Cambridge, a local helped us locate it. We found her!"

Leo chuckled. "Why am I not surprised? You're so much like your father."

"The Professor told me the same thing."

"How is she?" Leo asked. "Does she have the lists?"

"No, we still do. She wants to identify the mole before we reveal them."

Leo nodded his understanding. "Does she know about your sister?"

"No, I tried calling her cabin, but no one answered," Hattie said. "She might be in Washington, I suppose."

Leo rubbed his face. It was rough, with a day-old beard. "Let's hear what the kidnapper says, then we'll regroup."

Minutes later, Leo parked in Frank's driveway. Everyone grabbed a piece of luggage and went inside. It was not quite two, twelve hours after Hattie had learned of her sister's disappearance. No one was downstairs, but the sound of children giggling upstairs was loud and clear. Hattie told Leo and Maya to wait there while she located the family.

Hattie stood outside the doorway of the kids' room, discovering a mixed scene. Matthew was tinkering with a truck on the floor, making motor noises. Sarah was on her bed, playing with dolls. Frank was sitting on a small children's chair. Although dressed, he had messy hair and looked pale and shocked. The sight broke Hattie's heart.

Her niece and nephew went wild when she walked inside, calling her name and begging her to lift them. Matthew was too big, so she messed up his hair before picking up Sarah.

"Hey, kiddos, I need a word with your dad. Can you play up here by yourselves for a bit?"

"You just got here," Matthew cried.

"This is really important. I promise to spend time with you later." Hattie addressed her brother-in-law. "Frank? Can you come downstairs? Leo and Maya are waiting."

He pushed up silently from the chair and followed Hattie to the living room.

"Have you heard from the kidnapper yet?" Hattie asked.

"No," he said through gritted teeth. "What are you doing to find her?"

Hattie invited him to sit on the couch with her. "Until we identify who took her, all we can do is wait for him to call."

"Whoever wanted those lists took her," Frank snarled.

"That pool of people is larger than you think," Hattie said. "We need to figure out who in the US is desperate enough to kidnap Olivia to get their hands on them."

"So, an American took her?"

"We can't rule that out," Leo said.

"My money is on the traitor my father was looking for," Hattie said. "If we learn who he is, we'll know where he's keeping Olivia."

"What about that woman you were supposed to hand the lists to?" Frank asked. "She can find him, right?"

"I found her. She's working on getting the documents we need to determine who the mole might be, but she won't resurface until Sunday. I talked to my mother. My father is awake and on his way here. He'll be in New York City tomorrow afternoon. We need to talk to both of them before agreeing to any demands."

"I'm glad he's okay, but Sunday?" Frank was frantic. He popped up from his seat and formed his hands into fists. "That's too late."

"Maybe not. When the kidnapper calls, I'll stall for time." Hattie stood and tried to coax Frank back to the couch.

He threw off her touch and sneered. "Someone came into my home and took my wife, the mother of my children, and all you have is stalling for time." He looked furious enough to throw a punch.

Leo wedged himself between them to get Frank to back down. "I know what you're going through. I'd do anything, kill anyone to protect my wife."

The image of Beverly in her leg braces flashed in Hattie's head. She could see Leo going to the ends of the earth to find the woman and taking out any obstacle that dared to get in his way.

Frank relaxed his fists. Leo's ferocious words seemed to have knocked some calm into him.

"We can't put her in more danger than she already is," Leo continued. "We need to think this through and develop a plan."

Frank let his shoulders slump, letting go of his anger, at least for the moment. "Fine. I'll call someone to take the children."

"And what will you tell whoever takes them?" Hattie asked. "Whatever you tell them might make them suspicious, and we can't afford anyone bringing in the authorities. The kidnapper wants to deal with me. I'll make sure you're left out of this so the kids are never left alone."

"Okay." He took a deep breath, appearing a bit relieved. "What do we do until he calls?"

"Anyone else hungry?" Maya asked.

"Sarah and Matthew should be," Frank said. "I gave them cereal this morning."

"I'll whip up a late lunch for everyone," Maya said. "We all will think better on a full stomach."

Hattie had believed her love for Maya could not grow, but the next few hours proved her wrong. Maya prepared a wonderful meal and set it at the table to make things normal for the kids.

"Where's Mommy?" Matthew asked.

Maya replied, "She's doing something important, and she asked Auntie Hattie and me to help watch you while she's gone."

"When will Mommy be back?" Sarah asked in a sad little girl's voice.

"That's hard to say," Maya said, pulling Sarah into her lap. "Until then, can you show me some of your toys? I'd love to see them."

Sarah and Matthew cheered up. The three went upstairs to play, giving the others time to prepare for the kidnapper's call.

Hattie wandered upstairs when they took a break and leaned against the doorframe, watching Maya laughing with her niece and nephew. The woman was a natural with kids, and Hattie imagined her with one or two of her own. Maya would make an incredible mother. A thought more melancholy immediately followed that pleasant one. Because having children of their own was impossible for Hattie and Maya. Unless fate intervened, neither would know the joy of motherhood and watching a child grow.

"Hey, you," Hattie said.

Maya peered at the door, but the little ones continued to play. "Hey."

"That call should come soon. Do you want to come down for it?"

"Yes, I would." Maya turned to the kids. "Will you two be okay up here alone? I have something to do with Hattie and your daddy."

"Sure, Auntie Maya. We'll be fine," Matthew said.

"All right." Maya pushed herself up from the floor and met Hattie in the hallway.

Hattie bumped her playfully on the shoulder. "Auntie Maya, huh?"

Maya blushed. "That was Sarah's idea."

"Well, I like it," Hattie said.

"I do too."

They joined Leo and Frank in the living room. Frank leaned forward, resting his elbows on his knees and rubbing his hands together, willing the telephone on the coffee table to ring. Hattie understood his anxiety, knowing it stemmed from his feeling of helplessness. She would have felt the same, but her father's training had taught her that knowledge, skill, and ingenuity usually ruled the day. She harnessed her apprehension, turning it into heady determination.

The phone rang.

Frank snatched the handset off the receiver and brought it to his ear. "Hello... Yes, she's here... Let me speak to my wife... But... Fine." He extended the phone to Hattie. "He wants to talk to you."

Hattie took it. "This is Hattie James."

"I know Karl hid the lists in the sheet music, and you have the photographs of them. Bring them to the National Mall tonight, or your sister will die." His voice sounded muffled, as if he were speaking with a portion of cloth over the mouthpiece.

"Whoever this is, you have made a grave mistake. Family has always been off-limits. You have broken the rules. I hope you are willing to live with the consequences because now your family is on the table."

"I need those lists."

"The photos aren't clear enough, but I can get the originals. I check in with my father at regular intervals and can reach him in forty-eight hours. I can arrange to bring the sheet music here, but that will take some time."

"You're stalling."

"Whether I am or not is irrelevant. Sunday evening is the earliest. I will only do it if you give me proof you have my sister and that she is still alive, and it better not be a body part."

The man said, "You'll have it tomorrow."

"Make it in the morning."

"You're in no position to make demands, Miss James."

"But I am. You need those lists. Not want, need. That means you are desperate and stupid enough to involve family. The walls must be closing in rapidly, and I am the only person who can stop them. You will give me the proof. Otherwise, I will take my chances with the FBI."

"Fine, in the morning. I will call Sunday night at six o'clock."

"Nine."

"Yes, yes. Nine. Answer, or the sister gets it."

"And that would be the last thing that you accomplish. If you hurt her, I'll hunt you down and everyone you care about," Hattie threatened before hanging up.

"Well?" Frank asked.

"He's delivering proof of life tomorrow, and I bought us until Sunday at nine for the next call. That gives us time to see the Professor."

"The Professor?" Frank asked. "Is that the woman Karl trusts?"

"Yes," Hattie said. "Leo works for her too. Once Father arrives, we'll meet with her and come up with a plan."

"I hope so," Frank said.

"So do I, for all our sakes." Hattie was now convinced the kidnapper was the mole. He was the only person in the United States who would be desperate enough to take drastic measures to keep those lists from returning to American hands. If he failed after taking Olivia, he would continue to escalate and take more people she loved. She needed to stop the traitor and end this now.

The next morning, Alexandria, VA, Saturday, December 13, 1941

Leo still had to return from sleeping overnight at his DC apartment. Frank was outside raking leaves in the backyard; staying busy was his way of coping with stress. Meanwhile, Hattie, Maya, and the children were at the kitchen table, finishing breakfast and making up games to entice Sarah to eat her scrambled eggs.

The doorbell rang.

Hattie went on alert.

Maya stopped her tickling attack on Sarah and sucked in a playful breath. "Who do you suppose that is?"

"Mommy?"

"No, silly," Matthew said. "Mommy wouldn't have to ring the bell."

"I'll get it," Hattie said. "Stay with the kids."

She went to the door and looked through the peephole, discovering a man wearing a messenger's uniform. The man appeared genuine, but Hattie refused to take any chances. She grabbed the pistol Leo left on the top shelf of the closet, out of the children's reach, readied it behind her back, and opened the door.

The man smiled and dipped his cap. "I apologize for the early hour, but I have a delivery for Hattie James."

"I'm Hattie."

He raised the clipboard he was holding and removed a manila envelope half the size of a regular sheet of paper. "I'll need your signature, Miss James."

"Of course." Hattie slipped the gun into the back of her waistband, signed the log, and tipped the man a quarter from her pocket. The man thanked her and gave her the item. He turned to leave but stopped when Hattie called out. "Excuse me, but does your book say who sent this?"

The man reviewed the document on his clipboard. "It says someone walked into our Arlington office on Glebe Road and brought it in when we opened." He provided the address before leaving.

Hattie returned the pistol, grabbed her jacket, and went back to the kitchen, flashing Maya the envelope. Maya acknowledged with a nod and stayed with the kids while Hattie went to the backyard. Frank was transferring the pile of leaves from the lawn to the metal trash bin. She approached, holding up the item.

"Frank, it's here."

He dropped the rake and removed his work gloves. "What does it say?"

"I waited to open it with you."

He nodded his appreciation.

She slid her finger under the flap, breaking the glue seal and tearing the paper in spots. Feeling something hard at the bottom, she tipped the container with her other hand at the opening to catch whatever fell out. A gold ring with a small diamond in the center landed in her palm.

Frank picked it up and inspected it. "This is Olivia's wedding ring."

Hattie looked inside for anything else and found a folded piece of newspaper. She opened it, discovering the upper part of the front page of the *Washington Post*, displaying the headline, "Congress Approves War on Germany and Italy." It was yesterday's edition. Several handwritten words were above the headline. The text read, "The lists by Sunday or he will kill me. Olivia." She showed it to Frank.

"That's her handwriting."

"I know." The distinct curl at the top of the capital *O* in her name was proof. "Olivia is alive. That's the important thing. I have something to do, and I want to take Maya. Are you done here?"

"Yeah, I'll be right in to watch the kids."

Minutes later, while on the way to Arlington, Hattie explained to Maya that she wanted to check who dropped the package off. She parked Karl's car in front of the messenger service, and they went inside. No one was at the front desk, so she rang the bell on the counter. Moments later, a middle-aged man wearing the same uniform as the courier had appeared from the back room.

"Morning. How may I help you?"

Hattie showed him the empty envelope. "Your man said someone brought it here earlier today with delivery instructions. Can you tell me who that was? It's important."

The man scratched the back of his neck. "We normally don't give out that information."

"I understand. You see, I'm a professional singer, and sometimes I receive things that are... let's say, disturbing. I don't want to involve the police, but—"

"Hold on." The man put up his hands in a stop motion. "Let me check the book." He flipped through several pages and pointed to a handwritten passage. "Yeah, I remember this guy. It was a little strange. He appeared to be down on his luck and had had a few. He said it had to be delivered today and gave me an extra dollar to get it done."

"Did he leave a name or address?"

"He said he called himself Dick Tracy. That's it."

"What did he look like?"

"Kinda tall. He had a jacket and hat on and hid his face. Sorry I can't be of more help."

Hattie walked out empty-handed. The trail was dead.

18

———

New York City, NY, Saturday, December 13, 1941

It had been a while since Karl had been on a plane, but he was no stranger to flying. His jobs, plural, had required abundant travel, but this was an exceedingly long trip. The twenty-four-hour journey across the ocean, involving refueling and crew changes, was almost over, but new challenges awaited. He would be returning to the United States, to New York, where he was a wanted man.

This was the greatest risk he had taken in his twenty-year career as a covert agent. He could have stayed in Rio and trusted Hattie to find the Professor, but his country was at war against Germany. The War Department needed to know who the Nazis had embedded in the States to feed intelligence to Berlin and who among its ranks to trust with secrets. Hattie was capable, but too much was at stake. He knew the players and all their tricks. Without a question, he had to come. If he failed to evade the FBI... Well, he trusted the Professor to produce the evidence needed to clear him, including the decoded lists.

The plane made a smooth landing on the East River and motored to the dock. Karl deplaned with his two bags, blending in with the crowd. While in line to process through customs, he kept his coat and hat on to remain as unrecognizable as possible. During the half hour in the queue, Karl felt several sets of eyes watching him… and watching everyone else waiting to enter the country.

At the doors, uniformed police controlled entry and exit. Another officer walked up and down the line, observing new arrivals from a short distance. Two men dressed in suits were standing behind the check-in desks and also scanning the people in line. They were likely FBI, looking for anyone on the most-wanted list.

When his turn arrived, the clerk called him forward and had him remove his fedora. After reading his passport, the man looked at Karl, back at the photo, and again at Karl. Understandably, he was giving Karl and his German passport extra scrutiny. The United States and Germany were at war.

"What is your purpose in the United States, Mr. Fuller?"

"Personal. To see family and friends," Karl said. The key to not drawing attention to himself was to keep his answers short.

"And how long do you intend to stay?"

"Two weeks."

The clerk flipped a page in the booklet and stamped it, documenting his entry. "Enjoy your visit, Mr. Fuller."

"Thank you." Karl returned his identification papers to his inner coat pocket, picked up his bags, and exited the security area without glancing back to determine if anyone was following him. It would look too suspicious at that point.

It was mid-afternoon. Cold filled the air, clouds blanketed the sky, and the streets bustled with people and cars. He walked toward the curb, looking for where the taxis lined up. He pivoted, but a new Cadillac pulled up, and a platinum blonde exited from the driver's side.

"Uncle Joe, you made it." It was Maggie Moore. She hugged him. Her appearance was unexpected but not out of the realm of possibilities. Hattie would utilize people she trusted. Maggie was one such person.

"Thanks for picking me up, Maggie." He tossed his bags in the back seat and hopped in the front passenger seat.

Maggie swung into traffic and slung her expensive vehicle around like a pro. "Hattie sent me."

"I figured as much."

Maggie handed him a piece of paper. "She wants you to meet her at this address in Maryland by noon tomorrow. You can take my other car. It will be faster and safer since you probably don't want to be recognized."

"Have you seen her?"

"She and Maya were here for two days. They had to leave yesterday, so she asked me to pick you up."

"If she knew I was coming, why didn't she stay?"

Maggie turned onto another street. "We're a few miles from my home. I'll explain there."

Her cryptic response had him on pins and needles as she drove through the Upper East Side. She pulled into a gated courtyard of a double-lot brownstone and parked beside the house. He left his suitcase in the car, bringing only his smaller satchel as she guided him into the house. They settled in the living room on the main floor and sat near the fireplace. "Can I get you anything to eat or drink?"

"I'm fine," he said. "Now, why did Hattie have to leave? And what is this place in Maryland?"

"Someone abducted Olivia overnight Thursday, actually very early Friday morning. The note said they would call with instructions."

Fear and anger twisted Karl's stomach and shortened his breath. "Is she all right?"

"Hattie called today. She was vague but said to tell Uncle Joe that his precious cargo was safe but hadn't reached its destination."

Karl nodded. "Good. If I know Hattie, that means Olivia is alive and unhurt, but the kidnapper still has her."

"Before she left, she gave me that address and phone number and said you were to meet her there. She also said that she had found the Professor. Do you know who that is?"

"I do."

Maggie offered him a thick envelope. "She mentioned you might need cash. A thousand was all we had in the house. Will that be enough?"

"A hundred should do." Karl slipped a few of the bills into his coat pocket with his fake passport.

"I loaded my old Ford Model 48 with maps covering from here to Maryland so you can find your way. It's about a six-hour drive, so I had my aunt prepare a picnic basket and jugs of water for the trip."

"Are you sure about loaning me the car? There's no telling what I might run into."

"My cousin has been driving it since I got the Cadillac. Using the subway for a while will do him some good. Is there anything else you need?"

"Unless you have an arsenal hidden in your purse, you've thought of everything."

"Wait here." Maggie left the room and returned minutes later carrying a small black leather satchel. It showed signs that years of travel had worn it in. "These were my father's from when he was with the NYPD. Will they help?"

Karl opened the bag and discovered two pistols—a Colt Official Police with a four-inch barrel and a Detective Special with a much shorter barrel. Both were still in their holsters and were in need of a good cleaning. There were also several dozen rounds of .38-caliber bullets. "Your dad was a detective?"

"Fifteen years pounding the streets and another ten behind a desk."

"I can't take these."

"He spent twenty-five years on the force and never once had to fire his gun. He said they brought him luck. You're going to need all the luck you can get. I'm sure he would want you to take them."

"Thank you, Maggie. I'll ensure everything gets back to you as soon as possible."

"Hattie can bring them up on her next trip."

"You're a good friend, Maggie."

～

Maryland Eastern Shore, Sunday, December 14, 1941

Leo drove his car off the morning ferry, and Maya directed him to Route 50, which would take them south toward Cambridge. Hattie, in the back seat, contrasted their journey today to the day she had left her sister's house to take the ferry.

Five days ago, Olivia had been so disgusted to learn that Hattie loved differently that she ordered her and Maya to leave and never return. This morning, her brother-in-law had begged her and Maya to come back. The departures could not have been more different, but both were filled with gut-wrenching emotion. One way or the other, Hattie feared she may have lost her sister forever.

An hour later, they reached Cambridge and passed the store-slash-café, where the waitress had helped them determine the location of the Professor's cabin. Maya guided Leo down the wooded road to the gravel access road that led to it. He slowed the car, approaching cautiously.

The cabin looked much the same as before, including the same sedan parked out front, suggesting the Professor was there. Curiously, though the temperature was colder than before, there was no smoke wafting from the chimney. Surely the Professor would have started a fire to warm the place. Something did not feel right.

"Stop," Hattie said.

Leo coasted to a stop. "What's wrong?"

She explained her hunch about the fireplace. "It could be nothing, but she seems like a creature of habit."

"She is," Leo said. "We should scout the area before going in."

"I'll come up from the lakeside on the north," Hattie said. "I know the terrain there. You come up through the trees on the south. Maya, I need you to stay here, watch the front, and alert us if anyone comes."

Leo popped the glove box and distributed the pistols. "Meet back here in five minutes. No one goes in alone."

Hattie reached over the seat and rubbed Maya's shoulder. "I'll be right back."

"Be careful." Maya's concern bled through those two words. Whoever took Olivia was likely desperate enough to kill.

"I will."

Hattie cut across the gravel road to the north side and slipped into the trees, keeping her gun at the ready. The leafless vegetation offered less cover than it would in spring. However, moving amongst them was better than being in the open. She stayed in them for as long as she could, then dashed beyond the path to the pier from which the Professor had fished the other day. The dock was unoccupied, so she continued toward the house. The front windows had their curtains drawn, preventing a view inside.

She pushed to the side of the cabin. The kitchen window had no curtains, so Hattie moved as close as she dared and peered through it. No one was visible. Only the back of the cabin remained to be checked. As she rounded the corner, she noticed movement among the trees and raised her weapon. A deer appeared in the shrubs for a brief second and scurried off.

Leo emerged from around the corner of the house on the other end. He waved, indicating everything was okay on his side.

Hattie glanced along the building on her side. The bedroom window was closed, but someone or something had shattered the upper pane. She backed away and signaled Leo to stop. He acknowledged, and they both retreated. She arrived at the car seconds before Leo did. They climbed in to get out of the cold.

"Something is wrong." Hattie panted, slightly winded from running through the woods. "The back window is broken. It wasn't like that when we left." She feared things had gone sideways.

"We go in, but with caution," Leo said.

The three got out and clicked off the safeties on their handguns. They approached on foot in a staggered line. Leo would go through the door first, they had decided, followed quickly by the others.

As if someone had turned the knob and let it go, the door drifted open.

They froze and raised their weapons.

The door stopped in the middle of its arc, offering them a glimpse of a darkened interior.

Hattie's senses heightened, the rustle of leaves on the ground growing louder and the saltwater scent of the river becoming brinier.

"Songbird, it's Nightshade," said a familiar male voice from inside the cabin.

"Father?" Hattie lowered her gun but kept her finger resting on the trigger guard. She stepped forward, stopping when Leo called out in a hushed tone.

"It could be a trap," he said.

"I have to be sure it's you, Father." Hattie also had to be sure he was not under duress. She thought back to the lesson he had given her on clearing a room and hoped whoever was in the cabin could provide the correct answer to what she was about to ask. "Where are you hiding this time?"

Leo squinted at her, confusion in his eyes.

"Not in the broom closet, sweetheart," the man said. "It's safe to come in."

Hattie relaxed. He had been able to ambush her that day—just three weeks ago?—because she had neglected to search the closet. He would have provided a different answer if someone was holding him at gunpoint.

"Father." Hattie rushed inside—and an awful stench hit her so that she nearly threw up. Her father was seated on the leather couch, leaning forward with his elbows on his knees and holding his pistol loosely in his hand. Nearby, in the overstuffed chair, a putrefying body was slumped in an unnatural position.

Karl looked up, meeting Hattie's questioning stare. A deep sadness was dancing in his eyes. "I found her like this an hour ago with this note pinned to her sweater."

Hattie maneuvered to get a better look and glanced at the note. It read, "The lists or more will die." She focused on the woman's severely beaten and grotesque face, which made it impossible to discern precisely who it was, but Hattie recognized the knitted sweater. "The Professor," Hattie gasped.

"It certainly looks like her," Karl said. His voice was monotone.

Hattie had been around her father and death many times this year, but this was the first time she had seen it numb him. He had told her how the Professor had brought him into covert work, training and mentoring him. But the drained look on his face made her finally realize how important the Professor had been to him. She was more than his handler. She was his family.

"I'm so sorry, Father."

When Leo and Maya came inside, gagging at the rancid stench, Karl turned and assured them. "I've already cleared the place."

As Leo and Maya went from room to room, opening the windows to dilute the smell, Hattie stepped closer to her father and placed a comforting arm on his shoulder.

"When did you last see her?" Karl asked.

"Maya and I found her on Tuesday and left the next day. We have the cipher, but she insisted there was nothing more we could do until you looked at a compilation of suspects who might be the mole. We were supposed to meet here this afternoon. She had said she needed the time to determine if it was safe to reveal the lists."

"Do you have those names? The one she wanted me to look at?"

"No, she kept them. She said they were people you may have worked with at the Black Chamber."

Karl nodded. "I've long thought the traitor and whoever framed me was someone I served with at that place."

"I told her about Jimmy."

He sucked in an unsteady breath. "How did she take the news?"

"It rattled her. I was worried about leaving her alone, but she insisted she would be fine since she arranged for a friend to stay with her for a while."

"That's good." He rubbed the back of his neck. "I've searched every inch inside but didn't find any lists."

Hattie pivoted, looking for the papers the Professor kept near her chair. The woman had not outright identified them, but Hattie had the impression they were the documents she had used to narrow the suspects.

"Her papers are gone." Hattie swiveled her head, inspecting other surfaces in the room, but nothing was obvious. "Were any there when you arrived?"

"No, but there were ashes in the fireplace. They were either burned or taken." Karl stood and patted the woman's rotting body on the knee of her slacks. "We'll finish the job, Victoria." He had a sad, solemn look about him. "Count on it."

"What should we do with her?" Hattie asked.

"We'll just have to leave her, I'm afraid. We close the windows and the door to keep the predators out. The police will eventually find her. The State Department will see that she gets a decent burial."

They departed in two cars, Leo's and Maggie's, which Karl had hidden in the woods a quarter of a mile up the road. After driving their vehicles onto the Annapolis-bound ferry boat, Hattie left Leo and Maya and slipped into the front seat of Maggie's Ford. The trip was an hour and a half, and she did not want her father to be alone in his grief.

She scooted closer and leaned her head against his shoulder. "I'm so glad you're better."

"Your mother did an incredible job of keeping me alive."

"Yes, getting Dr. Navarro and the nurse."

"More than that." Karl described how Eva had saved them from armed Nazi agents, killed one in her kitchen, and enlisted Javier and Monica to get him to his jungle cabin.

"Mother did all that?" Hattie's jaw dropped open. She knew her mother was strong and independent, but this was beyond anything she dreamed Eva was capable of.

"I couldn't leave until I knew she was safe, so she served as my wheelman when I went around town taking care of those who broke into her house."

"Is she safe now?"

"I believe so. It will take some time for Berlin to get more agents in place, and after the message I sent about going after family, they likely won't bother her again."

"That firms up my suspicion that whoever took Olivia is the mole," Hattie said. "He said something that made this whole thing sound very personal. He's the only American we know of with everything to lose if those lists get into the right hands. I have no doubt he's desperate."

"I agree, sweetheart." He sucked in and released a deep breath. "Do you think Olivia is unhurt?"

"I asked for proof of life. We received her wedding ring and a portion of Friday's *Post* with her handwriting on it. I stalled for time until today, hoping the Professor could help, but you're here now. I'm positive we'll get Livvy back."

"Don't underestimate yourself, Hattie. You're a natural at this."

"I feel like I left the door open for the mole to take her."

"Don't think that way. Once you start, it's hard to trust any choice you make. There's no walking away from this business, not completely. Even if you retire, there will always be someone who will think you're still in the game. You have a lifetime of decisions yet to make. Many will be the right ones, but some won't. You can't swim in regret because, in the covert world, the tide is always rising. All you can do is your best and never look back."

"It sounds like you're ready to walk away."

"I am once I clear my name," he said.

Hattie sighed, knowing the situation with Olivia had not changed. They were still at a disadvantage. "What do we tell the kidnapper tonight?"

"We need time to find him. We stall."

After the boat docked, they drove to Alexandria. Karl was cautious and did not take a direct route to ensure no one followed them. They pulled into the driveway of Olivia's home, and Leo parked beside them. Karl donned his fedora and flipped up the collar of his winter coat to lessen the chance of someone recognizing him.

Hattie let everyone in through the kitchen door, using the key Frank gave her that morning. The house was quiet and dark, as the children's bedtime had passed. She pushed through to the living room, where she found her brother-in-law sitting in his chair with a small reading lamp on and a cocktail glass in his hand. His eyes were puffy as if he had been crying, and he was slow to recognize that they had entered the room.

"Holy hell, Hattie. It's almost nine. I was beginning to think something had happened." He was clearly drunk.

"Something did happen, but we can talk about that later."

Karl came in behind her. After greeting Frank, he grabbed the cup with a finger's worth of dark amber liquid and placed it on the table. "I think you've had enough, son."

Frank looked into Karl's eyes. "They took her, Karl. They came into our home while I wasn't here, and with my kids in the next room, they took her."

"And Hattie and I will get her back and make them pay. I promise we won't stop until my little girl is back with you and the children."

Maya returned to the kitchen and put on some coffee. Frank had gotten one cup of partially sobering caffeine down when the phone rang. He still was not speaking coherently, so Hattie answered.

"Hello."

"Do you have the lists?" The voice was muffled, but Hattie was sure it was the same kidnapper she had spoken to before.

"I contacted my father. He has them and is taking the next flight into the country. I need three days."

"That's unacceptable."

"I'm not Dorothy. I can't click my ruby slippers and have him magically appear. If you know about the sheet music, you know he's been in Brazil. It takes time to get from there to here."

"Fine. Noon on Wednesday. I will call with instructions."

The line went dead.

"He agreed," Hattie said.

Frank broke down into tears and clutched Karl's sleeve. "You have to save her, Karl."

"We will." Karl pulled him to his feet. "Come on, Frank. Let's get you to bed." Leo grabbed Frank's other arm. "Let's reconvene in the kitchen after I get this one asleep and check on the kids."

"I'll gather everything we have," Hattie said.

Maya readied more coffee while Leo and Karl took care of Frank. Hattie went through her bags, retrieved her father's coded spy lists and the Cicero book containing the cipher, and came back to the kitchen. As Hattie fixed her drink with sugar and cream, Maya flipped through the book, studying the illustrations and looking for anything unusual. The back inside cover caught her attention for some reason. She touched the cover repeatedly. "This feels bumpy."

"Let me see." Hattie ran her fingertips across the hardback surface, and she felt ridges. They made four connecting lines in the shape of a rectangle. "I feel something." She became curious but kept her optimism in check. A myriad of things—moisture, rough handling, or a flaw in the production process could have caused the anomaly.

Maya went to the kitchen counter, found a knife in the top drawer, and brought it to the table. She performed surgery, separating the hardcover carefully from the lining, and flipped up the loosened sheet, revealing a piece of paper. She unfolded it and handed it to Hattie.

Hattie studied its contents, a smile gradually forming on her lips. The page contained a handwritten roster of twelve names, three of which appeared to be women. Beside each name were one or two capital letters. She let her optimism run wild. "This has to be it."

"What has to be it?" Karl said, entering the room.

Hattie directed his attention to the note. "Maya discovered this hidden in the Cicero book."

Karl glanced at it. "Cicero was an inspiration to the Professor. It looks like her handwriting."

"This could be the suspects she mentioned. She said they all held government positions the previous year. All of them had clearance to access the agent list, and all worked in the Black Chamber near the time you were there."

Karl studied the collection of names. "Yes, they all look familiar."

"The Professor wanted to know who among these names might have known she had recruited you into clandestine service. Did you talk to anyone about her offer at the time?"

Karl plopped down into a chair. His face went pale, and he rubbed it with his hand. "We were the three musketeers back in the day. We did everything together and kept each other sane because our work was monotonous and sometimes felt wrong. I can't believe either of them did this."

"One of them did."

"I was about to make the biggest decision of my life, so I talked to both." He inhaled deeply, lifted a pencil from the table, and circled two names. He threw the pencil down angrily. "Andy Hobbs and Gene Stanton. One of you betrayed me, damn it!"

"Now what?" Leo asked.

Karl met Leo's stare with a determined look. "We use you to smoke him out."

They devised a plan for Leo's office to plant information that would entice the mole into contacting his German handler. They would follow both suspects, and Karl would soon know which one of his friends was the traitor.

19

Washington, DC, Monday, December 15, 1941

Eugene Stanton walked briskly down the corridor of the Munitions Building, headed for the urgent intelligence briefing to the General Staff that had just been called. He had been out for a few days to follow Hattie James, faking an illness to explain his absence. The atmosphere in the facility had changed since the Pearl Harbor attack. It was the business of the War Department and its staff to prepare for war, but its inner workings seemed chaotic today. The advent of one with two fronts—real ones, not academic exercises—made it obvious who was ready for the job and who was in over their heads.

Except for a handful of units on the leading edge—military intelligence units around the world and forces stationed in Hawaii, Panama, Newfoundland, and the Philippines—their work had been primarily theoretical. The cerebral types were confronting a steep learning curve as they hustled to catch up as the department transitioned from paper-pushing to a wartime footing. Things had gotten real. This was no drill. People were dead. Ships sunk. Aircraft destroyed. The United States had to regroup, quickly catch its breath, and figure out how to throw a lethal counterpunch.

His job had not changed. War planning was based on resources, enemy positions, and political will. When he and his boss met at the door to the conference room then, they walked into the room with confidence. They had made progress on revamping Rainbow Five, the plan Senator Wheeler leaked to the *Tribune*, and were well ahead of General Marshall's deadline to complete it. Though they were not part of the corridor fray, they were attending to stay abreast of operational and intelligence changes that could alter their strategies.

The room was fuller than usual, likely because more people wanted to hear the latest intel firsthand. Everyone took their seats, and the head of Military Intelligence took the podium.

The colonel followed the typical format, providing updates by geographic region and focusing on recent significant military and political happenings. The clerk operating the overhead projector kept up with his reports, changing slides at the right moment. This new machine was a game-changer during briefings, keeping the audience engaged and on the same page.

When the briefer reached the section on the United States and the slide changed, staff members began to whisper, their murmur growing louder by the second. Eugene sat frozen.

"Last night, an American operative assigned to Brazil recovered and decoded Karl James's missing list of covert American agents in Germany," the speaker said. "Our people appear safe at the moment, but we are continuing to withdraw the covert personnel on the list and replacing them with new assets. James's list of German spies within our borders remains missing, but we are confident we will have them soon."

Eugene broke into a sweat and loosened his necktie a fraction to give himself a chance to breathe. The man sitting on his right elbowed him in the side. "You okay, Colonel?"

"Something I ate. I'll be fine." Eugene straightened and looked at the projected image, hoping to appear engaged. However, he could not concentrate on anything other than the suffocating sensation of the walls closing in on him. Sam, his German handler, would not be happy to learn about this change of events. Different scenarios of how he would react to the news raced through Eugene's panicked mind. All of them ended with Sam firing a bullet into Eugene's head.

He scrambled to come up with a plan. If one list had made it into American hands, it was only a matter of time before the other did. Sam had probably lied about his name being on the list, but if there was even a remote chance of that being so, it justified drastic measures on Sam's part and on his.

He picked up a copy of the briefing notes, preparing to leave as soon as the meeting concluded. He was turning to leave when General Gerow asked him to wait so they could return to the office together. Eugene continued to sweat, physically and mentally, while his boss spoke to another flag officer.

Minutes later, Gerow waved him over, and they started their walk toward their wing in the building. "Are you still sick, Stanton? You're sweating buckets."

"Maybe I came back too soon. Would you mind if I knocked off now? It's only a half hour early."

"We have a lot of work ahead of us. I need you back and focused tomorrow. Pass along the intel to the junior officers and then leave."

"I will, sir."

Once back in their work section, Eugene gave the meeting notes to his assistants, highlighting the parts he considered essential to their planning. He then went to his office, where he gathered his belongings and stuffed an empty envelope into his coat pocket.

"I'm heading out, Mabel."

She grunted her disapproval, but he did not care. The woman could grunt all she wanted. He had more important things to worry about. Life and death matters. Beginning with getting a message to Sam, signaling that they needed to meet.

Leo had stayed by the door at the briefing, preparing for an early exit. Both of their targets, Andy Hobbs and Gene Stanton, were in the room when his section chief stepped up to the podium and began the meeting.

Leo had had to get someone's blessing for this maneuver. He had turned to Admiral Drummond. Drummond was the only man in Military

Intelligence he trusted to not let slip details of this operation. For good reason. Given the egg that had landed on the man's face after the Japanese attack debacle, Drummond was rightly gun-shy about ignoring any intel that Leo brought to him.

The discussion they had had this morning when he proposed putting out the fake story had been... tense. "You want my office to mislead the entire General Staff intentionally on a hunch," Drummond had said.

"It's more than a hunch, Admiral," Leo had said. "Yesterday, I discovered the body of Victoria Cooke in her cabin on the Maryland Eastern Shore. During our last communication, she said that she had narrowed the list to two suspects, one currently working in G-2 and the other in G-3." The number of suspects was an exaggeration, but Leo could not reveal that Karl James had helped them narrow down the list from twelve to two.

"My intelligence operations? Who?"

"I'd rather not disclose that information yet. You might tip this person off if you act differently around him. I think it best that no one knows the identity of our targets."

"How will you follow two targets?"

"I have a team in place whom I trust."

"I'm not ready to stick my neck out on simply your word, Bell."

"That's what you said the last time I brought something to you directly. Look where that got us." Leo had paused when Drummond shifted uncomfortably in his chair, worried about overstepping. "All I'm asking is that we drop this bombshell at a briefing where both of our suspects will be, and we see how they react. We give it a few days, and if it doesn't pan out, we retract the announcement, saying it was part of an ongoing intelligence operation. Other than the shock value, the information impacts no current operations but our own, and you control that piece of it."

When Drummond hesitated further, he offered a carrot. "And if it does pan out, sir, you will have helped identify and stop a traitor who could do the war effort irreparable damage." That had done the trick.

"All right, Bell. Type up the notes. I'll pass them to today's briefer."

"Thank you, sir. You won't regret this."

"I won't, but you might."

Leo kept an eye on Hobbs and Stanton now as the clerk flipped the slide on the overhead, dropping the intel bomb in the room. It was hard to tell from his position on the far side of the room from them, but both men's reactions seemed in line with the others there.

Leo slipped out of the briefing room as the meeting drew to a close and made his way to the door in the Munitions Building that was open for entry and exit. The beefed-up security posture put in place since the attack played right into Leo's plan. Hobbs and Stanton both would be leaving through this door, making it easier to tail each of them.

Exiting, he spotted Maya sitting on a bus bench near the parking lot and waved to her. He joined her, greeting her with a friendly hug.

"I brought you coffee." Maya handed him a cup. "But I'm afraid it's cold now." She tipped the opening of a small paper bag toward him. "Popcorn?"

"Thanks." He dipped his hand in and scooped out a handful. The drink and food would provide a reason for them to sit there for an extended period. Anyone watching would think they were on a break enjoying a snack.

"Why are you Americans so in love with this?" Maya asked, stuffing several kernels into her mouth.

"During the Depression, it was cheap, plentiful, and fun to make. For some, that was all they could afford or find."

Maya nodded and slowed her chewing as if giving its significance a bit more reverence.

"Are Karl and Hattie in place?" he asked.

"Yes."

Because of heightened war footing, security had blocked off the War Department parking area. People could walk to the entry point from the street, but only official personnel could park in the lot. Hattie and Karl, in separate cars, were parked across the street at the corner, waiting to follow their targets. As they emerged, Leo or Maya would trail a target to his vehicle once he came out of the building. After identifying it, they would hurry back to the street and inform the first car on standby, hopping in if time allowed to help Karl and Hattie keep the suspect in sight.

Leo and Maya continued enjoying their snacks and chatting while keeping an eye on the exit. Leo had intentionally scheduled the briefing toward the end of the duty day so they would not be out here suspiciously long as they waited for the targets to leave.

His strategy paid off.

Colonel Andrew Hobbs was the first of their targets to exit the facility. "You're up, Maya. Short army colonel with the briefcase in his left hand."

"Got it."

They stood and hugged before Maya left. She trailed Hobbs from a distance, keeping as close as possible to the street-side end of the parking lot. Leo split his attention between watching them and the building exit and eating more of the popcorn Maya had brought.

When Hobbs got into his vehicle, she walked toward the road and crossed it. By the time Hobbs backed out and the guard raised the security arm blocking the exit to the street, Maya had reached the group's first waiting car, Karl's sedan, and jumped in. Hobbs pulled onto 17th Street, and they followed.

One target tagged. One to go.

Leo threw another bunch of popcorn in his mouth and chewed. He was on his third handful when Stanton appeared at the exit. Leo picked up the paper cups, crumpled the popcorn bag, and tossed everything into the garbage can beside the bench. Prepared to see Stanton turn right toward the parking lot, he saw him instead pivot left.

Leo trailed on foot but kept a cushion of space between them to avoid being too obvious in his uniform. Stanton passed the building, walking to 17th Street and continuing north before turning west when he reached Constitution Avenue. Leo signaled Hattie to wait as he passed near her and then hustled to keep sight of Stanton. He slowed soon afterward. Stanton had stopped at a Postal Service mailbox about five yards down the avenue. After placing an envelope inside the box, he bent to tie his shoelace, doing something to the side of the maildrop at the same time. He stood then, and started retracing his steps, heading straight toward Leo.

Leo had a choice to make. Pivoting suddenly in another direction would look suspicious, so he continued walking down Constitution, angling his face to traffic so Stanton could not get a good look at him. When he glanced back, he discovered that Stanton had started to jog. Checking out the mailbox seemed important, but following Stanton was critical. He doubled back, managing to achieve a safe trailing distance again as Stanton returned to the parking lot. Leo followed loosely, watching more than walking, until Stanton got into a sedan. Crossing the street, Leo hopped into the front passenger seat of his car. Hattie was at the wheel.

"Blue Buick. It's coming out now," he said.

"Got it." Hattie turned on the engine and pulled into traffic.

They had succeeded in putting tails on both their targets as planned. Something told Leo, though, that Stanton was their man.

20

Washington, DC, Monday, December 15, 1941

Karl had to double his concentration as he trailed the white Chevy through heavy afternoon district traffic, darting between cars so as not to lag too far behind and get caught at a traffic light. Thankfully, he had Maya to keep her eyes on Hobbs and he was driving his sedan, not Maggie Moore's. He was familiar with his own car and knew how to sling it around in traffic without hesitating.

Once he got onto Georgia Avenue, Andy Hobbs settled down and flowed with the cars ahead of him. This street was a primary artery running north out of town to Silver Spring, Maryland. Based on the information Leo had found in army personnel records earlier today, he probably was heading home.

Karl reassessed his assumption at the next intersection when Hobbs turned onto Missouri and pulled into the parking lot of a small grocery store. Maya followed him inside to avoid Hobbs seeing and recognizing Karl. Minutes later, both reappeared and returned to their respective sedans.

Once they were on the road again and Karl could divide his attention, he asked Maya, "What did he do?"

"He bought eggs and milk, and when he was at the counter, he picked up a bouquet of roses," she said.

Karl thought hard, trying to bring out a stubborn memory. "What is today's date?"

"December 15th. Why?"

"Today is his wedding anniversary."

Karl increasingly doubted his friend was meeting a Nazi handler. When Hobbs pulled into a driveway and a tail-wagging German shepherd met him at the front door, he was even more confident this was not their man. It did not feel right. The Andy Hobbs he remembered was a standup, by-the-book guy, but someone who would also give his last dime to a starving man.

Despite his conviction of Hobbs's innocence, Karl and Maya had to stake out his house and follow his movements until tomorrow morning. Karl parked across the road at the corner, a few houses away from Hobbs's place, and turned off the engine. It would be a frosty night, but they had dressed warmly and brought blankets and thermoses of hot coffee. They had plenty to eat and ample drinking water, too, so the only difficulty would be bathroom breaks. Karl's dilemma was much easier to solve than Maya's, but she said she would improvise.

They would surveil in two-hour shifts, but neither was tired enough at the moment to try sleeping. Karl was glad he had Maya as his partner tonight. Their forced proximity meant they had abundant time to get to know one another better. Initially, she appeared reserved in her comments, but he suspected that ingrained habit was the cause of that rather than animosity.

Eventually, of course, their conversation steered toward Olivia.

"She and Hattie didn't part on the best of terms on Tuesday," Maya said.

"What do you mean?" he asked.

"She learned about me and Hattie, and it didn't go well. She told us to leave and not come back."

"I see. Hattie has yet to mention it." Karl rubbed his brow. Olivia would be a hard nut to crack, given her prejudice against Hattie's lifestyle. Like Eva once was, she had bought into the strict church teachings and put her faith above all else. As for himself, he believed in the divine but not in the box that religion tried to stuff him into. His loyalty was to his family, his country, and to himself.

"I doubt she will mention it. The rejection cut her to the bone, but she has set that aside because Olivia is family."

"That's because she has an enormous heart. Thank you for telling me."

"De nada. Family is important."

They settled in for a long, chilly night. Karl took the first shift.

Hattie eased Leo's car into the thick late-afternoon district traffic, tailing Eugene Stanton. It rivaled that of New York City. As she dodged a speeding station wagon, she reflected on how she had become much more skilled and confident since her last driving experience in the Big Apple. Maybe she would drive more instead of taking a cab or subway when she returned home.

"I think Stanton is our guy," Leo said as they relaxed at a red light three cars behind Stanton.

"Why is that?"

Leo explained he thought he had seen Stanton do something to the side of the mailbox he had stopped at. "Leaving a mark on something like that is an old spy trick. I think he was sending a signal to someone."

The light turned green, and she proceeded through the intersection. "Did you have time to look for a mark?"

"No, but I'd bet my bottom dollar that he left one."

"We have to be sure, Leo. If we get this wrong, Olivia will pay the price."

"Whether it's Hobbs or Stanton, I don't get why either would turn on his country like this. They're bird colonels with over twenty years of service and family men with wives and kids. They have it all."

Hattie remembered what the Professor had said to her in passing last week regarding her living a closeted life because of how she loved. "We all have secrets, Leo."

"But what is his?"

"Whatever it is, it has to be big enough to destroy that idyllic life he has."

Hattie followed Stanton to the Spring Valley neighborhood in the westernmost part of the district. After he pulled into the driveway of a two-story house with an ample yard, she parked across the street a few houses down.

Leo said, "According to Stanton's file, this is his home of record."

Stanton walked to his door, and when he opened it, a mangy, long-haired retriever jumped with his two front paws to greet him. Stanton pushed the dog back, yelled something, likely a string of curse words, and slammed the door shut.

"It looks like we'll have to wait for him to take the bait."

"Whatever he did at that mailbox tells me he already did," Leo said. "It's just a matter of time before he and his handler meet and take us to where they're holding your sister."

"We have until the end of tomorrow to figure it out." Hattie's reply sounded almost as desperate as she felt when it came out. She had stalled with the kidnapper for as long as she could, and time was running out.

"And we will." Leo shifted in his seat. "By the way, Beverly really enjoyed meeting you. She'd like to have you and Maya over for dinner."

"I'd like that." She considered him for a moment, deciding to raise the question that had plagued her since meeting his wife. "When were you going to mention Beverly's affliction? Is it polio?"

"Yes, but it's not something we talk about. It just *is* and has been since the day I met her." He smiled. "Rock Paper Scissors to see who takes the first shift?" He always had a way of lightening the moment for her, which was why she considered him a good friend. They had each other's backs and lifted the other up.

Hattie regarded him approvingly. Based on everything they had gone through, from the yacht, the bombing, a murder charge, Eva's kidnapping, and now Olivia's, not to mention his acceptance of her relationship with Maya, she knew he had a courageous and good heart. However, his love for Beverly was the icing on the cake.

"You're a good man, Leo Bell."

"Last chance for Rock Paper Scissors."

"I'll take the first shift. If he's going anywhere, it will probably be after dinner. I want to be wide awake for that." She grabbed a blanket from the back seat and wrapped it around her, covering herself from the shoulders down. "I might as well be warm."

"Suit yourself." Leo snatched up the other blanket and settled in for a chilly night.

If Jill had not had such a soft spot for that dog, Eugene would have found another home for him long ago. The animal was a jumper, and every time he walked in, the damn thing snared threads in his wool uniform coat. Fortunately, the damage was not anything that a pair of scissors or a lighter could not dispose of, but it was the principle. The animal needed discipline. Eugene was not there enough to instill it, and his wife lacked the heart to try.

After brushing away the dog and hanging up his coat, Eugene placed his briefcase near the door and headed for his liquor cabinet. As if the bombshell dropped during the briefing was not enough, he groused, he had to deal with the damn dog, two teenage girls, and his adult son's inability to stand up for himself in a household full of women. The only bright spots in his life now were the woman in the kitchen making dinner and the whiskey bottle in his liquor cabinet. He depended on both greatly. His wife kept the house running and his kids mostly pointed in the right direction. The bourbon prevented him from going over the edge. Admittedly, it had its downsides, too. His inability to keep it in his pants, particularly when he had been drinking, had put him in a hole so deep he no longer saw daylight. Only by nonstop digging could he hope to find a way out.

He poured himself two fingers' worth of Johnnie Walker and downed half before trudging into the kitchen. When he walked in, Jill had three pots going and was chopping the carrots for the salad.

"Hello, beautiful." He kissed her on the cheek.

"Good, you're on time. Can you get out the plates and silverware? We're about ready."

"And where are the twins to help with this?"

"You know teenage drama. If it's not fretting over homework, it's boys.

Sometimes, letting them be is easier than forcing them down to set the table."

"That's the problem with kids these days. They're too wrapped up in their own misery." The second he said those words, he realized he was just like them. He had become so entangled in the mess he had made of his life that it had engulfed him. Keeping Sam from crushing him, getting out from under his control, had become a full-time second job that left no time for anything else. He could not remember the last time he did something with the family or even took that damn dog for a walk.

"Uh-huh." Jill pointed her comment and salad tongs at him. "Plates."

"Yes, ma'am." He gave her a two-finger salute and did as she instructed.

Dinner was delicious and filling, as were all of Jill's creations. The children talked about high school and college, including the associated dramas of the people in their circles. Eugene did not need to know who had kissed the head cheerleader under the bleachers. However, by the time dessert came, he knew the entire dating history of both parties.

Eugene waited until the leftovers had been put away and most of the dishes cleaned to make his grand gesture. "Go upstairs, Jill, and take a hot bath. I'll take care of the rest."

Jill threw her dish towel on the counter and put her hand on his forehead. "Are you feeling all right? You must be out of your mind tonight."

"Nope. Fit as a fiddle. You've done enough for this house today. You should enjoy what's left of it."

"I'll be darned," Jill said, a smile creeping onto her lips. "Someone might get lucky this evening." She turned, removed her apron, and hung it on the hook beside the fridge.

He slapped her on her bottom. "Go, woman. I'll hold you to it."

Once she disappeared, he rushed through the remaining cleanup work. After ensuring everyone was upstairs, he prepared a bowl of leftovers, grabbed the trash, and went out the kitchen door. It was cold, but he would not be in the elements too long.

The back light was bright enough for him to see the leaves still needing to be swept from the porch. He stuffed the bag in the garbage can inside the gate and replaced the lid tightly to discourage the neighborhood raccoons from throwing a party in his yard again.

Leftovers in hand, he continued to the detached garage, which he used primarily as a workshop and storage for all the junk that did not fit in the house. After pulling the string to turn on the one bulb in the room, he closed the door behind him and walked to the small door on the other side. He turned on the stairwell light and descended the steps to the cellar. This dark, dank little gem was what had attracted Jill to the house. She had said she wanted the space to store her seasonal canning. However, she never got around to it. This section of the property had remained unused for three years. The cellar had the benefit of being deep enough underground and far enough away from the house and neighbors that no one would know anyone was down there unless they came down.

Once at the bottom and past another door, the stench of human waste hit him. Hattie James's sister, his most recent fiasco, was sitting on the ground on a pile of blankets and an old sleeping bag. The chain securing her to a nearby post was intact. She perked up when he walked in, looking less loopy than when he checked on her this morning. Time for another dose.

"It's dinner time," he said. "No tricks. Otherwise, the oven mitts and gag go back on, and you'll have to pee and crap on yourself."

She shook her head and her wild, unkempt hair. "I promise. No tricks."

When he first took her, she was hell-bent on escaping and calling for help. His solution had been to tape mitts over her hands so she could not use them to get loose and stuff a rag into her mouth to prevent her from screaming. When bodily functions became an issue, he devised a way to keep her docile.

"Are you out of water?" he asked.

"I still have some left. I saved it since I wasn't sure when you would be back." Her speech was slow but more coherent than it should have been. She needed to drink more.

"I told you. You'll get food and water twice a day. If you don't want it, I'll stop bringing it."

The woman started to cry. "No, no. Please. I want it. I'll drink it all this time."

"All right."

A glance at the piss and waste pail confirmed it still had plenty of room to add to it, so he was not about to touch it. He placed the plate in front of her and snatched her cup. After filling it from the pitcher he had left yesterday, he positioned himself to block her view and added a few drops of the morphine elixir he had pilfered from his mother's belongings after cancer claimed her. Every time she drank, she drugged herself enough to remain docile, allowing him to go to work.

He walked the cup over and placed it on the floor so she could grab it. "Eat and drink all of it. I'll leave you a full cup when I go."

"You said you would release me when Hattie gave you the lists. Hasn't she done that?" She scooped the potatoes with her hand, devouring them like a wild animal.

"You let me worry about that."

The woman cried, drooling food and spit. "She hates me. She's going to let me die."

"If you don't shut up, you'll get the mitts and gag again." The last thing he needed was a hysterical hostage creating a racket in the middle of the night.

She sobbed more quietly and stuffed in more leftovers. When she finished her food and water, he reclaimed the plate and refilled the cup, which should keep her sufficiently drugged until morning. He kept the cellar light on, his one act of kindness, and returned to the house, securing the doors and other lights as he went. He gave the plate a quick rinse and put it in the cupboard.

Upstairs and armed with another whiskey and a glass of wine, he went to the bathroom, where he found his wife of twenty-two years soaking in the tub. After three kids, she could still turn his head. His straying had nothing to do with her. It was all on him. Beyond the few moments of pleasure, those women all meant nothing. This was the only woman with whom he wanted a relationship, to have children, and to share a house.

"All done?" she asked.

"Yep." He handed her the chardonnay.

"You better be careful about spoiling me. I could get used to this."

"You deserve it," he said. "How would you like to take a trip after we've revamped Rainbow Five? I'm due some leave and would like to use it while we still can."

"I'd like that. Where do you want to go?"

"I was thinking about a cabin in the Blue Ridge Mountains. No kids. Just you, me, and a warm fireplace."

"I'd love that." She drank more of her wine. "Did you take the cans out? Tomorrow is trash day."

"Damn." He worked on his whiskey again. "I'll get it."

She stood, dripping and naked, and loosened his uniform tie and unbuttoned his shirt. "Get it in the morning."

"Grand idea."

Eugene would forget about the woman in the cellar and the man named Sam breathing down his neck. He would ignore the walls closing around him, at least for a few hours, until he woke, and the living nightmare started again.

21

Washington, DC, Tuesday, December 16, 1941

The last shift change occurred at five o'clock. Leo was sound asleep in the passenger seat now, his head leaning against the window. Overnight, they ran the engine to heat the compartment sparingly. The vapors rising in the cold could give away their presence. Hattie opted for a second blanket because the windows might fog up again.

She ducked lower in the sedan as the first bit of activity turned onto the street, the first she had seen in three hours. A garbage truck was making its rounds, its bundled-up workmen jumping off the back, jogging between homes, and returning to dump their loads into the compactor.

A light flicked on in the Stanton side yard, and the wooden gate swung open. Stanton appeared, dragging a trash can to the concrete driveway. He wore a robe and slippers and had comically messy bed hair. After stubbing his foot on something, he grunted loudly and hobbled back to the house.

Hattie laughed, stirring Leo from his sleep. "Huh?" he asked. "What did I miss?"

"Stanton almost missing trash day."

The garbage truck rolled up. A man in dirty coveralls jumped off the back, emptied his can, replaced it, and continued to the next house.

Leo rubbed his eyes and stretched. "What time is it?"

"A little after six."

"Things should start happening soon."

"I'd offer you some coffee," Hattie said, "but it's gone cold."

Up and down the block, cars periodically backed out of their driveways and rumbled down the street. After the sun rose around seven, Stanton made another brief trip to the detached garage moments before a sedan stopped in front of his home. The driver honked, and a young man lugging a book satchel, perhaps a teenager, ran out and hopped in. They drove off. Minutes later, identical teenage girls with book bags burst from the house and dashed to the corner barely in time to be picked up by a school bus. More neighbors warmed up their cars and took off to start their day.

Soon, the door opened again, and Stanton emerged carrying his brief-case. A woman appeared at the door with him, and he kissed her. She stroked his chest and straightened his tie. He patted her on the bottom and walked to his car.

"We're up," Hattie said, tossing the blankets to the back seat. Leo did too.

She started the engine and tailed him when he drove off. When he arrived at the parking lot of the Munitions Building, they were at a standstill.

"I'm going in," Leo said.

"You're still in the civilian clothes you changed into overnight."

"It will be fine. I have my ID card. I'll check on both of our guys and come out to the corner in an hour. If I think I should stay, I can change into my spare uniform in my office."

Hattie pulled over, and he got out and hurried toward the building entrance at a brisk walk, hoping to beat Stanton inside. Noticing Karl's car while searching for a place to park, she found a spot on the opposite side of the street, crossed it, and hopped into the back seat. "Morning. Any luck?" she asked, squeezing Maya's hand, extended between the headrests. They mouthed to one another, "Hi."

"Hobbs went home for his wedding anniversary and came back to work," Karl said. "How about Stanton?"

"After mailing an envelope, he went home, too," Hattie said. "He spent some time in the garage last night and this morning and had to race to get the garbage cans to the curb. It doesn't sound like either took the bait."

"Where's Leo?" Maya asked.

"He went into the Munitions Building to check on them. He said to pick him up in an hour."

"Does he have a plan?" Karl asked.

"No. He's winging it," Hattie said. "What do you suggest?"

"One of these guys is the traitor who framed me and who likely has Olivia. We only have until noon tomorrow. The mole will slip up. They always do. We have to be there when he does."

Hattie detected anger and desperation in her father's voice. He appeared worn out, and his injury was probably contributing to the sharpness of his response. She rubbed his shoulder. "We'll find her, Father."

He twisted the steering wheel. "We need twice as many people to do this correctly."

"Should Leo bring in his people?"

"Hobbs works in his shop. He's bound to find out if we start pulling personnel. We have to make do with the four of us," Karl said.

"But for how long? I say we have Leo watch them for the rest of the day and follow them when they leave. If they go straight home again, we regroup."

Karl sighed. "I think you're right. We're running out of time."

As they crossed the bridge into Virginia that night, Hattie held onto a sliver of hope that Maya and her father had better luck than she and Leo. Stanton had stayed in the Munitions Building all day and then gone straight to his house. Like the night before, Stanton went inside for dinner, tinkered in the garage for a while, and returned to the house. When the porch light went dark, she and Leo had decided to pack it in.

Driving into the well-lit Alexandria neighborhood now, the sight of Karl's car parked at Frank and Olivia's house crushed those hopes. Neither target, it seemed, had made a move to meet with their handler or tipped their hand on where they were keeping her sister. Now, they had to devise a Plan B.

Leo parked on the street, and they entered through the front door. It was after ten, so the children were long asleep. Frank and the others were in the living room with long, dejected expressions. Hattie and Leo sat on the couch.

"Any ideas about what we should do next?" she asked.

"I do," Karl said, "but it's risky."

"I'll do it," Frank said. "Whatever it is, I'll do it." He was still unshaven but appeared more in control. Most importantly, he was sober.

Karl patted Frank's knee. "For the children's sake, we can't risk security catching you. This is something I can't do either."

"What do you have in mind?" Leo asked.

"I'd do it, but someone would recognize me, and you already have the right clearance, Leo. I need you to break into their offices at the Munitions Building and see if you can come up with anything that points to one of them being the mole."

Leo stood. "I'm on it."

"It would go faster if you had somebody helping with the search," Maya said. "I'll go with you."

"No offense, Maya, but I think Hattie is better suited for this job. Security is tight, and the guard might not allow you in this late, even with me serving as your escort. But a famous singer—"

Maya put up a hand in a stop motion. "I get it. The man will be so starstruck that she'll easily get a pass."

"I'll change into something a little more convincing." Hattie winked at Maya before turning her attention to Leo. "When do we go?"

"Now."

"And what if they don't find anything?" Frank asked, leaning forward in his chair and running his hands through his hair.

"I made you a promise, Frank," Karl said.

"We both did." Hattie reached across the coffee table for Frank's hand. "We'll give them what they want and get Olivia back."

22

Washington, DC, Tuesday, December 16, 1941

The near-freezing night reminded Hattie of how inadequate a dress was in the winter. The weather in Rio had spoiled her for the last year since it changed little, and dresses had been a frequent choice for their airiness and appearance. However, tonight, halfway along the walk through the Munitions Building employee parking lot to the only personnel entrance, she regretted her choice of attire. It was darn cold.

Hattie walked in first. Four uniformed armed men were standing post at the security station a few feet inside. Leo approached the one sitting on a stool behind the desk, showing him his official credentials.

The man read his ID card and popped to attention. "Good evening, sir."

"I'll need a pass for my friend," Leo said.

"I'm sorry, sir. It's after duty hours and with the new rules and all." The guard dropped off when Leo leaned closer.

"Look, she really wants to see where I work. Do you know who she is?" Leo glanced over his shoulder at Hattie. Considering the mixed reaction of the people Hattie had encountered since returning to the States, there was no telling what direction this would take. "That's Hattie James. You know, the singer." The man's eyes lit up, and Leo laid it on thicker. "If you men scrounge up a camera by the time I'm done, I'm sure I can convince her to take pictures with you all."

The sentry smiled broadly and drew out his response. "Yes, sir." He scribbled something in a logbook and handed Leo a visitor's card with a clip.

"Thanks, Sergeant." Leo gave it to Hattie, and she clipped it to the collar of her winter jacket. He ushered her down the corridor before a supervisor could show up and correct the security violation.

Their heels clicked against the hard, shiny floor, and, with no one else roaming the halls, the sound echoed off the walls. Hattie wondered how far that noise traveled at night and how much of a warning they might have if someone came looking for them.

Leo took her to the office suite they visited the day after arriving in the United States. Where officials had dismissed their warnings about a possible Japanese attack due to it being the weekend. Despite the declarations of war this week, she hoped the Monday-through-Friday duty hours mentality was still pervasive enough to allow them to go unnoticed while they searched Hobbs's and Stanton's offices.

After flicking on the overhead lights, he unlocked the main door and closed it behind them. Turning down an interior corridor, he stopped at an office door near the end. He tested the knob but found it locked.

Hattie pulled a bobby pin from her hair and offered it to Leo. "Here."

"You do the honors," Leo said with a half laugh.

She had not picked a lock beyond practice for a while, but maneuvering the pins to manipulate the tumblers was simple for her. She raked them inside the mechanism and felt each obstacle release in succession. Once satisfied, she twisted the knob again, pushed the door open, and smiled. "Easy peasy." It came as quickly and naturally to her as singing.

"Showoff." He turned on the lights and went in. "You take the desk. I'll check everything else. The shelves are tall."

Hattie narrowed her eyes at his dig at her height. While Leo searched the bookshelves, file cabinet, and framed photos on the wall, she started with the cluttered drawers. She was not sure what they were looking for, but she would know it when she saw it. She hoped. The shoeshine kit and bottle of bourbon in the bottom drawer were not it. Neither were the office supplies, chewing gum, and half-eaten chocolate bars. However, the folders interested her.

Hattie grabbed them one by one and inspected each document. Most appeared to be copies of files related to his military career, rosters of personnel, and other unclassified documents detailing office procedures. She pulled the lists and went to Leo, who had made it to the filing cabinet.

"Do these names look right?" She held them up for him.

He scanned them briefly. "Maybe. I'll have to compare it to my copy. Take it." He eased the bottom drawer back. "I got nothing. Let's move on to Stanton's office, but first, one more thing to check."

They eyeballed things, ensuring every item was back to its initial position, minus the roster sheet. After turning off the lights, Leo locked the door, went to the outer suite, and stopped at the desk in the entry area.

"Whose is this?" Hattie asked.

"The secretary's. I want to see what messages she's taken for Hobbs in the last few days. She takes them in duplicate, so she has a record in case the original gets lost."

He opened the top desk drawer and located the collection of carbon copies in a small file box. The secretary had organized and divided them by date. "Let's go back a week. Pull out any to Hobbs."

They sifted through the memos and found four addressed to Colonel Hobbs. Hattie jotted down the names, numbers, and notes for each message on a slip of paper. After returning everything to its proper place, Leo led Hattie to the hallway to the next building wing. They stopped at a door labeled "Military Plans."

"My turn." Leo extended his hand for the bobby pin. It took him two tries to get it right, but Hattie was not counting. Not really. Well, maybe a little.

They walked inside, and Leo hit the lights. This suite was much smaller than the one where Hobbs's was located. They went to the door with Colonel Stanton's name on it. Leo was kneeling to jimmy the lock when Hattie leaned over him and twisted the knob. It turned, and she pushed it open.

Leo looked up. "Showoff." He stood, flicked on the light, and went in.

Hattie followed and strode to the desk. She sifted through the drawers while Leo addressed the bookshelves and file cabinet. Stanton stored several of the same items as Hobbs, including a shoeshine kit and liquor.

"What is it with army officers and booze in their desks?" Hattie asked.

"It's the culture," Leo said. "Many leaders have made agreements over a glass of whiskey."

Hattie also discovered that Stanton kept shaving stuff with a bottle of Old Spice aftershave in his desk. The files and office supplies were generic, and the waste can was empty. She shuffled through the papers on the desktop and lifted the leather desk pad. A bunch of messages and handwritten notes lay hidden underneath. She read through them. They seemed related to his job, though three business cards were telling. One was from an antique shop, another from a real estate agent, and another from a fashion magazine. All had one thing in common—they were all from women.

"Interesting," Hattie said, waving Leo over.

He came closer and studied the cards. "Women. You're thinking he's a ladies' man?"

"The real estate agent could be innocent, but the others?"

"Under the Articles of War, it's a crime to commit adultery. As a senior officer on the General Staff, General Marshall could make an example of him by dishonorably discharging him and sending him to Leavenworth," Leo said.

"Then having affairs could be blackmail material."

"My thought exactly. Did you find anything else?"

"Nothing."

They put everything back in place, closed the door, and returned to the reception area. Leo went through the secretary's desk and pulled out the box with carbon copies of the office telephone messages. The secretary here had organized them in the same fashion as were those in Military Intelligence. They divided the work and set aside Stanton's memos. Most had to do with his job. One was from his wife, and the three were from a dry cleaners shop. All of those were from different days but close together.

"Stanton gets an awful lot of dry cleaning done," Hattie said.

"It's the wool uniform. They require special care," Leo said. He studied the notes. "Though it does seem overboard. And why is he picking up his laundry and not his wife?"

Hattie slapped him on the shoulder. "As if a man is incapable of running his own errands."

"You gotta understand military culture. Navy wives have it different because their husbands are at sea for months at a time. However, army wives, particularly those of officers, take on all the household tasks because their husbands have such long duty hours. That includes getting the dry cleaning." Leo picked up the three messages. "The dry cleaner could be a cover."

"The FBI used a dry cleaners shop in Rio as a front for their operations. Maybe Stanton is working for them?"

While putting the box away, Leo asked, "Who in the FBI would want to leverage Stanton, especially if they think he's giving away national secrets?"

"Only one person comes to mind," Hattie said, walking toward the exit.

Leo was right behind her.

The door swung open. An armed military guard had his sidearm pointed at her. "Hands up."

Hattie complied as her stomach twisted into knots.

Leo did too, but said, "Corporal, I'm Commander Bell. I'll show you my ID."

The sentry kept his weapon trained on them. "Slowly."

"It's in my hip pocket." Leo reached backward, retrieved his wallet, and pulled out his identification card. "I'm assigned to G-2."

The enlisted man inspected Leo's document, lowered his gun, and glanced at Hattie.

"She's with me. Look at the visitor's pass," Leo said.

"I understand, sir, but what are you doing in War Plans?"

"I left something here today and came to retrieve it."

"You're not authorized to be in here, Commander. You two will have to come with me."

"Look, Corporal." Leo came forward.

The guard raised his pistol and retreated a step. "Don't make me use this, sir." He grabbed a whistle dangling from a chain hooked to his shirt and lifted it to his mouth.

Leo raised his hands again and stepped back. "My apologies, Corporal. There's no need to call for backup. We'll come with you and get this cleared up."

Hattie remained silent and walked beside Leo as the guard directed them from a few steps behind them. They went to the farthest wing and entered the security section at the end nearest the parking lot. The room was bright, with lots of overhead lights.

The enlisted man at the front had his feet propped atop the desk and brought them down when he looked up. "What do you have, Bryson?"

"They were in an unauthorized area. Is the lieutenant in?"

"He's having chow in his office," the duty guard said.

"Get him," Corporal Bryson said. "I'll put these two in lockup."

Once the desk guard hurried out, Bryson gestured toward the inner offices. "Please, sir. Regulations require that you wait in the holding cell."

"I understand," Leo said.

The guard led them to the back. There were two adjoining cells. Each had a barred door and a metal bench bolted to the cinderblock wall. The guard placed Hattie and Leo in the cell on the right.

"Sorry, sir." The guard secured the door and left.

The two sat. They were no strangers to authorities locking them in a confined space together, waiting to question them. On Mother's Day last spring, Brazilian police had held them in a room much more primitive than this place. They had spent hours in that room until someone came for them, passing the time by singing Hattie's songs. Doing so had taken the edge off the wait to learn whether David and her father had survived their gunshot wounds while thwarting an assassination plot.

Tonight, Hattie again found herself detained and fretting over the fate of a loved one. "Are you feeling a bit of déjà vu?"

"Do you want to pick the song?" Leo chuckled, which sounded forced.

"Singing doesn't feel right this time." The somberness of Olivia still being held captive and the country being at war hung heavily over them.

"No, it doesn't."

"What do we do now?" Hattie said.

"We're screwed."

"What about that general in Military Intelligence? Didn't you say he knows about our operation to fish out the mole?"

"He does, but he was called out of town today. He won't be back until Thursday. That will be too late for your sister."

"We're not screwed yet," Hattie said.

"What do you have in mind?"

The corporal returned with an army officer who looked young and right out of college.

"Trust me," Hattie whispered. She and Leo stood.

"Good evening, Commander, I'm Lieutenant Clark. I understand my man found you in the War Plans office."

"Yes, we were there," Leo said.

"I need to know what you were doing there. That section had a recent security breach."

"Which is why I was there. I'm assigned to Military Intelligence and can't get into the specifics."

"Then we'll have to hold you until we can clear this up."

"I'm afraid that won't do, Lieutenant. I'm on a time-critical mission."

"With Miss James?" Clark asked.

"Yes, with Miss James."

"I'm sorry, sir, but I can't release you without authorization."

"Who can authorize it?"

"The chief of security, Major Street."

"Get him," Leo said in a commanding voice.

Hattie dug a business card from her purse and gave it to the lieutenant. "While you're at it, call this man. He can clear up everything tonight."

The officer glanced at the card. "The FBI?"

"Yes. Speed is of the essence, Lieutenant. Please hurry."

The two men left, leaving Hattie and Leo alone in the cell. She sat, and Leo sidled beside her. "I hope you know what you're doing," he said.

"So do I."

23

Washington, DC, Wednesday, December 17, 1941

Hours had passed, and Hattie had begun to worry that her maneuver had already backfired. She had expected the head of security to appear the soonest, but the early morning hour likely was delaying both men's arrivals. Leo had taken the delay in stride. He fell asleep quickly, sitting on the bench, something Hattie attempted, but its metal surface was too hard for her to get comfortable enough.

Leo's calmness did not surprise her. They had been through a myriad of dangerous situations, several life-threatening, and he always remained even-keeled. The only time he had shown any overt worry was after finding a picture of the wife of a man who died during one of their operations. He had not mourned the dead man as much as he had felt for the man's wife, probably imagining his own wife in those circumstances and worrying about the possibility of failing Beverly and leaving her alone with no one to help her.

Yes, Leo Bell was a good man.

The door finally opened. Hattie glanced at Leo's wristwatch before he stirred. It was three o'clock. She elbowed Leo awake when an army major and the FBI agent walked into the holding area.

Leo and Hattie stood.

"Trouble seems to follow you everywhere you go, Miss James," Agent Knight said.

"We need to talk in private," Hattie said.

Knight cocked his head as if sizing her up. He looked more curious than he had in the past, precisely the state Hattie needed him to be in. She was depending on his unreasoning thirst for her father and his record of going rogue to get what he wanted.

Knight turned to the army officer. "Can you give us a few minutes, Major Street?"

"I'll be right outside," Street said before walking out and closing the heavy metal security door.

"Care to explain why you got me up in the middle of the night, Miss James?" Knight asked.

"We need your help."

"That much is obvious."

"If you want those lists, you'll help us," Hattie said.

"First, tell me what you were doing in War Plans, and I'll think about it."

"Someone abducted my sister. We have until noon tomorrow to produce the lists. Otherwise, the kidnapper will kill her. We believe a man who works in that office is the one who took Olivia."

"Do you have proof of any of this?"

Hattie reached into her purse, retrieved a folded newspaper section, and handed it to Knight. "The kidnapper sent us this and her wedding ring as proof of life."

Knight glanced at the paper and back at Hattie, returning the paper. "What do you want from me? For the last ten months, you've claimed to know nothing about the lists and the whereabouts of your father."

"I'm asking you to get us out of here so Leo and I can find Olivia before it's too late."

"And what do I get in return?"

The threat Hattie was about to lay at Knight's feet was based partly on conjecture, but the more she thought about it, the more possible it became. "Perhaps you'll get to keep your job. I know my father is innocent and that someone in the War Department framed him. His G-2 handler told me so."

"You're saying Karl James is an American spy, a double agent?" Knight asked.

"He works for Victoria Cooke. She is the mother of James Cooke, the vice president's aide murdered in Rio. He was there to pass along a message from his mother that she was onto who implicated my father." That part was an exaggeration, but Hattie needed a convincing argument. "She's how we knew to look here. Whoever framed my father is also Olivia's kidnapper. Vicky believes that person had access to those lists last year and knew she had recruited him into clandestine service when he worked in the Black Chamber with her."

"Karl was part of the Black Chamber? Those names are top secret."

"Yes, he was. Military Intelligence and the State Department can confirm that. Two men he served with met Vicky's criteria. One works in War Plans, where a guard caught us tonight. Either man or both of them could be involved in Olivia's kidnapping, which is why we are here."

Knight rubbed the back of his neck.

Hattie sensed the virtual wheels turning in his head as he digested her story, so she continued. "At first, we thought whoever took Olivia was working for the Nazis. We have found evidence that at least one of those suspects is a philanderer and a foe is blackmailing him to hand over secrets. However, we also unearthed evidence that the blackmailer uses a dry cleaner as a cover to contact him. That is a play right out of the FBI handbook. Do Agent Butler and Cohen Dry Cleaners ring a bell, Agent Knight? Have you gone rogue again and had my sister kidnapped to get those lists, no matter the cost? Are you the blackmailer?"

Hattie did not honestly believe Knight was behind Olivia's kidnapping, but she needed him to think that she did.

"Of course not," Knight said. His hard swallow meant Hattie may have succeeded.

"We're sure Attorney General Biddle would be extremely interested in what we've uncovered. So would a certain reporter associated with the *Chicago Tribune* and *Washington Times* who had no trouble leaking the nation's secret war plan. I have the backing of Admiral Drummond in Military Intelligence. Who is in your corner, Agent Knight?"

"If Drummond is behind you, why isn't he here to bail you out?"

"He's on a plane to the West Coast," Leo said. "By the time he lands and sorts this out, it will be too late for Olivia."

Knight turned to Leo. "Explain why your office recovered half of Karl's lists and did not notify us directly. We first heard about it from a major in G-2 at a counter-intel meeting."

"It was a ruse to draw out the suspects, get them to tip their hand," Leo said.

"You have a choice, Agent Knight." Hattie drew his attention back to her. "If you get us out of here, I won't spill what I've learned. However, if you leave us here, my sister will die and I will ruin you. You'll get a taste of what it's like to have the entire American media bearing down on you. I'll spend my last penny to ensure your picture is on every newspaper from coast to coast for months."

The tips of Knight's ears and his cheeks turned as red as a candy cane stripe, telling Hattie that she may have pressed the right button.

"After what we uncovered in the jungle, thwarting the German bombing attack and bringing you the Kessler brothers, I've earned credibility. You know what I've told you is the truth. And trust me when I say I will follow through with my threat. If my sister dies, I will blame you and take immense pleasure in taking you down. What will it be?"

Agent Knight stood motionless for several beats, absorbing and clearly weighing his options. Nothing gave away which way he would lean, not even a sign or an eye twitch. He opened the heavy metal door. "Major Street, come in."

Street returned with a questioning expression. "Well?"

"I need you to release these two into my custody and erase all record of their being here tonight."

Relief weakened Hattie's legs, but she leaned against Leo so as not to show it.

"I'll have to verify this with FBI Headquarters."

"Then you'll have to wake Director Hoover because I'm walking out of here with them in the next five minutes. I report directly to him on this matter. He is the only one authorized to confirm the joint Military Intelligence operation we're working on." Knight reached into his coat's breast pocket. "I'll give you his direct line. Go ahead. Wake him up and see how that goes. Either way, he will learn what you decide here, Major. The clock is ticking."

Street inhaled deeply. "Fine, but it's your ass." He opened the door and ordered the guard to release them.

Once the cell door was open and the sentry left, Knight said, "Destroy any paperwork of their presence here tonight, including the visitors' log. Speak to your men. No one is to know they were here. Understand?"

"Understood."

"The FBI thanks you for your cooperation."

Knight, Hattie, and Leo departed the building through the private security entrance on the National Mall side, which security used to transfer detainees. They entered the government parking lot and walked toward Leo's vehicle.

"Thanks for the Get Out of Jail Free card," Leo said. "We'll be seeing you."

"You're not getting rid of me that easily." Knight offered a crooked smile. "Both of you are in my custody now. Consider all of us attached at the hip until this is over. So, wherever you two plan to go, I'm coming with you. What car did you come in?"

Leo matched Knight's insincere grin. "Mine."

"My sedan is right here. Miss James is with me."

"Afraid you might lose us if I drive?" Hattie snickered.

"I'll follow you, Bell." Knight guided Hattie by the arm but not too tightly. He would not dare risk her ire at this juncture.

Leo mumbled something and walked to his car.

Knight unlocked his door, slid into the driver's seat, and reached over to unlock the passenger side. He did not bother to hold the door for her before getting in, and Hattie did not expect it. He had never shown her one ounce of courtesy.

When he turned around to go out the controlled gate, the Lincoln Memorial, backlit by the full moon, came into view. Hattie thought briefly about the words inscribed in granite in that shrine. In his Gettysburg Address, Lincoln praised the sacrifices made there to defend the union and hailed the government by and for the people. She believed in that sentiment but felt the government had lost its way in the seventy-eight years since Lincoln spoke those memorable words to rally a bitterly divided nation. Most of its guardians kept true to their oath, but some, like Agent Knight, used the people as pawns to get what they wanted. No greater good could justify what this man had done to her family, which was why Hattie's threat had such teeth with him.

Once they pulled onto Constitution Avenue, Knight asked, "Where are we going?"

"My sister's house in Alexandria."

Hattie leaned back in her seat, worried about the two problems they would face when they arrived at the house. Firstly, the abductor had instructed Frank not to alert the authorities, and Knight defined that position. Hattie and the others frequently checked out vehicles on the street, but they could not be positive that no one was watching the house. Knight's sedan did not scream federal agent, but seeing another car at the house might spook the kidnapper if he had someone there. Secondly, Knight had upended Hattie's life in two hemispheres, looking for her father, and she was bringing the man right to him.

When they entered her sister's neighborhood, Hattie said, "Can you park a few houses down? The kidnapper told us not to involve the police."

"It's a little late for that, and I won't have you separate me from my car. Across the street will have to do."

After Leo pulled in front of the house, Knight flipped his car around, parking parallel to Leo's sedan. Leo walked briskly toward Olivia's door but not so fast that someone could construe it as running.

"Come on, James." Knight hurried up the concrete walkway. By the time he reached the door, Leo was already inside. Finding the knob locked, Knight drew his service weapon and prepared to rush the door with his shoulder.

"Hold your horses," Hattie called out, increasing her pace. Even in a hushed tone, her voice seemed to travel in the wee hours of the morning. "I have a key." She opened the door.

Knight pushed past Hattie ten seconds behind Leo, and she was right on his heels. The living room light was on. Leo stood beside Maya near the couch, but neither her father nor Frank were in sight. That was a slight relief but failed to put Hattie at ease. Karl was somewhere in the house, within capturing distance of Knight.

Hattie asked, "Is Frank asleep upstairs?"

"He is," Maya said. "What happened tonight? And why is he here?"

"Security caught us," Leo said.

Hattie hung her jacket in the closet and went to Maya, giving her a hello hug. Before she let go, Maya whispered, "He's in the guest room."

Hattie pulled back and winked her understanding. "Our options were limited, so we had to bring in Agent Knight." She turned to Leo. "Do you need to use the restroom first, or can you wait?"

"I can wait," Leo said.

"Thanks. Fill in Maya. I'll be right back." Hattie went down the hallway toward the bathroom but continued past it to the guest room. She slipped inside the dark room and closed the door, looking instantly at the hinge side. "Father?" she whispered.

"What the hell is Knight doing here?" he asked.

She turned on the light. "Security caught us. Leo's boss was unreachable, so I played my trump card."

"Are there more FBI agents coming?"

"Only him. We told him about Olivia, the Professor, and that G-2 sanctioned the ruse about the lists. We found some evidence in Stanton's office—"

"So it's Gene."

"I believe so," Hattie said. "The evidence was such that it allowed me to maneuver Knight over a tenuous barrel by threatening to bring in the media if he didn't get us out. Now we're attached at the hip until this is over."

Karl nodded. "You've always been quick on your feet."

"Well, I'm out of moves. I don't know how much longer we can hide you from him. And having him here sidelines you when we have to do the exchange. I don't know if I can do it without you." Hattie sensed her calm slipping and took a deep breath. She could not afford to fall apart at this point. "We could overpower and tie him up until we get Olivia back."

"The kids are upstairs." Karl placed his hands on his hips and lowered his head. "I won't chance a gunfight in this house." He looked up. "Our backs are against the wall. It's time to lay out our cards. This all has to come to an end."

Hattie knew what he was suggesting. He planned to surrender himself, hoping Knight would cooperate, just as he had surrendered to the Nazis in Rio in order to reach Wagner and the airfield.

"No, Father. I can still use the lists to get Knight to back off."

"No, sweetheart. The playing field has changed. We are at war. I can no longer use them as leverage. Now that we know Stanton is the mole, we must get the lists into the right hands. If we do it correctly, we can save your sister and finally get you out of this world."

Everything was about to change. Hattie's lips quivered, but she refused to let herself cry. Every choice in this situation came with grave risk. Olivia would undoubtedly die if they did not turn over the lists, and her father would face a death sentence if they failed to prove his innocence.

Karl touched Hattie's back. "Warn the others. I'd like this to go as peacefully as possible."

She wrapped her arms around him, memorizing the feel of his firm embrace. He had been her rock through the good and troubled times. And she knew this was his way of stabilizing her life, and the lives of Olivia and his grandkids.

"I love you, Father."

"I love you, sweetheart." He pulled back. "Go."

Hattie kissed him on the cheek and left the room without looking back. She reentered the living room, where Leo was giving Maya details about their night. Knight was standing next to Leo, which was the position she wanted them in.

"Much better," Hattie said. "Did you notice the nightshade when we came in? I think it's about to appear."

Leo and Maya nodded their understanding of her father's code name.

Knight squinted in confusion. "What's nightshade?"

"I am," her father said from the hallway, stepping into the room.

Knight turned his head in Karl's direction. "You!" He raised his right hand and reached into his coat under his left arm, where he likely kept his weapon. Leo swooped in quickly and shoved him off balance. Knight teetered. Maya stepped forward and kicked Knight on his bottom, sending him tumbling to the floor.

"Stop fighting," Leo said, struggling to keep Knight down as he thrashed. "Don't make me hurt you."

"We won't harm you, Knight," Karl said, but the agent flailed harder and grunted like a wild animal.

Hattie and Maya pounced, grabbing his legs. Maya moved up when Leo secured Knight's arms and flipped him to his side. Hattie held on tightly, but Knight got one good kick on her thigh. It stung like hell, and she would undoubtedly have a shoe-sized bruise there for a week.

Maya snagged his pistol from his shoulder holster and aimed it at him. "Stop," she said in a loud, clear voice.

Knight gave up and went still. Leo pulled something from Knight's waistband, handcuffed his hands behind his back, and dragged him to the couch. "Stay," Leo ordered.

"I knew I couldn't trust you." Knight sneered at Leo.

Karl sat on Frank's easy chair close by. "I need you to listen."

"I don't care what you have to say," Knight snarled.

"Fine." Karl turned to Maya. "Hand me the photos."

"What?" Maya narrowed her eyes in confusion before shifting her attention to Hattie.

"It's okay, Maya," Hattie said. "Give my father the photos and the book."

Maya padded to the china cabinet in the dining room where they had stored the items, returning moments later. She handed everything to Karl.

He placed them on the coffee table in front of Knight. "These are pictures of the sheet music in which I had encoded the lists of covert agents. Hattie took them before I altered the originals because we thought Wagner was closing in. We were right, because he had turned David Townsend, blackmailing him to get those lists. If you have these blown up, you'll find Morse code hidden in the stanzas. Each line represents the city and cover and real name of an agent. The cipher is based on a passage in this book. I've marked the page and written down how it works."

"You're giving them up just like that."

"Yes, just like that. I never intended them to serve as leverage. They were my insurance policy."

"What do you mean?"

"Hattie said she mentioned my other job with Intelligence. My State Department position was the perfect cover. Those jobs overlapped in one respect—maintaining the list of covert agents. I got that responsibility because I was one. When I received back-to-back requests for both lists of spies from multiple sources, I suspected something was up and refused all requests. The following day, I noticed somebody had tampered with the lock on the classified safe. The lists were no longer secure. I knew that the Germans would kill for them and that someone in the War Department wanted them badly enough to try to steal them. So, I encoded them in the sheet music and altered the originals so no one could access them. The next thing I knew, you were arresting me for giving secrets to Nazis. I believe whoever tried to steal the lists also set me up."

"That's quite the fantasy, Karl."

"It's not fantasy," Leo said. "Everything he said is true. I also worked for Victoria Cooke. She dispatched me to Rio to watch over Karl and the lists."

"And Admiral Drummond will confirm all this?" Knight asked.

"Half of it," Leo said. "He can verify mine and Karl's history and that Cooke recruited him and sent him to Germany on a post to gain their trust. The Nazis were to think he was one of them since he was born in Germany. Beyond that, you'll have to trust me when I say that Karl fed Cooke intel for years. When he returned to the States, the SS had him feed them intel. It was all fake or strategic to misdirect the Germans."

"Who can vouch for the other half? This Cooke woman?"

"She could, but..." Leo looked as if he was about to say more but stopped.

Karl glanced at Leo before refocusing on Knight. "But she's dead. Hattie and Maya located Cooke at her Eastern Shore cabin days ago to bring her the lists. However, she wanted time to identify the mole so that she could expose them safely. They agreed to meet on Sunday. In the interim, someone took Olivia hostage. Thinking the mole had taken her, we went to the cabin on Sunday to work with Victoria to identify him. Instead, we discovered Victoria's body."

"So nobody can confirm your story," Knight said.

"The secretary of state and Admiral Drummond can verify her existence and the role she played, but only she could have attested to her knowledge." Karl turned to Leo. "Uncuff him."

"Are you sure?" Leo asked. "There's no going back if I do."

"There's no going forward if you don't," Karl said. "I have done plenty of killing in this job, but I never killed anyone on our side. I won't start now. Uncuff him and return his service weapon."

Leo unlocked the handcuffs and handed Knight his pistol.

Knight spun it around and trained it on Karl. "Even if I believed your story, give me one good reason why I shouldn't shoot you right here for killing two FBI agents."

"All I can say is that I didn't kill them. Two SS agents broke me out, thinking they were saving one of their own. They put me on a Rio-bound freighter, escorted by one of them. I killed him before reaching port. His name was Joseph Fuller."

"The other one was Erik Weiss," Leo said. "Cooke and I captured and interrogated him. We learned in the process that the SS had embedded someone, David Townsend, as we later discovered, in Hattie's inner circle. So, Cooke sent me to Brazil."

"What happened to Weiss?" Knight asked, still holding the gun on Karl.

"He's dead."

Knight's expression softened a fraction, and he rubbed his chin with his free hand. "Let's say I believe most of your story. What do you want from me?"

"Help us get my daughter back alive," Karl said. "Once she's safe, and the mole is in custody or dead, arrest me and help Leo surface those lists so they can do some good. I'm tired of hiding and want my life back. The only way to make that happen is to trust you'll do the right thing. So, what will it be?"

24

___

Alexandria, VA, Wednesday, December 17, 1941

Muffled but heated voices stirred Hattie from what she had hoped would be a few hours of rest. She shot up from her pillow, knocking the haze of sleep from her head to focus on discerning what had awoken her. A ruckus was going on outside the guest room door. She hurried to put on a top and slacks and bolted to the hallway. The shouting grew louder and clearer, joined by a little girl's sobs and a little boy yelling, "Stop, Daddy! Stop!"

Hattie rushed to the living room, horrified by what she found. Frank and Agent Knight were engaged in a brawl on the carpet while two children stood watching in terror, clutching one another.

"Stop, Frank!" Hattie moved closer to break up the fracas, but they were thrashing about so wildly that she feared being struck by an errant punch.

Maya ran in from the kitchen, dismayed. The front door swung open, and Leo and Karl ran in. Each grabbed a different man's arm and peeled them away from each other like twisting apart an Oreo cookie. Frank looked to have an egg developing over one eye, but he was still up for a fight. Knight, his nose bleeding, appeared more than ready to call it a draw.

Hattie picked up Sarah, who continued to cry. Matthew was clinging to her leg for dear life.

"What are you doing, Frank?" Karl was a bit winded, but his question was firm and demanding.

"Why the hell is he in my house?" Frank slung an index finger toward Knight instead of another punch.

"He's here to help." Karl firmed his grip around his son-in-law's torso to keep him from inflicting more damage.

"I know what he tried to do to my family." Frank spat his words like they were on fire. "I don't want him anywhere near this house or my kids."

"Just listen to me for a damn minute," Karl said. "He's agreed to help get Olivia back and arrest the man responsible." He loosened his hold when Frank ceased resisting.

Frank's face went slack. "We weren't supposed to bring in the police. They'll—" Frank shifted his attention to his children and stopped mid-sentence.

"Let me get the little ones some breakfast," Maya said. She turned to Hattie, extending her arms. "Come on, Sarah. I was about to make pancakes."

Sarah shook in Hattie's embrace, burying her face into her neck.

"It's okay, Sarah. You and Matthew go with Auntie Maya while Grandpa and I talk with your daddy."

"When is Mommy coming home?" Sarah asked in a timid little voice.

"Soon, sweetheart. Now go with Maya."

Maya took the kids into the kitchen. Once the swing door closed behind them, Hattie slapped Frank on the shoulder. "What were you thinking, fighting in front of the children like that?"

"Yeah, what the hell?" Knight said, pressing a handkerchief against his nose to stop the bleeding. "Striking an FBI agent is a federal—"

Hattie spun around, stabbing Knight with an index finger in his chest. "Be quiet. He has every right to be livid after what you tried to pull. Those kids could have ended up in a foster home. And for what? You've been chasing an innocent man." She turned to Leo and her father. "And where were you two? You were supposed to intercept Frank and warn him about this."

"We were checking the perimeter," Karl said, "and making sure no one had staked out the house." He turned to Frank. "I'm sorry. We should have woken you last night to warn you, but I wanted you to get some sleep. That's on me."

"Would someone please tell me what is going on in my own house?" Frank's muscles still appeared tense, but his chest had stopped heaving in anger.

"Let's sit down," Hattie said. Everyone took a seat. Frank was in his easy chair, and Hattie took her sister's. Leo sat between Knight and Karl on the couch, providing a cushion since their dislike for one another was as strong as Frank's for Agent Knight.

Hattie recounted last night's events, from the guards catching her and Leo, Knight bailing them out, Karl giving him the lists, and Knight promising to rescue Olivia without involving more agents.

Frank turned to Karl. "But he'll arrest you."

"We'll worry about that later," Karl said. "The important thing is to focus on getting my little girl back."

"We have five hours until the kidnapper calls," Leo said. "I suggest those of us who can should get more sleep before he does." He looked at Frank. "Can you promise to set an alarm to wake us all by eleven and not take Knight's head off in the meantime?"

Frank lowered his head in embarrassment. "I can do that. You can take the couch. Karl, you can use my bed." He glanced at Knight. "You, I don't care. Just stay out of my sight."

Hattie patted Frank's knee. "Be nice. He's helping."

"I'll see if I can locate Stanton," Leo said. "If I do, I'll call the house. If it's a bust, I'll come back."

Frank stood after Leo left. "I'll relieve Maya in the kitchen and apologize to my kids." He left the room, rubbing his neck several times. The tell revealed his lingering frustration.

While Karl climbed the stairs and Knight leaned back and put his feet on the coffee table, Hattie returned to the guest room. Maya joined her there moments later.

"How are Sarah and Matthew?" Hattie asked, removing her slacks and crawling back into bed.

"They seemed a little better when Frank walked in, but they really miss their mother." Maya crawled in, clothes and all, and cradled Hattie in her arms.

Hattie said nothing. She could not let her emotions dictate today, not when they were close to facing Olivia's kidnapper.

Maya held her tighter and whispered, "I know you miss her, too."

The kids were playing at a friend's house for the afternoon, and the group had gathered silently in the living room, ready to take the kidnapper's call. The tension among them was thick and oppressive, like the air in the Brazilian jungle this time of year. Everybody waited, nervous as cats with their knees bobbing up and down.

The phone rang at ten after twelve. Hattie's heart thumped harder, and everyone zeroed in on the device on the table as its bell vibrated.

Frank answered it. "Hello... Yes, we have them. Now let me speak with her... One, but—" He held out the receiver. "They hung up."

"What did he say?" Hattie asked.

"He asked if we had the lists, and I said yes." Frank returned the handset to its cradle. "Then he said Hattie and Karl are to come alone and unarmed with the sheet music and the cipher. They're to meet him at the National Mall side of the Smithsonian Castle at one o'clock and sit on the bench closest to the Capitol building facing the castle."

"That's a thirty-minute drive this time of day, which doesn't give us much time to scout and set up," Knight said.

"You three leave now," Karl said. "Figure out a plan on the way there. Hattie and I will go in my car."

Knight, Leo, and Maya hurried to their feet and checked their pistols.

"What about me?" Frank asked. "I'm coming too."

"No," Hattie said, signaling the others to take off. When the door shut, she returned her attention to her brother-in-law. "Things might not go as planned. We'll need cooler heads at the exchange point, and that's not you. You're a wreck today. Think of the kids. What will happen to them if something happens to you and Olivia?" Hattie cupped his hand. "Stay here and stay sober. We'll be back as soon as we can."

He shook his head hard but said nothing.

She grabbed the book of Cicero letters, the sheet music photos book-marking the cipher page, and rushed out the front door with her father. He backed the car from the driveway and started toward the primary artery that would take them to DC.

Hattie glanced over her shoulder at the house Olivia and Frank had bought after they got married. She remembered hauling their belongings in boxes with them the week before their wedding. Both were so young and joyful, looking forward to raising children there. They had wanted to watch the sycamore grow from a sapling into a shade tree so their children could play beneath its protective canopy. That hardwood had grown larger, and so had their family, but its branches were barren now. She hoped that was not a foreshadowing of future events.

She peered out the windshield and clutched the Cicero book against her chest. "Are we doing the right thing by giving him the lists?"

"I swore to never put anything above the safety of my family," Karl said. "Right or wrong, this is what we must do today."

"After David died, you'd said the government had successfully recalled many of our agents. I'm glad they got out."

"I'm sure there are a few they cannot risk bringing out of the cold, but those people knew the risks going in."

"At least most of them will be safe," Hattie said.

"But not the work they did. Once the Germans get the list of American spies, they will know what intelligence to distrust. Some of our assets have spent years embedded, providing false information to misdirect the Nazis. All their effort will have been for nothing when we hand over things today."

Hattie had been focused so intently on the human element of those lists that she had not fully realized the impact on Military Intelligence. Germany would dissect the lives of every American operative, interrogating anyone they had come in contact with and analyzing every detail they had provided. This was a nightmare of colossal proportions.

They crossed the bridge into the district, parked near the castle, and walked up the garden concrete pathway.

"How are we on time?" Hattie asked.

Her father glanced at his wristwatch. "Four minutes." Traffic through Alexandria had been heavier than expected because of holiday shoppers clogging the streets. The pathways leading to the National Mall were also more crowded than Hattie remembered. Then again, perhaps people were flocking there to chase away their war worries by taking in the bright Christmas colors in the shape of bows and candy canes decorating all the light poles in the area.

They located the park benches. There were eight, and all were unoccupied at the moment. Two wide decomposed granite walkways separated them into pairs of two. The caller had said to sit on the one nearest the Capitol, facing the castle. The location was horrible. Their backs would be unprotected at the open expanse of the National Mall. They would be looking south, where the sun was low on the horizon, and would not have a full view of the area.

Hattie performed a casual inspection of the area the way her father had taught her during his lessons on conducting surveillance. He did the same as they walked to the bench. The Smithsonian Gardens had many entrances and easy access to multiple streets. She spotted Maya with her camera a ways off, appearing to take photos of the Capitol. Knight was a bit closer. He was a cinch to spot, working on a bag of peanuts and throwing the empty shells on the ground. Leo was a mystery. He had blended in so well that Hattie could not find him.

When they sat on the designated bench, Hattie realized why no one else was sitting on them. The metal was cold, permeating the wool of her long coat. She placed the book in her lap under her purse. "I got two, but not Leo," she whispered.

"Ten o'clock. Man in a park worker's vest sweeping leaves."

Everyone was in place, but the setup felt wrong somehow. Their orientation limited their field of vision. There were too many avenues of egress and not enough people to cover them.

A man sat on the bench beside them. Hattie glanced in his direction but for only a second. "Do you have the lists and cipher?" he asked.

Hattie turned her head and studied his profile. He wore dark, fairly anonymous clothes. A fedora hid his head, but he had a fair complexion and not a hint of beard stubble. He was either freshly shaved or grew facial hair slowly. The lack of lines around his eyes suggested he was younger than she expected, perhaps in his thirties.

"First, I see my daughter," Karl said.

The man raised his left hand, waving the folded newspaper in it.

Two figures emerged at the trailhead Hattie and Karl had walked through when they passed the castle. One was a woman based on her clothing and shape, but the sun's angle made it difficult to discern her features.

"Hattie! Father!" the woman called out.

Karl stood. Hattie did, too, trying to get a better look. It was Olivia. She appeared beleaguered. In fact, she looked terrified. The man holding her by the arm partially obstructed his face by his hat.

"Liv. Everything will be all right, sweetheart," Karl shouted.

"The lists."

As Hattie clutched the book and her purse tighter, something drew her attention to the gaggle of people who had passed behind them moments ago. She focused on a short figure, a woman, who had stopped near a tree. Her stature, hair, and the way she stood looked familiar, but the shadows made it hard to see her clearly. Hattie blinked and looked again, still unsure of what she was seeing. "Who is that?" she whispered, mumbling a name under her breath.

"Who?" Karl asked, turning his head to follow her gaze. When he did, the woman disappeared into another passing group.

"I'm not sure, but something is off."

Karl grabbed the man by the collar. "What are you trying to pull?"

The man broke Karl's hold and pulled a gun, holding it at his belly.

A DC police officer walking by on foot approached. "Is there a problem here?"

"No problem," the man said, slipping his pistol into his pocket before the police officer saw it. "Just a minor disagreement among friends."

"Let it go, fellas. Holiday spirit and all." The cop continued his patrol after both smiled and patted each other on the shoulder.

"Let's try this again," the man said.

Before he could walk away, Karl grabbed him by the wrist. He studied his eyes for several seconds before saying, "Call the house at three."

When Karl released his grip, the man took off, shadowing the officer. Leo followed them.

Karl took Hattie by the arm and hurried her toward the trailhead where Olivia had been, but she was already gone. A vehicle was speeding away from the private parking area, likely taking away her sister and their one chance to get her back alive.

Knight and Maya converged on their position.

"What happened?" Knight asked. His narrowed eyes said he was angry.

"The cop spooked him. Get your car and try to catch up with Leo. I don't want to lose him."

"I don't think so," Knight said. "After that stunt, I'm not losing sight of you again."

Karl snatched him by the collar using both hands. The muscles in his jaw twitched, and his lips arched into a sneer. "You're focused on the wrong man. If Olivia dies, I will blame you."

"Don't make me regret agreeing to this," Knight said, slapping away Karl's hold.

"I already do." Karl turned to Hattie and gave her the keys. "Go to the house. If we're not back by three, tell the kidnapper to call back at midnight for instructions. We set the terms now." He squeezed her hand and took off at a jog with Knight.

Hattie and Maya walked to Karl's sedan at a normal pace so as not to draw unwanted scrutiny. Once they were driving toward Alexandria, Maya asked. "What happened? Why did your father lose it?"

"I think he did it on purpose to get the attention of the passing cop."

"Why would he do that?"

"I told him something wasn't right. I thought I might have seen...I don't know." Hattie thought back to the woman she saw behind the bench, but she had been too far away to be sure who it was. "Anyway, Father told the man to call at three. We need to be there and give Frank the bad news."

"He's going to be devastated."

"I know."

Twenty minutes later, Hattie pulled into the driveway. The moment she engaged the emergency brake, Frank burst through the front door, worry written on his face.

Hattie let out a breathy sigh and opened the driver's door.

He bobbed his head left and right, looking in the passenger compartment. "Where is she? Liv?" he called out.

"She's not here, Frank."

His face went pale, and he went weak in the knees.

Hattie buoyed him, and Maya came around to his other side. "She's okay. I saw her. She looks tired and worn out."

"What happened? What went wrong?" He regained his strength enough to stand on his own.

"Let's go inside before the neighbors see us."

They went into the living room. Hattie waited until Frank sat to tell him that two men were involved and that the exchange had not gone off because a police officer had come by. She omitted the part where her father had intentionally tanked the meeting and she had seen something that was likely nothing but was still gnawing at her.

He pulled at his hair. "What do we do now?"

"The others are trying to follow one of them. In the meantime, the kidnapper should call here at three. If Father isn't back by then, we'll stall for more time."

"More time." He pounded his fist against his thigh. "Always more time. I doubt she can take this much longer."

Hattie doubted Frank could either. He had become more unhinged after each contact with the abductor and would likely lose complete control if their next attempt failed. "I know, Frank. We're being extra cautious because anyone who would take an innocent person hostage is extremely dangerous."

"I'm starting to think that your fight with Olivia has clouded your judgment. That you're more interested in keeping those damn lists from getting into their hands than in saving your sister's life."

"That is not true and not fair," Maya said, coming to her feet. "Hattie would do anything to save her. You have no idea the lengths she has gone to in the past year to protect the people she loves. She barely knew me when Baumann took my sister, but she risked her life time and again to save her. Hattie is doing the same, if not more, for Olivia. Don't ever doubt her love for that woman and this family."

Hattie was speechless. This was the most beautiful thing Maya could have done for her.

Frank buried his face in his hands and wept. "I'm sorry, Hattie."

Hattie came closer and rubbed his back. "It's all right, Frank. We're all on edge." She popped her head up and listened to the silence in the house. "How long can the kids stay at Shelly's house?"

"Until five."

"That's good. I don't want them to see you this upset."

They waited another hour for the phone to ring. When it did, neither Karl, Leo, nor Knight had returned. Hattie answered, not trusting Frank's mental state. "Hello."

"That was a mistake, Miss James," the man said.

"I don't know which one you are, but tell Gene Stanton that my father is very disappointed in him."

"How—" The man stopped mid-sentence but not before positively identifying himself. The fear dripping from that single word said it was Stanton.

"It's you then, is it? Hello, Colonel. I know where you, your wife, and your three teenagers live. If you hurt one hair on my sister's head, your entire family is fair game."

"If you touch them—"

"Now you know how it feels. You should have followed the rules about not involving family and found another way. Now, we do things my way."

"You're in no position to make demands."

"Oh, I know I am. Call back at midnight tonight. We will tell you the time and location of the exchange. Otherwise, you will never get those lists of spies, one of which has your name on it." She guessed the last part and was probably wrong, but it made for a convincing threat.

He breathed heavily over the line, a sign she had gotten his attention.

"Midnight, Colonel." She hung up, hoping she had done the right thing by tipping their hand.

Half an hour later, Karl and the others returned. The long looks on their faces said they had lost the man from the park bench. Leo confirmed it, explaining he had gotten away among the vendor tents selling holiday gifts, hot cocoa, and roasted chestnuts for some event in the mall. "We thought we had him, but he gave us the slip. We went to Stanton's house and the Munitions Building but couldn't find him."

"How did it go with the caller?" Karl asked.

"I could tell the call wouldn't go well, so I used our last card."

"So Stanton knows that we know his name?"

"Yes, he knows."

"Which means he will be desperate and might make a mistake. Actually, that was the right move. We want him scared and off his game."

"She threatened his family, for God's sake." Frank shook his head in disgust and looked Hattie in the eye. "I thought I knew you."

Karl stood firm, positioning himself between Frank and Hattie as if defending her. "These men aren't Boy Scouts, Frank. They kill for much less than a list of spies. The only thing that has kept Olivia alive is the threat of the lists exposing them. Sometimes, good people have to do terrible things to protect the people they love. I know Hattie. She may have threatened his family, but she would never lift a finger against them. However, I would. That's the only way you survive this game."

"My wife's life is not a game."

"You don't think I know that already? This is as real as it gets, but as far as everyone else in the world of espionage is concerned, it's all one giant chessboard. Opponents try to outmaneuver one another by moving pieces around endlessly until the other side makes a mistake. Then we go in for the kill. Hattie has set us up for it. We control the board now, and this will end tonight."

25

Washington, DC, Thursday, December 18, 1941

Another check of Stanton's home and office building looking for him was a bust again, so the exchange was a go. Leo and Knight were in the lead car. Karl was behind them in his sedan with Hattie and Maya. As they crossed the bridge into Anacostia at midnight, Hattie thought back to the tense planning session that had taken place in the living room once Frank calmed down.

"When that phone rings," Karl had said to Frank, "tell them to be at this address at one o'clock. If they are one minute late, the lists will go to the Americans. Then hang up. Do not engage with them or ask to speak to Olivia. These men have to believe they will lose their chance to get what they want if they don't do precisely as we say. Do you understand?"

Frank had nodded.

"This will be the most important call of your life. I need you to repeat it back to me." Karl had made Frank recite the instructions until he could say them from memory. "That's great, Frank. By the time you give them the message, we'll be minutes from setting up. This time, we'll be ready for them."

Frank had stood by the front door when they were preparing to leave and clutched Hattie by both arms. The lost look in his eyes was heartrending. "Bring her home. Otherwise, I'm not sure I can do this on my own."

Hattie had a feeling he meant more than he would need help raising those kids if the worst had come to pass and would lean on her to pick up the load. She would readily assume that responsibility, though she fervently hoped it wouldn't be necessary. She was also worried that losing Olivia would break him.

When Leo took her and Maya to the abandoned industrial section of Anacostia last week, Hattie had seen how useful it could be as a place to conduct sensitive interrogations. Tonight, it would provide an ideal trap for their adversaries. The warehouses were dark, offered high ground from which to defend a position, and acted as an excellent funnel. They could lure in a target and pluck them off before they knew what hit them.

When they reached the warehouse, they blocked the back entrance and rolled up the front door, creating their choke point. They set up lanterns at the open entrance and at the exchange spot. The lighting was strong enough to identify faces but insufficient to illuminate the building's second level. Leo positioned himself there on the high ground atop a catwalk near the old foreman's office. Thanks to Agent Knight, he had a rifle with a sniper's scope and a submachine gun. Maya and Knight, armed with pistols, were hiding among old barrels on opposite sides of the warehouse, flanking the opening to prevent a sneak attack or escape. Karl and Hattie, also equipped with handguns, had stationed themselves in the shadows behind some old crates near the wall, a position that offered an unobstructed view of the entrance and the meeting point.

Wintry air seeped into the cavernous industrial space, which was littered with leaves, trash, and material rusted after years of neglect. The only sound was the light breeze rattling the warehouse door pull chain. The chessboard had been set up, and Hattie and Karl were about to move in for checkmate.

"I never got a chance to say," Karl said in a hushed tone, "thank you for staying in the back seat and holding that tourniquet." For three harrowing hours, his life had literally been in Hattie's hands as they raced through the jungle from the secret Nazi plane factory to Rio. If she had let up for one moment, he could have bled out.

Hattie swallowed past the thickness in the back of her throat and flexed her fists inside her coat pockets to keep them warm. "You would have done the same for me. Now, we have to do as much for Olivia. She's depending on us to not let go."

"And we won't," he said. "No matter what happens here tonight, neither of us will let go. Not of Olivia, not of Frank and those kids, not of your mother, not of Maya, and not of each other." He squeezed her hand. "Because we're family."

Hattie gave his hand a firm squeeze. "Family."

A glow made its way through the open warehouse door and grew in intensity, signaling that a vehicle was approaching. Its tires crunched the gravel road, and its brakes squeaked as it pulled to a stop near the entrance. Headlights shined like spotlights into the interior.

The passenger door opened, and a man stepped into the beams a few feet outside the building, making it impossible to make out his face.

"Turn off the headlights," Karl shouted.

The man glanced over his shoulder toward the car and issued a hand signal. When the lights went dark, he faced them again and said, "Show me the lists."

"Come inside," Karl said. They wanted to give the others an open shot at him. The man moved forward until he was two steps into the structure. Warm amber lantern light there provided enough illumination from the side to see him clearly. "You disappoint me, Gene."

"Your daughter said as much last night on the phone. Now, the lists."

"You know the order of things. Once I see Olivia, I'll produce them."

"And demonstrate the cipher," Stanton said. The sweat on his face made him appear nervous.

"After I know Olivia is unhurt. First, though, tell me why, Gene. Why did you betray me? Betray our country. We were the best of friends at one time. And you were once a true patriot."

"I painted myself into a corner."

"With your drinking and women."

"What else? They were going to destroy me, Karl."

"I understand turning over secrets because some idiot is extorting you, but you chose to frame me too. Why?"

"The SS already had their claws into me. After you decided to hide those lists from everyone, they said you needed to pay the consequences. That told me you had turned, so giving you up was easy."

"That's why you framed me? You thought I had gone to the other side?"

"It was hard to believe at first, but they showed me intel you had given them. It became either you or me. I chose me."

"I thought you knew me better than that."

"You did all this based on an illusion," Hattie said, breaking in. "You're a damn fool, Stanton. Was killing the Professor also your doing?"

"She was an accident. I took a chance that you would lead me to the lists, and I was right, but the old woman refused to give anything up." He ran a hand through his hair and stiffened his posture. "What's done is done. Let's get down to business."

"Olivia first," Hattie said.

Stanton waved again at the sedan. Its driver got out, pulled a woman from the back seat, and pushed her forward. She stumbled several steps but then got her balance. Stanton grabbed her arm and pulled her into the light cast by the lantern.

It was Olivia. Her sluggish movements suggested to Hattie that Stanton had drugged her. She showed no outward sign of having taken a beating, but that was inconclusive.

The click of someone cocking a rifle behind Olivia and Stanton was unmistakable. It was followed by the sound of another car door opening and then another. Two armed men got out and stepped closer to the warehouse opening. There was no telling how many lingered outside.

"Olivia," Hattie called out. "Did they hurt you?"

"Hattie?" Olivia cried. "I want to go home."

"We'll take you there. I promise."

"Enough," Stanton said. "You've seen her. Now show yourselves and the lists." He shoved Olivia back toward the vehicle, where an agent took her by the arm.

Karl clutched Hattie's hand and kissed it before releasing it.

"Family," she whispered.

"The Germans, then Stanton," he said. She interpreted it as the implied priority for when the shooting commenced, an inevitable event.

They emerged from behind the crates, stopping near a glowing lantern on the floor.

"Come get it," Karl said.

The idea was to draw Stanton in for an easier shot and keep the list from getting out of the warehouse. He complied, coming forward to stand in the cone of light emanating from the lamp.

Hattie handed him the Cicero book, along with the envelope of pictures. "The photos of the sheet music are there. The book is the cipher."

"I thought you said the photos weren't any good, that you needed the originals," Stanton said.

"I lied."

Stanton grunted. "Of course you did. Tell me how to find the code and how the cipher works. When I can decode the first name, we'll give you Olivia."

"I hope you have a piece of paper to write it out. My father embedded the lists in Morse code in the stanzas. Each row contains a name and city. The cipher is based on a Cicero quote, 'Trust no one unless you have eaten much salt with him.' The passage is on line four in Volume One of *Cicero's Letters*, Section Nineteen. I placed the envelope there to mark the passage. It's simple. Add four positions to any letter in the first half of the alphabet. Line four. Then, add nineteen positions to any letter in the second half. Section Nineteen. Always keep letters in their original half. A becomes E, and M becomes D. But since the second half has thirteen letters, you're really adding six. So, N becomes T, and Z becomes S."

"You're confusing me."

"It's intended to confuse," Hattie said. "Numbers are all shifted higher by one position. Volume One. Reverse the process to decode."

Stanton glanced at her father. "You're one tricky bastard, Karl."

"I can't take full credit. The cipher was the Professor's idea. The Morse code was mine to make the markings appear like printing errors."

Stanton removed the photos from the envelope and placed the book under his arm. "They're too small to make out."

Hattie pulled from her coat pocket a magnifying glass they had picked up at a drugstore and handed it to Stanton. "Here. A through M, shift up four positions. N through Z shift up nineteen, but if you think about it, just go down six. It's faster."

"You'll have to walk me through it."

"Fine. Do you know Morse code?" The last thing Hattie wanted was to help, but it was the only way to get Olivia and everyone else out alive.

"Of course. Pick a German agent to decode."

She selected a photo she had identified before leaving the house as one that would not pose a loss of intelligence. She used the lantern light and magnifying glass to read off the dashes and dots of the first word. Once both confirmed the jumbled letters, she stepped him through decoding each one. "There. Those letters become Erik." They repeated the steps for the rest of the words in the same row. "This line is Erik Weiss, known as John Davies, living in Baltimore."

"Let me verify it." Stanton turned to walk to the entrance with the lists and book.

Hattie grabbed his arm and whispered, "I have multiple guns trained on you, Colonel. You don't leave with those lists until we get Olivia."

Stanton glanced at the grip she had on him and back at her eyes. "I don't believe you."

"Look up at the catwalk above my right shoulder." Hattie gestured his chin toward Leo's perch. "He will shoot you where you stand. Verify the name from here."

"Okay." He called out the names and the city and received a confirming thumbs-up from the driver.

"Now give us my sister," Hattie said.

Stanton waved at the man again and yelled, "Release her."

The driver sent Olivia forward and shouted, "If he dies, she dies."

Olivia and Stanton walked toward each other. When they were two steps past parallel, and Olivia was out of his reach, a woman's voice bellowed, "That's far enough, Colonel Stanton."

The men from the car all raised their weapons and motioned like they were ready to fire.

Stanton looked back at them and froze, apparently as confused as Hattie.

"Don't shoot!" Hattie called out, putting her hands up. The unexpected voice sounded nothing like Maya's, and it had come from behind her, not from where Maya had set up. There was not another woman here except Olivia. At least there should not have been. Hattie did not care who this was or what her motives were. Her primary focus was Olivia. She rushed to her sister, latched onto her arm, and intended to pull her to a place of safety. When she pivoted to do so, though, the sight before her stopped her in her tracks. She had not been seeing things in the park.

"Professor? It *was* you at the mall."

The Professor stepped even with Karl. "It's good to see you, Karl."

Karl smiled and nodded. "And you."

"I'm sorry, my friend." The Professor's expression turned hard and cold. "Family first." She confidently strode to the center of the warehouse, holding a short stack of newspapers. "If you want the list, gentlemen, all you have to do is open the special editions of the *Chicago Tribune* and *Washington Times*." She fanned out the paper, displaying the headline "Spies Everywhere!" in bold, black letters. "It's all right here. Nicely decoded. Hot off the press. Erik Weiss from Baltimore and everyone else."

Karl walked up. "What are you doing, Victoria?"

"Burning it all to the ground."

"I don't understand."

"You will," the Professor said. She turned to Hattie. "Get your sister to safety." She continued toward Stanton, slapped a newspaper against his chest, and threw another one in the direction of the car and the driver. "There are your precious lists. My son died because of them." She turned to Stanton. "And you killed my dear Celeste, all for these wretched names which are nothing more than pieces on a chessboard. Your secrets are no more. The entire world knows them. Knows you!"

"You stupid, crazy old woman." Stanton spat his words.

"This crazy old woman will be the last thing you see."

The Professor flipped her right hand, spilling the last newspaper onto the concrete floor and exposing a pistol in her hand. She aimed and fired, striking Stanton in the chest.

His body jerked. Before he fell, more shots rang out.

Acting out of instinct, Hattie wrapped an arm around Olivia. Someone pulled them to the ground.

"Stay down," her father said in a hushed voice, as if no one being able to hear them equated to no one seeing them.

Someone shot out or doused the lamps, and the place went dark. Amidst the chaotic gunfire and a racket of consecutive crashing sounds, her father slipped from their sides.

Olivia whimpered, covering her head with her arms.

Hearing rapid footsteps coming toward them in the darkness, Hattie gripped her pistol and told Olivia to stay down. She looked up. The driver ran forward, picked up the Cicero book and music sheet photos, and turned. She could not allow that information to leave this warehouse. The Professor had claimed to have released the lists to the media, but that could have been a ruse.

Hattie fired once, twice, three times. She was unsure which shot had hit him, but at least one sent him to his knees.

"Stop!" Maya yelled from the stacks of barrels on one side of the warehouse near the open door.

A hail of automatic fire pierced the air. Sparks from bullet strikes appeared on the car Olivia had arrived in. The angle was such that they must have come from Leo's position. The headlights and windshield shattered. When the burst stopped, a few final bits of splintered glass fell to the ground.

"We need light," Knight shouted, though who he was yelling at was not clear. "Keep your hands up, or I'll plug you right here."

Karl rolled Stanton's body over, and the space lit up. Stanton had fallen on the lantern, blocking its light, when he tumbled to the ground dead.

Footsteps clomped on the metal stairs to Hattie's side. That meant Leo was approaching.

Hattie glanced back. Olivia and her father were fine. Knight had called out, but Hattie had not heard from Maya since the gunfire stopped. Her stomach knotted as the worst possibility formed in her head. "Maya!" Hattie pushed herself up and looked around frantically.

Stanton and the driver lay motionless on the concrete, blood pooling around them. Her father had rushed over to check on his old friend and mentor, who was lying face down near them. She heard him say in a broken voice, "Victoria, no!" before she stood and rushed toward where Maya had positioned herself, concealed among the stacks of metal barrels. Footsteps from behind her got louder, but she paid them no mind. She reached the corner where Maya had set up. The barrels were a scattered mess. A mountain of metal. And Maya was nowhere in sight.

"God, no!" Hattie shouted. Maya was likely under them. "Maya! Call out! Maya!"

She frantically tried shifting the containers, but they were too heavy for her. Leo came up beside her, placed his rifle down, and lifted one after another like Hercules. Within seconds, Maya's legs appeared. They were not moving.

Hattie pushed back her panic, and she rolled another barrel away. Leo removed more until they had uncovered Maya entirely. Her eyes were closed, and she remained still. Hattie dropped to her knees and stroked her face.

"Wake up," she whispered.

Maya did not move. Hattie was too terrified to check for signs of life. She did not want to make that horrible discovery herself. She touched her face again and pleaded, "Please wake up. Don't leave me."

Leo kneeled on Maya's other side and placed a hand on her chest. "She's breathing."

Hattie's lips trembled, and a floodgate of tears opened. Alive. Maya was alive. Hattie continued stroking her face and hair until Maya finally moved her head and groaned.

"It's okay, Maya," Hattie said. "Try not to move too fast."

Maya brought a hand to her head and fluttered her eyes. "I feel like a truck hit me."

"All those barrels hit you. Is anything broken?"

"I don't think so. Just achy."

"Can you stand?"

"Yeah, I think so."

Hattie and Leo helped her up and walked her to the center of the warehouse. The scene there was heartbreaking. Knight had thrown a pair of handcuffs onto one agent from the car. Two more were dead in a pool of blood. Stanton was too. Olivia lay on the ground weeping. Karl was kneeling next to the limp, bloody body of Victoria Cooke, his face blank.

They had won this game, but at what price?

26

Washington, DC, Thursday, December 18, 1941

Hattie could not be sure, but she estimated little more than half an hour had passed since Leo had left to get help following the bloodbath at the warehouse. An ambulance arrived first, though it was largely unnecessary apart from having the attendants examine Maya's head and scrapes and check Olivia for injuries. The rest of the injured were dead, including the Professor.

Hattie had never seen her father cry except for a few tears of joy when his first grandchild was born. However, he had shed several over Victoria Cooke's body tonight. He mumbled one word repeatedly before the medical attendant placed a blanket over her.

He had said, "Why?"

Hattie still had yet to wrap her head around what the Professor had done. She had pieced together that Stanton had killed Celeste by mistake. And that the Professor had faked her death by disfiguring the corpse of her lover drastically enough to make a positive identification impossible. Hattie could only imagine that the devastation of this loss, on top of grieving the death of her son, had broken the Professor, cleaving all rationality from her. Why else would a woman who had dedicated a lifetime to the service of her country set it back so drastically in a single act? Yes, the US had now rounded up most of the German agents. And yes, it had safely recalled most American agents in Europe, but the groundwork those operatives had laid meant nothing now.

Hattie felt betrayed. She had spent the last ten months keeping secret after secret and telling lie after lie to keep those lists safe. So much bloodshed. Baumann had kidnapped, hunted, and killed so many women, one of them Maya's sister, in his search for those once sacred names. Hattie had lost David. Her father and sister had nearly lost their lives. Frank had almost lost his wife. Matthew and Sarah could have ended up motherless. All that loss and anguish were for naught now that the lists were being delivered to millions of households.

That was the part Hattie could not understand about the Professor's drastic actions. They had rendered meaningless the deaths of her son and her lover, who had died for something the Professor handed over with little more fanfare than a fireworks display.

Other people arrived while Leo and Knight secured the prisoner and the ambulance attendants evaluated Maya and Olivia. Three district patrol cars, a half dozen FBI unmarked sedans, and two coroner vehicles had cluttered the narrow road between the warehouses.

Hattie snickered when the cops tossed up barriers and rope to keep out anyone who was unauthorized. They had selected this place for its remoteness. No one would know to come there unless they were monitoring the police bands.

After being examined by medical personnel, Maya and Olivia walked toward the warehouse where the coroner's attendants were wheeling out the bodies on gurneys. Karl wrapped an arm around Olivia, and Hattie pulled Maya into a brief but tight embrace.

"Are you sure you're okay?" Hattie asked Maya.

"Other than a slight bump on my head and several future bruises, I'm fine. I know you're worried about your sister. Go to her."

Hattie had put off talking to Olivia other than giving instructions until now. The way they had left things after Olivia walked in on Hattie and Maya hugging was weighing heavy on her. Despite everything she had gone through to get her back, Hattie was unsure whether Olivia would be able to set aside her prejudices. Nonetheless, she took a deep breath and approached her sister.

Hattie rubbed Olivia's arm gently. "How are you feeling?"

"Much better now that I've gotten some water." Olivia sounded less groggy, but an awkwardness still swam between them.

"I can't imagine what you've been through after a week in captivity."

Olivia's lips quivered. "It was horrible. That man kept me in some cellar underneath a garage. He fed me twice a day, but he always drugged my water. I had to use a bucket as a bathroom. My God, it was awful."

"Where was this place?"

"I'm not sure, but I think it was his house."

Hattie nearly doubled over. She had camped in front of Stanton's house for two nights and had seen him enter that garage. Her sister had been right there.

"Are you okay, sweetheart?" Karl steadied her with a hand on her elbow. "You went white as a ghost."

"I'm so sorry, Olivia." Tears escaped Hattie's eyes. "I was there. I followed Stanton home and could have saved you days ago." She covered her mouth and wept.

"Don't blame yourself." Olivia offered a sad smile. "You didn't know." She raised her hand and grazed Hattie's cheek with her palm.

"You're safe now." Hattie cupped her sister's hand and squeezed it. "Frank and the kids will be so glad to see you."

"How is he? Is he holding up? My gosh, what did he tell them?"

"He told Matthew and Sarah that you had to go away on a trip. He's had it rough with worry, but we've been helping as much as possible."

"I don't know how to thank you."

"There's no need. We're family."

Maya approached their group. "I'm sorry to interrupt, but Leo gave me a heads-up. Knight finished with the man he captured, and he and the other agents are taking him to FBI Headquarters." She turned her attention to Karl. "That means he's coming for you next."

Karl sighed, but he and Hattie knew this was the consequence of getting Olivia back.

"What's going to happen to you, Father?" Olivia asked, her voice and expression filled with worry. "Can you escape?"

"I'm done running, Olivia. I promised Agent Knight I wouldn't try to flee if he helped us. He kept his word, so I'll keep mine."

Olivia pressed her head against Karl's chest and sniffled more tears. "But I just got you back."

Karl wrapped his arms around her. "The truth has come out. I have to trust that Knight will do his duty."

Knight came over. He tipped his hat to Olivia. "I'm glad you're safe, Mrs. Windom."

"Poppycock," Olivia said, turning her nose up at him. "You threatened to put me and my husband in jail and my children in foster care. You should be ashamed of yourself."

"I won't apologize for doing my job, which is why I must do this now." Knight turned to Karl. "Karl James, you're under arrest for the murder of two federal agents and espionage against the United States."

Olivia flung a once-in-a-lifetime expletive at Agent Knight before Hattie calmed her down. "It will be all right, Liv. Father is still a wanted man. They have to sort all this out at the FBI building." She pivoted to her father. "I'll have Albert Wright meet you there or send over a criminal lawyer from his firm."

"Thank you, sweetheart. He's going to love you waking him at this hour." Karl chuckled.

"The rest of you are free to go," Knight said. "We'll need you at headquarters today to sign your statements."

Karl kissed his girls goodbye before Knight stuffed him in the back of an agent's car and drove off.

"He'll be all right, Liv." Hattie wrapped an arm around Olivia's shoulder. "Let's get you home where you belong."

～

Six days later, Washington, DC, Wednesday, December 24, 1941
Hattie had developed a healthy dislike for the FBI Building. Every time she walked inside, an agent would put her in an interrogation room and

grill her for hours about something her father had allegedly done. Today, however, that all would change. She had come willingly and prepared to answer any question hurled at her. Her father had, too, though Leo had advised her that he and Knight would do most of the talking and that she and Karl might not have to say a word.

When Hattie strode into the executive briefing room, the proceedings had yet to begin, and people were chatting. Leo had told her that top American intelligence officials had gathered to hear about the leaked spy lists. Those covert names, which the FBI accused Karl James of stealing, had become sensational headlines like the Rainbow Five war plan story. The conference table's far end held the heads of the military and FBI intelligence services, along with the deputy secretary of state and the DC chief of police. At the other end sat Agent Knight, Commander Leo Bell, Karl James, and Karl's lawyer, Albert Wright. Several lower-ranking officials filled the chairs lining three sides of the room.

Today marked the second time Hattie had seen her father since Agent Knight had hauled him away a week ago from that government-owned warehouse. Authorities had granted her and Olivia one visit between his interrogations. Karl assured them of receiving excellent treatment and that Albert was carefully safeguarding his interests during every interview. However, she had no idea what direction this briefing would take or whether someone had already decided her father's fate.

Hattie went to him. He looked good in one of his double-breasted dark gray wool suits. The outfit hung better on his frame with his slightly broader shoulders and trimmer waist. He looked more like his old self, perhaps an improved version of himself before all this started when she had considered him a bland and boring diplomat who doted over his children. This dignified, professional look no longer befitted him, in her opinion. She had gotten accustomed to seeing him in casual attire or a basic coat and tie designed to let him blend in, rather than make a statement.

He rose from his chair and hugged her. "Good morning, sweetheart. You look nice today."

"So do you." She smoothed his jacket collar. "Ready to impress."

"Whichever way this goes, this will be the last time I put on a suit like this. It's time for a change."

Hattie patted his chest. "I get it." She took a seat next to him. On her other side was Leo. They had seen each other nearly every day since the warehouse confrontation, meeting for lunch or dinner with Beverly and Maya at his house. Today, he was in his service dress uniform with a rack of ribbons depicting an honorable naval career. She squeezed his hand. "It's good to see you."

"Likewise."

"Who's in charge?" she asked.

Leo pointed his index finger across their end of the table toward the other side of Karl. Agent Knight, his face buried in a stack of documents, was mumbling to himself. "He's nervous as a cat. Knight is a field agent, not a briefer."

She would have enjoyed his discomfort if her father's freedom had not been dependent on the reception of his recounting of last week's events. "Please tell me you're prepared to step in."

"Don't worry." He winked. "We've been working on this for days."

That was easier said than done.

Knight went to the podium. "It appears everyone is here. Thank you for coming. I'm here to brief you on Operation Nightshade, a joint FBI–Military Intelligence effort to uncover a major War Department security leak that spanned a year and two continents." He fumbled with his notes and stumbled over his words for nearly a minute before Leo stood and touched his shoulder.

"I got this," Leo said. Knight sat, looking relieved, and Leo took his place. "Gentlemen, imagine you've served your nation for twenty-five years, during half of which you perform a job you cannot share with a soul beyond the person who recruited you. Not your wife and not your children, whose lives are at times as much of a mystery as yours because you've missed a considerable amount of their childhood. Your entire professional life is a trail of lies except for one core anchor point—unwavering loyalty to country. Let me tell you the story of Karl James."

Leo stepped the senior intelligence officials through the salient points of Karl's journey, which had resulted in him being labeled a traitor for nearly a year. He started with the back-to-back requests for rarely accessed classified lists of covert agents that had led Karl to suspect sinister motives from someone high up in the War Department.

Leo touched on the accusation that resulted in Karl's arrest for treason and his deadly escape from custody. He continued, saying, "We'll return to this critical aspect soon. Distrustful of the government he loved, Karl James encoded the names, hid them in sheet music, and entrusted them to his daughter, a person he knew was loyal. Hattie James unwittingly carried them for months, including when she relocated to Brazil to evade the backlash of her father's troubles."

Leo paused and glanced at Hattie and at Agent Knight. He had glossed over Knight's highly questionable tactics to coerce Hattie into going to Brazil, and she understood why. Getting into it would muddy the waters. Leo and Knight needed to present a united front about the relevant facts in this forum, not pick bones. To do otherwise might muddle the officials' understanding and alter any decision made there today.

Leo went on to explain briefly about the FBI's and Nazis' search for those lists by a powerful man who kidnapped and killed women along the way. "That is when Victoria Cooke, the intelligence coordinator who recruited Karl into covert operations, brought me into the picture. Known in our circles as the Professor. She told me about the suspected War Department mole. My job was to gain Karl's and Hattie's trust in Rio, protect the information, and keep my identity secret. I saw firsthand the lengths the Jameses had gone to in order to prevent those secrets from falling into anyone else's hands, particularly the Nazis."

Admiral Drummond spoke up. "Gentlemen, I assure you that Commander Bell is one of our most experienced and trusted field agents and well-qualified for such an assignment."

Leo acknowledged the compliment with a nod and continued with the briefing. He detailed that with Agent Knight's help, Hattie had unearthed a Nazi plan to bomb the United States in coordination with the Japanese. "Once we foiled the German involvement, we knew it was vital to resume the search for the infiltrator so we could safely resurface the lists. That effort brought us to the Maryland Eastern Shore and the Professor."

Leo explained that the Professor was the keeper of the cipher and that she had narrowed the list of suspects who could have been the War Department mole. "Meanwhile, someone took Karl's younger daughter hostage to force Hattie into giving up the lists with the cipher. Logic told us the abductor and mole were one and the same. When I returned to the cabin days later, as scheduled with Karl and Miss James, we located what we believed was the Professor's body. This is when we pulled in Agent Knight and things turned murky."

"Define murky," the FBI deputy director said.

"Hattie had inadvertently led the infiltrator to the Professor. He broke in to get the lists but accidentally killed a woman who surprised him there. He assumed the woman was the Professor, but she wasn't. The Professor was still reeling from learning of her son's death when she found her."

"Who was this woman?" the DC police chief asked.

"A long-term lover." Leo paused when several officials squirmed in their seats at the implication. "Both losses sent the Professor off the deep end. Unbeknownst to us, she met with Chesly Manly of the *Chicago Tribune* and arranged for him to publish the names in the lists in a misguided act of revenge. Once we identified the mole as Colonel Eugene Stanton, Agent Knight helped set up the hostage exchange at the warehouse. At the location, Stanton confessed that Nazi operatives had been blackmailing him into handing over classified information. He also admitted to being the mole Karl was searching for, setting up Karl to be arrested, and killing a woman whom he believed was the Professor. Then the Professor appeared and killed Stanton. A shootout ensued, resulting in the death of two SS agents and the capture of one. The prisoner thus far is not talking.

"In conclusion, we have yet to determine the full impact of publishing the lists. Our agencies have brought in all but two American operatives in Germany, and we have already rounded up four Nazi agents attempting to flee the United States."

"This is an incredible story," Drummond said.

"Believe me when I say that it feels even more incredible from the perspective of someone who lived through it."

"Do you have anything else to add, Agent Knight?" the FBI official asked.

Knight stood. "Without reservation, I can say that Karl and Hattie James are nothing short of national heroes. I recommend dropping all charges against Karl James."

"I concur," the deputy director said. "Mr. James, you have our gratitude and are free to go."

"I have something to add," Albert said.

"And who are you?" the deputy director asked.

"Albert Wright, legal counsel for Mr. James."

"Go ahead, Mr. Wright."

"When the FBI arrested my client and German agents later broke him from custody against his will, federal agents went out of their way to malign his and Hattie's reputation. The FBI's actions ruined both their careers. I expect a full public retraction, clearing them of any wrongdoing. If that is not forthcoming in the next thirty days, I will file a defamation lawsuit on their behalf."

"I see." The deputy director shifted uncomfortably in his chair before standing. "We'll make that happen."

When he left the room, Hattie surmised the meeting was over. She was ecstatic about how everything had turned out. Her father was about to walk out a free man, and without either of them having to provide more details, some of which might not have gone over well.

Several officials filed out. However, Admiral Drummond gathered his things and walked to the other end of the table. He shook Leo's hand. "Great job, Bell. You've earned the assignment of your choice after this."

"Thank you, sir," Leo said. "I'll think about it and get back to you."

Drummond pivoted to Karl and also shook his hand. "Welcome back from the cold, Mr. James."

"It's nice to be back, but you'll get my retirement papers before the end of the month."

"I understand. Your departure will leave a big hole in the intelligence service. You will be hard to replace." Drummond shifted his attention to Hattie. "But I hear from Commander Bell that you have acquired some unique skills. He's quite impressed with you. If you're interested, I'd like to offer your father's shoes to fill. The Germans' activities in the jungle are far from the only ones they'll conduct in Brazil. Having an observer there as astute as you are could be of real value to your country in the conflict ahead."

Drummond's offer took Hattie aback. As much as she had taken to Karl's teachings and as comfortable as she had become in dangerous situations, she had never considered doing the work officially. Agent Knight had forced her into that life, and that genesis still left a bitter taste in her mouth. She had to rebuild her career as a musician in Brazil and the US with Maggie as well as by partnering with Maya in establishing the Halo Club as a major competitor to the Golden Room at the Copacabana.

"Thank you, Admiral," Hattie said. "I'll think about it and get back to you."

27

Eleven days later, New York City, NY, Saturday, January 4, 1942

Hattie was lying on her side in bed, her head supported by an upturned palm, watching Maya as she slept next to her. Typically, Maya rose before her, but this day marked an important milestone. Today, she would lay down two final songs in Maggie's recording studio and complete her first contract with her. The band did not work on Sundays, and Hattie and Maya had a seaplane to catch back to Rio on Monday, so she had to squeeze them in today.

First, though, she wanted to take in the woman beside her, bathed in filtered morning light, for a few more minutes. Maya's face was so peaceful when she slept, with none of the day's worries taking their toll. The corners of her lips drew up occasionally, forming a satisfied smile more genuine than anything Hattie had witnessed.

Her mind drifted back to several nights ago. She and Maya had arrived in New York after Christmas. Between recording sessions, she terminated her apartment rental, arranged for the donation of her furniture, and packed her personal belongings to ship to Rio with them. When New Year's Eve rolled around, she had been ready to celebrate.

Despite the recent attack on Pearl Harbor and America's official entry into wars with Japan and Germany, thousands of New Yorkers had gathered in Times Square to mark the occasion. Hattie and Maya had been among them. The wartime atmosphere had subdued the celebration, but bringing in the new year with Maya stirred memories of the year they spent together. They had a rough time, beginning with the disappearance and death of Maya's sister Anna, multiple harrowing encounters with Nazis, and other personal losses. Still, a common thread had kept them together—their love for one another. Their bond, built on kindness, acceptance, and respect, was unbreakable, Hattie was certain.

Maya shifted a little and smiled more broadly, her eyes still closed. "How long have you been watching me?"

"Long enough to know I want this every day for the rest of my life."

Maya opened her eyes. "Now you know why I wake before you."

Hattie entwined their legs and pulled their bodies closer with a hand to Maya's back. "We'll have to take turns now that I know what I've been missing." The slamming of a door on the floor below them meant someone was up and going inside Maggie's brownstone. "I better get ready. The band is coming early."

Hattie shifted to pull the covers back, but Maya held her in place and said, "I'm so happy for you."

"Why are you happy for me?"

"Because I can see how much joy you get from being in the recording studio. I hope you take Maggie up on her offer to extend the contract if sales go as expected."

"It would mean more time away from you, recording and touring."

"If we hire the right people for the Halo Club, I could come with you. You can call me your manager."

"I'd like that," Hattie said. Music brought her endless delight, but it would hold less meaning if Maya was not with her.

They got ready and went to the kitchen on the main floor, where Maggie's Aunt Ivie was preparing breakfast. "Good morning, Ivie," Hattie said.

Ivie glanced over her shoulder from her position in front of the stove.

"Morning, ladies. I have your plates in the warmer. I hope scrambled eggs, potatoes, and toast are okay."

"It's perfect," Maya said. "Can I pour you coffee or juice?"

"Juice, please," Ivie said. "I've had my fill of coffee with Maggie. She's still at the table."

"She's up early," Hattie said, lifting their dishes with a towel to avoid burning her hands while Maya filled their glasses.

"Something about sitting in on today's session."

"Interesting," Hattie said. She and Maggie had completed their duos days ago. Hattie's solo songs were the only ones that remained.

Hattie and Maya entered the dining room, where Maggie was reading a newspaper and sipping from a mug. She looked up. "Hello, you two. Anxious to start the day?"

"It will be bittersweet. I've enjoyed recording all week, but finishing means we'll be leaving soon." Hattie put their plates down, and she and Maya sat. "I'm going to miss you, my friend."

"I'll be down in a month for your opening. And you'll be back to hit the club circuit in the spring. We're going to get sick of each other."

"Never." Hattie laughed. "Ivie said you plan to sit in today."

"I wanted to do background vocals today. It should be a pleasant surprise for people who buy the records, and it will play well when we perform on stage to promote them."

Hattie smiled. "You're very good at the marketing end of this business." Everything she and Maggie did together turned to gold. If given a little nudge, word would spread like wildfire about a Maggie Moore–Hattie James duet hidden in one of the songs, and sales would go wild.

"I tired quickly of being at the mercy of the men who rule the music industry. I watched and learned for years, biding my time until I had the startup capital and the right artist to make the leap with me. From the first time I met you, I knew you would be that person."

"That's why you mentored me."

"That, and you make me laugh. There's never a dull day with us."

"Not a one." Hattie laughed. They both did.

"Which is why, after seeing you work with the musicians and sound engineer this week, I know you're ready for the next step."

"And what is that?"

"Being partners. The buzz we've generated with the newspaper and billboard ads about our upcoming songs tells me this little label is ripe for growing quickly. I have my eye on plucking some artists from RCA and Columbia whose contracts are up this year. To do that, I'll need a managing partner I trust. Again, that person is you. What do you say?"

"Wow." Hattie leaned back in her chair. First, the head of Military Intelligence offered to make her a full-fledged covert operative. Then Maggie asked her to become an equal in her company.

Her career in the last twelve months had been feast or famine. Before all this mess with her father, she had had a lucrative RCA contract and was performing at the Copacabana in New York City. She had felt she was at the pinnacle. Then Knight had caused her to lose everything, and she was performing in piss-stench dives. When she arrived in Rio, she had imagined her future would be much the same. However, meeting Maya Reyes changed her life forever, launching her on a trajectory she never thought possible. Headlining at Brazil's most sought-after venue morphed into her partnership with Maya to build a nightclub to surpass anything the continent had seen.

Maggie turned to Maya. "I don't intend for her to choose between the Halo Club and Harmony Records because I believe she can do both. I want her to do both. My vision is to make a mark in North and South America. Your nightclub could serve as a major focal point in the south. I want to open a club of the same quality in New York."

"You want to control recording and the venues," Hattie said.

"The only missing link would be distribution, but that's in the ten-year plan."

"You are ambitious, Maggie Moore."

"Just think about it, Hattie. We can talk more when I'm in Rio."

"I'll think about it."

Maggie folded the newspaper in half, handed it to Hattie, and pointed to an article. "By the way, you made page two."

Hattie scanned the print and read the title of the second story, "Hattie James's Father Innocent." The brief snippet was to the point. "The federal government has dropped all charges against Hattie James's father, an American diplomat accused of giving national secrets to Nazi Germany. After a year of hiding in the wake of two murdered FBI agents during a brazen escape from federal custody, Karl James has returned to the United States. The leak originated from a military source at War Department headquarters, a person whose rank is unknown. Federal operatives fatally shot this individual while trying to apprehend him. Authorities have exonerated Hattie James, whom they previously suspected of aiding and abetting James after the fact."

That was it. A story sandwiched between the year in review of books published in 1941 and a three-car pileup in New Jersey resulting in one fatality, that was the FBI's retraction. Their sensational stories about Hattie and her father, of course, had been front-page headlines for weeks.

She showed the article to Maya. "I guess it's better than nothing."

"Karl's lawyer will look it over," Maya said. "If it's not enough, I'm sure he'll pursue it."

"Getting this little offering was like pulling teeth. I doubt we'll get anything else out of them."

"Tell you what, ladies," Maggie said. "You should have some fun tonight. I want you two to be my guest at the Copa. I have a one-night performance there to promote my last record with RCA."

"We'd love to," Maya said.

The country being at war seemed to have no dampening effect on the Copacabana. Well-dressed people in gowns, suits, and tuxedos packed the dining room. The din of conversation and laughter was robust. The smoke-filled atmosphere buzzed with the excitement of flowing money, copious booze, and Maggie's upcoming performance.

Other than a bit of turnover in the waitstaff and cigarette girls, the place had not changed since Hattie was last there a year ago. The jungle décor and plaster columns fashioned to resemble palm trees throughout the room created a tropical feeling. After spending so much time in the rainforest around Rio, the recreation seemed oddly fake to Hattie. Nonetheless, New Yorkers and wealthy tourists appeared to be eating it up.

The hostess, who recognized Hattie by sight, escorted her and Maya to a reserved table near the stage in the center of the dining room. "Miss Moore has opened a tab for you ladies tonight and has already provided your drink preferences—tonic waters with a twist of lemon and two olives. Your server will be by shortly with beverages and to take your orders. Is there anything else I can start you with?"

Maya blushed.

"What is it?" Hattie asked.

"I've always wanted to try a milkshake," Maya said.

"What flavor, miss?" the hostess asked.

"Chocolate."

Hattie smiled. "Make it two."

"Of course, Miss James."

After a while, the waitress delivered their drinks and milkshakes and took their dinner requests. Their meals were delicious and prompted Hattie and Maya to spend much time discussing ideas for food selections at the Halo Club when it opened next month.

Maggie's performance would begin soon, so Hattie excused herself. "I have to use the restroom. How about you?"

"I'll pass. You go."

Hattie weaved her way through the sea of people, dodging servers hurrying to clear the tables before the start of the show. She entered the ladies' room and stood in a short line, waiting for a stall to become free. The wait for the women's bathroom was such a common complaint in nightclubs that Hattie had insisted on doubling the number of toilets at their club.

After a flush, the stall door at the far end opened and Hattie walked toward it. A second later, a blond woman stepped out. Her face, blond hair, and figure were unforgettable.

"Hello, Hattie. I thought that was you at the center table."

Hattie momentarily froze at finding herself face-to-face with the woman who had broken her heart and haunted her for years. She had done the same out of the steamy desire generated whenever Helen Reed entered her orbit. Today, though, she had frozen out of simple surprise.

"Hello, Helen."

The name rolled off Hattie's tongue more easily than it had in years. It no longer had a hold on her, no longer made her pant for the thing she could not have. She smiled to herself at the realization. She did not want Helen Reed. The scars in her heart were gone, as if they never existed, thanks to Maya and the abundance of acceptance and love that Eva and Karl provided. The past no longer haunted her. It shaped her. It informed her. Whatever Maya Reyes offered was enough and always would be.

"I heard you were in Rio. What are you doing back in New York?"

"Business."

"I read that story about you and your father today. I'm glad the FBI has cleared both of you. Does that mean you'll move back to the States soon?"

"We'll see. I'm incredibly happy in Rio."

"Yes, yes. My cousin said she went to your show at the Palace. Are you still performing there?"

"Not any longer. I gave my notice in December."

"Who is the woman with you tonight? I've never seen her before."

"No, you wouldn't have. She's why I'm happy in Rio." Hattie angled herself to shimmy past Helen and into the stall. "Now, if you'll excuse me."

Helen placed her palm on the door, blocking Hattie's path. She leaned closer and whispered, "Your eyes tell me differently."

"My eyes are saying I have to pee and flush away the excess and anything else toxic that's not worth keeping. It's a very cathartic process. You should try it." Hattie peeled Helen's hand from the door and closed it behind her, hearing a loud, disappointed harrumph on the other side.

After conducting her business, Hattie returned with a satisfied grin to her table, delighted to have chosen what of the past to bring into her present rather than the other way around.

Maya leaned over. "What did I miss? You look pleased with yourself."

Hattie slipped her hand under the white tablecloth and touched Maya's leg, giving it a loving caress. "I couldn't be more pleased with how things are."

The lights in the dining room dimmed markedly, and the conversation in the room hushed. Once the overhead lights were dark, leaving only the candlelight glow at the tables, a spotlight came on with a dramatic, echoing thump. The light poured onto the microphone standing at center stage, illuminating part of the band behind it, and an announcer came over the speaker system. "Ladies and gentlemen, the Copacabana proudly presents Miss Maggie Moore."

The crowd roared, and Maggie strode out. She opened with her new song, the one that had flooded the airways for a month, and then, for half an hour, sang more of her RCA titles. The performance electrified the audience; whistles and cheers erupted after each number.

She signaled the musicians to stop, wiped the sweat from her brow, and spoke into the microphone. "Everyone having fun?" The audience went wild with applause and shouts. Next, placing a hand above her eyes as a shield from the spotlight's glare, she asked, "Where are you?"

Hattie shrank a bit, guessing what was next. She expected as much after today's invitation, but truth be told, she welcomed Maggie's maneuver. This stage had marked the height of Hattie's career before it all unraveled. She had nothing to prove, but joining Maggie on it tonight would reinforce what Hattie already knew—no one should have forced her from the limelight.

Maggie smiled, ending her search. "There you are. Ladies and gentlemen, there is a special guest in the audience tonight, and with a little encouragement, she might join me." She extended her hand toward the center tables. "What do you say, Hattie James?"

The crowd got louder with more inviting cheers and applause.

Maya spoke into Hattie's ear. "Show them what they've been missing."

"In spades."

Hattie took the stage with Maggie to thunderous clapping and covered the microphone with her hand to whisper, "Let's give them everything we got."

"Precisely why I called you up. I've had this planned for days."

They put on a performance for the ages. They sang Maggie's songs, Hattie's numbers, and their unreleased duets. Each number, including the three encores, was fun, exciting, and sometimes seductive. It had a wow factor the Copacabana had never seen. They even teased the news about their new recording label and the planned opening of the Halo Club in Rio the following month. And when they finished, they rejoined Maya, toasting their tonic waters to an incredible show.

As the crowd thinned, several customers stopped by their table, asking for autographs and pictures with them. They were all respectful, and a few asked questions about more performances together in the States, to which Maggie replied, "Only time will tell."

Then Helen Reed approached. She had hiked her glittery dress up a little, showing more above the knees, and adjusted the neckline to reveal a hint of cleavage. "That was a wonderful show, ladies." She turned to Hattie, licking her lips. "I enjoyed reconnecting with you in the restroom. It was"—she glanced at Maya—"invigorating. We should do it again sometime soon."

Maggie raised her eyebrows and snickered.

"Where are my manners?" Hattie said. "Helen Reed, this is Maya Reyes."

Helen shook Maya's hand. "Hattie says you're from Rio."

"I am."

"What do you do in Rio?"

"I run a nightclub."

"Don't be so modest," Maggie said. "This brilliant woman was the manager at the Golden Room and owned her own club before that. Now, she and our dear Hattie are in business together, opening the Halo Club, which will blow the socks off everyone in Rio."

"It sounds like you're quite the little water carrier."

"I'm not sure what that means," Maya said, furrowing her brow.

"It means Helen has worn out her welcome," Hattie said. "You need to leave, Helen."

"The only one carrying water around here is you," Maggie said. She lifted the pitcher on the table and emptied its contents over Helen's head. The curls in her hair flattened and stuck to her neck. The water soaked her glittery gown, making it droop and cling to her body like drenched rags.

Helen yelped and stiffened her arms in shock.

Maya and Hattie covered their mouths but could not contain their laughter.

Helen shouted several expletives and stomped away, furious.

Hattie patted Maggie's hand, laughing. "That was amazing."

"Helen Reed is all wet in my book." Maggie raised her glass of tonic water. "Here's to washing away the past."

Maya and Hattie held theirs up. Hattie studied the two women with her at the table, deciding once more that the world offered no better friend than Maggie Moore and no better keeper of her heart than Maya Reyes.

They clinked glasses, and Hattie said, "And to only looking forward."

28

Rio de Janeiro, Brazil, Friday, February 13, 1942

The Brazilian government had canceled official Carnival activities because of the war. However, this year, like last year, a sizeable number of Rio's citizens would be holding their own celebrations, some of them at the Halo Club, which would celebrate its grand opening tonight. Hattie and Maya passed groups of men and women dressed in vibrant colors and hats, playing instruments, and selling food and trinkets on the streets as they drove to the club to oversee final preparations.

Hattie turned the corner, and the new marquee came into view. A large, elegant arch, trimmed in the same granite and antique brass accents found inside, spanned the double-door entrance.

"It's beautiful." Maya crouched down in the front seat to better see the top of the sign.

"Wait until tonight. The electricians added the finishing touches last night," Hattie said. When lit, multiple embedded lights would create an angelic glow resembling a halo.

She pulled into their spacious parking lot. Their decision to purchase two adjacent properties across from the Halo Club to expand parking was one of the best things they could have done to make the club an attractive destination. While it lacked the space to accommodate all the cars associated with a packed house, it allowed them to offer valet service for those desiring it.

Javier jogged up from the attendant shack, dressed in his new tuxedo uniform. "Hello, Miss James and Miss Reyes. What a beautiful day for a grand opening."

"It is." Hot weather was unavoidable this time of year, but the sky was clear, and no rain was in sight. "When does the rest of your crew arrive?"

"At three, since we open at four. Everyone knows valet parking is by reservation only tonight. We have the list Miss Reyes gave us."

"Thank you, Javier. I'm sure your men will do an outstanding job."

He raised the arm barrier, and Hattie pulled inside to park in the owner's reserved slot. She and Maya walked to the main entrance instead of going through the service doors; they wanted to experience the club as their customers would in a few hours.

Maya took a deep breath before inserting the key into the front door's lock. Hattie did the same. They had returned to Rio over a month ago and, after overseeing the final renovations, had delegated staff training and stocking the kitchen and bar to the relevant managers. There had been some bumps along the way, but nothing they could not iron out.

"Ready for this?" Hattie asked.

Maya looked at her, her eyes shining with pride.

"Anna and I worked at bars and clubs for years, always dreaming about running a place of our own one day. When we bought this club with the money we got when our parents died, we thought we had hit the jackpot. We quickly discovered we were in over our heads. The first few months were rough, but we were getting the hang of it." She reached for Hattie's hand. "Then you walked in, and my life changed forever. I'm not only more experienced now, but I also know I can't fail with you by my side. So, yes. I'm ready for this."

And so was Hattie. They turned the key together, unlocking the club and their future, and stepped inside, examining their prize as one of their VIP guests might.

The hostess station was more elaborate than the Golden Room's, featuring rich woods and smart benches where people could sit while they waited for a table, something their competitor did not have.

They relocked the door and moved further inside to the club's vast main dining room. The waitstaff had the house lights on as they completed their last-minute preparations. Fine linen covered rows of tables, each adorned with matching napkins, silverware, water glasses, and miniature lanterns for a romantic glow.

The head waitress approached them. "Good, you're early," Monica said. "I need the final count for the VIPs."

"I'll get that," Maya said. "The list is in my office." She led Monica toward the back of the club.

Hattie turned her gaze to the club's focal point—its raised stage. The curtains were open, and the band's shining instruments were in place. An arch that mirrored the marquee at the building's entrance formed the backdrop. It, too, held a fixture that would light up like a halo during performances.

A woman in casual slacks and a blouse walked onto the stage from the wings, there early to test her instrument. Of course. At rehearsals, she was always the first to arrive and the last to leave, not satisfied until she had perfected her performance for every song.

Hattie called up to her. "Hello, Zoya. Ready for tonight?"

Zoya came to the edge of the stage. "I will be, Hattie."

"I'm so glad you decided to join us."

"This is the only venue I want to work."

"And you're the only pianist I want backing me up."

Hours later, Hattie, Maggie, and Eva peeked out the wing curtains of the stage to assess how things were going. The band was in place. Elites packed the house, all dressed to impress. Some of Hollywood's most revered stars, top international singers, and other rich and famous business owners and politicians dotted the audience.

"Wow." Hattie blew out an uneasy breath. Crowds of this caliber never made her nervous, and she had performed in front of many of the guests before. This, however, was the first time that more than her career rested on a single performance. Her future and Maya's and the club's future did as well.

Eva placed an arm around Hattie's shoulder. "You and Maya did this. It's an incredible thing you've built, sweetheart."

"What if it doesn't take off?" Hattie faced her mother. "We've poured everything we have into it, our money, our hopes. Maya will have nothing if the club fails."

"You'll have each other, and you'll have us. Family"—Eva glanced at Maggie—"blood and chosen, is all that matters."

The three held hands when Maya appeared behind them. "Ready?"

"Let's do this."

"You do the talking, Hattie. I'm too nervous."

Hattie winked. "Happy to."

The crowd's noise came to a slow hush as the lights dimmed. When the spotlight came on, Hattie and Maya strode onto the stage to whistles and roaring applause. They stopped at the microphone. When the warm greeting died down, Hattie said, "Welcome, everyone. I'm Hattie James. Thank you for coming tonight to witness the incredible realization of one woman's dream. As many of you know, last year's tragic fire destroyed the nightclub originally located on this spot. If not for the vision and commitment of my business partner, Maya Reyes, the Halo Club would still be a pile of ash and rubble. We dedicate this evening to the memory of Maya's sister, Anna Reyes, whose light still shines brightly in this club and in our hearts. So, eat and drink well and enjoy the show."

The band started to play.

Hattie extended her arm to the wings. "Ladies and gentlemen, I give you two great artistic treasures, Eva Machado and Maggie Moore."

Maya squeezed Hattie's hand as she left and hugged Eva and Maggie as they emerged to join Hattie on stage.

Together, their threesome put on a show that nobody in the crowd would ever forget. Three of the world's best singers together on a single stage, performing the music of two generations. The audience refused to let them leave for nearly two hours. They departed exhausted but energized nonetheless by the audience's excitement.

They tumbled onto the couch in one of the dressing rooms.

"I've never had so much fun," Maggie said, grabbing a glass of ice water Monica had left in the room.

"And that's saying something." Hattie laughed.

Eva grabbed a towel and wiped her brow. "Goodness. You two are hard to keep up with."

Hattie pushed up from the sofa. "We better freshen up and make the rounds again."

After changing their outfits and making themselves pretty again, the three entered the dining room together to another round of applause. This was an exhausting but essential part of opening night. Everyone in that audience was a big spender, but they needed to make each of them feel like they were Halo's most important guest.

With their rounds complete, the crowd began to thin, and they finally were able to join the family at the table of honor in the center of the room. Leo held out a chair for Maggie, sandwiching her between him and his wife, Beverly. Karl greeted Eva with a lengthy kiss, signifying their reconciliation was on track. Maya met Hattie with a firm hug but did not let it last too long. Hattie sat between her and Frank, with Olivia on his other side.

Once everyone had taken their seats and servers filled their glasses with their drinks of choice, Hattie asked, "Do you have any numbers yet?"

"Excellent. Receipts are better than expected," Maya said.

"Any feedback from the waitstaff?"

"All positive. Not a single complaint, and we're booked solid for a month."

"That's wonderful," Eva said. "Word will spread. I knew this place would be a hit. Hattie was right when she said you had vision, Maya. This location is perfect."

"Thank you, Eva, but Hattie and I could not have pulled off tonight without you. Thank you for tending to things while we were in the States."

"It was my pleasure, girls."

Frank leaned over to Hattie. "How much longer do we have the babysitter at the house?"

"As long as you need," she said. "She's paid through the morning if you two want to dance, hit the beach, or do whatever." Hattie winked.

"Thanks for lending us your room at Eva's. I hope you and Maggie are comfortable in Maya's guest rooms."

Hattie patted his hand. "We'll be fine."

Conversation flowed around the table as it should with family and good friends. Someone asked how Beverly liked her trip to Brazil so far.

"It's lovely here," she said. "It's too bad I'm here for only two weeks."

Leo rubbed the back of his neck. "Yeah, about that. You know how the admiral said I could have my assignment of choice?"

"Yes?"

"Well, I put in for Rio, attached to the diplomatic corps."

Karl laughed. "That's great news."

"What's great news?" Beverly looked confused.

"It means," Leo said, "that you can come too, and we stay for as long as we want."

"Really? No more months at sea?"

"Nope. We can find us a little house and settle in for a few years."

The group toasted to Leo's new assignment, and Hattie could not be happier knowing he would be around for some time.

Hattie whispered to Maya, "I'm going to the ladies' room. I'll be back."

Frank helped with her chair when she pushed back and said she was going to freshen up.

"I'll go with you," Olivia said.

When they were at the sink washing up after conducting their business in the stalls, Olivia said, "The bathroom is beautiful here. I've never seen one so grand."

Hattie looked at her in the mirror. "We ordered the granite from Mexico. Selecting the right floor tile to complement it took a while."

"Well, you and...and Maya did a wonderful job."

Karl had told Hattie about the talk he had with Olivia on Christmas. He had recounted the journey of acceptance he and Eva had gone through after learning of Hattie's truth and how she loved. He had reminded her that Hattie was the same woman who had helped raise her after Eva returned to Brazil. The same woman who doted over Matthew and Sarah like they were her own children. The same woman who risked life and limb to save her from Gene Stanton. He had gotten through to Olivia enough to convince her to come to Rio with the family for the grand opening. It was obvious, though, that she still had a long way to go toward acceptance.

"Thank you, Olivia. That means more than you realize."

Her sister scanned the restroom as if ensuring they were alone. "I haven't said anything to Frank yet."

"I gathered as much."

"It's because I don't know how to broach the subject with him, and I'm not sure whether I want him to know."

"I'm sorry that this upsets you, but I won't apologize for who I am," Hattie said. "I'm glad this is no longer a secret between us, and I hope one day I won't have to hide it from Frank and the kids. Until that day, I will respect your wishes."

"Good." Olivia's shoulders slumped, maybe out of relief or perhaps out of frustration. In either case, it still did not bode well for their relationship.

Hattie turned to face her. "I love you, Olivia. I'll never give up hoping we can be as close as we once were. Even if you never come to terms with this, please don't cut me out of the children's lives." Hattie's voice cracked through the emotion building in her throat. "That would be too much to take."

Olivia sniffled and shook her head. "I won't. Just..."

"I know. I've lived in the shadows all my adult life." Hattie pulled her into a brief hug before someone entered the restroom. "We should get back to the family."

As she returned to the table, Hattie noticed that Karl and Leo had left and were engaged in what looked like a deep discussion at the bar's far end. After telling Maya where she was going, she joined them, signaling the bartender to bring her a drink.

"You two look too serious. Tonight is for celebrating."

The bartender dropped off a glass of tonic water with her traditional garnish.

Karl looked at Hattie. "Leo told me who you requested to be your handler."

"Ah." She wished he had waited until tomorrow to pass along the information rather than letting it intrude on their big night. "Well, what do you think, Father? Will you do it?"

"What if I say no?"

"Then I won't accept the position, even as part-time as Admiral Drummond has made it sound. If I'm going to do this, keep an eye on American interests in Rio, I'll only do it with someone I trust controlling the assignments."

"You've put a giant wrinkle in my retirement plans, sweetheart."

"Only part-time. To the world, you'll be retired, but to the department, you'll still be on the payroll. Leo and I would be your only agents."

Karl smiled. "How can I turn down an offer like that?" He raised his glass, and Hattie and Leo joined him. "We make a pretty good team."

Maya locked the club after their family guests departed. Leo and Beverly had gone to his apartment, and Olivia and Frank had headed to the house with Karl and Eva. Maggie would go with them to Maya's. The waitstaff continued cleaning up and prepping the dining room for tomorrow while the kitchen crew cleaned the cooking surfaces and the last batch of dishes and glasses. Every employee had one thing in common—they lauded the night's success.

"You three must be tired," Monica said. "Go home. I'll close up."

"Thank you, Monica." Maya hugged her, and they exited through the service door to the club parking lot across the street.

Javier was the only remaining attendant, having stayed late to drive home with his wife. He had pulled Hattie's sedan up and had it waiting by the lot entrance. "Spectacular night, ladies," he said, tipping his cap.

"Thank you, Javier," Hattie said. "It went well."

He opened the car doors. As Hattie got in, she reflected on the couple's kindness in helping Eva hide the injured Karl from the Nazis. She would never forget their generosity. They were indeed family.

She drove to the corner and stopped to allow Maya and Maggie to admire the marquee's halo-like arch.

"It's magnificent," Maya said. "I have to admit that I was a bit worried when you refused to tell me your plans for the marquee, but I'm glad you didn't. It's the grandest surprise of the evening."

"You done good, kid." Maggie laughed.

Hattie pulled up to Maya's home. At least it was Maya's until Hattie and Eva closed next week on a "little mansion," as Eva called it. The best solution they could come up with to allow Hattie and Maya to continue living together without raising suspicion was to live under the same roof as Eva. And Karl, who had agreed to move in with Eva. Knowing that space would be an issue whenever Olivia and her family decided to visit, she and Eva had pooled their resources for an upgrade. Having primary suites on opposite sides of the house would provide each couple privacy.

Once inside Maya's, the three tossed their purses on the entry table.

"I'm still wound up from tonight," Maggie said. "Any chance you have something in the house that could help put me to sleep?"

"I think there's an old bottle of Cachaça in the cabinet. I'll pour you a shot." Maya went to the kitchen and returned moments later with the drink. "Watch out. It's sweet but has some kick."

Maggie sipped it and raised her eyebrows. "Wow. I guess so. Just a few sips to unwind." She went to the couch and patted the cushion beside her. "Sit, ladies. This is as good of a time as any to discuss my offer for Hattie to join me in managing Harmony Records. As I see it, Maya is the brains of the Halo Club and will probably take on the day-to-day management responsibilities. Hattie will be the entertainer, getting butts in the seats every night, but unless you become a housewife and learn to bake, most of your days will be free. Why not spend them building an international record label the right way?"

"Boy, you have my entire life mapped out, don't you?" Hattie chuckled.

"You know me, as shy as a politician at a Manhattan fundraiser."

Hattie and Maya laughed.

"Well?" Maggie sipped and looked on expectedly.

"You tell her, Maya," Hattie said.

"We've discussed it at length, and the answer is yes, with two stipulations."

"What are those?"

"I get to come with her on tour."

"Done. What else?"

"You have to spend at least one holiday with us each year."

Maggie laughed. "Done. This is great, ladies. We're going to make an incredible team."

After a long night, the three headed to bed, Maggie in the guest room and Hattie and Maya in the primary bedroom. Hattie crawled in first, and Maya followed. They faced one another with their legs entwined and arms wrapped around the other's torso.

"We did good, didn't we?" Maya asked.

"We did great," Hattie said, "and this is only the beginning."

In the morning, Hattie woke before Maya and lay there for some time, watching her sleep. Despite the chaos at their first meeting, Hattie felt incredibly lucky to have found her perfect match in Rio. She planned to cherish every moment of their life together, regardless of how they met.

She padded to the kitchen, put on a pot of coffee, and retrieved the newspaper from the front porch. After pouring a cup and dressing it with sugar and cream, she dove into the report on the bottom half of the front page, the one with the headline that read "Halo Club a Hit." The story detailed the evening, reporting that the guest list was a "who's who" from Hollywood and many other corners of the world. Although the article praised the unparalleled food, it said that the evening's show-stealer was the two-hour performance by Eva Machado, Maggie Moore, and Hattie James. They had brought the house down.

It was a tremendous relief to read this great review. The praise helped confirm that last night's success had not been merely wishful thinking. It was real. Her life with Maya was genuine and perfect.

Hattie scanned the rest of the page, the other articles bringing her down from her high. The United States had opened internment camps for Japanese nationals living in America, it reported, and it was preparing to send troops to the European Theater.

The war had been going on for years in Europe and elsewhere. But it had just started for Hattie James.

AUTHOR'S NOTE

The Rainbow Five plan was a United States strategic military plan developed by a joint board of the army and navy in 1941. It was part of a series of color-coded war plans created to address potential conflicts with various nations. Rainbow Five specifically outlined the US strategy for a two-ocean war against the Axis Powers, including Germany, Italy, and Japan. The plan called for the United States to take an initial defensive posture in the Pacific while building strength for European offensive operations. The ultimate goal was to defeat the Axis Powers through coordinated efforts with allied nations.

This top secret war plan was published in the *Chicago Tribune* and the *Washington Times Herald* on December 4, 1941, just three days before the attack on Pearl Harbor. The leak detailed plans for an army of ten million, including an expeditionary force of five million men to invade Europe to defeat Hitler. The leak embarrassed Roosevelt and undercut his claims that he had no plans to involve the country in the war.

Journalist Chesly Manly was pivotal in the Rainbow Five war plan leak. On December 2, 1941, Manly, a reporter for the *Chicago Tribune*, obtained the top secret war plans and recognized the significance of the scoop. He believed the public had the right to know about the plans and received the go-ahead from *Tribune* publisher Robert R. McCormick, a staunch isolationist and critic of President Roosevelt. Manly's article, "F.D.R.'s War Plans," was published two days later.

In his 1962 memoir, Senator Burton K. Wheeler (Montana), an isolationist supporter of the America First Committee, said he was involved in the leak. Wheeler said he obtained a copy of the Victory Program, which included the Rainbow Five plan, from a source within the Air Corps—an army captain. Motivated by his opposition to Roosevelt's foreign policy and desire to prevent the United States from entering the war, Wheeler passed the information to Manly. Wheeler died in 1975 without ever revealing the name of the army captain who originally leaked the plan.

In 1987, Thomas Fleming wrote an article in the *American Heritage Magazine* detailing the leak and the mystery surrounding it. In "The Big Leak," Fleming said, "So big was the leak that it might have caused us to lose World War II. So mysterious is the identity of the leaker that we can't be sure to this day who it was...or at least not entirely sure."

I join in Fleming's characterization of the leak's impact and wish the real leaker could have faced justice. While I attribute the leak to Colonel Eugene Stanton, his name and actions were purely fictional. I hope you enjoyed this story.

If you want to learn more about the Rainbow Five plan and its leak, you can find Fleming's article at https://www.americanheritage.com/big-leak.

30% Off your next paperback.

Thank you for reading. For exclusive offers on your next paperback:

- **Visit SevernRiverBooks.com** and enter code **PRINTBOOKS30** at checkout.
- Or scan the QR code.

Jubilee
Book #1 in The Clandestine War series

Before the triumph of D-Day, there was the tragedy of Dieppe—where a secret operation altered the course of World War II.

The summer of 1942 finds the Allies desperate for a foothold in Hitler's Europe. Operation Jubilee is born in the smoke-filled rooms of the War Office—a daring raid that will test not just military might, but the moral fabric of those who command from safe distances.

Arthur Cutter, a haunted SOE operative barely out of Oxford, is forced back behind enemy lines for one final mission: infiltrate Dieppe's defenses to gather intelligence critical for the raid.

In the skies above Scotland, American-born RAF instructor Ian Faraday battles to prepare his pilots to provide air cover for the operation, even as his own demons threaten to ground him permanently.

In Occupied France, resistance fighter Talia Crevier becomes Cutter's unlikely ally, risking everything to map Nazi positions around Dieppe while battling the prejudice of her male comrades.

American Ranger Malcolm Parker, embedded with British Commandos slated for the raid's first wave, uncovers disturbing truths about Jubilee's planning—an operation compromised by ambition and miscalculation before it even begins.

As dawn breaks on August 19, 1942, four lives converge in a maelstrom of violence. Like pieces on a chessboard, they are moved by forces beyond their control, each forced to grasp the cost of sacrifice and the brutal truths of waging a clandestine war.

Get your copy today at severnriverbooks.com

ACKNOWLEDGMENTS

Thank you, Barbara Gould, my plotting partner in crime. She is still the best sounding board I could ever ask for.

Thank you, Kristianne and Nancy, for reading my rough, rough, rough first draft, providing your unfiltered thoughts, and pushing me to be a better writer.

Thank you, Jacquelin Cangro, my amazing developmental editor, for helping me whip this story into shape.

Finally, to my family. Thank you for loving me...and keeping the pantry stocked with popcorn.

ABOUT THE AUTHOR

A late bloomer, award-winning author Stacy Lynn Miller took up writing after retiring from the Air Force. Her twenty years of toting a gun and police badge, tinkering with computers, and sleuthing for clues as an investigator form the foundation of her Lexi Mills thriller series, as well as her Manhattan Sloane novels. She is visually impaired, a proud stroke survivor, mother of two, tech nerd, chocolate lover, and terrible golfer with a hole-in-one. When you can't find her writing, she'll be golfing or drinking wine (sometimes both) with friends and family in Northern California.

Sign up for the reader list at
severnriverbooks.com

9 781648 756931